SING

HER

NAME

SING HER NAME

a novel

ROSALYN STORY

A Bolden Book

AGATE

CHICAGO

Printed in the United States.

Library of Congress Cataloging-in-Publication Data

Names: Story, Rosalyn M., author.
Title: Sing Her Name / Rosalyn Story.
Description: Chicago : Agate, [2022] | "A Bolden book." | Summary: "This
    third novel by Rosalyn Story, whose critically acclaimed books treat the
    central role of Black people in American music, is her most rewarding
    yet, telling the intertwined stories of two singers whose lives connect
    across time"-- Provided by publisher.
Identifiers: LCCN 2021038449 (print) | LCCN 2021038450 (ebook) | ISBN
    9781572842977 (paperback) | ISBN 9781572848504 (ebook)
Subjects: LCGFT: Novels.
Classification: LCC PS3619.T694 S56 2022 (print) | LCC PS3619.T694
    (ebook) | DDC 813/.6--dc23
LC record available at https://lccn.loc.gov/2021038449
LC ebook record available at https://lccn.loc.gov/2021038450

9 8 7 6 5 4 3 2 1

Bolden Books is an imprint of Agate Publishing. Agate books are available in bulk at discount prices. Single copies are available prepaid direct from the publisher.

Agatepublishing.com

The impeded stream is the one that sings.
—Wendell Berry

PART I

CHAPTER 1

New Orleans, 1919

When Celia saw the light shift to shadow in Henri Benoit's eyes, she knew she would not sing. Not here, anyway. And maybe never again.

At dusk, the maestro had summoned her to his apartment on Rue Dauphine in the French Quarter, as he did every other Thursday. It was the day his wife visited her ailing mother in a nearby parish. For his lover, he'd planned a quiet dinner and chosen an excellent wine.

Celia wore her newest frock, white lace over golden silk, the color that made her brown eyes sparkle—or so he once told her. At the door, he took her coat. She removed her gloves and twirled for him so the ruffled hem of her satin skirts flared.

She stopped when he turned away. "What's wrong?"

"I am so sorry. There's been a change. Let me try to explain."

She saw it in his eyes. Their unspoken bargain—her unharnessed affections in exchange for a place in history—was broken. Every other Thursday evening, the maestro and the diva ascended the stairs to the small apartment above his office. He poured wine. His eyes glistened with desire. *And now this?*

"Beloved, someday, perhaps. You are brilliant, you are beautiful, your voice is a miracle, but the world is not yet ready for…It was not my choice. The decision was made. It is out of my hands."

But she had been born to sing Carmen. He had told her so himself.

She wanted to scream. Instead, she locked a long, hard gaze on him. She had already been fitted for costumes. Rehearsals were to begin tonight.

She narrowed her eyes at him. "You tell me this now."

Just months ago, she reminded him, *the president of the United States* had been moved to tears when, during her fourth White House recital, she had lingered on the heartbreaking C of Puccini's "Un bel di," as she always had. She had heard the gasps and applause from the audience. Even when Celia was a young singer, Queen Victoria had bowed to her as if *she* were royalty. Thousands of people had cheered her in New York at Madison Square Garden.

They had not cared that she was black.

He knew all this. He knew the marvel of her voice. He had read the reviews in papers from New York to London. But there had been complaints, he told her. He had also been disappointed when the powers above him—the entire board of directors—had ordered him to replace her.

She saw it immediately—the end of her career. Her pulse raced. She struggled for words. Finally, they came.

"Burn in hell, Maestro."

At 8:00 p.m., while the orchestra tuned and Benoit raised his baton for the overture, she sat alone in her cottage on Rue Conti, sipping peach brandy. Bizet's music spun in her head alongside thoughts of what could have been.

Instead, the rehearsal for *Carmen* at New Orleans' French Opera House would feature The Great Adeline Donatella in the role of Carmen. Petite, golden-haired, she was the most famous diva in America and Europe. Long ago, Celia had been dubbed "The Black Donatella," even by her own press. This betrayal had sealed her fate, placed her forever in the shadow of Adeline. She would never sing in the world's great operas. The minstrel troupe of black jugglers and comedians she'd formed in desperation to feature her talent had gone bankrupt. She'd been forced to dismiss the ensemble, unable to pay the thousands she owed them. Where she once had riches, she was now almost penniless. To star as Carmen at one of the nation's great opera houses had been her last best hope.

And now, if she could not sing…

The streets were cold. With purpose, she walked toward the river.

The French Quarter was quiet that January night, except for the occasional moan of a tugboat on the water and the click of her heels on the cobblestone. In the morning, they would find her still fully dressed, river stones tugging at the lining of her coat pockets, and her long white gloves ballooned with water. The gown, now crisp, would billow, washed out by the tide of the sea.

She walked for an hour. Turning east, she headed past the blacksmith's shop toward Decatur and the river. Gas street lanterns threw smoky veils of light on the cobblestone. The scent of dry leaves rose as she passed the cigar factory, then the old absinthe house. When she got closer, she took a deeper breath. The Mississippi, America's Nile. She loved its rhythm, its deep bass hum. The perfect place of rest.

But the air changed. A sharp scent stung her nostrils: the smell of smoke, heat in the air. She looked in the direction of the opera house.

The building was in flames.

When the Great War ended, the streets had roiled with rowdy celebration. A cheering crowd gathered around the grand French Opera House, the pride of the city.

She walked toward the blaze, drawn to it. Two men, their silhouettes swollen by firelight, spotted her and pointed in her direction. In the distance, a woman's high-pitched scream. Then there were the fire wagons, the horses, the calls for action as the firemen assembled. Flaming rafters and roof tiles fell to the street below.

Now that she was barred from the French Opera House's stage, it paid for its crime.

Burn in hell, she thought.

She kept walking. The two men rushed toward her, yelling, "Stop her! Stop that woman!" Something inside her turned. A vision grew in the fire's light: She was on that stage. She was singing.

Now, only now, that stage will be mine...

She arched her shoulders back, head high as she walked to meet the adoring crowd. The applause, the shouts, *Brava, diva!* swelled in her head. She smiled, clutched at the gold locket on her bosom, and bowed. And with every thought erased, she walked toward a bouquet of flames, the grand stage, her heart singing, and the music burning like fire in her head.

CHAPTER 2

New York, 2006

Eden raced through the door of Estelle's Café in Midtown, breathless and bleeding from the knee, praying Enriqué hadn't noticed. She'd never been this late before.

As far as waitresses went, Eden was confident she was one of the best. Everybody in the fried chicken and Creole restaurants where she'd worked in New Orleans had said so, and even here in New York, where she and her younger brother had lived since the storm, she got her share of customers' praise.

But today, from the beginning, nothing had gone right. When she met Marianne's eyes, she knew she'd have to explain, but not now.

"I know, I know," Eden said. "I should have called. My phone died. Is he looking for me?"

The restaurant was finishing the breakfast rush. Marianne shifted the tray of iced tea glasses on her forearm for better balance and looked down at Eden's knee, where blood leached out beneath a white gauze bandage.

"Enriqué? Haven't seen him. Jesus, what happened? Did you fall or something?"

"Yeah," Eden said. "Trying to help this woman up who fell getting off the train. Big woman. Pulled me down with her."

Marianne suppressed a giggle and shook her head. "No good deed…" she said.

"And I had to stop and get a bandage. Knee's killing me and I'm stressed. You got any Tylenol?"

"My coat's on the hook near the door. Left side pocket. There's some rubbing alcohol on the first aid shelf by the window in the break room. I'll cover for you."

"Thanks, girl! I owe you one."

She threw back two Tylenol caplets with a swig of water and cleaned and dressed her wound. Her knee throbbing, she headed toward the restroom and regretted not telling her friend the whole truth: she'd forgotten to re-set the alarm clock last night after the power went off during the rains yesterday, and then chased her brother halfway to the subway that morning because he'd left behind his chemistry book. Mistake. At sixteen, he was old enough to take care of his business. That boy. And what had it gotten her? Late for work for the first time in…forever.

Thank God for Marianne. Almost fifteen years separated them; Marianne around fifty and Eden just shy of thirty-five. But they had arrived in New York around the same time, months ago, each fleeing disaster—Eden, a devastating flood, Marianne, an abusive husband—and each one had dropped into the city as if parachuted from a burning plane.

Their distinctions—one young and black from Louisiana, the other a middle-aged blonde from Kansas—might have distanced them. But since they met at Estelle's, their bond was unspoken but quietly understood, like parched nomads sharing the same desert spring. For each, New York offered a way out, a hand up.

At the station near the bar, Eden filled water glasses, wound napkins around silverware, cut lemons into slices, and thought about how

Enriqué, the manager, was already giving her grief about the singing. Arriving late to work didn't help.

"Hey, Eden!"

From behind her, she heard Andre Delaney's voice. He was a deep brown-skinned, chubby-faced, twenty-something line cook with a tattoo of a mermaid on his forearm and a wild, untamed, throwback Afro.

"Heard you in the break room yesterday. *Damn*, I didn't know you could blow like that! You sound like that singer…You know, the one on that car commercial all the time. Can't think of her name, but you sound just like her!"

"Thank you, Dre." This made her smile—a compliment, but also a heads-up. As much as she loved to sing, and as much as her customers in New Orleans restaurants had loved to hear her, it did not work at all in New York, or at least not at Estelle's. Enriqué had caught her, just once, or maybe twice, singing along too loudly as the speakers pumped out an Alicia Keys tune, and had looked at her as if she'd pulled up a chair to her customers' plates and taken a bite. She couldn't help it. There were rare moments when she could actually forget the hell of the last year—the flood, the displacement, the long bus rides from one evacuee outpost to another—and feel good about nothing in particular. It was always music that slowed her racing brain, made her insides smile. Alicia Keys, or even Mary J., placed her squarely in that feel-good groove. And so she sang. Like an unconscious exhale, the music spilled from her.

"Please don't do that," Enriqué had told her the last time, adjusting his glasses on his broad forehead.

"Do what?" she'd answered. She really didn't know.

Breaking into song while waiting tables was undignified and unprofessional, he explained. If people want to hear singing, they can walk over to Broadway and pay to see a show, or to the subway at Columbus Circle where the homeless drunks would oblige for free.

"Yes, sir. I'm sorry, Mr. Enriqué," she'd said. And wondered what in the hell was up with a city where a woman couldn't sing when she felt like it.

She'd tried to dial it back, quash her impulses. This job was important, for her sake and her brother's, who, unlike most New Orleanians, had benefited enormously from the storm: he'd had at least one brush with the law just before the big flood, but his records, like those of so many others, had been destroyed. Countless criminal trials had been thrown into confusion.

It was more than a second chance. It was a bona fide rebirth.

She would never have thought of New York this way, but here is where she could fulfill her promise to her father. *Keep him safe.* Not back in New Orleans, where broken schools spat out young black boys like chewed snuff and where they often landed just as easily on the street, trampled underfoot. But up here, beyond the reach of Louisiana law, her brother could disappear. *Just a couple more years*, she told herself. Then, he would be grown, and hopefully, on his way to a good job or trade, something, anything.

For now, though, she needed to keep this job.

"Just don't let it happen again," Enriqué had told her.

A hand went up in her section from a woman with half-glasses slipping down the bridge of her nose. Eden had been in town long enough to know the tourists from the locals, and Estelle's West Side Café, unassuming and inexpensive by Manhattan standards, attracted both. This lady was of the tourist variety: white, well-heeled, well-dressed, and with designer shoes unsuited for the foul New York streets. The man with her confirmed it—they were definitely tourists. His combover had to have been pasted down with some sort of glue-like gel, and he was far too overweight to have spent much time walking the avenues of New York.

"Hi, there! I'm Eden. I'll be your waitress. What would you like today?"

The man closed his menu. He smiled and ordered the steak and eggs.

The woman now looked perplexed. "Oh, dear. There are so many choices…"

"Take your time." Eden took out her pad and arranged her best smile. The man asked Eden, "Are you from New Orleans, by any chance?"

Eden gave him a look of surprise. "Yes, sir, ummm, how…"

He pointed to the back of her hand. She had been fifteen and her father'd had a fit. A night of wilding with her high school girlfriends after a Saints win and the impulse—*Let's go get tattoos!*—had all but been forgotten except the mark was still there, no bigger than a thumbprint, as it would forever be. She couldn't have known then that the fleur-de-lis (now everywhere, on car bumpers, t-shirts, and backpacks around the flooded city, and wherever evacuees had fled), would become the city's recovery symbol and mark her as a survivor. She covered the small emblem with her hand.

The woman continued deliberating. "I'm thinking lunch now. Maybe the salade nicoise…"

The man smiled sympathetically at Eden. "I hear the city's still pretty bad. We're so sorry for what happened to all you folks down there."

Eden stuttered a thank you.

The wife looked up. "Maybe I'll have the red beans and rice! Although I know It's not as good as your people can make it, right?"

Eden decided not to dwell on "your people" and "you folks" and waited. Surely, the woman would change her mind again.

"We spent our thirtieth anniversary in New Orleans!" the woman exclaimed. "We just loved it down there. The culture! The music! And the interesting way you all talk! How do you say it? 'Where y'at?' I think that's so…poetic! And '*making* groceries!' The whole world shops for groceries, but in New Orleans, they *make* them!"

How the hell you gonna make groceries, Miss Eden? It had been her second or third day at Estelle's, but the sound of the laughter still echoed in her head. "I'm gonna make groceries on the way home," was all she'd said, and the two Cuban busboys looked at her as if she'd spoken in tongues. Eden had never thought about this. Even her father, with his correct speech, had used the expression.

"It's just something we say," she said. "Need another minute?"

"Oh, no. I'm ready. I'll have the gumbo."

Seriously? Here? Horrible choice. "Yes ma'am! Excellent choice," she said.

The woman furrowed her brows. "Now, I hate to ask you this, but are you OK? Did you lose much? And are you going back?"

"I'm here for now, ma'am. And I'm OK. Thank you for asking." Eden shifted from one foot to the other. Her gashed knee began to throb again. "So!" she said. "You said the gumbo, right?"

The woman opened her menu again. "Oh, I don't know. Maybe I should take another minute."

Eden put her order pad in her pocket. "Take your time. I'll be right back."

The man who had been sitting at a nearby booth since the earlier shift caught her eye. Eden exhaled her relief and tried to put the couple out of her mind before she headed for his table.

"How can I help you, sir?"

It was only on the occasions when she saw him—once, twice a week—that she realized how few black men came into Estelle's, and he was the only regular. She had never actually talked to him, as he often sat at the bar with black coffee and a copy of the *Times*. She'd always thought he was older, but now, in the afternoon light, he looked not much older than her.

He smiled at her. "It comes from the French, you know."

"Excuse me?"

"Making groceries. *Faire l'épicerie.* To make or to do grocery shopping. See, 'make' and 'do' translate the same in French."

"Oh, right."

"Next time somebody says anything to you about that, tell them that the French inspired that phrase."

"Got it."

Dang. A brother speaking French without even a touch of Creole. Polished, smooth, like the woman who taught the high school French class she'd nearly flunked. She fingered the ends of her hair and wished she had washed it the night before and wondered if her knee bandage needed changing. And did she have any lipstick on at all? She stood with her bad knee tucked behind her good one.

"Can I get another coffee? A cappuccino this time?"

"Sure. Anything else? Dessert?"

As he removed his glasses and rubbed the lenses with a corner of the white cloth napkin, she noticed the dark mole just beneath his left cheekbone. The light from the sun turned his eyes from deep brown to amber, and she could tell by the way his knee brushed the tabletop that he was tall.

Definitely not from here. Midwestern maybe, or maybe even from the South.

"Well, how about a verse of...whatever that was you were singing last Thursday?"

"Beg pardon?"

He let out a small laugh. "You've been quiet lately. No singing. Did something happen?"

Now she was embarrassed. This man had actually heard her sing. Listened to her. And liked it.

"Just something I do, something to make the time go by. I do it when I don't even know I'm doing it. My manager says it's not 'professional.'"

Been singing my whole life, she wanted to say. *I don't know how not to.*

"Too bad. I thought it gave the place a little color."

She smiled. *Color? That'd be the last thing they're looking for here.*

"Be right back with that coffee, sir." When she returned with his cup, he asked, "So, what was that song anyway? The one you were singing last week?"

She turned to glance behind her, making sure Enriqué wasn't watching. She had no idea what the song was. Maybe something she'd heard on the radio, on the street, or passing the open door of a shop. There was always music in her head, and she was often unable to place where it came from or even when she began to sing it. She looked over her shoulder again and spotted Enriqué walking to his office and closing the door.

"Was it this one?"

She didn't know the words, so she hummed lightly, starting high and descending to the lower octave. It was just a small melody, a four-bar phrase or so. Since the storm, she sang it to herself whenever she needed to go away in her mind. Whenever she thought of that last night with her father, or when she remembered her mother. Or whenever she thought about home, the way the city used to be. Or whenever she woke up from a dream of water rising. She hummed it when she feared for her brother's life, or worried about what would become of him. Or when she had a morning like this one. It felt good to sing now, to hear herself and feel the music coming out, to feel it unspool from her, a golden thread of peace.

"Yeah, yeah, something like that." His smile was approving, appreciative. "That's the one, I think."

"My daddy used to love that song so," she said. She remembered it from when she was a girl. It was the only song he played on his stereo that wasn't jazz, blues, or gospel. There was a sadness to the melody. He played it a lot after her stepmother left them.

"Miss Malveaux. When you finish with your customer, I'd like to see you in my office."

Enriqué stood just five feet away, a pencil tucked behind his ear.

The customer looked alarmed. "Oh, I'm so sorry. I didn't mean to get you into trouble."

Eden's heart thumped. "I better go see what he wants. Excuse me."

Once inside Enriqué's office, she felt a chill even though the tiny room was windowless and humid. It reeked of cheap cigars. With his white sleeves rolled to his elbows, Enriqué sat behind a paper-cluttered wooden desk and pushed his wire-rimmed readers up on the bridge of his nose.

He looked up, but didn't meet her eyes. "Going to have to let you go."

"Excuse me?" A sinking feeling in her gut. "I don't understand, Mr. Enriqué. What did I do?"

He took off his glasses and rubbed his forehead. A ropy vein bulged at his temple. "Look," he let out a sigh of exhaustion. "You were twenty minutes late today." He took a sip from a half-filled coffee cup in front of him. "You should have called. And what did you do to your knee?"

Eden looked down. Blood had soaked through the bandage.

"And while you were talking to that guy—while you were *singing* to him—I saw a woman trying to get your attention for another glass of water. I had to get it for her."

She apologized. She was so, so sorry. Her phone's battery had died because the power was out in her house after the storm and then her brother forgot…and then she fell. She stuttered silly excuses. "It won't happen again," she said, her voice breaking.

Barely looking up from his desk, he told her she was a good enough waitress. It wasn't that. She just didn't fit in. And she'd been warned about the singing. And one of the customers last week had complained. She could work until the end of the week, then pick up her check.

Bile rose in her throat. She wanted to apologize again, to beg. She wanted to get down on her knees, even the bleeding one. As clearly as a vision, she realized how useless it would be. "No, thank you," she told him. She'd leave today.

Dazed, she cleared out her locker, filled a brown grocery sack with the contents—a Thermos, a bag of Oreo cookies, a slightly smashed box of Kleenex, extra panty hose, an unopened bag of Cheetos, and a white coffee cup that said *I* ❤ *NY*—and walked toward the door.

The customer in the corner, his *Times* still open on the table, watched her. "Is everything OK?"

She walked toward him and stood by the window. Sunlight illuminated the tears in her eyes.

In her New Orleans neighborhood of Holy Cross, right after any big storm, sunlight blinked silver flecks on the surface of the river, sprouted jewel-green grass along the levee, and coaxed wildflowers of red and purple from dead swaths of earth. Thinking of it emboldened her.

"You know, I 'member the song now." She was afraid she would cry, but she cleared her throat a little, then sang, her voice in full bloom.

Her high notes had never rung truer. When she finished, her shoulders spread wide. She felt warm and powerful. *Everything will be OK.* The double doors of the restaurant, facing the slender trees on 106th, barely made a sound when they closed behind her.

At 9:30 that night, in the sixth floor Harlem walk-up Eden shared with her brother, Reginald Jr., she poured herself a third glass of red zinfandel and put her still-swollen leg up on the brown velour Salvation Army sofa donated by the church. The room was drafty, so she wrapped her cotton bathrobe around her neck. Her eyes, finally dry, were rimmed red.

The apartment building, a brick high-rise built just after the Second World War, was just a few blocks away from the IRT station at 125th. Besides the bathroom, there were two rooms, a bedroom, and a living room that doubled as a kitchen and had a small sink, a refrigerator, and an electric stove pressed against one wall. The apartment was small, but just big enough for a woman and her teenaged brother clawing their way up from rock bottom. From beyond the thin walls came the restless cadence of the street below: cats fighting and people arguing, couples making noises of love, war, or both, all around the sounds of people living the best they could.

"I was thinking, you know, I could get me a job. I could work after school."

A toothbrush dangled from Reginald Jr.'s mouth as he came out of the bathroom and stood looking at her on the couch. She realized how tall he was getting to be and wondered if by now he had passed his father's height. And his face—his jaw was beginning to jut, his rounded boyish bones angled sharply, just like his father's.

Reginald Jr. had been only three when their father died, leaving eighteen-year-old Eden to assume the role of mother, father, and whatever else a boy needed in the way of guardianship. Eden remembered her father, Reginald Malveaux, Sr. as a dapper man, a proper man, a gentleman with apple-butter skin and a Hollywood smile that flashed wide whenever someone put on Dinah Washington's "This Bitter Earth," or an LP by young Aretha, when her soprano bubbled way above the staff. His Duke Ellington hair gleamed, laid to the side with Murray's Pomade, and his eyes shone like small suns. His big palms had coarsened from years in the shipyard near the river. But his wing-tipped Florsheims were always polished to a mirror shine. When a man wore steel-toed brogans Monday through Friday, sharp Sunday morning shoes reaffirmed his dignity and pride.

A mostly self-educated man, Reginald Sr. spoke "proper," his eloquent speech crisp as a starched dress shirt, meant to mask the absence of a college degree. Book smart, obsessed with libraries and used bookstores, he read constantly, favoring poets like Yeats and Langston Hughes and the *New York Times* for news. She was smart, too, he'd always told her, smarter than she believed she was, as smart as anybody needed to be. He was a thoughtful man, proud, always dispensing advice: *Make sure you got on decent shoes. Nothing cheap and no run-down heels. And make sure your grammar is correct. Folks like to size you up from head to toe, so make sure they don't go cross-eyed at what comes from your mouth or covers your feet.* She had the shoes part down; flip-flops were for the shower, not the street, and soles worn toward their outer edges were a sure sign of triflin' trash. But try as she might to affect her father's tony speech, "he do" and "she don't" slipped from her tongue as easily as spit. Her verbs and subjects did not just disagree, they were in armed combat.

On the night he died, she remembered him struggling to speak, to get his final words out. His faint voice slipped, inaudible, beneath the whir of the fan, and she could only imagine what he'd wanted to say. But she'd remembered his instructions for her brother: *Keep him safe.*

She was trying, but there was so much to remember. So much to pass on. From that night on, she'd done all she could, but she'd been only a kid herself. Or she might as well have been.

"Ain't no reason why I can't work, till you find something." Reginald Jr. was still standing over her. "What's wrong with you? You ain't talking?"

She held in her hand a stack of final notice bills and a letter that had arrived a week ago bearing the arthritic scrawl of Aunt Baby's handwriting. In the letter's three pages, her only living relative in New Orleans, her father's maternal aunt, was filling her in on the gossip of neighbors—who'd gone and who'd come back in the past year, who'd been seen, and who'd not been heard from. She glossed over that part to the final paragraph: *If you ever need anything, you just let me know. I got something special for you, something that can help you. But now I need to see you. I need you to come see about me as soon as you can.*

Tucked into the fold of the last page were a hundred-dollar bill and three twenties. *For bus fare,* Aunt Baby had written.

Was she sick? Was she dying? Maybe the old woman, close to the end, just wanted to see her. She folded the money and tucked it into a zipper pocket in the purse at her feet.

The thought was fleeting—*no.* No way, she decided, that she would use the money for some other purpose. Bad karma. She'd read about it. What if she ignored the letter, spent the money on groceries or new shoes, and the woman died? She had to go home.

And maybe there was more money where that came from.

She took a sip of wine and looked up at her brother.

"We talked about this. You don't need to be working now. You need to get your grades up."

"But—"

She held up a hand, took another sip. "You ain't gotta worry about it. I got everything under control. I can get another job. I'll get me another job soon as I get back. Go finish brushing your teeth and get in that shower. You sweating like you been shooting hoops again."

"Only played for five minutes."

"Well, still—"

"Get back from where? Where you going?"

A small roach crawled across the dull gray carpet of the living room and headed toward the bathroom. She sighed wearily. Maybe a trip home was what she needed. Maybe it was a sign. Being home might help. The river was still there. She could sit on Aunt Baby's steps, look at the Mississippi, and figure out what the hell to do next.

"I gotta go 'way for a couple of days." She nodded, the decision made. "Aunt Baby," she said to Reginald Jr., holding up the letter. "I gotta go back home."

CHAPTER 3

New Orleans, 1919

"Do you remember this man?"

She glared at the man speaking, at his cool ice-blue eyes, and his wool uniform, at least a size too small for him, exaggerating his protruding belly. Did he think she was crazy? She glanced over at the man in the topcoat who was standing next to him. Of course, she remembered him. She answered with a dismissive head turn, too annoyed to speak.

"Let me start this way. What were you doing, a woman alone, walking that hour of the night?"

That was the more curious question. Her head was splitting. A single lamp lit the room; shadows flitted on the dark gray walls. The stench of stale cigarettes, unwashed wool, and sweat filled the cramped space. She had never been inside a police station before. Why in God's name was she in one now? She'd never broken the law in her life, and whatever she'd intended, tonight was no different.

Two blank, white faces stared at her.

"Beg your pardon, please?"

The one in the topcoat, his handlebar mustache a thick bristle beneath his angular nose, gave her a narrow-eyed look. And then she remembered she'd only answered in her head, not aloud.

A woman alone. Don't you mean a colored *woman?* There was no way this officer saw anything but dark skin before him. No doubt, he had already fixed her in his mind as one of the Mahogany Hall clan, one of Miss Lulu White's girls, even though Storyville, where the women plied their trade with the sailors, had closed two years ago. *Do they have any idea who I am? No, of course not.* The insult of it burned like hot ash between her eyes.

"Yes. Sir."

"'Yes, sir,' what?"

"Yes, sir. I remember him."

"And you were out walking alone at night because…?"

I wanted to go to the river, was all she could think to say. *I wanted to go down to the river as I had every right to do.* What she did was her own business.

But, again, she couldn't speak. The man in the topcoat moved toward her and revealed something she hadn't noticed before, a row of framed portraits of five presidents of the United States. The one in the middle was of a man with wire-rimmed spectacles.

It was a lovely portrait, but didn't look anything like the same man, the President Theodore Roosevelt she'd met twelve years ago. The man in the portrait had the gaze of a lion. In person, his eyes were kinder. He dearly loved the Stephen Foster songs. "Swanee River" was his favorite, he'd told her, then bowed and took her hand. And no one he'd heard had ever sung it more beautifully. His faint smile curled his bushy mustache and crinkled the lines around his eyes.

She had sung for three of his predecessors including President McKinley, the one he had replaced. She had looked into Roosevelt's eyes and thought, *Dear Lord, I hope they don't kill you, too.*

Instead of answering the officer's question, she looked into the white porcelain cup on the metal table before her. "What kind of tea did you say this was?"

"We managed to find what you asked for, sassafras."

Sassafras. Cleanses the body and the blood. Her throat was dry. She was in need of a hot liquid for her vocal cords. It was important, whether she was going to sing again or not.

"What were you thinking, going toward that fire?"

"Fire?"

"You were trying to walk into the building as it was burning to the ground."

She took a sip of the tea. The two men turned away from her and exchanged a whispered conversation.

"What in the name of heaven were you doing there? Did you set the fire?"

She raised her eyebrows.

"I asked you, did you set the opera house on fire?"

She blinked. Had she? Had she willed it? Had something in her created a force that could set a building ablaze?

She thought back to when she'd returned home to New Orleans from her triumphs in Europe. London. Paris. They had all loved her. The night after her arrival, she went to the opera. The French Quarter was alive, vibrant. She remembered the grand stage from high up in the colored balcony. *I will sing on that stage,* she vowed, *if it is the last thing I ever do.*

Now she glared at the officer. The brass buttons of his dark blue uniform glinted in the artificial light. Set the fire that destroyed the greatest opera house in the nation? Did these men think she had that much power?

Do I?

There was a knock on the door. The top-coated man answered it. When he returned, his face was ghostly pale. He leaned over her and lightly rapped his large knuckles on the metal surface.

"This was not our decision," he began. "Someone has arranged…" He cleared his throat. "We, ah…have been given instructions to allow you to go."

The top-coated man snorted and huffed as he escorted her out. At the door of the station, a cool wind nipped and the moon's soft gray light was already giving way to the sun. Her unlined coat and her satin gown, while perfect for the back of a chauffeured motorcar, were not so for walking in the early morning air. She wrapped her white-gloved hands around her waist.

A black Tin Lizzie was parked at the curb, billowing gray smoke from its exhaust as it waited for her. She turned away from it and walked in the other direction.

The river rolled in the receding moonlight, its silver-tipped waves shimmering on the surface.

It was no secret to her who had arranged for her freedom. The only question was why. Bribery? A favor? A threat? Apparently, there was no limit to a wealthy maestro's power and influence.

The streetcar stop was only four blocks away, and as she walked, she realized the men in the station had never once spoken her name.

CHAPTER 4

New Orleans, 2006

The camelback shotgun squatted behind a warped chain-link fence, a stone's throw from the levee. A four-foot-high water mark stained the peeling white siding. A sun-bleached calf's skull, a stack of worn tires, and a white porcelain commode sat in the front yard. Next to the commode stood three crudely carved wooden crosses, two feet high. Like many of the houses in the Holy Cross neighborhood of the Ninth Ward, even months after the storm, Julia "Aunt Baby" Claremont's house looked uninhabited.

The taxi had pulled away a few minutes before, and there was still no answer to Eden's knock at the door. Eden stood on Aunt Baby's front stoop as her Motorola flip phone vibrated in her purse. *Reginald Jr., finally*. She'd been trying to reach him since she got off the bus.

"So, what you been doing? You just now finding time to return my call?"

"I called you," he said. "Twice. No answer."

She remembered. It had rung while she was finding her luggage.

"Oh, yeah, well. Finish that homework. You find that hamburger in the freezer and thaw it out? Good. It's some pickles on the door of the fridge. Make you a sandwich for dinner. You need anything, ask Mr. Wembly up in 8C. All right, Boo Boo Head. See you Thursday night."

Eden knocked once more. *Aunt Baby probably doesn't hear that well anymore, probably takes her a while to get to the door anyway.* Sitting cross-legged atop her wheeled luggage, she surveyed the front yard of random objects, the weedy grasses, the vacant street, and nearby on the river, a quiet barge floating south. She sucked in a deep breath of river breeze and lifted her face to meet the sun. It was so much colder in New York, but spring had come to the South and it was good to be home. There was a comfort here not found in any corner of New York, storm or not, and this holy mess of a city welcomed her back like a warm, unmade bed she'd just left. Her pulse slowed. Here, by the river her father loved, where the wind feathered the hairs on your arms, the whole world slowed to a crawl and gave you time to think. Waited for you, wrapped its arms around you, if that was what you needed. Even after all that had happened, there was a peace in landing back in the nest from which you had sprung.

"Eden! Child, how long you been out here?"

Short and frail, Julia "Baby" Claremont stood smiling in the half-open door. She wore a red kaftan, and her black turban revealed a fringe of black curls.

"What you doing out there, child? Come on in here! Why you didn't knock?"

Eden rolled her bag to the door where Aunt Baby stood. Eden could see her own reflection in the thickness of the old woman's glasses, a reminder of her battle with glaucoma. Aunt Baby still bore a seasoned elegance; in her sculpted cheekbones, rounded forehead, and sable skin, Eden was reminded of being told how stunning Aunt Baby had been when she was young.

"So, how you doing, Aunt Baby?"

"Still above ground, praise Jesus. Come on in."

Aunt Baby closed the door behind Eden and faced her with one hand on her chest. She looked down at Eden's bandaged knee, then looked up, sucking her tongue.

"So, New York, huh? Eating you alive, ain't it? Baby, that place can be a bitch."

She led Eden into the shell of a living room, just two-by-fours and unpainted drywall, muttering to Eden to be careful where she stepped. Eden followed closely behind. There was a heaviness in the woman's walk, as if she was staggered by some old weight, long forgotten but still there.

"Come on back this way," Aunt Baby said. The back of the house looked somewhat finished. At the end of the long hallway were two bedrooms, side by side.

Eden followed Aunt Baby into the bedroom on the left. A full-sized bed was draped in an orange and yellow flower-print spread. Curtains of the same fabric hung over newly installed windows. She parted the curtains to reveal a yard of foot-high grass and weeds and an angel trumpet tree, drooping in the afternoon sun.

"Child, volunteers been coming in from everywhere—even back east. Helping us get our houses together, those that want to. Mexicans working everywhere! Everybody speaking Spanish, playing that Mexican radio music! I got a whole team of 'em here! The men polite and cute as can be, although who knows what they're saying!"

Aunt Baby sat in an armchair by the window while Eden sat on the bed and rearranged herself as the thin mattress sank beneath her weight. *Shocking*, she thought, *how finished the two bedrooms look compared to the front of the house.*

"Just got your room fixed up yesterday," Aunt Baby said, looking proudly around at the spartan furnishings of Eden's room: the bed, a four-drawer wooden chest, and the small, hinged mirror atop it, and a side table of black plastic with an imitation Tiffany lamp. Aunt Baby looked out the window at the neighborhood, or what was left of it. "Ain't much to look at back here. Folks coming back in dribbles and drabs, those that can make it back at all."

So far, Eden's great-aunt showed no signs of failing health, or anything that would require her to drop everything and travel home. Surely, she wanted more than company.

"How's your health, Aunt Baby? You holding up OK?"

"Me? Child, I feel fine!" Julia looked over her shoulder. "Good for an old woman. Had me a excellent BM this morning! Feel like a new woman."

Eden might have attributed the woman's candor to old age, but she had always been this way. If Aunt Baby thought it, it was as good as spoken.

Then Julia pointed out the houses on the block, who lived where and where they were now. Who was coming back, who would never come back, and who had not been heard from since the storm. Eden tried to remember the families in the neighborhood from her childhood. The Carters with the big German Shepherd? They hadn't lived in New Orleans for years. The folks who lived in that yellow house on the corner, a retired couple from Bogalusa? They went back home. The Mandervilles? Never left, but waited out the storm with their son over cross the bridge on the West Bank. Took on five feet but planning to rebuild. Never did find her cat. The Hobson twins' grandmother, Juanita Maye? A sweet old lady with a scary-looking goiter and tightly curled, blue-rinse hair. Eden remembered her.

"Juanita Maye, bless her. Gone on to a better place," Aunt Baby nodded, matter-of-factly.

Eden's face shadowed. "Oh, I'm so sorry to hear that." Aunt Baby shrugged. "Mmm-hmm. Nashville. Nephew sent for her. Better place for her than here."

"Oh, you mean…Right." Not heaven, Eden thought. Just Nashville.

And what about Randy Marvais? The name seemed to come to Eden from nowhere. She hadn't thought of him in years, the man with whom she'd almost managed to ruin her own life.

As if reading her mind, Aunt Baby said, "What's that boy's name used to chase around after you? Jesse Marvais's grandson. Long, tall, drink-a water. Randy, that's his name, saw him down to the Rite Aid. Think he works there when he's not hauling trash to the dump. Baby, I tell you. You wanna make some money now, get you a trash-hauling job. You be working day and night for the next twenty years!"

Wood creaked as Aunt Baby rose from her chair, gave a steadying knock of her cane against the floor. "You know that boy stuck around here during the storm? Heard he pulled Ludelia Banks out of a tree, carried her on his back through all that water and mess. You seen Ludelia. You know she ain't no small woman. Anyway, he asked after you just the other day when I was down to the store. Always thought y'all would hitch up together. You got you a man up in New York?"

"No, ma'am."

"Well, child, you need to find you somebody! Especially up there where it gets so cold at night—you know what I mean. I know you got your brother to look after, but he ain't gon' be there forever and ain't no sin in finding a little company." She sucked her teeth. "You young, child. Too young to give up. Look at you. You looking kinda tired, but you still got that smooth skin like your mama and a good head-a hair. Nice little figure, too, just like me when I was your age." She laughed. "Child, I was a fox back in my day!" She let out a long, low belch as she steadied herself on her feet. "'Scuse, me, baby. My own cooking done turnt on me here lately! Glad you back! So happy to see Reginald's girl again! I got a pot of gumbo on—I know you ain't had no decent gumbo in a while! Bathroom's right over there. Help yourself, you want to freshen up or anything. Come on out when you're ready to eat. Gumbo's just about ready. Welcome home, baby."

In the bathroom, she found an array of wood studs, unfinished drywall, and naked plumbing behind the sink. Eden splashed cold water on her face. The humidity here, she had forgotten the weight of it. She'd been back only once since the flood. The first time, a few months ago, was after the death of her father's best friend (a trumpet player and former postman from La Place), and his funeral coincided with the mayoral election. Because she'd sung solos at church as a child, Eden had been known around town early, and had topped the church's A-list for funerals and weddings. The postman's widow had summoned her to sing at the service, so for a bus ticket and seventy-five dollars for her trouble, she took the all-night Greyhound home to pay respects and cast a vote.

At the two-hour service, she'd sang a soulful "Soon I Will Be Done," setting off a chorus of "Amen, sisters!" that could be heard blocks away. Then she marched in the second line, her tears obscuring the devastation. Friends had warned her, "Don't look too deep, 'cause it was worse than you could imagine." She took their word for it—she couldn't imagine it and didn't want to try. After the service, she voted at the high school, then took the first bus back to New York.

She hadn't seen her great-aunt then. But being back in Aunt Baby's house triggered memories of childhood, and the last time her father brought her here.

She was about twelve years old when she'd first heard the rumors about Julia "Aunt Baby" Claremont, a (mostly) single woman who was rarely employed, but never poor, had a racy past that was dark and shady as the Mississippi, and nearly as deep. The women among whom she grew up at Holy Trinity Catholic Church narrowed their disapproving eyes and shared tales of Aunt Baby's adventures and exploits during her youth. "Hussy." "Street woman." The language of the neighbors and churchwomen would have been much worse had it not been restrained by Christian propriety and decency. Rumors fanned through the neighborhood like a storm breeze from the Gulf.

Some said, for instance, that Julia Claremont had a liaison with a famous New Orleans politician in the 1940s who ended up in the cabinet of the president of France. Years later, photographs surfaced, showing the politician's wife with a young child who, some believed, was the spitting image of Aunt Baby herself. Others said the famous lover in question wasn't a politician at all but a former merchant marine turned shipping magnate who somehow managed to get rich during the Great Depression. Aunt Baby, they claimed, stole off with him to Parma, Italy, on his wedding night while his new wife sat waiting in the bridal suite at the Roosevelt Hotel. Two months later, a bored Aunt Baby supposedly returned to New Orleans, having dusted her hands of that affair, and awaited the next.

Years passed and the rumors continued: She'd had an affair with a Catholic priest, then extorted money from him. She'd been the mistress of an English lord. Some members of the church where Aunt Baby had been christened as an infant claimed that, at barely nineteen, she'd been the proprietor of an illegal house of ill repute just a few blocks from the French Quarter. Some claimed this was just not true; she had simply entertained there.

Aunt Baby did nothing to quash the rumors and instead conducted herself in such a way as to keep them aloft. Her wide-set almond eyes embellished a secretive, flirtatious smile. Her wavy, dark hair framed a symmetrical, valentine-shaped face. With smooth, copper skin and a showgirl's legs, she was a self-proclaimed fox in her day; Eden knew this because as a child, she had often seen Aunt Baby strike a pose and say, "Child, I was a fox in my day!" With that, she would wink, twirl around on four-inch heels with her hands on her hips, flip a black feather boa across a naked shoulder, and cock a wide-brimmed, red-flowered hat to a seductive tilt over one eye. Even years past her prime (How old was she now? Ninety? Older?), she was as self-possessed as a siren; her lipstick choice showed a preference for darker hues before they were vogue and her Max Factor foundation could well have been applied with a palette knife. Her wardrobe leaned toward bright reds and violets, but in the finest fabrics—silk and cashmere for winter, linen for spring—and stitched by the best couturiers.

Even though her father had forbidden Eden from going to see Aunt Baby after her mother died, the lure of legend was too great. She ducked her father's watchful eye one night to go dance with the devil herself, knowing the woman who had done just about everything would allow her to do just about anything. "Child, your daddy know you here?" Aunt Baby had squinted her eyes and looked sidelong at the girl. When Eden said, "No, ma'am," Aunt Baby shook her head and sucked her teeth, but opened her door wide.

It was a world Eden had never seen. Thick plush drapes. Velvet-embossed walls. Furniture fit for a royal drawing room, and photographs of people she had only read about. Louis Armstrong and Duke Ellington. Lena Horne and Huey Long. Their hair shining, eyes smiling, and shoulders nudging Aunt Baby's. Dressed to the nines and flouncing around her living room to the music that suited her mood—worn vinyls of Bessie Smith or Billie. Julia had invited Eden to smoke some of her unidentified herb and sip her sweet tea, sweet wine, or champagne while the older woman regaled her with highlights of her heyday in the blues clubs of Memphis or Chicago or beyond.

Try as she might, Eden couldn't recall the specific reason her father forbade contact with Aunt Baby. For years, the rule stuck: Do not go there. Do not speak of her. One evening, when her father found out she had gone against his will, his face flushed, his eyes blazed. He ordered her into the car and drove to Aunt Baby's house.

The sky was clear that October night. A full harvest moon rose over the river. She remembered the moon because at school that day they had talked about how it made dogs howl, crops grow, and tides shift. And a full one, folks said, could make some people do outrageous things.

That had to be the reason.

Reginald Sr. parked in the yard and told her to stay in the car while he went inside. The calm evening air outdoors belied the storm within—two voices, both enraged. Then a horrific wail and a grown man's desperate tears. When he got back in the car, stone-faced and silent, he said nothing all the way home and never spoke of Aunt Baby again. His silence lasted until the day he died.

Years later, the letters from Aunt Baby began: first, Christmas cards, then notes, and then pages detailing her travels to Chicago, London, and Barcelona. Finally, the letters were only postmarked from New

Orleans. "Come see me, whenever you can." An invitation, despite her
father's admonitions, to come back to family. All that time, Eden had
wondered, *What really happened between you?*

"Gumbo's ready now!" Aunt Baby's voice echoed throughout the house.
"Got some collards and cornbread, too! Whenever you ready."

In the middle of what Aunt Baby swore would someday become
a living room, she had set up a card table draped by a red plastic
tablecloth with purple and green Mardi Gras masques painted on it
and placed a huge stock pot in the center. Two large red candles, casting high shadows against the bare walls, stood between their bowls.
Mouth-watering. Saliva pooled around Eden's tongue at the expec-
tation of thick, peppery roux. While they ate, Aunt Baby ranted like
a woman who hadn't had a real conversation in years, which for all
Eden knew may have been true. Eden was content to listen because
the gumbo, so rich, so authentic with its succulent shrimp and tender
chunks of sausage and chicken, made her want to cry. How could she
have forgotten the sacred marriage of okra and bell pepper, celery and
onions, properly spiked with Creole spice and gumbo filé? The first
spoonful held June night breezes by the river, languorous and sweetly
lazy, the way her father's trombone spun out sultry, backwater blues.

"Aunt Baby," Eden closed her eyes. "This...it's so good. I missed
this so much."

Aunt Baby waved her hand, dismissively. "Ain't they got gumbo in
New York? Don't even answer that. I was in New York with my second
husband Ralph Edward, back in '67, ordered gumbo at the Everest
Hotel down in SoHo. Little sorry-ass pieces of chicken and shrimp
in some kinda nasty gravy so thick you could stand a fork up in it.
Wouldn't serve it to a dog. And I don't care for no dogs. I sent it back
to the kitchen with a few choice words for the chef I wrote on the back
of the menu." She sighed. "Eat all you want! I'ma do these dishes now."

Aunt Baby got up from the table and Eden started to get up, too.

"No, no child. You sit yourself right there and keep me company while I straighten up."

Eden listened while Aunt Baby went on about the house: the new roof, the paint color she'd chosen for the almost-finished kitchen, and the new furniture she planned to order. Aunt Baby's soft Louisiana tones were as comforting as a hymn, and when she finished sudsing and rinsing the last dish, she sat down, folded both hands in her lap, and looked at Eden. "I'm old, child. Got a lot on my heart I need to get off before I go on to my reward."

Eden sat up straight.

"I look at you, child," she began, "and I see my nephew Reginald. More him in you than your mama. She was a pretty thing, like you, but you had Reginald's ways. And you got Reginald's heart. Now your step-mama, that's a whole n'other story, you know. Your daddy was a lonely man after your mama went, but he shoulda never married that girl. Too young. And then that depression thing some women get after birthing a baby? Well, she just couldn't shake it after your baby brother was born. When I heard one day she just grabbed her purse and left, well, I was not a bit surprised."

Eden nodded but looked away. Whenever she thought about all of this, her mother's death and the young woman who became her step-mother and the way she left, it was as if it was happening all over again.

Aunt Baby shifted in her seat. "But maybe I wasn't much better. I think at the time she walked out on y'all, I was off somewhere, France, I believe it was. Provence. My third husband had a retail wine business there. When that fell apart, I fell apart. I went back to my old ways. I drank, did a little of this and that, you know. I went from one man to another. I was shameless. And long about the time Reginald died, well, them was some hard times. I was so strung out I couldn't see straight. Anyway, what I'm trying to say is, I wasn't there for y'all kids and I know it and I'm sorry. Reginald was right. I wasn't fit to take care of children, even if I had been willing, which I sure as Jesus wasn't. I just couldn't do it."

Eden let Aunt Baby's words dissolve into the quiet of the room. "Aunt Baby," she began, "That's all in the past. It's over."

Making amends. If the woman isn't dying, she's getting all ready for it.

"That was all before I came to the Lord. It was Cherise, watching her go down with that monkey on her back, that's what did it for me. That changed me. Swear to God it did."

Eden remembered. She'd heard the stories. Cherise and Aunt Baby were women who lived with abandon, women who flaunted their wiles, sashayed through life free and easy as men. They were as thick as thieves, according to her father. Whatever reckless habits Aunt Baby had, her best friend Cherise Duvelle Johnson had them in spades.

Aunt Baby pulled the black cotton turban from her head and placed it in her lap. She fingered the spirals of thinning curls around her forehead.

"I just want you to know that I'ma leave my house to you and Reginald Jr. after I'm gone. 'Course, right now, I ain't never felt better, so don't count on it too soon! But I'm fixing it up for you and your brother.

"And when I get it all fixed up, I'll have plenty of room. I know the projects y'all was living in, well, they closed 'em down for good. But I'm hoping y'all will come and live with me." There it was. Aunt Baby was getting her house together, literally and figuratively. She wanted to set things right, and Eden and her brother were part of the picture. Eden struggled with the thought. *Come back to New Orleans? With the police looking for him?* Aunt Baby didn't know about Reginald's troubles. And even if there was no police trouble, Reginald Jr. wouldn't last a day here. He would slip back to his old ways, fall prey to the streets, as he had since he was thirteen.

"Aunt Baby, I don't know what to say. Uh…thank you. I mean, I don't know if we can come back here to live, at least right now, but thank you."

Aunt Baby gave her a quizzical, hurt look, then rubbed her hands together in her lap. She nodded as if the matter was tabled for now, but still open for later discussion. "Well. City's on the way back, things changing fast. You used to love it down here. Now, you got your own place coming, if you want it. Right here by the river."

For a moment, Eden allowed herself to dream—living with her brother in this house with the river she loved right at her door. Back home where she belonged.

Impossible.

"Aunt Baby, I got a favor to ask." Eden sighed, composed herself. Now seemed as good a time as any. "I...I need some help. I don't know nobody else to go to. I lost my job. I can't even tell you how it happened. It was just crazy." She stopped and lowered her head, touching her hand to her forehead. She hadn't said these words to anyone except Reginald Jr., and her voice came out ragged, frayed. The thickness in her throat, the swelling of emotion surprised her.

"Well, there you go. You just move on back here. My place'll be ready, they tell me, two, three more months."

And do what? Eden thought. She'd changed sheets at the Monteleone in the Quarter and waited tables at The Praline Connection on Frenchmen Street. But even if her brother's street ways and cop troubles didn't prevent them moving back, what were the chances of her getting a job at either place? "Well, we just can't...not right now. Maybe someday. But if you could spare a loan, a few hundred even, I know I can get me a job when I get back to New York 'cause they always need good waitresses. I mean, I could pay you back."

Silence stretched like a blanket between them.

Aunt Baby got up from her chair. "Come with me," she said. She led Eden to a storage room off the kitchen. In the corner was a large metal box. "Look in there, child."

Eden reached down, her heart racing. She had heard stories of houses where stashes of cash or valuables long lost had been revealed after the storm. The top of the metal box was slightly concave, as if it had been recovered from the bottom of a pile of heavy objects.

Inside, beneath a stack of ruined photographs in cheap plastic frames and a dozen rippled copies of *Life and Look* magazine was an object wrapped in yards and yards of water-stained fabric—a ledger of buckled pages bound in brown leather.

"What is it?" Eden unraveled the cloth and held the ledger up to the light.

"Somebody's scrapbook. Can you believe that thing survived all that water and mess? Must have been in just the right place all these years, nobody messing with it."

Just inside the cover was a photograph of a black woman, her hair tied back and loosely knotted at the nape of her neck, wearing a white lace gown. Her eyes were large and brown, and her ivory-gloved index finger delicately curved under her chin. Layers of eggshell ribbon bordered her bodice and neckline.

The book and the photographs looked as if they had been sitting for a century, but they were remarkably intact. Eden turned the delicate sheets of press clippings and news articles, crudely glued in, every page crackling. Incredibly, the print had barely faded. Among the clippings were picture postcards of foreign landmarks: An opera house in Paris. The Eiffel Tower. Buckingham Palace. There were handwritten letters on thin and faded stationery, and now and then a handwritten paragraph or note alongside the clippings.

Eden looked up. "Somebody famous, a performer, a singer, or something? How'd you get this?"

Aunt Baby smiled and shrugged. "Storm," she said. "When I come back from Memphis after the flood, I went over to see Mildred Fountaineau. Don't suspect you know her, a nurse over at Charity. But she used to do hair sometimes. Did mine in fact. Lived a few blocks from here, over toward the bridge. Anyway, don't you know that house, the whole damn thing, moved off the slab and was sitting in the middle of the street? Part of the back end came clean off the house. Whole big pile of debris left behind. That box was just sitting there where part of the house used to be."

Eden remembered Mildred Fountaineau. A fellow church member. She often checked in on her father in his final weeks. "Is Mildred OK?"

"Yeah, she's all right, neighbors said. Her people sent for her. Texas. Far as I know, she's doing fine." Aunt Baby smiled. She poked her cane inside the box. "Look down into that box some more."

Eden reached further and felt something with a rough, hide-like texture. She pulled out a small pouch of dry, stiff leather. Her heart raced. She placed it on the floor and looked at Aunt Baby.

"Well, go on. Open it."

Eden loosened the drawstrings. Inside the pouch was a handful of medallions, like military medals, strung on red, blue, and yellow ribbons with gold or brass chains.

Her heart sank. *No money in here.*

"Got foreign writing on them," Aunt Baby said. "Look to me like gold or something. Anyway, look how old they are. And they belonged to the woman who collected them clippings."

Eden took one of the medallions in her hand, feeling its heft and weight. There were five of them, each one inscribed with writing in a language she couldn't decipher. One read, PREMIER PRIX, 1888. Another was from 1893.

"Awards," Aunt Baby said. "Medals for something, a contest maybe. Something like that."

Eden put it all back in the box. "You said there was money in here?"

Aunt Baby frowned, impatient. "Look in there some more. You haven't seen all of it."

Eden tugged at a heavy object caught at the bottom of the pouch: a necklace, a round pendant with edges of braided metal, heavily tarnished, with a thick chain. It was crusted with decades of grime, but it was interesting-looking. Not something she would have described as beautiful, but the weight of it was impressive.

"Something from somebody's jewelry box," Aunt Baby said.

Eden held it up by her fingertips. "Doesn't look like much to me."

Aunt Baby laughed. "Child, you looking at money! Even if there's no gold or nothing, just think how old they are. Somebody somewhere collects that kind of thing. Pawn shop, antique dealer probably give you some decent money for them. Take them with you. See what you can get."

Eden put the necklace back, dusted her hands off, and stood. She couldn't think of a thing to say.

Aunt Baby looked defeated. "Truth is, child, I ain't got no money. Outlived most of it. Used to be money would just fall into my hands—one man, then another. But those days been over a long time. Then the storm…insurance company wasn't a goddamn bit of help, 'scuse my French. No flood insurance. Little bit of money I saved up, I put into fixing up this place. For you and your brother, so y'all'll have something for yourselves."

Eden could see how excited Aunt Baby was and didn't want to disappoint her, but this was a far cry from what she'd hoped to find by coming home. A house for a future she couldn't imagine. Trash. Old mementos, rusted and worthless. She looked at her great-aunt and forced a smile.

"Aunt Baby," she began. "This is real nice and everything…"

Her mobile phone buzzed in her purse.

"Hello?" A woman answered and identified herself as a nurse at Reginald Jr.'s school. Eden could barely wrap her mind around her words. When the woman finished speaking, she said, "I'll be there as soon as I can."

Aunt Baby placed a hand on Eden's arm. "What, baby?"

She hung up, then swallowed hard. "My brother," she began, her voice shaky. "Something happened, some kid at school…there was a fight." She sat back down and put her head between her hands.

"Some kid stabbed him with a knife."

CHAPTER 5

New Orleans, 1920

The noon sun blazed on a dusty lot off Rampart Street near the Quarter as two young black boys tossed a baseball back and forth between them. Another pair of boys danced, grinning—tap-a-tap-tap-a-tap—on worn soles fitted with bottle caps. A peanut vendor, his white shirt-tail billowing in the humid breeze, passed them by: "Peanuts! Fresh peanuts!" A lean, young, brown-haired white man in knickers pushed a cart of fresh-caught fish. A stately Creole woman, wearing a red-and yellow head wrap and a long white skirt that flared around her ankles, carried a wooden basket of hot stuffed crabs. She stopped to sell them to a couple passing by. Waffles, bananas, taffy candy, fish, nuts—the bounty of goods sold on the street was endless.

When Celia got off the crowded streetcar and stepped into the unusually warm January weather, the smell of food was nearly intoxicating. She hadn't eaten much that day, and the scent of the ripe bananas made her head light.

The banana man's straw hat was rimmed with grime and his handlebar mustache curled as he smiled at her.

"I only want one," she told him.

"Fifteen for a dollar," he told her.

A dollar? Something she had not seen in a while. "I have…I don't have…" she started. "How much for two?"

He handed her a banana. "A gift," he told her. "Have a good day."

Charity, she thought. *Pity.* She was suddenly aware of how he must have seen her: weary, weak, hungry, and poor. She couldn't deny she was all of those things. But she was grateful for the banana and stopped to eat it beneath the shade of an oak tree just beyond the streetcar tracks.

They had told her it was not far, but the leather pouch she carried grew heavy as she searched the shop windows along the street—Gallier's Tailoring, Mondrian's Baked Goods, a bicycle shop, and a haberdashery. Next to the shoeshine parlor and before the barbershop, she'd been told. Finally, the green and white awning for J&D's Loan Shop came into view. She opened the door.

"May I help you?" The short pale man looked at her above the rims of his thick-lens wire spectacles.

She placed the pouch on the glass counter. "These things," she said. "How much would you give me for them?" She emptied the contents of the bag on the glass: three gold rings, a sapphire brooch, and a diamond-studded tiara. One by one, she picked up the five medals.

"These are very, very valuable," she said. "This one, this one here," she held the brooch in her hand, "this was given to me by…someone very famous. And this one, it contains real gold, as you can see."

She smiled at the recollection. A day in June, a bright sun warming a salt breeze from the Gulf. Louis Armstrong was brash, young—his talent a flame about to ignite the jazz world. A personality as fiery as the sun—a smile nearly as dazzling. And a proper gentleman. She'd wondered what was in the box he'd held. "A gift," he'd told her as he pressed it into her hand, "to the greatest singer in the world."

The man looked through the articles on the glass, incredulous. He palmed them, separated them and shook his head. He held up a medallion tied with red-and-yellow ribbon. "Some kind of medal or something, from some foreign country? Cheap metal. Not much value here." He looked at her again and raised an eyebrow. "Where did you say you got these items?" Now there was judgment in his stare.

Do you know who I am? Do you have any idea? I have sung all over the world, for presidents and kings. What have you done?

But she only lowered her head. Finally, she pulled the ring from her finger. One and one-half carats, set in a ring of small rubies. She fingered it thoughtfully, then held it out to him. "This was a gift from someone…very special."

He looked at it, then looked at her. "Where? How did you get this?"

How did a poor black woman like you acquire something like this?

"How much?" she asked him.

When he told her, she laughed sarcastically. "It's worth six times that much. You know it is. Maybe more."

"Take it or leave it," he said.

"As you say," she replied, gathering up the jewelry.

"Wait." He frowned and folded his hands on the glass. "I'll take the ring. I'll double the offer if you throw in the watch."

She looked down at her wrist-watch, an item she'd promised herself she'd never part with. If she had told him it was a gift from the Prince of Wales, he would have thrown her into the street.

She would not allow herself to be ridiculed and would not tolerate his laughter, his look of utter disbelief, his conviction that she was not only desperate but delusional.

She sighed.

It would only be enough to get by another few weeks or so until the sale of one of her houses came through, if it ever did.

How long had it been since she last sang? Minutes after the final curtain, in the dim light of the backstage at The Winslow Theater, the somber troupe had gone silent. It was the last show of the tour and the end of the bankrupt company. She had called the cast together— costume designers, actors, comedians, banjoists, fiddlers, drummers, tambourine players, jugglers, acrobats, and even the singers who performed subordinate roles to her featured opera selections—and told them there was no money to pay them.

"It breaks my heart," she'd told them tearfully, "but I will make it up to you all, somehow."

She'd wanted to believe she was telling the truth, but she knew what the cast knew: it would never happen. But now, the matter was not paying off debts, but survival.

"You are a remarkable artist," Prince Edward VII had told her before he bowed and gave the watch to her. "This once belonged to my mother. I want you to have it."

A clock for the wrist, like a bracelet. It was the latest fashion and she'd heard all the women in Paris were wearing them. Now she removed the watch from her wrist and, along with the ring on her finger, pushed it across the glass.

When she left the shop, a new hunger surfaced she hadn't allowed herself to feel before. Now she could eat without guilt. What was the name of the little Sicilian food store on Decatur Street? She could almost taste the olives, the warm bread, and the thin-sliced meat of the sandwich made by the little man with the drooping right eye. The walk would be long but worth it.

Every piece of jewelry she had of value. All gone. Almost.

If she had sold the gold pendant necklace, how much might she have gotten? Hundreds? More? Maybe enough to keep her living well for another year.

Impossible. She could never betray the trust of the old man. Never.

She touched the pendant to her cheek. *As long as there is breath in my body...*

CHAPTER 6

New Orleans, 2006

Reginald Jr.'s stab wound was not as serious as it could have been. There was no sign of infection and the knife had missed arteries and vital organs. Blood loss, but not enough to cause real concern. On the phone with the nurse, Eden was furious and anxious. *What the hell? How could something like this happen at a school where kids without daddies beat half the schools in the city at chess? Where armed guards patrolled the halls?* She demanded a conversation with somebody "in charge." Somehow, the assistant principal had explained, a fifteen-year-old sophomore had slipped a six-inch fishing knife past the metal detector. "It happens," he'd said.

She'd not been in New Orleans a full day. But there was no thought in her mind except getting back to New York.

Taking the Greyhound again would have taken forever. She managed to find a last-minute flight that got her home by noon the following morning. The ticket was expensive, but not as much as it could have been, thanks to the Newark and Manhattan New York Baptist Pastors' Alliance, which paid for discounted emergency air fares for New Orleans evacuees. But the cost of the ticket left her with less than three hundred dollars in the bank, and she still had an electric bill to pay, groceries to buy. And, with no insurance, there was the emergency room bill to pay, somehow. One more check was coming from Estelle's, but she would have to get some kind of job as soon as she got back to New York.

Aunt Baby had no money, she'd already told Eden, and she wasn't sick. There had been no reason to come back home. No reason at all.

Sixteen. Wasn't that old enough to be left alone for three days? She hadn't been much older than that when she'd become her brother's guardian. Hadn't younger kids lived without supervision, put themselves out into the world with no adults in sight? She never should have left him, even for three days. *Stupid.*

She sat on the stoop in front of Aunt Baby's house and watched the branches of the cypresses dip and sway in the breeze, listened to the river's drone, watched the fading sky. She pondered her predicament and took another drag on her cigarette, crushed the inch-long ash and filter tip beneath the sole of her sneaker. When she reached for another, she realized the pack was empty.

It'll be OK, she told herself. *He will be OK.*

"Stitches, but nothing to worry about," the nurse had said. He'd made an emergency room trip and the police had been called. He'd been sent home, heavily bandaged, and she needed to visit the assistant principal before he would be allowed back.

A police report. *What are the chances of his school finding out about what happened in New Orleans?*

She waved her hand in the air, fanning away the thoughts. She needed a cigarette, a drink, or both. But most of all, she needed to get out in the open air, away from the house, to think.

"I'm going out for a little walk," Eden told Aunt Baby. When she saw the city bus stopped at the corner, she changed her mind. She hopped on with no particular destination in mind.

Her hands were still shaking as she got off the bus a half block before the Rite Aid on Robertson. She hadn't taken it all in before, hadn't allowed what she might see in the city to penetrate her steely core of purpose and obligation. The first time back to New Orleans, a funeral and election, and this trip, Aunt Baby's mysterious (false?) claim of life-and-death urgency. But now, there was the stunning quiet, the emptiness of the streets, the shade of night closing in. It unhinged her. The darkness brought an unfamiliar desolation to the changed neighborhoods this side of the bridge, where flood waters rose roof-high, and higher. So many streetlamps still unlit. Towers and banks of debris fronted buildings along the streets, and water lines stained the clapboard houses. Battered trees tilted against winds and waters long gone. Missing street signs. Businesses dark and shuttered. A quiet void still hovered, an unnamed absence. It had been seven months. The city still looked shaken, barely removed from the biggest catastrophe of its three-hundred-year history.

Pre-storm, the Rite Aid pharmacy at the end of the busy block was where young women stocked up on Revlon lipstick and founda-tion and Dark and Lovely perm kits and young men bought Red Bulls, smokes, or condoms. Weather permitting, they gathered outside to drink and talk cars, sports, women, and whatever else was on their minds. Post-storm, the Rite Aid was a muted version of its former self, and a sign outside, WE ARE OPEN, announced the store's recent return to business. She walked up and down the aisles between the half-stocked shelves and remembered what she'd come for. She headed for the front counter, eyeing the row of cigarettes.

But as soon as she saw him, she wondered. Maybe beneath all her muddled thinking, he was the reason she'd come inside. Maybe the unfinished business between them so many years ago lay tucked somewhere in the back of her mind. They'd been just a couple of kids and she hadn't seen him in what seemed like a lifetime. Odd seeing him now, as if the storm had turned the city upside down and shaken out the things stuck deep in its corners.

"Hey, girl! You just gonna walk right past me?"

"Hello, Randy."

He was stocking one of the middle-aisle shelves, arranging packs of adult diapers. He hadn't changed all that much: still the same lanky build, same gold-capped smile, and the bill of his dark blue baseball cap was cocked sideways. One ear sported a single sparkling gold stud. He might have lost a little weight; his jeans sagged a bit at his hipbones. His dreadlocks, which now looked a little thin, were flecked with gray.

"You back here now? Ain't seen you around. Where you living at now, baby? I heard you ended up in Chicago."

She remembered how striking his light brown pupils were with his dark skin. "Chicago for a little bit. New York, now. I'm just here for a minute. Gotta go back tomorrow morning."

He pulled out a stick of gum and tossed it into his mouth. "New York! Damn, girl! How much space you try'na put between you and home?"

He made small talk while she eyed the door. *Stupid to come in here. Just let me get my smokes and go.*

"Got me a trash-hauling thing going, you know, making good money. This here just a temporary deal," he said, looking around the store. "I'ma have my own business pretty soon. In a place like this, ain't nothing but a cash cow, know what I mean?"

It came out "na-meen." She looked away. "OK. Good. Nice to see you again."

He ignored her move to walk away. "You real smart to get out before everything happened. Smart. I shoulda left too. You see how it look now. Shoulda seen it before, all that damn water. It was a mess." He shook his head. "Thought this place was all over with. Just like everybody else. I mean it was just…horrible, you know. You cain't even imagine. Thought I wasn't gonna make it my damn self."

"I know," she stammered. "Must have been awful."

He changed the subject, his mood lighter now, and talked about his new business, how much money he'd planned to make. *Really?* She thought, *You gonna talk to me about money?* She could not listen any longer.

"Randy, you just gonna stand there and talk to me like nothing went on? Like nothing happened?"

"What you mean?" His eyes widened. "Aw, that, yeah. Well, you know. I meant to come through. I really did. But stuff got real complicated. It just wasn't a good time for me. Anyway, we was just kids back then, you and me. I heard you made out OK, just the same."

"I don't care how long ago it was. You don't remember what you owe me? What you promised to do?"

He let out a long sigh. "Look. I get off in ten minutes. Wait for me. Come on with me to the crib. Got me a place just five blocks away. I got what you want. I'm sorry 'bout what happened. I'ma make it up to you. For real."

He looked at his watch, then flashed his gold-trimmed grin. "Eden Malveaux! You still looking good, girl, you know? Fine as ever."

Apologetic and slightly embarrassed, he made his way around the four-room apartment, picking up a beer can left on the glass coffee table and a single sneaker tucked just under the edge of the maroon plaid loveseat. "'Scuse all this mess. I didn't know nobody was...Here, sit down here." He removed a wadded t-shirt from the loveseat and gestured for her to sit. Once seated, she remembered what it was about him that she found attractive.

He looked at her bandaged knee, and without even asking what happened, gently lifted her left leg to place it on the glass coffee table before her. He offered her a beer and a glass of wine. She nodded toward the wine, sipped it, closed her eyes, and allowed herself to float inside the feeling of lightness it created in her head. She wanted to feel nothing except the alcohol drift, to step down from the earth's spin, stop every movement of the whole world for just an hour or two, and be no one, nowhere, doing nothing.

"You know, I went to your daddy's funeral. Sat in the back." His voice was softer than it had been in the store. He sat opposite her on a worn, fake leather ottoman and turned up his bottle of Abita, drinking long and slow. "Heard you sing, too. Wow."

"You never told me you were there," she said.

"Yeah. Well. It was a long time after…us. Always liked your daddy, always thought he was so cool, way he dressed and all. Sharp. But I know he didn't like me too much." She sipped more of the wine and looked toward the only window in the small living room. The light and noise from the nearby gas station—a car horn, a radio blaring Marvin Gaye's "Let's Get It On"—filtered through the single-paned window and thin walls.

Yes, he never liked you, and yeah, I was a fool for not listening to him.

Stupid. Stupid girl. She never thought about that day with her father without that word coming to mind. How many times had he warned her? *Stay away from them.* The slit-eyed, grinning boys who sport their cap bills sideways or whose gaze can find your breasts, but not your eyes. Or whose mouths flash grills of gold where white should be. "Gold in the mouth means none in the bank," he'd always told her.

Her daddy had sized Randy up. "No-count. Never looks me in the eye, and that boy's got a skulk about him." Randy Marvais had broken every one of Reginald's rules, but Eden couldn't help it. The slim, hard waist and his muscled arms, the confident swagger, the way his one dreadlocked braid fell across his sad-puppy eyes—had first taken her breath away, then her virginity. He had told her she was his beautiful, black queen, and every moral wall she'd built—the unbreakable fortress of her father's wisdom—crumbled at his touch. She hadn't planned to get pregnant, just hadn't planned not to. Only ten weeks along, and somehow her father had known. She'd been late before—this hadn't been the first time—but this time, she suspected, the new seed inside her had ballooned with invisible heft and weight. Her father's accusatory look might as well have had been the back of his hand across her face.

He'd confronted her. When her silence confirmed what he already knew, his shoulders sank and his eyes widened. "Dear Lord. Dear God. No." He took it personally, as if he'd failed, if only he had been a better father.

One day, however, his smile returned. Time and reason had

realigned something in him, and it was as if everything he'd believed before had been reversed. Hadn't he been a decent single parent to one baby-in-arms? How much more difficult could it be to help his daughter raise another? And if it was a boy, so much the better; the new baby and Reginald Jr. could grow up together, uncle and nephew, but as tight as brothers.

He'd wanted to surprise her. He'd repaired the broken spindle on Reginald Jr.'s old wooden crib, repainted the old bassinet a robin's egg blue, and unearthed a box of newborn clothes and blankets. *There was a reason for everything*, he'd decided, and who knows? Still grieving the loss of Eden's mother and being abandoned by his second wife, he'd figured, *There were two gone, but a new somebody coming.* He'd told her this, pointed to the bassinet and the box of baby blankets he'd retrieved from the storage shed. "A baby is always a blessing, no matter what," he'd said, and beamed. "A new life in the world? Nothin' but a blessing from God."

The look on her face told him exactly what she had done.

He had been stunned and heartbroken. His expression had gutted her.

She hadn't thought it through, not really. Her only thought had been to fix it, to make his pain go away.

From the leather recliner, he'd leaned forward with his elbows on his knees, head resting between his large hands. His silence was thick, brick-hard, and heavy, and Eden wondered if he would ever speak to her again. Finally, he got up and headed for his bedroom.

"Daddy, I…" she began. "I thought you…I only meant to…"

He'd closed the door.

Reginald Jr. had been fourteen months old then. It would take a while, but finally, her father's wounded heart healed, and though he never told her, she knew he had forgiven her. But something shifted in his eyes; the father love-light, while still there, shone dimly, as if through a scar, one that lasted until the day he died. It wasn't that her life had been a failure—a disappointment—it was only that it hadn't yet proven itself to be anything else.

The night Reginald Sr. died, she'd swore she would raise her brother as her father would have, somehow, some way. Her father's child, now hers. It was the very least she could do.

I shoulda never left him alone.

Rap music blared from the gas station across the street. "I can't stay," she told Randy. "I told Aunt Baby I'd be right back. And like I said, I'm leaving tomorrow."

"Look, baby, I know I owe you four hundred, to pay for the…thing."

"Seven hundred. All my tips and babysitting money for a year. And you promised you'd meet me there. I had to go all by myself."

"I know. I know."

He refilled her glass. "Just…stay with me a little while. You ain't got to go till tomorrow. Just relax, baby. Keep me company. You know, for almost a year now all I been doing is work. Hard-ass work. This right here?" He waved two fingers in a back-and-forth motion between the two of them. "This feels real good, real nice."

As he talked, she waited and remembered that one of his eyes was a lighter shade of brown than the other, and that his left cheek showed a deep dimple, but only when he flashed his broadest smile. She studied his forearms, trying to imagine him wading through high water with big, wailing Ludelia Banks flung across his back. She took another sip. It had been so long ago and so much had happened. He was right, they had been children back then.

Later, she would wonder what possessed her. Loneliness, or maybe just wanting to feel something, if only the pleasant heat of pulsing, human flesh. One minute, she was sitting and sipping wine on his love seat. The next, she was lying on his bed, his body a coverlet over hers. He moved gently, blocking out all sound and light.

She'd never figured him the type to stop the world from spinning. But stop it, he did, for almost an hour, while she caught her breath in the curve of his neck. She remembered his touch, the sharp, spicy scent of his cologne, and the coarseness of his facial hair. His capacity for gentleness, lacking when he spoke to her, was present in how he moved around her. It took her back to a younger time when he had filled her need to be somebody's someone, however briefly. He may not have been the best answer, but he was the one who showed up, all broad chest and beating heart. She thought about the girl she had been then, and said to her, *I don't blame you, not at all.*

Afterward, when the sky had turned dark, a car horn from the gas station woke her.

"You leaving?" He watched her as she got up, rubbed the sleepiness from his eyes, and stretched his arm toward the ceiling.

"Gotta go." She looked back at him, found her denim capris, and pulled them up around her waist. "Aunt Baby'll be wondering where I'm at."

"Stay a little while longer." Without looking, she could hear the smile in his voice, low and calm, as he raised one elbow onto a pillow. "The Sweet Spot over on St. Claude opened up again last week. Let's go get us some po'boys."

"Ate already," she said, fastening her bra. "You said you had something for me."

He yawned, then rolled back over on his side. "Yeah, OK. Leave me your address. I'ma send you that money, soon as I can. Promise." Then he was asleep again, snoring softly.

His jeans lay across a straight-back chair near the bedroom door. She found the pocket, reached inside, and felt the paper bulge. *Paid in cash and wearing it. Only in New Orleans.*

Some things never change. Even at sixteen, he'd carried what he called his "gangsta roll." Back then, it had been a band of ones and fives. From this thick wad, she peeled off seven one-hundred-dollar bills. *That'll work.*

Without a backward glance, she slipped quietly out the door.

CHAPTER 7

"I'm sorry?"

The young woman flight attendant flashed a smile. "I asked what would you like to drink."

"Oh. Coffee, please?"

It was still dark, the cabin quiet, but she was in no mood for a nap. Her seat was upright, the scrapbook Aunt Baby had given her was wide open on her lap and the metal box in a Winn Dixie bag she'd carried through security sat beneath her seat. The coarse, yellowed ledger paper in the scrapbook held articles from every stage in Celia DeMille's life after 1888, which must have been the year she began to sing in public. But how did the daughter of a Virginia slave get to be so famous? A *New York Beacon* article, written by somebody named Arthur Flanagan, laid the whole story out: Her father, owned by a cotton planter, had moved North after Emancipation to somewhere in New England. Her mother, a fine seamstress, stitched clothing for a wealthy doctor's wife, who overheard the eight-year-old girl singing while her mother worked. Eventually, Celia DeMille sang at a Presbyterian church and a Massachusetts congressman's wife heard her. Lessons were arranged.

The Beacon interview quoted Celia, who remembered the woman's generosity: "The woman helped me, yes, but I always knew I had something special. I could see it in the faces of the people who listened to me sing."

Ah, Eden thought, reading further. *That's how it was. It had been that way with me, too, hadn't it?* She remembered the first time she had known about her own voice, that it was special. More than special. Brilliant.

She was twelve. She'd been asked to sing at the monthly meeting of the Prince Hall Order of the Eastern Star, one of those black masonic groups that the elder ladies at church prized as much as membership in a royal court. "How Great Thou Art" in the key of D suited her mood, and she was feeling herself that day. The applause was deafening. "Child, you got a gift!" chorused the women afterward, nodding, sipping their cinnamon clove tea.

The second time was even better, a late-night watch service one New Year's Eve at Blessed Redeemer, a sanctuary packed to the oak doors with the faithful. The congregation lost its collective mind when she sang, "At the cross, at the cross, where I first saw the light," rocking the simple hymn upside down and sideways in 6/8 time.

At the second, she took it up an octave, couching the melody in a flurry of blues-tinged gospel riffs. Her accompanist, young Joseph Wainwright, home on Christmas break from his sophomore year at Tennessee State, pulled out more stops on the Hammond B-3, coaxing swells of sound from the wooden beast as his feet danced across its pedals. Feeling dramatic and feeding the rising spirit in the room, Joseph flipped his right hand over and swept his knuckles left-to-right across the white keys in a loud glissando while his massive left hand pounded out big bass chords:

At...the cross (clap, clap)
At...the cross (clap, clap)
Where...I first (clap, clap)
Saw...the light

Three pews of church folk in the back jumped to their feet, started swaying in rhythm, while others clapped on the offbeats and the rest stomped their feet. The oak planks beneath the choir loft shook with the weight of the sanctified Johnson sisters, three big-chested women who raised their hands skyward, their foreheads dripping sweat as they beamed and shouted praise, "Lawd, Lawd. Praise Je-sus!"

When Eden finished, Reverend Malcolm Jenkins spoke. "Thank ya, little Miss Malveaux! Can I get a amen, church? Umm-hmm… 'Where I first saw the light!' Can you see it? Can you see the light? Can I get a amen, brothers and sisters?"

Eden saw the light. Not so much of The Spirit, but of her own power. She was in awe of the awe she'd inspired, the teary-eyed women, the nodding, smiling men. She sensed the magnitude of the moment. Twelve years old and fearless as the night is long. Just give her a full room and a good tune.

Singing was like breathing, just as natural and just as necessary. The muscles in her golden throat never failed her, and from that point on, when she wasn't singing, there was always some sort of tune in her head. Gospel. Jazz. Hip-hop. Rhythm and blues, or just plain blues. Her daddy had been right when he'd told her, when she was just six, that music would be how she would make her way in the world.

Then Ethel came along.

After school one day, Eden found her daddy sitting in the living room with a smile like she hadn't seen since before her mother died almost two years past. The woman he had his arm around was smiling too. Her tight black curls framed her round face. Her green dress was too bright, her heels too high and pointy, her makeup too thick and pasty for any woman claiming the mantle of lady. She leaned toward Reginald and looked like someone he would have, years ago, pegged as a woman of easy virtue. And here he was, eyes bugged, mouth set in an adolescent's grin, gripping this woman's shoulder tightly, as if afraid she'd fly away.

They both stood, caught unawares, like guilty teenagers on the brink of sin. The woman was tall and leggy, as tall as Reginald Sr., and she smoothed her skirt across her wide hips in a manner that set Eden's teeth on edge.

"Eden! This is Ethel. You remember her from the Memorial Day church picnic? Ethel Kinsley is my…well, she's going to be your step-mama. Just as soon as we can get it all worked out!"

Ethel stuck her hand out and stepped toward Eden, who resisted the urge to step back. "Nice to see you again, Eden!"

Eden tucked her own good news, her shock, and her resentment deep inside, observing the change in her daddy since the woman showed up in their lives. *Intruder.* It was a word she didn't know at the time but sprang to mind whenever she was confronted with Ethel Kinsley's presence.

They had been fine without a woman in the house, just fine. There was no need to find another. Eden had taken up that space. She had peeled the potatoes while her father studded the ham with cloves for Sunday dinner. Brushed and combed her own hair when her father had made a mess of it. Watched the pot of red beans bubble on low flame while he did the weekly laundry. They were fine.

After one Sunday school class, she'd heard the church women talking: "Look at that child's hair. Malveaux need to get him a woman in that house." "And is he colorblind? Red plaid skirt with that solid orange blouse?" "And what about when the girl gets her monthly? What he gon' do then?"

His answer to their complaints stood in front of Eden now; Ethel Kinsley had her hooks so deep in her daddy, Eden could almost see the blood. She couldn't stop what was about to happen. But she didn't have to like it. She did not show her displeasure openly, but in her own quiet, clever way.

Little things. The wedding had been a sad affair, as she saw it. Or rather, as she didn't. Her father and Ethel had gone to the justice of the peace after Eden refused to take part in a backyard ceremony, claiming a stomachache for three days. "She's just missing her mama," Reginald explained to Ethel. She spilled milk on Ethel's just-mopped linoleum, then left her size-six Keds prints in the spill. Sent to the store for two large red onions, Eden conveniently forgot them, leaving Ethel's dinner of liver and onions lacking the latter. She lied about turning down the heat beneath the étouffée. Smiled in self-satisfaction at the charred, gluey mess.

Taking the child's willful unruliness in stride, Ethel suspected grief, not mischief, and tried to win her over. New shoes from the tip money Ethel made at the Cosey Inn Diner in Bywater failed to cool Eden's quiet rage, which boiled daily as she watched the father she adored float in the rare air of new love. Still, Ethel tried. An occasional, "You look pretty today!" followed by, "And what a sweet voice you've got!" did little to dent the girl's jealousy. But there were moments. Eden had to admit that the yellow and white polka-dot dress Ethel picked out for her was pretty, and that her hair, now adorned with ribbons of red satin, had never looked better. The years passed and an icy intolerance gradually melted into a truce.

But when the new baby arrived, Eden assumed an unexpected share of childcare, and her resentment returned. The words Eden learned years later—*postnatal depression*—looked to Eden's twelve-year-old eyes like laziness. A willful unwillingness of Ethel Kinsley to care for a baby who never should have come in the first place.

Ethel's long spells of silence, her blank stares at walls when she should have been nursing, the tears which came out of nowhere, and the hours in bed gave Eden further proof of Ethel's maternal incompetence. But the final straw was when Ethel stayed in her bed for four straight days, unresponsive to Reginald Sr.'s pleading or Reginald Jr.'s crying.

Eden had not meant any harm—at least, not serious harm. She had only meant to wake her father up to the notion that Ethel Kinsley did not belong in their lives.

When Ethel up and left, it was her father who faced the walls, his wet eyes blank and bewildered. It was a while before Eden and her father accepted the departure of Ethel as permanent, thanks to the constant needs of an infant who neither noticed nor cared about her absence. Mother or not, the baby needed tending, and Eden came to view his persistent wailing as a signpost of coming peril.

Eden put Celia's book away, and by the time she got off the plane, she'd put her childhood recollection aside. On the bus into Manhattan, she checked her watch—no time to go home first. Talking to Reginald Jr. earlier, she'd been unable to read him: Was he OK? Her breath got short as she braced for the meeting with her brother and the principal. The memory of their last days before the storm—the cops, the questions—came racing back.

CHAPTER 8

Artemis Johns, the assistant principal, was a big, dark-skinned man with a shaved and shiny pate, dressed in a pale blue mock turtleneck and baggy brown pants. "Have a seat," he told Eden and Reginald Jr., gesturing to the two wooden armchairs near a window in front of his desk. He explained the school's position. As far as violence was concerned, there was a zero-tolerance policy. So the rules were clear: strict disciplinary actions with no appeal. Any participation in violence resulted in automatic suspension, and possible expulsion, for all involved parties.

What's this got to do with my brother? Eden thought. From what her brother told her, he'd been bullied, then stabbed. Why wasn't the other boy, Tyrone, in the office with them? Reginald Jr. was the victim, not the perpetrator. She sat straight up, her eyes on the principal as he spoke, and felt like *she* was the student in trouble. Johns explained there were no witnesses to the incident, so they only had the students' word for what happened. They were here now to get Reginald Jr.'s version. Did he provoke Tyrone? Did he draw first blood? What words precipitated the attack?

Slumped in the seat next to her, Reginald Jr. lowered his eyes. He fidgeted with the zipper on his jacket and shuffled his feet beneath the chair. He'd always been the kind of boy who could get into trouble simply by being in the wrong place at the wrong time. Unsuspecting, trusting, until it was too late.

"My brother said Tyrone called him a name." Eden was defensive. "Tyrone attacked *him*. Tell him what you told me."

"He called me a name," Reginald Jr. whispered.

"What did he call you?" Johns sat back in his chair and twirled a pencil between his fingers.

Eden leaned forward. "Reginald, go 'head. Answer Mr. Johns."

"He called me swamp nigga."

Reginald said when he heard the words, he'd shoved Tyrone in the shoulder. He didn't even see the knife before he felt the burn of it.

Eden's hands folded and unfolded in her lap as tears filled her eyes. *Swamp nigga*. The words might as well have been spoken to them both. She'd seen the news reports for the last year, how people from home were viewed by the rest of the country—poor, undereducated, without the good sense to come in out of the rain, let alone see it coming and leave before it began. Every time she saw a TV report with people trudging through the water on mattresses, desperate-looking, eyes glazed, their wet clothes sticking to them, she knew the kind of judgment it provoked.

In their last phone conversation, she'd asked her brother, "Was the boy white?"

"I don't know," Reginald had said. "Not sure. Maybe. Maybe Mexican or Puerto Rican or something. Or he coulda been white. Or black."

After seconds of silence, Johns sat forward in his seat. Eden thought, *Surely, this black man understands.* But when she searched his eyes for understanding, she saw nothing.

Finally, he spoke. "Have you seen the nurse yet today?" When Reginald nodded, Johns told him he was dismissed and would be allowed back in class tomorrow. Wait in the hallway, Johns instructed him, while he spoke to his sister.

When the boy was gone, Johns leaned back in his swivel chair, steepled his fingers and closed his eyes. He leaned forward toward Eden. "I'm sorry for what happened to your brother. We regard both bullying and fighting as violent acts, and we don't tolerate either." He was also sorry, he added, for what happened to them during and after the storm.

To Eden, his speech seemed rehearsed.

They hadn't had many students from the Gulf Coast region since the storm, he told her, but they had a few. "Was your brother ever in trouble with the police in New Orleans?" Please understand, he assured her, he had no reason to suspect such a thing, and her brother had not been a problem, no more than any other kid. But he was obliged to ask these questions. Many of the kids from "down there" had been assimilated into several school districts across the country, and there had been some "issues." He understood that, in many cases, police records had been compromised by the "situation"—the flooding of government buildings, courts, and police stations.

Eden stared at him, unblinking. *Down there.* Why hadn't she seen this coming? Why would the school administrations up here think any more of them than the managers of the restaurants? They might as well have had *sad-ass refugee* tattooed across their foreheads.

The fact that the correct answer was yes was irrelevant. He had no right to ask, and besides, Reginald Jr. was innocent. He hadn't done anything wrong. *How was he supposed to know that one of them had a gun? As soon as they pulled up to the store, he got out of the car and ran.* That's what he'd told her, and she believed him.

Johns waited while Eden composed herself. Her heart raced. If she lied, they might find out anyway, someday. Or they might not.

"I understand," he told her. He knew how boys were; he'd been a youngster himself and occasionally got into some mischief. Little stuff. She didn't have to worry about police here. They just wanted to know what they were dealing with when it came to the newer students from other regions. Wanted to be as helpful to them as they could. And did they plan to return to New Orleans? Would they be looking to rebuild their home? That would also affect how they 'assisted' Reginald during his stay here.

"What about that other boy?" Eden ignored the questions. "That Tyrone boy that hurt my brother?"

He would be dealt with separately, Johns said. The school handled minor skirmishes between the students, but this was a little different. If she wanted to press formal assault charges against the boy, she would need to take that up with the police. "I can set that up, put you in touch with them," he said.

Police. No way. "That's all right, sir," Eden said. "No, I don't wanna do that."

"Are you sure?"

She nodded.

"All right, then," he said, and repeated his earlier question. "Did your brother have any trouble with the police in New Orleans?"

Eden fixed an unblinking stare on the big man. She'd been a pretty good thief. She could be an even better liar.

"No sir," she said. "None at all."

After the meeting, Eden and Reginald took the subway to the apartment, where Eden dropped off her bag, then gave her brother strict instructions: *Stay home 'til I get back.* During the meeting with Johns, Marianne had texted. "If you're back in town, can you meet me for coffee?" There was a place she wanted Eden to see.

She arrived first at Divine Grind on 66th Street in Midtown and surveyed the chrome-trimmed retro tables, the huge windows, and the vintage wall posters of Broadway shows. She chose a booth near a window that allowed a view of the street bustle; around Lincoln Center and The Juilliard School, the city teemed with the young and fit. Music students loped along to classes and rehearsals, their shoulders and backs strapped with violins or cellos or the odd French horn, while young techies laughed or talked or stared into their phones.

Shoppers and weekenders over from Jersey or down from Connecticut fanned themselves with Broadway matinee Playbills, hoping to hole up in a trendy café before the commute home.

Lately, evenings and nights were mild, temperate. The sky between the city's towers was a rich, chalk blue. Eden spotted a packed Grayline tour bus passing north along Broadway, its passengers peering out while a guide undoubtedly pointed out points of interest: The most famous music school in the world! The greatest opera house in America! Columbus Circle was named for Columbus! They would, Eden figured, learn more about New York in the next hour than she had learned in the seven months she'd been here. She knew for many visitors that the city was a place of fascination and curiosity, but for her and her brother, it had been an escape to higher ground and a good place to hide.

When Johns had asked her earlier if she'd planned to stay in the city or someday return home, she'd had no answer. The future was hazy. But if the city meant little to her, there were moments, she had to admit, when there was comfort and even pleasure in sitting by a window with a view. Pedestrians clumped together at crosswalks. Stoplights flashed green and released the huge huddle into a forward march. It was as if this city, like New Orleans, was parade-obsessed, and all that was missing in the promenade from one intersection to another was a nine-piece brass band.

What if Johns found out about her brother's troubles back home? What if he made some calls and found out she'd lied to him? A joyride once in a "borrowed" car and a gram or two of weed in his school locker didn't amount to much, but recalling the convenience store episode always brought a rush of heat to her face. And leaving the state after the cops had already questioned him—was that a crime? The storm had happened, turned the police department upside down, and the message could not have been clearer: get as far away as possible. They'd come here and they would make the best of it and that was that.

Except she needed a job now, in the worst way.

"Sorry." Marianne tossed her trench coat across the back of the booth. "Something happened with the trains. Something fell on the tracks. Practically ran here. Sorry to keep you waiting."

Eden smiled. "Sit down and take a breath. You look like somebody been chasing you."

"Feel like it, too." She sighed. "Getting too old for this."

With her blondish hair pulled back into a ponytail, Marianne had a youthful look that betrayed the gray edging her temples and the crow's feet sprouting from the corners of her blue eyes. A month ago, she and Eden had gone with two other employees at Estelle's to a local bar after work and celebrated what Marianne called a milestone birthday, though she wouldn't say which one. Eden and Javier (one of the line cooks) figured it must have been her fiftieth, although they both agreed that except for being a little overweight, she didn't look it. Marianne wore well the scuffs of life and had a way of dusting off hard times like so much lint on her shoulder. She seemed always to be in a good mood and smiled easily and often, which crinkled the W-shaped scar just above her left eye. Eden figured the freedom from her ex-husband's fist had added years to Marianne's life.

They ordered coffee. Marianne looked back at the baristas and the cashier and then turned to Eden. "I know it doesn't look like much, but the coffee is good, and you should see the folks lining up in the mornings. It wouldn't be the tips you're used to, but hey…"

Eden sighed, nodded. She'd seen the placard about the job opening. Pay couldn't be that great, but maybe she could work two jobs—nothing she hadn't done before.

"I got the number," she said. "Somebody said the manager's not here. I'll check into it tomorrow."

"Good."

When the drinks arrived, Marianne took a sip and said, "Cream and sugar? And can you bring a menu? I'm starved."

Eden was a little hungry too. She reached for her purse to check her cash.

"No." Marianne put a hand on her arm. "Yours is on me. The least I can do."

Marianne reached in her bag and pulled out a white envelope, Eden's last check from Estelle's, and a business card. She handed both to Eden.

Eden put the check in her purse. She held up the business card. "What's this?"

Marianne smiled. "The guy. The one who wanted to hear you sing."

She explained. The customer Eden had sung to when Enriqué fired her had come back a day or so later and asked Marianne if he could sit in her section. "He blamed himself, said you wouldn't have gotten fired if it hadn't been for him. He thinks he can help you find another job. So, he asked me, *begged* me, to give you his card."

The waitress returned with cream, sugar, and two menus. Eden remembered the man at Estelle's. Brown-skinned. Tall, maybe. Slender frame, short beard flecked with gray, and nice teeth. What she recalled most was his speaking French with ease, and the fact that he liked her singing.

"Tell him thanks, but I don't think it made all that much difference. Enriqué woulda got rid of me sometime, no matter what." She read the card: EVAN SMALLWOOD, ANTIQUES AND COLLECT-IBLES, BROOKLYN, NY.

Marianne said, "I talked to him a while. Interesting man. A kind of lonely vibe to him. Got the feeling he was single—divorced, widowed, maybe. Guess that's why he came in so often. Said he lives mostly on disability after an injury he got on the job a while back. Likes to find old furniture and restore it, then sell it out of a little shop on Fulton in Brooklyn."

He really wanted to help her, Marianne said. And he seemed pretty sincere.

"OK," Eden said. "I'll think about it."

When the waitress returned, they both ordered Cobb salads and Eden switched from coffee to iced tea. Eden told Marianne about her trip home to see her aunt, her brother's trouble at school, and the meeting with the principal. Eden hadn't told her much about Reginald, except that both their parents were gone and that for years, it had been just the two of them.

When the sky's light began to fade and the traffic and noise subsided, they decided to leave, Eden to check on her brother and Marianne to get ready for an early morning shift.

But as they reached for their bags, a man approached.

Tall and lean, he wore a deep blue blazer and white, button-down shirt with an open collar. With his hands clasped in front of him, he had an almost professorial air.

Evan Smallwood nodded to them both. "I don't mean to intrude on you ladies," he said softly. "You mind if I sit with you a minute?"

CHAPTER 9

Marianne and Evan did all the talking while Eden sipped coffee and feigned interest, nodding occasionally. Her face grew hot. She was still shaking off the shock of Evan's appearance out of nowhere. She studied his face. The pendant lamp's glow over their table sharpened his jawline. He was smooth—she gave him that. Elegant even, with the kind of formality that always made her a little self-conscious. *So, the guy just shows up here in this coffee shop, like some kind of a coincidence? Really, Marianne?* For sure, there was going to be a conversation about this later.

As Evan apologized to Eden, his head bowed, he was nearly groveling. "I'm so, so sorry," he repeated. "I didn't mean to get you into trouble with your boss...forgive me."

She'd wanted to interrupt, "Dude, come on, stop it already." Instead, she looked up from her drink, shrugged. "Hey. You know, it wasn't really your fault." She took a long sip. "No big deal, really," she said, the second lie easier. "The manager didn't like me. He woulda fired me anyway. Maybe not that day. But he woulda done it."

He shook his head again. "No, no. It's on me. I felt horrible after. I practically dared you to sing. I just didn't know the guy would react like that. Anyway, I have an idea, a way I can make it up to you." He looked at Marianne, then back at Eden. "Look," said. "One drink on me before you head out?"

Before Eden could reply—she really needed to get back; her teenaged brother was at home by himself, his eyes likely trained on ESPN instead of homework—Marianne smiled, sat up straight. "Sure! I'll have another cappuccino."

Night set in. By the time the waitress arrived with two cappuccinos for Marianne and Evan and a raspberry tea for Eden, the thick-paned glass had darkened, an opaque curtain against the street view. Around them, the customer chatter amplified with high-pitched laughter and louder conversations as the doors facing Broadway opened and closed to abrupt bursts of street noise.

If he had an idea of how to make it up to Eden, she thought, he was taking his sweet time bringing it up. Evan and Marianne chatted like old friends around the punchbowl at a high school reunion. Meanwhile, as Eden drank tea her gaze shifted from Marianne to Evan to the time on her phone. She'd lost track of their slow-rolling small talk minutes ago, and she was thinking about calling Reginald Jr. when she realized they were talking about her voice.

"A couple of folks asked me, 'What happened to that girl that used to sing?' Eden, remember the woman—maybe in her sixties—who always sat on the east wall next to the ficus and wore those funny little hats?" Marianne let out a laugh. "She asked Enriqué what happened to you and I almost spilled the coffee I was pouring, I was leaning so far so I could hear. He mumbled something and the woman said, 'Well, is she coming back?' Whatever he said, she didn't like it. That made my day."

Eden smiled. "Yeah, she always came in on Tuesdays, sat with her crossword puzzles." The woman had once told Eden her niece sang, too. "Not as well as you," she'd added.

Evan set his cup down. "So, there's this place I think you'd like. It's a restaurant called Maestro's, a waitress job, but really different. You'll see. I know the guy, the owner. You'd be perfect."

Her eyes narrowed a little on the word. *Perfect?* She wondered how this man assumed to know so much about her. Whatever Marianne told him, Eden hoped she hadn't mentioned Katrina or evacuation, anything that would set him off on some do-gooder crusade. She thought about what a kid at school had asked Reginald Jr. "You from Katrina?" Like the storm had its own damn zip code.

Thanks, anyway, she told him, but she had some things planned. "Got a couple of leads. Probably have something by tomorrow or the end of the week. But I appreciate it."

Her plan? Nothing more than some serious hustle. She'd go out before sunrise and wouldn't return until she found a new job. Simple. She'd done it before, in New Orleans. She'd start with Pastor Fleet from the Holiness Church in Harlem, who had sent for them and gotten them housing. He'd told her to call if they needed anything. And this coffee shop. There'd been a HELP WANTED sign in the window with a number to call. She'd never made one of those fancy cappuccinos, but how hard could that be?

"Mr. Smallwood?" She looked at his card again. "Well, thank you. If I haven't got anything in a couple of days, I'll call you."

Surely, that was the end of the conversation, and she drained her cup while she reached for her bag. But Evan took a long drink, leaned back, and asked Marianne where she was from.

Seriously?

A fellow midwesterner. His eyes lit up when Marianne mentioned Kansas. They went through the customary home-folks routine: What brought you to New York? How long have you been here? Real culture shock, right? Born in Bronzeville, Nebraska, he had grown up the youngest of six, the son of an airplane mechanic and a kindergarten teacher. A stint in Kuwait during the first Gulf War. Then, while back-packing through Europe, he searched out "the cool places I'd only read about:" London, Paris, Zurich, and Venice. It was the best time of his life. Primo pasta in Italy. Great wine in France. And good jazz everywhere. He sat in piazzas and squares and sipped strong coffee, watching good-looking women parade by and contemplating the rest of his life.

When his money ran out, he'd returned to Nebraska, logged two years at a community college in Omaha, and married a high school sweetheart. Divorced after three years (she left him for an economics professor she met in her yoga class), he headed east to New York. His father's side of the family was from there, and why not check it out? He spent two months sleeping on a buddy's couch. An amateur musician himself (he'd learned some piano), he sold life insurance by day and played jazz standards for tips with a small band on weekend nights.

He leaned forward, raised his voice above the roar of the blender in the back grinding out smoothies and frozen margaritas. "Music was big in our family," he said. "My mom, she sang. Church choirs mostly, but she had a great voice for the classics."

Before Eden could steal another glance at her watch, he looked at his. Evan stood and put a twenty-dollar bill on top of the check. To her surprise, he reached for a cane perched against the back of the chair. She hadn't noticed it before.

"Had a little injury a while back," he said, leaning on the cane. "Still doing rehab."

He buttoned his blazer. "Sorry, didn't mean to bore you. But I just wanted you to know I'm not some crackpot. You're probably thinking, who is this guy? But like I said, this place, Maestro's Bistro—I know you'd fit right in. The owner's out of town, but he'll be back in a few days."

Eden flung her purse strap across her shoulder. "Thanks a lot," she said. "I really appreciate it. But I got, you know, bills to pay and I need a gig soon, like now. But I'll call you if I don't get something. I got your card."

"Right," he said, and then his tone turned serious. "Look, don't hate me for this, but there's something I just have to say."

"OK."

He met her eyes. "I'm just gonna say it. Your talent. You're just wasting it."

"Excuse me?" Eden said.

"You're too good for what you're doing. How could you be OK with waiting tables? The way you sing."

Eden blinked.

Marianne looked at her watch. "Oh, wow, look at the time. Sorry, we better be going."

Evan said, "Well. You ladies have a nice evening," and left.

As she and Marianne descended the steps to the subway, Eden said, "Did you hear that? He got a lot of nerve, that man. He don't even know me."

When they reached the platform, Marianne said, "Well, he's just—"

"Out of line," Eden said. "And anyway, you coulda told me he was gonna meet us."

"He didn't say for sure he was coming. I thought he'd forgotten about it."

"So, I guess you told him, you know, everything."

"About you losing everything in the storm? About raising your brother on your own? OK. Yes. People don't think any less of you because of where you're from or what you've been through."

Yeah, right, Eden thought. She'd been the target of every reaction, from pity to racist loathing. "I want to make it on my own. I don't need anybody feeling sorry for me."

Marianne laughed. "Well, I sure as hell don't feel sorry for you." They held onto the overhead pole as the A train lurched away from the station. "Look at you. Young. Thin. Perfect cheekbones, big eyes and gorgeous as all get-out. And that voice! It isn't fair. I hate you, truth be told. Happy now?"

Eden laughed a little, shook her head. *Still. He had a hell of a nerve.*

"Homework," Eden said as she entered the apartment. "All done?"

Reginald Jr. shrugged, then nodded. "Didn't have too much."

She kicked off her shoes and flung herself onto the beige, faux leather side chair in the living room, which sagged so much, she just knew someday her butt would feel the floor. She hated this chair. But the price had been right—free at Blessed Samaritan Mission, about six blocks from the apartment. She and Reginald Jr. had carried it all the way home and up the four narrow flights of stairs. She leaned forward and rubbed her feet.

Her overnight carry-on bag sat open in the middle of the living room floor, a few items of clothing spilling out. She hadn't done laundry before she left New Orleans, so she sorted underwear and a few other items for a quick hand-wash in the sink.

"You ain't heard a word I said," Reginald Jr. said.

Eden flinched. Reginald Jr. sat on the floor, legs crossed. "What?"

He exhaled an exasperated breath. "I said, I want to go back home. How come you got to go back?"

Not this again. "You have school."

"School be out in a couple months. I can go then."

"No. You can't."

"Why not?"

Now he was working her nerves. "You know why."

"Like I told you, I wasn't even in there."

"You were in the car," she told him.

"Yeah, but—"

"And somebody got shot." She grabbed her laundry and headed for the bathroom. "I'm through talking about this," she said. "You are not going to New Orleans. Now, I'ma wash out these things and when I get through, your butt better be in bed."

She filled the bathroom sink with water, added a spurt of liquid Dawn, and tried to get that boy and his crazy-ass ideas out of her mind. She would get up at 6:30, just like always, put in a full day of work—only she'd be looking for a job instead of heading into one. Pastor Fleet. If she didn't find something by tomorrow night, she'd call him.

"What's this?" Reginald Jr. stood at the bathroom door, the metal box of mementos in his hand.

"Put that down. That's just some stuff from Aunt Baby's house. Some stuff she wanted me to have."

"Yeah, but what is it?" He held up one of the medals. The box was heavy, unbalanced in his hand. The medals fell to the floor, along with the worn, leather-cornered ledger scrapbook.

"Please," she said, her voice low, tired. "Pick that up and put it back where you found it. No, wait, put it in my room. Please."

She squeezed water out of the bra, hung it on the towel rack, took a slow breath, and decided this was not going to be one of those times. The feeling could happen any moment: while she rinsed out clothes, cooked dinner, or waited for a bus or a train. The quick, shuddering breathing, the racing heart, and then it would start.

There had been more than a few times in her life, since becoming the guardian of her brother, when she didn't know how they would possibly make it, how the rent would be paid, or how food would appear on the table. Whenever she sensed the death-grip of duty, her heart pounded and her breath got tight. Panic. Marianne had knowingly nodded when Eden had described the feeling to her. "Inhale deeply, then let it out," she'd advised.

This will not be one of those times.

Before she went into the bedroom, she checked the front room where her brother lay stretched out on the futon, a sheet loosely tucked in corners beneath the mattress, his long arms cradling his pillow. When she needed to get calm, to remember what was important, she watched him. He looked as innocent as he did at three, when his father placed the boy's life in her hands.

He opened an eye, looked at her, and closed it again.

"Hey," she said, grabbing one of his toes. "You change your bandage?"

"Ow. Quit doing that."

"You change it?"

"Yeah." He bunched his pillow under his head.

"Still hurting you?"

"Naw."

"You sure?"

He nodded. "What about you?"

"What do you mean?"

He pointed to her knee, where a small triangular bandage covered what remained of her wound. She had all but forgotten about it. She sighed. *Look at us, all scarred and banged up like we been through a war. What a pair.* "Oh, better now. Thanks." She sat on the futon. "Look. Sorry you had to go through all that trouble at school. By yourself, I mean."

He rolled over and turned his back to her. "I just wanna know when I can go back home."

She exhaled sharply. *Too young. Too young to know danger, that the world could change and you could be wiped out in a minute. Didn't the storm teach him that?*

What she never wanted to tell her brother, and never wanted him to find out, was that she was making all this up as she went along. She had no plan, no blueprint, no guiding force. Just the wisdom, the instinct of the moment, bad decisions and all, for whatever it was worth. Didn't he realize how badly she wanted to go back, not just to New Orleans but all the way back in time? Back to when her mama was living. Back to when her daddy was alive and she didn't have a care in the world. Back to when a storm would come, and then in a day or two, life would return to normal.

Go back? You and me both.

Growing up in New Orleans, the old folks always said it and you just knew a Big One was coming. But like everyone else, she was still shocked at its power, its unrelenting toll. She and Reginald Jr. spent weeks moving around the country after the storm, from church basements to rec halls, from YMCA bunks to gymnasium floors, in Houston, Dallas, Atlanta, and Chicago. In Houston, when the over-whelmed toilets in the YMCA gave up like a prizefighter throwing in the towel, she fought the urge to inhale. In Dallas, on the Convention Center floor, she convinced herself she had imagined those stranger's cold hands on her body in the middle of the night.

Then came the real journey, when it was clear, through the TV news reports, that the city was on life support and there was no telling when, or if, they could ever go back. Just the two of them, brother and sister, surrogate mother and man-child, waiting in the parking lots of the AME or the CME church or the First Baptist Church of Wherever, and in front of bus stations, backpacks bulky with donations from the American Red Cross—t-shirts, deodorant, toothpaste, six-packs of Dasani water, bags of Doritos, sanitary napkins, toilet paper, Snick-ers—and waiting, waiting, and waiting some more.

And when they finally landed in New York, they hunkered down with six men, five women, and two children in the kitchen/dining hall of Pastor Fleet's church. The long nights were longer with no sleep, her brother snoring next to her while she lay, wide-eyed and anxious, inhaling the odor of feet and unwashed bodies, staring at the ceiling and thinking about what, if anything, was left of the city she'd left, and how her father, if he weren't already dead, would surely die if he'd seen those levees break.

Enough of that. What had her father told her? *The past is something you just can't do anything about. Here and now were all that mattered.*

She raised the window next to her bed. On the street below, ev-erything was quiet except for the groans of two men struggling with an armoire that looked too big to fit through the front door. *It's a beautiful piece*, Eden thought. *A pretty piece of furniture bought new from a furniture store. How would that feel?*

The metal box sat on the floor at arm's reach. She reached for the half bottle of zinfandel she'd stashed behind her bed and filled her glass half-full. When the first hour passed without sleep, she pulled out the scrapbook.

On thick yellowed sheets, Celia DeMille emerged in four distinctive portraits. In one, she wore a sailing outfit in front of a painted background of a ship at sea. In another, she was seated on a chair as ornate and huge as a throne. From a high window, light fell on her soft eyes and hair. A cryptic smile defined her full lips, her expression secretive, knowing. The black and white photographs had clearly been taken in a professional studio. *The dress is like something out of a movie*, Eden thought. Miles of lace, silky, satiny fabric corseted neatly around a slim waist. In another, Celia wore what looked like a ballgown that could have been worn by Scarlett O'Hara, if Scarlett O'Hara had been black.

She took a long sip, plumped her pillow, and leaned back. Outside, a police car siren blared and tailed into silence. She took the scallop-edged photo out of the cardboard frame and held it beneath the lamp light. In a corner, there was a date: 1893. Clearly, Celia had money. Eden wondered what kind of black woman, in 1893, was able to dress so beautifully. She propped the photo up against the lamp.

The woman was so beautiful, it made her smile, but it might also have been the sweet, heady tease of the wine. Skin as smooth as the silk of her dress. Dark eyes as large and luminous as the shiny dark buttons that lined her bodice. Cheekbones set high, the hollows beneath them shadowed. Her beauty seemed to belong to no particular period; this picture was taken more than one hundred years ago, and yet there was something classic about her. Eden opened the pages with the crackling, clumsily pasted newspaper clippings.

Celia DeMille. Who were you, lady? You must have been some singer. You must have been somebody. "The Black Donatella," she read. Two and a half hours later, her eyelids thick and sleep-heavy, she was still reading.

CHAPTER 10

New Orleans, 1921

The Black Donatella Triumphs

*Fresh from her triumphs in England, where she captured the imagination
of the Royal Family and captivated sold-out audiences with her stunning
soprano voice, Madame Celia DeMille has returned to the United States,
where she has been called the greatest singer of her race. Indeed, it has
been said by many that her voice rivals that of the great Italian American soprano, Adeline Donatella. No wonder she has become known all
over America as 'The Black Donatella.' High praise, to be sure.*

Celia read the clipping for the third time. "The Black Donatella?"
Mio dio! Again? It had appeared over and over in nearly everything
written about her. And "the greatest singer of her race?" What about
any race? Her managers, Edgar and Victor, had insisted the nickname
would sell tickets, so she hadn't resisted when reporters used it; now
it seemed she was saddled with it for eternity. She had heard Adeline
Donatella twice—once at the French Opera House in New Orleans

77

when Celia was young and newly married, another time after her own recital at a black church in Chicago, sitting high up in the colored section of the city's opera house. The Italian diva ambled across the stage, a beautiful, if wooden, Carmen. It was a role that should have been hers. Celia knew every note, every turn of phrase, every gesture. She knew Carmen, knew the heart of the woman, her soul, blood, and bones. Knew how it must have felt to be a lowly cigarette girl, a gypsy, born poor and beneath the world's contempt. She, Celia, was the daughter of a proud black man who had been owned by a white man. How could she not know how Carmen felt?

That thin woman with the yellow curls and the pale eyes had no idea of such poverty. No idea how to use her body, how to strut and flaunt her *sexualité*, as if every man was hers to conquer. Had no idea how to use her eyes to portray her *puissance*, as the French would say. And more to the point, Celia could sing much higher, much bigger, and—why not say it?—much better than the slight, emaciated, and sexless little creature.

And now, in the hundreds of articles written about her, they called her not by her own name. No, they called her "The Black Donatella."

During the summer, the air in her upstairs apartment was thick and clogged her lungs. Still, her lungs were important; someday, she might sing again. She turned on the small electric fan near the oak dining table, a gift from its inventor, who had seen her perform in Chicago. She stirred sugar in her teacup, set it on the desk next to the scrapbook, turned the page, and glued in the next article. The cutting and pasting took time, and there was some catching up to do. There was her performance at the Academy of Music in Philadelphia, and a lovely writeup with a drawing of her in *The New York Age*. And my goodness, her performance at the fabulous Music Hall in New York. How they loved her there! She smiled as she remembered each one and pasted the reviews to the thick pages of the ledger. She took the last one, the longest, and held it closer to the light.

Ah, the reporter from the *New York Times*.

That reporter was handsome. Tall with an erect posture, a neatly trimmed mustache, and thick, wiry eyebrows that arched at every question. He had been patient, interested, and curious. Intrigued that she, a woman of such "unusual" background—a black woman? a slave's daughter?—could even imagine such a career. She had offered him tea, and they sipped together as southward breezes stirred the air in the front room of her apartment on the Rue de Conti, with the window that overlooked the shops on the street below. He had wanted to know all about her, and she had sat back, taking her time.

"Well, where shall I begin? Papa. Papa worked on a cotton plantation, in the Carolinas."

Papa had been a slave. Try as she might, and as much as she finessed her language and affected her tone, truth was truth. *Slave.* The word burned like acid. His whole life had been steeped in the indelible ink of bondage. Bought, sold, then bought and sold again before the spring of 1865, when the War ended and he'd been proclaimed "henceforth and forever free" to travel the country as he wished. He met her mother, a cook and a maid, while fitting stallions with steel shoes on a Virginia horse farm. From Virginia, he had gone to Boston, where he had gotten a job as the valet to a councilman of the city, and where he had provided an education for his daughter, and she had learned to sing.

She would not tell him about how her father, during slavery, was "promoted" from field hand to house servant. He had informed his master of a plot hatched by several of his brethren in the Quarter to run away to Tennessee and then Ohio at the next full moon. It liberated him from the unbearable sun, the overseer's lash, but burdened him with a guilt he took to his grave.

"And what about your personal life? A husband? Children?"

At the question, her eyes had glazed, and she had taken a long sip of tea. She had not wanted to talk about this. She had not wanted to discuss how her husband, Richard, a pretty man with acorn skin, sculpted cheekbones, and eyes like polished topaz, had wooed her, brought her to his home in New Orleans, where he'd promptly taken over the management of her career, been shamelessly unfaithful, and then disappeared with all the money from her concert tour. Nor did she want to talk about the loneliness that consumed her after he had gone. And then, afterwards, the maestro. She did not want to talk about the man who had been her lover, whose broken promise had pushed her to the brink of madness.

She bowed her head, her eyes closed. There was more. So many things she kept close to her heart. The awful time in Connecticut, when no hotel would accept the all-black company.

The troubles with her troupe as they moved throughout the South while Klansmen and Night Riders roamed the roads. The epithets, the long stares that promised harm, the traveling from city to city by train with her band of minstrel singers and jugglers in the dismal, colored cars, thanks to the laws separating black and white. The audiences where her own people were shunted to the balcony away from the whites, if allowed in at all.

"After the War ended and Papa was free, he went to Boston, where I was born, and where I learned to sing. The rest is…" She raised her hand in a gesture of conclusion. "The rest is…as you can see."

The reporter was kind; he had not pressed her for more. His father was an abolitionist from Boston. So, they talked about Boston. A good place to be free. He'd heard her sing at Mother Bethel AME Church in Philadelphia. He'd even known the Messrs Trotter, James and his son William, both champions in the cause of freedom and equality in their own rights. He and his father had joined them.

"More tea?"

He smiled. Lovely man. Rare that a white reporter would take so much time with her. So sad that it was now, at the end of her singing. Perhaps he would tell the story the way it should be told. Perhaps she should tell him all, trust him with her history. If she truly wanted her legacy to grow, she had to plant many seeds.

"It's late now," she told him. "Come back tomorrow, and I will tell you more."

"I will," he said.

She took her scissors and trimmed the edges of the last article, then pasted it into the book. The reporter had returned, but it was not the next day as he promised. He had gone back to New York. It was a long time before he kept his promise and returned to Louisiana.

CHAPTER 11

New Orleans, 2006

"Yes, sir, that's right! Louisiana born and bred."

"And, uh, you've been here how long?"

"Came up last September."

"And where did you say you worked?" His phone rang, and he reached inside his pocket. "I need to take this, sorry. Give me just a minute."

"Oh, of course, yes, sir."

She watched as he left the table where they'd been sitting and walked toward a window facing the busy street.

Sir? Nobody up here called anybody *sir*, let alone a manager who looked like a kid not much older than her brother. The restaurant, Hardy's American Grill in the South Bronx, was nothing like what she'd imagined and not what she'd pictured after all the hype from Xavier, her former coworker at Estelle's whose best friend's father owned the place. *Was Xavier joking?* The neighborhood was scary and the place was a dump. The front door trim was caked with layers of blistering paint, and she wondered how fresh were the bullet holes in the window. The air held the odor of something stale and foul, or possibly dead. Cracked leatherette booths, patched with duct tape here and there and flanked by grease-stained and peeling walls. The tackiest restaurant she'd worked in New Orleans was at least a cut above this.

A day after she'd returned from New Orleans, she'd called Pastor Fleet from the Holiness Church in Harlem, who months ago had sent for Eden and some of the other evacuees sheltered at his brother's church in Chicago. She interrupted the pastor's Wednesday morning staff meeting and prayer breakfast with a phone call, hoping to hide her desperation. He listened and, between bites and slurps of coffee, asked, "Have you tried the unemployment office?" He'd keep his ear to the ground for any job leads from his parishioners.

No help there. Even the Midtown coffee shop didn't pan out. The HELP WANTED sign, the manager told her, should have been removed days ago.

It was 3:15 in the afternoon, and a hard sun bounced from asphalt pavements to the glaring glass of high-rise apartment buildings. She'd been in and out of twelve restaurants, dry cleaners, bakeries, bodegas, supermarkets, fast-food chains, hair care supply stores, and a nail salon all with the same response: "We don't need anybody." Her arches were killing her and a bunion near her left big toe burned like crazy. To get to Hardy's, she had taken two trains and a bus, then, realizing she'd gotten off the bus too early, walked four blocks along the ugliest, most godforsaken street in the South Bronx.

The young manager returned to the table. "You were telling me about your experience. Where'd you say you cooked before?"

Cook? What had Xavier told this guy? "Uh, I've only waited tables and hostessed. But I can cook too, if that's what you need. When would you want me to start?" she asked.

He cocked his head and now gave her a doubtful look. "Sorry, I thought you knew. Right now, we just need a cook. We kinda need somebody with a little bit of experience."

"Right. Well, thank you."

"Thank you. We've got your number. We'll call if we need you."

Outside the restaurant, as buses and taxis passed, she checked the time; the bus was already twenty minutes late. She reached into her purse for a cigarette, found an empty pack. She looked around for a place to sit. A bench, a chair, anything. Her head throbbed. Her feet ached. She was as tired now as she had ever been in her life.

There was still plenty of daylight left, but she could only think of going to bed and pulling the covers up over her head the way she had done when she was ten and a mean, uncooperative world had had its way with her. Three days, and not a damn thing. Nothing. And not even a cigarette to chill out with. She thought about finding a store, but she'd been trying to cut back; her habit was expensive up here, and she needed to quit, again, anyway.

"How you doin', miss? Sorry to bother you."

She turned around. A young, fair-skinned black man who looked about her own age was smiling at her.

"Hey. Sorry, uh, I was in that restaurant where you just came from and I overheard what you were talking about. You from Louisiana, right?"

She looked down at his hands to make sure he wasn't carrying any religious pamphlets. Sometime in the last year, she'd lost all patience with strangers on the street with their flyers admonishing her to re-nounce her sinful ways and come to Jesus.

"I already got *The Watchtower*," she said.

"What?" He looked confused. "Oh, this," he said, and looked at the pamphlet in his hand as if it was flypaper. He flicked it into a nearby trash barrel. "I asked a dude where was a good place to get a pizza around here and he gave me that."

She laughed. "Oh, OK." She thought she heard something famil-iar in his tone, but before she could ask him, he told her he was from Gulfport.

She smiled. "Oh, yeah?" Gulfport, Mississippi, wasn't all that far from New Orleans. Another town battered by Katrina. Meeting this kid in New York was as if she'd met someone who'd grown up next door. He wasn't there during the storm, he told her. He'd come to New York four years ago when he'd gotten tired of dealing Black Jack at the Copa Casino, which he'd since learned had been completely destroyed. He'd come to New York to visit a brother, found a job as an EMT for the New York Fire Department, and never left.

His name was Doyle Dugan. He had "people" in New Orleans, he told her. "I love that place. I hope you and yours made out OK. You going back?"

She shrugged. "I'm not sure. I'm here for now anyway. Your folks down there all right?"

He sighed. "Put it this way—nobody hurt. We was blessed."

"Yeah. That's good. I'm glad for that." She looked down the street and down at her watch.

"This bus here is always late," he told her. "Might be in for a little wait."

They talked on. When the nearly empty bus came, they sat up front. The afternoon sun streamed through the dusty, streaked windows. He told her about his family in New Orleans, how they had fled the storm and scattered West and North, and his family in Gulfport, two cousins, who also worked at the casino and had lost their houses to Katrina. She told him about how she and Reginald Jr. had left New Orleans for Houston two days before the storm hit, and after they learned the housing project they were living in would not allow residents to come back, began a journey that included Houston, Atlanta, and Chicago before they ended up in New York.

They were talking so much, she missed her stop to transfer to another bus. He apologized for talking so much, and then invited her to go with him where he was headed, a New Orleans-type bar where he was meeting friends to watch a Hornets game. There would be karaoke afterward, a little food, and a chance for her to "meet some folks from down home." There were plenty of folks up here from the Gulf Region—Baton Rouge, Biloxi, and other cities nearby—even a friend just up from Pass Christian last month who was originally from New Orleans. Eden had been refraining from taking up with strangers in this city, but this situation seemed different. This guy was a homeboy whose tongue dripped the long, liquid vowels, softened consonants, and bayou rhythms that she'd missed and had been longing to hear since the day she'd arrived.

The place, Little Eva's, was tucked deep in a block of small businesses—a yogurt shop, a kosher deli, and a noodle restaurant—in the northeast part of Bushwick in Brooklyn. It exuded an overworked Big Easy theme, convincing only to those who had never been there. Louis Armstrong and Jelly Roll Morton winked and smiled down from wall posters of the artists in their prime. The sound system pumped out endless loops of tunes from second lines and brass bands, from the Dirty Dozen to Preservation Hall. Above the sleek granite bar, a flat-screen TV tuned to ESPN broadcast a game between the New Orleans/Oklahoma City Hornets and the Dallas Mavericks. The bartender, a tattooed and pierced twenty-something with buzz-cut hair and a bodybuilder's physique, crafted drinks with impressive prowess: daquiris, Sazeracs, and hurricanes.

Doyle proved a smooth, skillful host. He glided from barstool to table, speaking to friends with a wide grin and a gentle hand at Eden's back. "Just up from New Orleans," he announced. "A Gulf Coast homegirl. Make her feel welcome!" Raised glasses and friendly cheers washed over Eden. Rounds of happy hour drinks arrived, then more drinks, and before long, belly laughter rippled above the din of thumping bass lines, ride cymbals, and piano scales. When the Hornets lost, the fans drank more. Then, the pain of the game quickly drowned in booze, they switched their focus to karaoke.

A thick binder of popular song lyrics rounded the counter-high tables near the bar and a cordless hand mic appeared. Motown tunes gave way to seventies girl group songs. Then, the Philly sound of Ashford and Simpson. A dark-skinned, barrel-chested man crooning

Teddy Pendergrass's "Turn Out the Lights" brought a collective swoon to the largely female crowd.

Eden hummed along and Doyle took note. "Right over here!" he said, pointing to Eden. "This girl here, she got a voice."

Oh, what the hell. Tipsy, and with a failed day behind her, what did she have to lose? *No job, no prospects, the rent still due. Screw it. At least I can sing.* When the mic arrived in front of her, she grabbed it and stood up.

She had never seen *Dream Girls*, the film or the Broadway show, but had heard the torchy "And I Am Telling You, I'm Not Going" belted out by more than one Broadway diva on the radio or TV. It was the song's raw emotion that spoke to her: a woman's stubborn desire to turn the face of the world her way when it seemed bent on showing her its backside.

The women at the table egged her on. She'd made friends with the two retail clerks from Macy's in East Orange, one white blonde and another tall, cinnamon-skinned sister with cascades of silky brown extensions. All three women, their shoes kicked off and their shoulders shimmying to the pulse of the music, felt their groove coming on. Another table of young black music and dance scholarship students hailing from the smaller towns near the Gulf stomped their feet when Eden stood, then whooped when she held the mic close to her lips and lifted her arms in diva-drama style.

Her voice was raw and rough as she fought to even out the tones. But by the end of the verse, as she worked her way to the bridge, something powerful consumed her, and she had no choice but to open up her chest, her lungs, her voice. She closed her eyes. As she ascended the scale, the stirring in her chest came out in high, searing tones. She stretched her arm and pointed at three random figures standing in the back. "You, and you, and you, you're gonna love me!" She belted the words at the street beyond the doors.

As she sang, she thought of everything that had brought her to this point, this place. Her tones swept from guttural depths to piercing highs, called up memory after memory. Her father. Her mother dying. Her stepmother leaving without a trace. The storm. The flood. Aunt Baby. Her brother. His woes that had become her trial. His future that now shaped her life, it seemed, irrevocably.

By the end, the force moved so powerfully in her that she barely heard the sounds. People stood up and whooped and clapped—the whole bar erupted.

An hour and a half later, when the crowd thinned and it was time to leave, Doyle Dugan held the door for her, beaming with pride and blinking his misting eyes. "Girl, you something else." He held her arm as they both staggered out to the sidewalk. Except for the headlights of taxis and the golden halo of street lamps, night had darkened the streets. She could not remember how she'd gotten there. The streets were nearly empty; even this city, at least parts of it, were muted at 2:00 in the morning.

They laughed, stumbling along; she'd taken off her shoes and walked barefoot.

He told her there was a shortcut to the subway through the alley, but once there, he leaned against a wall of brick, reached in his pocket, took out a joint. It made Eden smile; she must have been seventeen the last time she'd even seen one. She giggled.

They walked on and he held her hand. Soon, the weed made her defenseless. She could have sat down and slept. "Let's catch our breath," he told her. "What a night. I'm so glad I met you." He sighed. She sighed. His smile was gone, replaced with a beatific gaze. He was in awe of her.

When they stopped, he held her chin in his cupped hand. His lips pressed against hers, softly at first, and then with force. He pulled back, looked her up and down, and stroked her shoulders. "You are beautiful," he said.

Later, she would not remember exactly what transpired, only that a force came from Doyle that felt all wrong, even though, she would later remind herself, she didn't know him at all. He pressed himself harder against her, reached his hand up her skirt, and tugged at her panties. With his other hand, he found her breast.

"No," she said, but he persisted. She pushed him. "No!" she told him again, but the liquor and the weed worked against her, made her weak.

"Wait," he told her. "I'm just...let me..." He pressed his whole body against her and pinned her to the wall. She turned her head and a small cry erupted from her throat. She tried to work her wrists free from his grip, but he was too strong. She shoved her knee into his groin and ran. Shoes still in her hand, she found her way to the subway entrance and descended the stairs, breathing hard, just as the train pulled into the station. Once seated, she buried her head between both hands. *Stupid*, she thought. *Stupid, stupid fool.*

When she woke, the train was above ground and there was a body of water visible through the window. FAR ROCKAWAY, the sign said. She had taken the wrong train in the wrong direction—east, not west—and was passing the waters of Jamaica Bay.

"Oh, hell, no." She looked out the window again in disbelief. She made her way to the end of the car, found a uniformed attendant, and told him what happened. "I'm trying to get to Harlem."

The attendant shook his head. "Miss, you are at the opposite end of the world from there."

At 3:47 a.m., she eased open the door to her apartment and found her brother sprawled across the futon in the living room and fast asleep, his mouth open and one arm flung out so his knuckles touched the floor. At the sink, there was a pile of dirty dishes, and an empty frozen pizza box sat on the counter near the stove. He needed to be up for school in three hours.

She sat on the side of her bed for a moment, kicked off her shoes, and watched as they thudded against the closet door. She leaned over, elbows on her knees, her head splitting. *Wow. You really know how to screw up, don't you?* It would be nice to just give up. Surrender. Admit defeat. Even if she wanted to give up, she didn't know how. What did giving up look like?

She turned on the lamp and fell back across the bed, her arms stretched out, staring up at the white stucco ceiling. A day that had begun badly had ended much worse. But give up? Not a chance. Not with that sixteen-year-old boy in the next room.

Life, for most people, had an annoying, continuous quality about it. No matter what kind of hell it put you through, you still had to get up the next day, gird your armor, and prepare to lose again. Tomorrow, she would do the whole damn thing all over. It was not a choice.

But the night hadn't been all bad. There was the singing. As she recalled the moment, holding the mic, and filling the room with music—her voice—her self-judgment softened. The music and the cheers from all those people in the bar had drugged her as much as that reefer, making her feel giddy with power. While she sang, the ground grew solid beneath her feet and the spinning world stopped and listened.

As she reached to turn out the lamp light, she spotted the small white card that had fallen from her purse onto the floor. Evan Smallwood. She had forgotten about him.

Then, as she had done every night lately, she felt beneath the bed and pulled out the scrapbook and box of medals. She turned the first page and traced a finger along the faded, fray-edged photograph. Celia DeMille. She spoke aloud, rolling the name on her tongue. Even in black and white, the woman's enormous, deep-set eyes shone bright, set wide above sculpted cheeks and a beautifully carved chin. The gaze held a reassuring power, a fortitude that Eden hadn't seen before. What had she been thinking? The look said, *I've had my troubles. But here I am.*

She tucked it all beneath her bed. All was not lost. Maybe Evan could help. It was worth a try. She placed the card on the crate beside her bed and went to sleep.

CHAPTER 12

*Good morning, good morning! What's up New York? This is One. Oh.
Seven. Point. Five! W-B-L-S! The class of New York City radio! You're
listening to Daniel D., your host for the next three hours, bringing you
everything you want to know and all the music you want to hear! We
got news. We got weather. We got traffic for you, all comin' up after this
message.*

Eden sat straight up in bed. The numbers on the alarm clock
made no sense at all: 10:17 a.m. *Shit.*

Reginald Jr. was supposed to have been to be up and out the door
by 7:30. Had he…?

She leaned over and looked through the crack of the open bedroom door into the living room. Gone. The futon folded up. No noises
in the kitchen or the bathroom. Thank God, he had gotten himself off
to school. Or somewhere. Did he eat something? Did he even go to
school? She'd call him. No. She'd wait till lunch. He was sixteen. He
knew how to get himself off to school, and besides, where else would
he go this time of the morning?

Not a question she wanted to answer.

She had sat up so abruptly and been so stunned by the hour that she didn't immediately notice the throbbing behind her eyes. Hangover. It had been years since she'd had one of those, but there was no forgetting the pressure, the pain that made you think twice about sudden moves. Her eyelids ached. She closed them, massaged her temples with her palms and tried to get the blood flowing again. She stood up, reeled, felt nauseated, and sat back on the bed again. Now her whole body ached and a weight, like iron, hung around her neck.

Her plan for the day was clearly shot to hell. She should have known that turning in at 4 a.m., still slightly stoned and buzzed, would not play well with that plan.

When the phone rang, it startled her so much, she flinched. Her voice was a raspy croak. "Hello?"

Marianne paused. "Uh…you all right?"

"Yeah, yeah. I'm OK. What's up?"

"You sound a little funny. How's the job search going?"

"Girl. You don't even want to know."

"What about Evan? You call him?"

"Oh, no, I haven't. Not yet. I was gonna call him today, but…"

Eden told her friend about the previous day without too much detail, except that she'd had too much to drink and smoked a joint, then got lost on the subway.

"Listen. I've got the day off," Marianne said. "Come to my place. You hungover? I can fix that. I'll make you breakfast and you'll be good to go in an hour, and then you can think about finding work."

"I don't think I can eat anything. I feel like hell."

"Put an ice pack over your eyes for a minute. Then come over, if you can find your way to the subway," she added, laughing.

"I guess I could probably figure out how to drag my triflin' butt over there." Eden put a hand on the top of her head to stop the tiny hammers pounding.

Marianne gave her detailed directions, and in twenty minutes, she was ready to leave. When she closed her front door, a small slip of yellow paper wedged in the doorway fell to the floor.

SECOND NOTICE: RENT OVERDUE.

She sighed, then shrugged. *Figures.* She crumpled it and put it in her pocket.

Marianne's apartment, a brownstone she shared with two waiters from a nearby steakhouse, sat in a recently gentrified neighborhood in Washington Heights. Only a ten-minute subway ride away, it was a simple journey Eden could manage even in the state she was in.

"Oh, my," Marianne said at the sight of Eden's bloodshot eyes and matted bed hair. She put a hand to her mouth, looking Eden up and down.

"I know, I know," Eden said. "I look like shit."

When Eden sat on Marianne's sofa, she felt a shift—the weight of the last two days sifted like sand in her body. She leaned, let her jaw drop, and allowed every muscle to go slack. Exhaling audibly, long, and slowly, Eden was suddenly self-conscious, aware of how she must look. She'd hadn't showered, just managed a quick wash-up. And her hair—she did a futile finger-combing—would have been a complete mess had she not decided months ago to give in to the trend of way-ward, corkscrew curls. She looked up and around at the clean white walls, the carefully placed furniture, and thoughtful touches of art—an African mask here, a clay pot there, an arrangement of dried flowers in one corner—and on the walls, sleek black frames housing posters of art exhibitions and paintings Eden recognized as famous, but could not name.

In the apartment Eden shared with her brother, her walls were heavily layered in stark white paint over plaster, and the building superintendent gave specific orders not to hang anything with nails. The few furniture pieces were worn, sagging, and decrepit Salvation Army and Goodwill specials, some donated by Pastor Fleet's parishioners. Two small windows, one in each room, and each an arm's reach from adjacent buildings of red brick, lit the entire space. Everything about the space said "barely getting by."

Looking around, she was aware she'd not been in anyone else's apartment in New York. The warmth of the room felt like a revelation. She took off her shoes and wiggled her toes in the thick pile of white shag beneath the coffee table, where a sheaf of papers was stacked. An application form or something. She remembered now. Marianne had told her she was thinking of getting a nursing degree. She'd always wanted to help sick people and didn't want to be waiting tables when she was sixty.

Marianne placed a white porcelain cup of ginger tea in front of Eden and looked up, surveying her own space as if for the first time.

"I found this place in an ad in the paper. Had my furniture shipped up from storage in Kansas, so most of what you see here is mine. My housemates were here for a year with absolutely nothing but mattresses! Drink that, sit for a minute, and then I'll bring out the big guns."

Marianne had set a place for Eden at a small oak dining table near a window in her galley kitchen. An oversized bowl of cereal, a small plate with a simple boiled egg, toast, and a thick, gray concoction in a tall glass sat before her. She picked up the toast, burned to a crisp.

"Don't ask, just eat. It works."

She ate. In a few minutes, the nausea went away. She leaned her head back and sighed, eyes closed.

Marianne went to a drawer and pulled out a scrap of paper and a pen. "Evan stopped in the restaurant yesterday for coffee. Asked about you. That place he mentioned—the owner's interested. He wants to see you as soon as possible. Tomorrow, if you want."

Eden looked up. "What kind of place is it?"

"Here's the name and address, but I'll let him tell you about it. There's a little bit of a catch to it, he said."

Eden smiled wryly. A catch. "Well, I'm too flat-chested for Hooters. And I was never very good with a pole. But don't think I haven't thought about it."

Marianne laughed. "I'm pretty sure it's nothing like that. By the way, how are things going? Money-wise. You making out OK?"

Eden's phone vibrated in her purse. Her brother. "'Scuse me," she said. "I need to take this."

As soon as she answered, Reginald Jr. began. What was up with her this morning? And last night—where was she? He would have called the police if he hadn't fallen asleep. Yeah, he went to school, and yeah he was on time. Breakfast? He'd had a slice of pizza from the night before. Did she get up and go off to look for work? Was she OK? She didn't look too good before he left. She was groggy and saying stuff that didn't make no sense. He was just wondering when they could get him some new shoes. A piece of his sole came completely off, and he'd almost tripped on it. Oh, and another thing, he was thinking of getting a job after school.

She had been dead set against him getting a job. But that was before she'd lost hers. "Uh…yeah, OK," she told him. "We'll see about all that."

A pause. "You OK, sis?"

Eden cleared her throat. "Me? Yeah. I'm fine. I'm at Marianne's. I'll be out for a few hours. See you back at home."

There was something in his voice, something new. Concern. The boy was worried about her. Was this what it had come to? Her brother, at sixteen, taking care of her?

Marianne asked again, "How's everything going? I mean, really?"

Eden put her phone away and ate a final bite of the toast. "We're still hanging in there. My brother needs stuff for school, you know. But it'll be OK."

It had only been ten days since she'd been fired, but to Eden, it felt much longer. Having a job to go to every day had done more than kept the lights on. It had also kept her in a reasonable state of calm. If she didn't get something soon, she didn't know how they would make it through the month.

"So, tell me." Marianne was looking, it seemed, right through her.

"Tell you what?"

"Everything."

Eden's gaze turned toward the window as her eyes welled up. She swallowed hard before she could bring herself to speak without breaking down. For the next few minutes, she unpacked it all—the futile job search, the guy she met who nearly raped her, waking up late and hungover when she should have been out looking for work. When she was done, she took a deep breath and closed her eyes to relive each failure, each mistake and stupid choice, one after the other.

"I don't know what I was thinking. I guess I just wasn't. I messed up. Totally."

Marianne pointed to the glass of thick liquid and told her to take another sip. "You never told me how your trip home went. Everything OK?" she asked.

Eden told Marianne about the house that Aunt Baby wanted to leave to her and her brother, and when she mentioned Reginald Jr.'s "issues" in the city—she left it at, "It's complicated"—she explained that it just wasn't a good solution for them right now. She told her about what it meant to see the city she'd grown up in reduced to such a horrible state; she was stranded, in limbo between two strange places, and neither one felt like home.

But there was the scrapbook she'd taken from Aunt Baby's house, the pictures and reviews and medals of the once-famous singer. Her nighttime refuge. It quieted her mind, eased her heart. There was some hope for her, in there, somewhere. This slave's daughter had sung for kings and queens and at the White House. And the more she read, the more she realized that despite all the articles and reviews praising her singing, the woman had probably never received the recognition she deserved. She was black after all, and a woman, living a hundred years ago. She had probably died poor, alone, and completely forgotten.

But while she lived, she must have been one fierce sister.

She did not tell her about singing at Little Eva's. She'd tucked that moment beneath more pressing concerns. It hardly mattered now;

the feeling, powerful as it was, could not be cashed in, could not be exchanged for food, rent, or electricity. No matter what, she still had no job, no money, and no prospects of either.

Marianne leaned forward. "I know. Feels like the world is beating up on you," she said. She placed a finger near her eye. "See this scar?" She touched it, then traced the W-shaped line from the corner of her left eye down her cheekbone.

Eden raised her eyebrows, nodded. She'd noticed the scar many times. *Her sorry-ass ex-husband*, she'd figured, though Marianne had never explained it.

"I'm grateful for this scar," she said. "Because it reminds me of November 14."

"What do you mean?"

Marianne sat back, shaking her head at the memory. "I went through hell with Edgar. I got tired of it all. So, one day, November 14, 1999, years after I should have been gone, I just fought back. This scar reminds me of how that man beat me down, and how long I stayed there, and how I left and never looked back." She put a hand on Eden's arm. "Listen. You keep your head up. You're stronger than you think, and there's always a way out. Always."

Eden smiled. "I sure didn't think this was gonna be easy. And if you had told me a year ago that I'd be living in New York right now, I'da swore you were crazy. But I swear to God..."

"That scrapbook of the woman, with the pictures and medals. If she was that famous, could you sell it? Maybe to a collector or somebody?"

Eden shrugged. "It's just a bunch of old pictures of somebody I never heard of. Haven't looked through it all, but the medals and other stuff look kind of cheap. I just thought it was kind of interesting."

"What about FEMA? Any more money due from them?"

"Got a check a few weeks ago. That's the last of it."

Marianne sighed and held up the paper she'd written on. "Then, at least do this," she said. "Give me a minute."

She went into the bedroom, got her phone out of her purse, and made a call. Minutes passed before she emerged again.

"OK." She sat down in front of Eden. "There could be a job waiting for you, if you want it. It's a little different from what you're used to. But before you say no to it, give it a try."

"What?"

Marianne pressed the paper into Eden's hand. "All the information is right here. Tomorrow at noon."

She added, "And by the way, it's not what you think. You won't need a push-up bra."

CHAPTER 13

New Orleans, 1921

Celia reached for the broom. "Get down! I told you, get down!"

The black, white-footed cat vaulted from a high-backed chair onto the windowsill, next to a flower box of red petunias. Celia had only made one move toward the Victrola with the record in her hand, and the cat jumped to stake out a place on the nearest perch. She'd wait there for the music.

It had been two years since the opera house fire, but Celia still walked evenings in the Quarter, strolled by the site of charred ruins, musing over her faded dreams. More than once, she'd seen the cat scale the pyramids of rubble and debris. *Do you miss the music, too?* She took the cat home and named her for the lead role in the opera she'd always wanted to sing. Aida, the Ethiopian princess, was desperately in love with the Egyptian enemy army captain—a role fit for a diva, and the role of a lifetime for a black woman, but one that no black woman had ever played.

"What did I tell you, Aida!?" she snapped. All Celia needed to do was reach for the broom. The cat jumped away from the Victrola, landed on a lamp table, then the arm of another chair—beyond the broom's reach but close enough to hear.

Celia pulled the shiny disc from its sleeve. Her old friend Bert Williams had sent her his newest recording. As soon as the wax platter began spinning at seventy-eight revolutions per minute and the vaude-villian's voice came to life in the room, the cat leaned in toward the horn, consumed with curiosity.

Along with the recording, the newest model of the Victrola pho-nograph machine had arrived at Celia's doorstep—another gift from Bert. The disc players were the newest invention, the sound of the phonograph records much better than the old Edison cylinder ma-chine she owned. The old machines, however, did something the new players could not—they allowed her to record her own voice at home. The sound was a little thin, but my God, what a revelation it had been! When she heard the recording of her own singing for the first time, she cried.

The new machines—they were the future.

Celia sat near the Victrola in a chair to listen and reminisce. She smiled at the sound of Bert's smooth tenor, remembering the song, one that he and his partner George Walker had done when they were part of her troupe, Black Donatella's Troubadours. Coon songs. Knock-knock routines. Lively buck jump music. The crowds loved them. Now, from Aida's throat came purring confirmation.

When the recording ended, Celia turned off the machine and put the record back into its sleeve. Memories of the touring days rushed back in waves. The cities. The crowds. The adoring fans. Celia's en-during fame and a place in history all but assured. Throughout the Northeast, the West, and the South, the Troubadours had played every opera house and auditorium in dozens of towns, until her husband bankrupted her and broke her heart. Thank God, Bert and George landed on their feet after leaving the company. She didn't even be-grudge them their good fortune—a recording contract from Victor, the same company that had ignored her.

But then the letter had arrived: The Victor company, Celia's managers reported, wanted to record her voice! She could barely contain her joy. Now at last, she would be remembered. Perhaps even her career would be revived. Recorded music was a revelation, introducing the great voices of all time to *tout le monde*. Finally, she would join the ranks of the great artists—Patti, Melba, and even the great Adeline Donatella.

This was the way, surely; the phonograph machine was colorblind, and the gods who parceled talent were not partial to paler skin. Now, her voice would be imprinted in the memory of all, absent the distraction of color.

But months had passed without further word from her managers. So, she wrote directly to the head of the Victor company, Eldridge Johnson.

Dear Mr. Johnson,

I am thrilled at the prospect of recording my voice, for the benefit of history, on your marvelous machine, the Victrola. I have heard many of your company's efforts, and have been pleased with the result. I would be honored to record one or more of my songs. Perhaps "Swanee River"? Or "My Old Kentucky Home"? Even though I am quite busy with performances, I am vocalizing every day and singing the popular songs, as to be ready for the recording.

Please let me know as soon as possible when and where this recording appointment should take place. I shall adjust my schedule in accordance with your time and convenience.

Yours in music,

Celia DeMille

The Black Donatella

She had added the last line only after much thought. It was that moniker that appeared on marquees and billboards from Fort Worth to Providence. Not her own name. Indeed, sometimes it seemed as if the name given to her by her mama and papa had begun to disappear. She often wondered how many of her most ardent fans remembered her real name, or if they had ever known it at all.

I shall adjust my schedule in accordance with your time and convenience. A joke. She had no schedule. Her popularity had waned long before the bankruptcy, long before the final performance. And then came the War. It was a sober time, and if America was no longer amused by madcap minstrel shows, they were even less interested in her.

But today, the young reporter, Arthur Flanagan from the *New York Times*, had asked to come by for tea. Would she mind an afternoon visit? Dear God! Yes! He regretted keeping her waiting so long for the article he promised months ago. The newspapers had lavishly written about Patti, Melba, and of course, Adeline Donatella. Every singer of worth, some who had never sung at the White House, the Academy of Music in Philadelphia, or for the king of England as she had, held forth in the pages of the nation's biggest journals. Why not her? It was long overdue.

Since selling her properties, a small Cape Cod bungalow in Newport and a larger colonial in Virginia, her furs (all four of them), and most of her jewelry (even the gold watch), her funds were still meager. Even now, when she looked at the depression on the hardwood where the seven-foot Steinway had once sat, she was crestfallen. Nonetheless, for this occasion, she had purchased a new, only slightly used sterling silver tea service from Edelman's Pawn Shop. She still had a sealed tin of oolong tea from China sent by an admirer years ago. And she would put out a lovely tray of sweet biscuits and pomegranate jam.

Finally, there was reason to celebrate! With an article in the *Times*, other newspapers would surely seek her out for interviews, and the world would clamor for her singing. Then let the Victor people deny her a recording!

She chose one of her most stylish chemises—red with black lace trim—and set out what remained of her wedding china cups and saucers. At precisely 4 p.m.—the young man was so prompt!—she opened the door.

"Madame!" He gave a small bow and kissed her hand.

He had grown a trim beard since the last time she had seen him, but was no less handsome.

"Come in!" She gestured toward the armchair and took a seat on the divan next to him.

Their talk was polite. Yes, the weather had indeed been beautiful since the storms ended. The phonograph? Oh, it was a gift from an admirer, she said. A recording of *my* songs? Well, it is being discussed. Did I tell you what President Roosevelt said about my "Swanee River"?

Finally, he reached into his black leather briefcase, talking as he searched among papers for the article, and she poured tea from the silver teapot into the English china cups. She talked to him as he ruffled the bag's contents. Had he remembered to mention the command performance at Buckingham Palace? The four White House recitals? Madison Square Garden and The Music Hall? Of course, he told her. He had not forgotten.

"Ah, here it is," he told her, extending the newspaper toward her, folded to the article.

She looked at it. The article was several inches long and three columns wide. But it was not the *New York Times*.

"This is an advance copy. It will run tomorrow."

She was silent a moment. "But…"

"I can explain." He looked down into his cup. His editor at the *Times*, he explained, was not familiar with the career of Madame De-Mille, and therefore, was reluctant, or rather, ah, unwilling to print a story about someone…

He stumbled, began again.

She helped him along. "He has never heard of me," she said, her voice low, her gaze drifting to the open window. "He refused to print an article about a black woman singer, and especially one who is…"

Past her prime, words she could not say aloud.

He said nothing. The paper he had handed her with the full-page story, titled "A Diva's Life," would be in the early morning edition of *The Black Beacon*, the newspaper of black New York.

"Yes, well." Her chest tightened while her wet eyes burned.

"I am truly, truly, sorry." His voice was both apologetic and hopeful.

She lifted the silver teapot and poured more tea into her cup. And then his.

The Black Beacon, he told her, was elated to publish the story and he promised that it would reach many, many readers.

"A small fraction of the number who read the *Times*," she said, setting the paper down next to the teapot. "And read only by the colored population."

The Beacon had written about her many times. It had always been generous, fawning, even. But it was small, a far cry from the *Times*.

"I know that you are disappointed."

Papa had taught her to smile in the face of disappointment. "A quiet smile stamps the offense in the mind of the offender," he had said. As a slave, and later as a servant, he had learned the practiced art of the smiling, sardonic gaze.

She smiled.

She listened to but barely heard his excuses and efforts at an apology. His promises. He would try again, and again. Maybe in another few months, or perhaps to another editor. Was her recording to be released any time soon? Perhaps then. She got up and cleared the small table of the tray, the tea service, and the tin of oolong.

Later. After I'm dead and gone.

As he was leaving, he turned toward her again. "Pardon me, but there is one more thing I would like to ask you."

"What is it?"

He paused and cleared his throat. "It's just that, well, when I was doing a little research on your story, one of my sources told me that you were at the site of the French Opera House, the night the whole building burned to the ground."

She paused, her eyebrows lifting. "Oh, who told you that?"

"My source. And, if you'll forgive me, I have also heard you were brought in by the police for questioning. But then, after a few minutes, you were let go."

She tilted her head and gave him an impatient, questioning look. "What is it you are asking me?"

"Do you mind if I ask what you were doing there? Near the building?"

"It was so long ago, I do not remember. Probably just out for a walk."

"A walk? I'm told it was well after midnight."

"As I said, I do not recall."

The night of the fire, and the night of her lover's betrayal. She was in such a state, even hours later. She'd felt as if the world had ended.

"Well, it was a while ago, I understand," he said, turning away to walk to the door. "I guess I will be going."

"Why does this interest you? It was so long ago."

He looked away, fingered the rim of his hat, then squared it on his head. "It's just that after all this time, no one seems to know how it happened. The opera house fire, I mean."

"And you think I do?"

"I think it is possible," he said. "Perhaps you saw someone? Or something?"

She looked at him straight. "No, I did not. Now, if you'll excuse me, it's getting late."

"Of course. Again, I am truly sorry about the paper. I did my best."

She nodded. "I'm sure you did."

Weeks passed. On an evening just after sunset, with the night air thick and balmy and the courtyard ripe with the sweet scent of jasmine, she stepped out and walked in the direction of the river. Not so long ago, the neigh of carriage horses filled the night and the streets were fouled with the horses' excrement. Now, the high-pitched whine and engine sputter of automobiles were more familiar as they motored past Jackson Square. Two sailors strode past her, and in the distance, a pair of silhouetted young lovers embraced under a gas lamp.

Charred heaps of bricks, fallen beams, hollowed window arches, and piles of stone and metal made the once stately opera house look like a toy castle of blocks and sticks kicked over by an angry child. Celia shuddered; a ghostly presence hovered amid the ash and dust, but remnants of song hung in the air. Bizet. Mozart. Puccini. The smoky ghosts of genius. Their melodies swirled through the ruins, threaded in the night breeze carried from the river.

She'd entered the site from Toulouse Street, remembering this spot as a once-bustling corner, where the motorcars once stopped to allow patrons of the evening's performance to disembark. The women floated in gowns of silk brocade or taffeta; the men wore swallow-tail coats. Sometimes she re-envisioned the fire, but struggled to remember the details of that night. The flames. The sparks and crackles. The firemen. The police station. Had it all been real? The more time passed, the more it seemed like a dream.

She returned to the apartment to find her nurse, Catherine, waiting outside the entrance gate off Rue Conti. Her dark-brown skin glowed in ascending moonlight. A waif of a woman, she was slightly stoop-shouldered and wore her thickly braided hair pulled back from her elfin face. *Mousy, yet a sweet girl,* Celia had thought upon first meeting her.

Catherine's services as a private nurse, three evenings a week, were a gift, a peace offering from the maestro upon hearing of the diva's ailment.

It was the least he could do.

Celia smiled and unlatched the gate to the courtyard.

"Good evening, Madame!" Catherine's voice rang in lilting Creole. "How was your walk tonight?"

"Peaceful out. Quiet."

"And the pain?"

Celia reached a hand to her side and massaged it. "Oh, tolerable. Feels good to move the body while one can. Doctor said I should have many months, maybe even a year or more."

"Ah, that's very good news."

They walked toward the back of the courtyard past the two banana trees and the wild hibiscus plants. As Celia held the arm of her young nurse, the wooden stairs creaked and whined as they climbed toward the balcony.

At the door of Celia's apartment, Aida rushed to greet her as she did each night after Celia returned from her walk, then scampered back toward the window and jumped up on the arm of the chair. Celia put her cotton shawl on the dining table next to the scrapbook, now swollen with pasted-in articles.

"I'll just get your medicine, and the things together for your bath," Catherine said.

In the kitchen, Catherine found the porcelain wash bowl, washing towels, castile soap, and the pain and sleeping pills. In the last several weeks, Celia's pain, which came and went randomly, had subsided to a dull throb.

After her bath, Catherine poured a greenish liquid into a small cordial and the aroma of licorice stirred the air. She sat next to the singer's bed, taking a chair close to her, a large metal box with a latch in her lap.

Celia looked at the glass. "Not tonight, I think. Tea. I'd prefer tea, please."

"Oh, yes ma'am."

The tea, served in a white china cup with a silver rim, perfumed the room with a wintergreen scent. "I'm almost done." Celia took a slow sip from the cup and turned to a blank page in the scrapbook. "There is one more article to be pasted in. Make sure my medals and my jewelry are nicely polished, please."

"Yes, ma'am."

"Remember, take it to him right after I am gone, which I hope won't be soon! Do it immediately. It's important all of this goes to the right place. It's important, if I'm to be remembered at all."

"I understand."

"And do you have a safe place to keep it until the time is right?"

"Yes. Yes, of course. It will be safe."

She reached in and found a necklace with a pendant, a round disk of gold. "And I want you to have this."

Catherine smiled. "But this was given to you by—"

"I know, it is very precious. But keep it. It's yours. And at the bottom of the box, you'll find my will. You, young lady, have made my life so much…easier." She smiled. "As I said before, I'm leaving most of my personal valuables to you to do with as you like. But you must do exactly what I ask. I am counting on you. I may be gone, but I will know if you have not."

Seeing the expression of dismay and alarm on Catherine's face, she reached and patted her nurse's hand. "I'm teasing you," she said, smiling.

The pills began their effect, making her drowsy, but sleep still eluded her. Whenever she drifted into that unconscious haze, thoughts roiled and tossed in her head, a chain jerking her back into wakefulness. The reporter. What was his name again? Arthur Flanagan. Arthur Flanagan of the *New York Times. A good man,* she thought. But his last questions bothered her. *What did he know? Who had told him she was near the fire that night?*

And simply being there didn't mean anything. She wasn't guilty of anything.

Was she?

CHAPTER 14

She entered the revolving door of the Welborne, Able, and Delacourt Building on 6th Avenue and stood against a wall inside the lobby with water puddling at her feet, twenty minutes early and looking a mess. She'd spent more than an hour with Marianne getting ready, and now, a bank of mirrors threw back a shocking sight. Her hair was a disaster. The cheap purple umbrella she'd brought had betrayed her—it had flipped inside-out like a giant tulip in the wind—her black leather pumps were rain-stained, and her black blouse and skirt clung like cellophane.

If there was anything worse than trying to find your way around New York City, it was trying to find your way around it in the pouring rain.

That morning before Marianne left for work, Eden had gone to her apartment; getting dressed for this interview required a team. Shoes, makeup, a blouse and skirt, and hairstyle had to be considered. Marianne took over: foundation, mascara, eye shadow, just a touch for daytime. Clothes that signaled maturity and professionalism—albeit on a budget. Hair...well, there wasn't much she could do about that;

it was what it was. She tamed her natural, frizzed-out, chin-length corkscrews with moisturizing dabs of Kurl-Renew.

Marianne had stood back and assessed her work. Eden's blank neckline needed something. Did she own a simple pendant? Eden pulled out of her purse the necklace and pendant she'd removed from Aunt Baby's box of medals and mementos. Eden had scrubbed it with soap and water, gave it a glistening, rustic shine.

Marianne cupped the piece in her hand to feel its weight, then held the necklace up to the light. "Interesting, and kind of beautiful in an antique-y way. Gold-plated, I guess? Or maybe it could be...You brought this back from home, didn't you? You sure this isn't worth something? Did you take this to somebody, have them appraise it?"

"No." Eden shrugged. "Figured it was nothing special. Crusted with dirt and stuff. Got them little nicks and broken places."

"Adds to the character. A little toothpaste wash and it'll look great. It'll be striking with the black top."

She was right. Marianne had scrubbed, washed, and polished the pendant, which now shone like a newly minted coin. Eden put it on and Marianne fastened the polished clasp. Her chin up, Eden threw her shoulders back to straighten her spine. No one could tell, she hoped, that apart from the necklace, her entire outfit, including her shoes, had cost roughly $8.75 and was courtesy of the clearance bin of the Salvation Army thrift store on 146th.

As she stood in the lobby, a small knot worked in her stomach. *Was Evan Smallwood serious? Me? Work here?* In the vast, circular atrium, she stood beneath a chandelier that looked like the size of her whole apartment. An alternate pattern of rectangular mirrors and marble panels lined the walls and an ascending escalator looked like it possibly reached the earth's atmosphere.

She leaned her head back to take it all in, then, self-conscious, pulled her lips together and glanced around to see if anyone had noticed her gap-mouthed awe. No one had. In fact, her whole existence seemed unnoticed. All around her, people, mostly dry and impeccably dressed, stepped briskly, chatting, with their eyes boring straight through her or focused on phone screens. She wasn't even on the right floor yet, but already she believed there'd been a huge mistake. *Was this the right building? Yes.* She'd double-checked. Smallwood had told her to take the escalator up to the mezzanine level, then find the elevators to the right and take a car up to the…what floor? She pulled the wadded paper out of her pocket and looked down again at the directions. The seventy-third floor.

Dear Jesus.

In her whole life in New Orleans, she had never been any higher than fifty floors up, and that was in the penthouse suites of the Omni where, as she changed sheets, made beds, vacuumed carpets, and changed towels for the week's onslaught of business travelers, she pulled the drapes closed and steered clear of the window. She would never look out from so high up, at least, not a second time. The first and only time she'd looked down at the street from the fiftieth-floor penthouse suite balcony, her legs staggered and she'd had to sit down on the bed.

Acrophobia. Fear of heights. Figures, since she'd spent most of her life several feet below the level of the sea.

But she did as Evan instructed: took the escalator up to the mezzanine, found the elevators, held her breath, and punched 73, the floor for Maestro's Bistro and Bar. Everyone she'd seen in the building looked polished and privileged and were white, except for the black window washer and the (maybe) Hispanic receptionists. Men as trim as models, doused in minty cologne and hair gel, strode alongside thin, Pilates-fit women, their five-inch heels clacking against the tiled floors, looking like the younger versions of all the people she had ever worked for. On the twenty-seventh floor, three dark-brown women in red, green, and yellow saris got in the elevator speaking in—Indian? Or what did they call it? Hindu? Hindi? She wasn't sure, but their melanin-rich skin provided momentary comfort, even if she couldn't understand a word of their conversation. They got off on a lower floor. Alone now, up, up, up, she went, and closed her eyes at floor fifty-three.

The seventy-third floor opened up to a vast, wide room of floor-to-ceiling windows fanning out into a giant convex back wall of glass. On the far-left side was a long, sickle-shaped granite bar, and to the right, the wall was adorned with a gallery of back-and-white photos of the Manhattan skyline in various shades of light—early morning, mid-day, night, and every hour in between. In the middle of the room were cabaret-style tables draped in white cloth and high-back chairs. She gave the room a quick assessment: *too rich for my blood, but the tips here have gotta be good.* This was nothing like Estelle's or any other place she'd ever worked. Lunch seemed in full swing. Bartenders dispensed tall iced drinks; waitresses and waiters hustled, smiled, and laughed from table to table. Ahead, the windows framed a view of what looked to be the entire state of New York.

She glanced at her watch—still thirteen minutes early. Good. Maybe her hair and outfit could air-dry in that time. She found a seat at the bar. Placing the dripping umbrella on the floor near her feet, she took up the black cloth napkin before her, blotted her clumped wet hair, and tugged at the clinging wet blouse.

"What are you having?" The young blond bartender in front of her wore a tight black t-shirt and striped horn-rimmed glasses. He smiled as he polished a wine goblet dry with a cloth.

"Uh, nothing, I'm just waiting for somebody. Supposed to meet them here. About a job. I'm early."

"Oh, you must be the new singer. Glass of water? Cup of tea? The singers, they're always drinking hot tea, so I keep bags on hand. Chamomile OK?"

"Uh, no. Water, I guess. Thanks."

"Gotcha." He filled a tall slender glass with ice, then water from the tap, and placed it in front of her with a napkin.

Singer? She couldn't figure out what he was talking about until, from the front of the room near the window, she heard a woman's high voice. A song she recognized, something classical, from a movie or some TV show. The woman had a light voice, vibrating sweet and silvery at the top of its range. *Nice,* Eden thought, though the words were incomprehensible, some language with rolled Rs and long Os.

"O mio babbino caro…mi piace é bello, bello…"

This is what Evan wanted her to do? Wait tables and then sing, in a foreign language, in front of these people, on the seventy-third floor?

She turned up the glass and finished the water. "Thanks," she told the bartender. She stepped off the barstool and made her way to the elevator.

In the lobby, she ran into Evan. One look at her and his smile vanished.

"What happened? You're leaving? Didn't you find David?"

She didn't know who David was and didn't care. "I'm just not…I appreciate what you were trying to do for me and everything, but I don't know. I just don't—it didn't feel right. Not for me."

His brows furrowed. He followed her as she walked to a corner of the lobby by the restroom door. She wrung her hands together, then rubbed her temples with her thumb and forefingers.

She turned to him. "I'm really sorry, but…They were up there singing in some foreign language, and they were singing that opera music, or whatever it was. I don't do that stuff. I can't sing in anything but English and I don't know nothing about that other kind of music."

She wanted to correct herself, the way her father would have. "'I don't know anything,' not 'I don't know nothing,'" He'd told her a million times. "I don't know nothing 'bout birthin' no babies, Miss Scarlett." He used the line from *Gone with the Wind* to tease her. It made her laugh, but the lessons never stuck when she was nervous, like now.

"Wait a minute." Evan put a hand on her forearm. "Just take a deep breath and come with me."

Outside, the rain had let up slightly; the clouds were higher and tentative light played through the leaves of the fenced-in trees along the avenue. Intermittent sun shimmered on the rain-soaked sidewalks, and pedestrians emerged from the shelter of awnings and doorways. Evan led her to a café only a few yards north of the doors of the Welborne Building, just before the entrance to the subway.

"Here, you look like you could use a little pick-me-up." He placed a smoothie on the table in front of her. "OK. Tell me what happened up there. What did David say to you?"

David? She told him she hadn't met anyone named David; she'd only sat at the bar and waited. David Kim, he told her, was the owner of the restaurant, a Korean opera lover who moved to New York five years ago, had a son who studied percussion at Juilliard, and from the moment he first breathed American air, dreamed of a restaurant where every member of the wait staff sang some of the most beautiful music in the world while they served the best food and drinks in town. Two senses satisfied at once—three, if you counted the beauty of the young people he would hire. He quickly learned the idea was not a new one. Opera-singing waiters had become something of a novelty in a few Italian restaurants and bars at least a decade ago. But he wanted to take it to a different level.

"I met David when I used to play piano at this little hole in the wall in the Village, Eddie Marvel's. David came in on Wednesdays, used to request all the old Jelly Roll Morton tunes. Anyway, David and me, we got to be friends, on account of us both being jazz fans."

She remembered he'd said his mother had sung. Stirring the smoothie with her plastic spoon, she looked at Evan's face and found something calming in it. She took a deep breath, tried not to think about how she was almost out of money with rent still overdue, and made a note to herself to call about another extension. She couldn't let another unemployed day go by and she decided, then and there, to follow her earlier thought. McDonald's, a new one, was on the way home. They might be hiring, and if they weren't, maybe one of their other stores was. She knew it didn't pay much, the hourly compensation hovering somewhere around minimum wage without the chance for tips she'd been used to. But she needed a job and she needed it now.

She'd stopped listening for a minute, then realized he was going on about her singing.

"High, light, kind of lyrical, you know, like a real soprano. My mother, she had a voice like yours…"

She stopped listening again at *mother*. Eden wondered whether he looked like her, and how come he never mentioned a daddy.

"I know you don't sing opera, and I told David that. But you've got that kind of talent, and I know someone who could teach you enough to do the work. You can sing anything you want. It's just that most of the singers at Maestro's are classically trained and have voices that are suitable for classical stuff. Like yours."

Hell, I know I can sing, she thought. Her talent was no mystery to her. *But what did he mean, 'suited for classical stuff'?* She'd always known that her voice was impressive from the awe on the faces around her. Eyes lit with wonder or closed in sublime joy—that was her doing, she figured out long ago. She'd always sung higher than anybody else she'd known at school or in the gospel choir at Blessed Redeemer back home. But no one had ever told her that her voice was suitable for opera since no one she knew had ever seen or heard one. Including her.

Evan's phone rang: David Kim. As fate would have it, the restaurant owner had been unexpectedly called away and needed to reschedule. Eden nodded. Another morning gone to waste.

"Well, are you hungry? Let's eat. Then there's something I want to show you."

He was not convinced, he told her, that she should just give up on the job at the Welborne Building, but they could talk about that later.

Eden's smile was guarded. "Listen, you don't owe me anything. Like I said, what happened at Estelle's was not really your fault."

That was not why he was trying to help her, he told her. It was her talent. What she didn't know about her special gift was how rare it was. And even if she chose not to pursue it, she should at least know what was possible.

She looked at him, speechless for a moment. It was his eyes. For the briefest moment, she was reminded of the air in her father's bedroom—the scent of rubbing alcohol, English Leather cologne, Wrigley's spearmint gum, and black Shinola polish was as palpable as a heartbeat. Why was she thinking of him now? It wasn't that this man's eyes were anything like her father's. Reginald Sr.'s dark eyes had been smallish, narrowing to near-closing when he smiled, while Evan's were hooded and deep-set, sleepy-looking. It was his manner that seemed familiar. Restful, calm. Assured, even protective. His eyes didn't dart or shift, but stayed straight and true. The eyes of a man who not only wouldn't lie or hide but also wouldn't know how to do either.

Walking in the warmish drizzle, they stopped at a pizza-by-the-slice restaurant across the street for lunch. Eden licked her fingertips from the best pizza she had ever had: gooey with mozzarella, thick with crumbled sausage, and dripping a spicy tomato sauce. Real New York pizza, he told her, then folded his slice in half lengthwise, biting a small section off the narrow end. She folded hers and took a bite that dripped red sauce on the counter. Giggling at her mess, she accepted his offer for a second slice with grilled onions. She was eating a little too fast, she realized; she hadn't realized how hungry she was. Evan was looking at her, trying to hide his amusement.

"Sorry," she said. "I always eat too fast when I'm hungry."

"Good to see a woman who appreciates food," he told her.

"I'm from New Orleans," she reminded him, smiling now.

He looked down at the gold around her neck. "That necklace. Very cool. Looks like an antique. How'd you come by it?"

She wiped her fingers on a napkin and touched the golden disk. She told him about the box Aunt Baby had given her. The name of the singer didn't register with him.

"She must have been pretty successful," he said.

"Yeah, I think she was real famous," she told him, remembering the news articles pasted in the scrapbook, reviews from cities and even countries she'd never heard of. "There are all these articles about her, singing for presidents, and even kings and queens. But I don't think she stayed famous. It seems like everybody forgot all about her after a while."

He changed the subject, asking her if, apart from here, she had ever been outside of Louisiana.

"I barely been outside New Orleans."

"And what about here?"

"What do you mean?"

"Been outside of your neighborhood? Seen much of the city?"

She almost scoffed. Seeing any place in this city other than where she worked did not interest her. *I'm just trying to survive*, she wanted to say.

"I got too much to do, responsibilities and stuff." *You know where I can get a good deal on some size-twelve sneakers?* she wanted to ask him. She would not bore him with talk about her real concerns: taking care of her brother, avoiding eviction, and keeping her head above water with a teenager in tow.

He wiped his hands on a paper napkin. "Let me show you some of my favorite places. Turn your miserable day around."

Another day without finding work? No way. "I was gonna go to the McDonald's up near me, check it out, and see if they need anybody. There's gotta be a fast-food place that'll hire me. I need to work, like, real soon."

"Take a day off from looking. I can just about guarantee you you'll have a job, a good one, once David hears you sing. Promise. Just let me show you around."

He wasn't hearing her. What was with this man? Was she speaking in tongues or something? "I don't know."

"I do. I know this will work. Give me a couple of hours today. Please. I know you can do better. Don't go to McDonald's. Not today."

Then he told her what the job would pay.

Her mouth flew open. "You kidding."

Now he had her attention. It was more than twice what she'd earned at Estelle's. And, he added, that was before tips.

"A little more than McDonald's, I would think."

"But I don't know if I can do it."

"So, you're not even going to try." His tone was firm, almost a challenge.

She exhaled audibly. With that much money on the table, even a wobbly one, she'd be a fool not to try for it. She looked at her watch. An hour wouldn't hurt, and she could stop by McDonald's on the way home if she wanted. She was about to respond when her phone buzzed in her purse: Reginald Jr.

Now what? Was he in trouble again? Or did he forget something? She remembered: he needed a field trip permission slip signed. The Museum of Natural History, or something like that. He'd mentioned it once, but had forgotten to give it to her, and was there anything she could do about it now? Missing a field trip with his class might help him learn. The last time he'd done that, she'd spent almost half her day off taking the permission slip to the school, and she'd warned him, "Last time I'm doing this." It was time the boy learned to take care of his own business.

She was out with a kind, interesting man who was being nice to her. How long had it been since she'd been with a guy who didn't want anything from her? A guy she could feel safe with?

She nodded. She was in.

"Good." Evan smiled.

When the phone rang again, she turned off the ringer and tucked it back inside her purse.

CHAPTER 15

"This way." Evan weaved through a mass of tourists and commuters heading to the Staten Island Ferry station. The Spirit of America, a massive ferry ship docked in the harbor, rocked gently as they climbed aboard along with dozens of others and made their way to the top deck. Evan held the tip of Eden's elbow as the winds shifted. The ferry horn droned a loud, bovine baritone. Breezes swirled off the water while the ship plowed out of its slip into the grayish-green expanse of New York Harbor.

As the ferry heaved away from shore, white foam churned behind it and a new chill spiked the air. Eden rubbed her forearms and shoulders. "Here," Evan said, removing his jacket and placing it on her. "It'll be even chillier farther out on the water."

The Mississippi. That calming, singing river was nothing like this busy harbor, but water was water and the scene pulled her back in time to another shore—the riverbank near Holy Cross in New Orleans. Eden and her father would watch the Steamboat Natchez roll across the Mississippi toward the bank of Algiers. But just as quickly, as the sea air cooled her arms and the salt spray nipped at her cheeks, as white gulls and egrets banked and leaned into the sun, the waves slapping the hull and the roar of diesel power brought her back to the moment. The ferry powered southward and the skyline of Lower Manhattan shrank.

From this distance, the whole borough seemed harmless and small, entire skyscrapers reduced to toy building blocks no more intimidating than a photograph. At the concession stand on the bottom deck, Evan bought two bottles of sparkling water and handed one to Eden. They leaned elbows and arms against the rails, and with the wind on their faces, the boat ferried past the Statue of Liberty and Ellis Island. Eden took out her phone and snapped a picture.

Funny how everything's changed, Eden thought. A few hours ago, wrestling wind and rain with an inside-out umbrella, feeling stupid, she had accepted another failure, another jobless, wasted day. She pulled Evan's jacket close around her neck and caught a whiff of the woody aftershave on his jacket collar.

She thought of Randy Marvais. Doyle Dugan. Those two had convinced her that men, except for her father, of course, meant nothing good for her. Yet, here was this Evan guy. Soft-voiced, kind-eyed. Easy. Was it true that he didn't want anything from her? Wouldn't he be just like the others?

It had been years. No men in her life, and she wanted it that way. She had no time for them, their sideways smiles, or their appraising stares, that "Hey, baby," and "Mind if I call you?" Maybe someday, she told that smiling stranger in her dream, once she'd fulfilled the promise to her father: raise her brother, keep him safe. Thirty-four years old now and so many years without the touch of a decent, caring man. Did she even care? She worried she'd become so numb to desire that if a man showed up with a good heart and honest intentions, somebody who wanted more than a new pair of sneakers for school, his tables waited on, or a warm pulse in his bed, she would wonder what the trick was.

Taking a deep breath, she tried to remember the last time, other than when she was singing, that she had felt this way—happy in the moment. What had her father said to her so many times on their levee walks? *If I could be anywhere with anybody in the world doing anything right now, I would be right here, with you, doing this.*

She rested her hand on Evan's forearm. "Thank you," she said.

He shrugged. "You can thank me after you get the gig."

"No, I mean thank you." She nodded toward the water. "For this."

He smiled, patted the arm she'd placed on his. The look he gave her—calm, generous, and maybe a little too personal—almost embarrassed her. Or something. She wasn't sure what the feeling was, but something flickered in her chest. She looked away.

They took a quick trip to Staten Island and back to Manhattan, where they disembarked. The subway took them to the West Chambers Street stop, close to the site where the September 11 Museum and Memorial was planned. "It's not built yet," Evan told her. But there was something else, another memorial he thought she might find interesting, something hardly anybody knew about.

It was a few blocks away. They walked along Chambers Street to Broadway, and on to a jumble of office and government-looking buildings where a large fenced-in lot was strewn with rocks and crowded with unmanned construction equipment: forklifts, bulldozers, excavators, and hydraulic hammers. When Eden looked perplexed, clearly wondering what in the world she was supposed to see here, Evan explained.

Three hundred years ago in Lower Manhattan, he said, not far from where the planes struck the Twin Towers of the World Trade Center, Africans, some free and some enslaved, blacksmiths, carpenters, artisans, craftsmen, longshoremen, and laborers had served the city's wealthy while building its bridges, sidewalks, and streets. They lived, worked, and raised their children, grew old, and buried their dead. Centuries passed. In the early 1990s, with construction underway on a new Federal Building, bulldozers plowed into about four hundred African graves, a fraction of the fifteen thousand or more Africans still there since the eighteenth century.

He went on. Over the years, progress rode roughshod over it, pummeling the cemetery deeper into the earth until it completely vanished beneath the upward sprawl of steel and glass. And with another shovel-ready building set to go, city officials swore there could not possibly be anything left of the ancient African burial grounds.

But when excavators and bulldozers struck coffins and bones, protests rang out loud and shrill from the city's black leaders. This was hallowed, sacred ground, they cried, and proper respect for the ancestors was due. After all, they'd practically built all of Lower Manhattan. The city conceded.

Evan nodded toward the fence. "Now, years later, the bones will finally be re-interred and a national monument, right in this place, will honor them."

Eden ran her fingers along the chain-link fence. Placards bore an artist's rendering of the planned memorial, some photographs of skeletons and artifacts, and a map of New York in 1755.

Evan had delved into his family history and learned that his father's side of the family could be traced back to New York in the 1800s. Some of the Smallwood men had been coopers, blacksmiths, and wheelwrights, or so the handed-down stories claimed. The Africans had not been permitted to live outside this part of Manhattan; this was the only area where they could be legally buried.

"So, if they lived in this city, my ancestors might've been buried right here."

Eden tried to imagine such a thing: Africans three hundred years ago, living right here. "So, will there be a list of their names? Maybe you can find your ancestors if they have a list of who's buried there?"

Too polite to utter the obvious, Evan shrugged. He shook his head. "No. No names. Just bones."

A beat passed.

Eden wanted to snatch her question back from the air. A flush of embarrassment rose to her face. They were slaves, weren't they? Most probably didn't read, nor write. Of course, there were no names.

"I uh...I guess not," she said.

"But at least we know they lived. They won't be forgotten."

Eden looked again at the photographs. "It's really cool, what they've done," she said.

"Yeah," he said and smiled. "Better late than never, huh?"

He touched her elbow. "Come on. Let's head uptown."

They traveled by train, by bus, and on foot, until Evan noticed Eden had begun to limp and insisted on buying her a pair of twelve-dollar sneakers to cushion the aching bunions she was too proud to mention. At 85th, they headed into Central Park. Where we are now was once a village, he told her. Seneca, as it was called, was where free and formerly enslaved black folks lived during the 1800s with their own AME church and a school, before the community was razed to make way for urban green space. Like at the African burial ground, coffins had surfaced during the razing that contained the remains of dark-skinned people.

"More history," he said. "This place is loaded with it." Evan gave her a look, almost apologetic. "So. In case you didn't notice, I'm really kind of into all this stuff."

"Yeah. Maybe you shoulda been a teacher."

"I was," he said, then shrugged. "For a couple of years when I came back from the service, a long time ago."

She wondered if Celia DeMille had ever sung in New York back then, and if so, where? Then she remembered one of the reviews for a performance at a place called Steinway Hall. A recital or something. She made a mental note to look up the singer's New York performances.

As the sky darkened, neon signs lit up—restaurants, coffee shops, bistros, bodegas priming for the evening rush—and street lamps illuminated. There was one more place where Evan wanted her to see. "A place I go to a lot," he said.

The Cathedral of St. John the Divine occupied a massive quadrant of Uptown real estate and was one of Evan's favorite places in the city. Not just a miracle of architecture, but of culture, too, he told her. Some of the best music the city had to offer. Bach, Mozart, or some Charles Mingus jazz. You just never knew what you'd find there. When he told her about the Feast of St. Francis of Assisi, when goats, llamas, donkeys, and even kangaroos are paraded down the aisle to be blessed, she laughed, then stopped abruptly at his deadpan look. Clearly, he wasn't joking.

The entrance was dark and cool. They left the scatter of tourists at the doorway and walked deeper beneath the arches into the space east of the entrance. Everywhere, there was something to study: a painting, a statue, or an ornately carved sculpture. The vaulted ceilings of stone loomed impossibly high; Evan and Eden's footsteps were amplified by the space. *Amazing*, Eden thought.

Eden stepped quietly, walking between pews and through aisles. From above, or left, or right, or everywhere, came a sound—a woman singing. Neither Eden nor Evan could see the woman, but the voice seemed to come from one of the small chapels away from the entrance.

Evan whispered, "Probably a rehearsal for Sunday's program. Let's check it out."

They stood behind a back pew of the chapel near a white statue of an angel. In the light from the stained-glass windows, Eden could see the woman beneath an altar, dressed in yellow. The chords of a pipe organ swelled as the voice powered above it.

As the voice grew, Eden moved away from Evan, weaving between the pews. The woman, now in her clear view, was black, taller than average, and large-boned. A substantial woman. With her eyes closed and head lifted, her skin was like red earth. *A queen*, Eden thought. *She looks like an African queen.* Her chin-length straightened hair loosely hung around her face; her hands rested at her sides.

Her voice is not as loud as it is big, Eden thought. *Big enough to pool into every corner of a cathedral.* Amplified by the towering vault and some miracle of acoustic stone, the woman's voice was big enough to block out all other sound and sight. At its core was a warmth that sent a chill up Eden's spine, and when the singer released a single feathered note up high and held it forever—the way one holds on to a last breath and heartbeat—her knees went soft. Another note, not high this time but wine-dark, round, and full, she could feel the blood rushing to her face. It was a sound that contained life, death, heartache, joy, and every truth in between. She went on, this singer, boundless, as if her voice knew no limits. Ocean wide and well-deep, yet intimate and as sacred as a prayer.

Earlier today on the water, Eden's ears flooded with the caw of seabirds and the diesel roar of the ferry. The rush of wind, the water lapping the hull, the rolling waves. The power of it. It was all here in this voice, a sea of sound reduced to a woman's song.

Her father would have called it glorious. Something glorious in this voice, as if everything she'd missed, dreamed, or hoped for her whole life was in the music. Love. Hope. And something more.

Forgive, the music pleaded. *Let it go.* Eden's eyes clouded. Why was she still punishing herself? Her father was gone, but he would have forgiven her, would have done the thing she could not. Surely. He had just died too soon. Once a thing was done, it could never be undone and she would have to live with that, as she already had. But if he forgave her for what she did to her unborn child, then he would surely have forgiven her for the other thing, the worst thing she had ever done. And not because she deserved it, but because of the man her father was.

How long had she been crying? A tear slipped beneath her chin. She bowed her head, wiped her face with the back of her hand.

The music still pulled, but she turned her head away, eyes closed. *Please, lady, stop singing. Please.*

"Are you OK?" Evan was looking at her, concerned.

A flush of heat warmed her neck. Somewhere in her stomach, something caved. She could not look at him, or at the woman whose voice had arms that wrapped around her chest, choking her breath.

"I'm so sorry, I can't stay here. I need to go."

And in a moment, she was outside on the dark, cool street. She dissolved into the clump of pedestrians crossing at the green light. A few minutes later, she was on the subway and headed home, the voice of the woman erased, mercifully, by the rattle and clatter of the northbound train.

The sky was as black as ink now, and the thick air teased more rain. Climbing the stairs to the apartment building, her thighs moved slowly and ached. How far had she walked today? The walk from the subway had calmed her a bit, but she didn't know what she felt more—hunger, exhaustion, or defenselessness against an overpowering force.

Reginald Jr. would be home, would have eaten his dinner of leftover spaghetti and meatballs, and should be doing his homework. She pictured the leftover Campbell's Chunky Chicken Noodle soup on the shelf in the fridge—and what else?—maybe some of the Lay's pretzels from the bag she'd found on sale at the bodega on the corner.

The fire escape, a glass of wine, and a Winston filter tip. Then she could settle down and put that woman and that voice out of her mind. That voice, taking her to places she'd rather not go.

Two mysteries crowded her head now: Celia DeMille, the slave's daughter in the crumbling pages of the scrapbook; and the singer at the cathedral in the yellow dress. When she pictured the image in the scrapbook, she heard the voice in the church.

She would give up years of her life to be like either one of those women, to be a singer the whole world might want to hear. When she was twelve and knew nothing, she might have believed it was possible. But she was not twelve. Hell. Who was she kidding? She couldn't even figure out how to pay the rent.

The rent.

She ran up the last two flights of steps, her heart pounding. When she arrived at the door, her breath stopped.

Oh, God. Oh, no.

A heavy lock box hung on the latch to the door of 8D.

She grabbed the metal box and shook it futilely. She took out her key, an equally stupid thing to do. A slip of paper was taped to the door: EVICTION NOTICE—BY THE ORDER OF THE CITY OF NEW YORK.

No, no. Shit. Rent, $865, due four weeks ago. The grace period, already up. She just didn't have all the money, not if she wanted to eat. She'd meant to call the landlord, Donald McGeavy, again. What had he said the last time? "I've got bills too, lady."

She checked her phone. Five calls from her brother: three she'd ignored; two she'd simply not heard. Had McGeavy called her? She found his number in her phone and listened to his last voice mail: "I'm sorry to have to do this to you, but I warned you. I had no choice."

She tried to call McGeavy. No answer.

And where was her brother? Surely he'd found the lockbox on the door, as she did, and left to go...God knows where. She sat on the top step and buried her face in her hands. For the second time that night, the tears came.

CHAPTER 16

Money. So cool in his hands, like silk. Just to have it, just to know it was there added an inch to his height. Or that's how it felt. The power of it. In all of his sixteen years, he had never known a better feeling than a pocket full of cash.

Puts a new kick in a man's stride. It wasn't like he'd never had money. Once or twice, and especially the last few months back home before that whole deal at that store, before the thing with the cops and all, there had been some cash. A taste of it, more than he'd ever seen at one time. But even then, even though Noodie and them told him there was a lot more to come if he'd just do what they told him, he had a feeling something would make it all end. Then the storm came.

The sun was long gone and night had settled in, but except for an occasional gust, the air was calm. Reginald Jr. passed the Shop 'n Save and Belkin and Son's Dry Cleaners on Lenox Avenue at an unhurried pace, like a man who had the answers. Because he was a man now, and if he didn't have *all* the answers, he had the one that mattered. He had fixed everything. *Things were looking up now. Yep, definitely looking up.*

He reached into his other pocket and pulled out a stick of wintergreen Orbit. He unwrapped the gum and popped it into his mouth.

Of course, Eden probably wouldn't admit it, wouldn't give him the credit. But that was cool. They both would know he was the reason they weren't out on the street, that he had been the one to find the lockbox, all their possessions boarded behind a door to which they had no working key. He'd been the one to make it right, the one who made the call to McGeavy, made the deal, and set everything straight.

His daddy would have been proud. Not that he knew that much about him. Just that he'd worked in the shipyard, went to church on Sundays, played trombone in a band, and had served in the military—the marines. Vietnam, way back, decades before he was born. She always said he looked just like him. The photo his sister kept in her wallet was pretty cool, him in uniform with both arms around his buddies' shoulders. Made him think of dudes he'd seen in the movies about Vietnam, like that one, *Full Metal Jacket.* Those dudes, man, sharp as a blade, and so tight. He sometimes dreamed about his daddy in some jungle war like in the video games, looking all badass and whatnot with a helmet on and a gun, looking over his shoulder for the enemy. Shooting the crap out of them. *Bap!, bap! Bap, bap, bap!* Coming home a hero with all kinds of medals and shit. His daddy was a hero.

Two blocks away and he made the corner as a blast of spring wind slapped him full in the face. The temperature had dropped so quickly; he hadn't dressed warmly enough. The fake leather of his black jacket was thin, so the wind sliced through to his bones. He pulled it close to his thin waist. The wind up here had teeth in it for real, and New Orleans' muggy bayou winters hadn't prepared him for this kind of cold. There had never been icy winds off the Mississippi like the ones that barreled up the streets of East Harlem. But now he could get himself a new coat, maybe something with a hood, some shoes, maybe even some Timberland boots, the kind everybody had except him. Now he could afford them. Or he could very soon.

As he reached Bonita's Baked Goods and passed the Ruggiero Bros. Deli, he thought about stopping in to grab a pastrami sandwich and a

Coke, and try some of his best lines on the cute little chica who sold the onion and poppy seed rolls fresh out of the oven near the back of the store. He felt the kind of confidence he needed to hit on somebody like that: "How you doing today?" "I'm fine," she'd say. Maybe she'd smile. "Well, ain't no doubt about that. You fine, all right. But how you doing?"

Yeah, that line was old and lame, but it didn't matter 'cause the ladies always smiled. The sister had that good, pretty skin, and those dimples. Cute little figure, short curly Fro. Big, dark round eyes, like she got a serious Latina thing going on. He could say that much about this city: the girls, a lot of 'em anyway, were off the chain.

She was one of the nice ones, smiled at him at school, even when nobody was looking. Some of the shorties up here had their noses all up in the air. But all in all, the girls were no different from the ones back home, except up here they tended to be a little skinnier and there were so many of them. Still, there was no one yet to make him forget Jasmine.

Whenever he thought about Jasmine, fine Jasmine, with that birthmark shaped like a feather on the back of her neck and her soft eyes, his mind always went back to his sister. She shoulda let him go back home to New Orleans with her. A couple days out of school wouldn'ta mattered and he coulda hung with Jasmine maybe, or at least found out if she was back from Houston. Making him stay up here while she got to go home was messed up. If he coulda gone home, then Tyrone wouldn'ta come at him like he did. It was her fault.

Well, maybe it wasn't. It was just that these dudes up here made him feel like he had some kind of disease or something. *Swamp nigga.* No way he could let that slide. No way.

What did they know about his town, those dudes? Nothing. Thinking New York was all that and ain't never been no place else. New Orleans was the place, or at least that's the way it used to be—the food, the music, the way they knew how to party. Sometimes when he thought about home, like late at night when he couldn't sleep, he just wanted to cry. Wanted to cry like some little girl. Sometimes he actually did, using his pillow so Eden couldn't hear him. He'd even thought about just getting up and going back to New Orleans by himself, hitch a ride like they did in the movies. He missed his boys, his crew. Missed hanging out in the Quarter, checking out the girls from wherever. Missed the whole damn city, the way it was. The news people said things were looking up, folks coming back. But from the pictures, he wasn't so sure. Still, the place was all he knew, and in his mind, going home wasn't completely off the table. He belonged there, not here. Soon as he could, he'd head back to New Orleans. Soon as he could.

He decided against the bakery; there wasn't much time before he was supposed to meet the landlord at the apartment, and besides, Eden might already be there. No need to make her sweat any longer 'cause the lock box wasn't going to open until the money was paid, and he had the money. As for the little chica, he'd catch her another time. Give him time to get a haircut, a dope shirt maybe, and some new kicks.

He checked his phone for the time. The guy, McGeavy, should be there by now, or at least close. Once again, he felt his pocket for the cash, reached in, and squeezed the cool thick wad that would be slimmer in a minute or two. Enough for this month's rent and the late fee and enough to get them another month (it was part of the deal he'd made), even if his sister didn't find a job. Plus, more to come. He decided not to call Eden again. She'd been ignoring his calls all day, and what was up with that?

She'd been acting a little strange for a while, especially since she lost that gig and ever since she got back from home, now that he thought about it. He'd seen her sitting out on the fire escape at night, wine glass full at 8:45 and empty by 9:00. Looking dazed, cigarette ash a full inch long before she flicked it. Reading that book she brought back from home, that scrapbook, like she was damn near hypnotized by it. He'd taken a look at it once when she wasn't looking and didn't understand what the big deal was. Some lady, a sister even, from a thousand years ago, dressed all fancy, a bunch of newspaper articles about her. A famous singer or something. And then he'd seen Eden with that necklace. When he'd asked her about it, she'd freaked, like she was hiding something from him.

"What's that?"

"What's what?"

"That thing you got 'round your neck?"

"It's just something Aunt Baby had. Nothing."

But she hadn't acted like it was nothing, wearing it all the time, rubbing it like was a magic lamp or something. He'd felt it once and it was way heavier than it looked, and shiny, like it was real gold. He wondered if maybe it was. Wouldn't that be something.

She'd been acting strange, no doubt. Like sometimes he'd catch her saying she was watching the tube, but really staring at space, biting her nails the way she'd always told him not to do. Then there was that night she came in really, really late and overslept. And was that weed he smelled the next day when he had to fix (his own!) breakfast? Weed? *Her?* That was so weird. He hadn't wanted to admit it, but he'd been a little worried.

And it took a while to notice, but the singing stopped. Used to be, back home, he'd be upset about some little thing, something some dude said or some girl he just couldn't get with, and he couldn't get to sleep. He'd hear Eden singing, her voice streaming out from the shower wrapped up with the steam and the lemon scent of shower soap, or from the kitchen, mixed with the smell of garlic and butter while she cooked, or later when she cleaned up the kitchen. She didn't do that anymore. Damn, he missed that voice. When he heard her sing, like when she went way up high the way they did at church, he'd lie back and let all that pretty sound hold him, block out his troubles. He knew everything would be all right. That voice of hers, it had the softest hands. It was the lap of the mama he had never known.

One more block to go and another strong wind kicked up. He

dug his gloveless fingers deeper into the pockets of his jacket. As he made the last half block before the apartment, his phone rang. *Speak of the devil.*

He let it ring because now he had to decide. The question about how he got the money was moments away. It needed an answer, a good one.

He thought about that night in New Orleans before the storm, when that whole deal went down. And just like then, the less she knew, the better. She didn't need to know the truth. It didn't matter, did it? They needed money, and he'd gotten it, so that was the end of it.

Messenger service. A buddy at school had a brother who was doing it, so why not him? He could even give her the name of the company; she'd never check. Delivering important packages and documents around town to the suits who worked in those fancy office buildings. The company even provided a bicycle to use. Paid decent money, and that would explain what he'd been doing after school the evenings he'd come in late claiming a pickup game of hoops with some ballers from school. And why hadn't he told her sooner? Easy. She told him she didn't want him working until he got adjusted. Working was her job, she'd made it clear, and school was his. Well, lucky for both of them, he'd stepped up and kept both their asses off these cold New York streets.

He answered the phone, spoke, waited through a thick silence. Once she started, she went on and on. The tears seeped through the fracture in her voice.

"Hey, don't worry, sis, I got you," he told her. "Everything's cool. I'm on my way."

PART II

CHAPTER 17

"Did you bring anything with you today?"

"'Scuse me?"

"Some sherbet, maybe?"

Odd, Eden thought. *Why would anybody bring dessert to a singing lesson? Is sherbet good for the voice? Like honey? Or hot tea?* "No, ma'am, I didn't bring any, uh, sherbet. But I can next time."

The tall, slender woman looked nearly sixty with deep brown skin and gray ringlets framing a face that now appeared as puzzled as Eden's. "What did you...? Oh. No." She smiled at the misunderstanding. "*Schu*-bert. Franz Schubert, the German composer. He wrote some lovely songs that many of the students sing. I thought, since Mr. Smallwood said you were a lyric soprano, maybe Schubert would be nice for you to sing today."

"Oh, wow. I'm sorry, I didn't hear—I thought you said—"

"—That's all right, darlin'. He'll work with whatever you've prepared. Just make yourself comfortable, and Mr. Blessing'll be with you as soon as he finishes up." The woman disappeared behind the door at the end of the hallway.

Schubert. Shit. Who the hell is that? Dear God, let this floor open up right now and swallow me whole.

No one had told her she needed to prepare something to sing. She mentally sifted through her repertory of radio music and her father's beloved jazz ballads and show tunes. What did she know by heart? She knew all the words, but she didn't think the Beyoncé tune going through her head lately, "Sexy L'il Thug," was appropriate for the situation. A church song, maybe. If she could even remember the lyrics. Damn. Another opportunity for her to embarrass herself. Again.

In the dark, high-ceilinged foyer of Professor Ernest Blessing's West Side pre-Second World War brownstone, Eden sank into a thick, silk upholstered armchair, and sank even deeper into her humiliation. Looking into the huge mirror framed in ornate silver hanging on the wall, she tugged at the collar of her Polo-style shirt. She should have at least put on a blouse, but there just hadn't been enough time to change into something more…what? Presentable. Her McDonald's shift had ended thirty minutes ago and allowed just enough time to make the 6:40 train from Uptown, and that was if everything was running on schedule. Even with a black cotton sweater covering up part of the logo, she damn sure didn't look like anybody's lyric soprano.

In New Orleans, she'd managed to avoid the burger chain grind—gigs with white to-go bags, drive-up windows, or corporate logo-laden uniforms. She swore "You want fries with that?" would never pass her lips.

There were many things she'd begun doing lately that were not part of the plan.

Treble tones of a piano chimed from the other side of the hallway door as a small, light voice followed an upward climb of warm-up scales. *Whoever she is, she's got some serious pipes*, Eden thought.

Three days ago, just two weeks into minimum wage hell, Evan showed up toward the end of her shift. She looked up from the counter after handing off six orders of burgers, fries, and Cokes to a group of rowdy middle-schoolers and saw him at the back of the line, towering above them.

When he reached the counter, his unsmiling stare surprised her, and she thought she might have seen a hint of embarrassment (for her) or even annoyance in his eyes as if, just after she'd turned down his invitation to a four-star restaurant dinner, he'd caught her digging in a dumpster for food.

"Hey," Evan said, his tone flat. His expression was hard to read. He placed a slip of paper on the counter and pushed it toward her. He leaned over the counter, his voice low. "You say you want to be a singer. Call this number. And I'll take a small coffee. To go."

There was an edge to his tone that quickened her pulse. She hadn't seen him since the day, almost a month ago, when she'd practically run out of the cathedral, unable to stand one more minute of the most extraordinary sound she'd ever heard.

Behind him stood another line of school kids armed with pocket change, pubescent energy, and attitude, laughing and striking gangsta poses into each other's cell phone cameras while they debated what to order. Evan left, coffee in hand.

She called him that night, listened quietly to his plea. "You see yourself serving up greasy burgers at forty-five? Is that your dream?"

Nobody had ever asked her that before.

A dream? Ain't nobody got time for that.

The number he gave her was for David Kim's friend, the singing coach who could get her into shape to be, as he put it, "the kind of singer she was meant to be." When she told him she didn't even like "that kind of music, opera and stuff," he'd asked her if she'd ever seen one, knowing the answer. He reminded her about the woman in the church, who had brought her to tears. What did she think the woman was singing?

Evan scoffed, impatient. "It's not even about opera. It's about your life being a little bigger than…than this." That day in the church, he'd watched her eyes. "I saw something there," he'd told her. She'd looked transformed. Or transfixed? Something like that. Either way, some-thing held her. "That could be you," he'd told her. "That could be you."

When Reginald Jr. showed up with all that money, money she'd not been able to put together herself, and handed McGeavy eleven one-hun-dred-dollar bills, she realized what was going on. *Messenger service. Where'd he even get that idea from?* Making more money than she ever had. Despite all the crap he'd put her through in New Orleans, he had started moving forward in his own life in a way she hadn't been in hers. It had already begun, the growing up. The manning up. He wasn't even shaving and yet he'd found a way to keep them off the street.

She made the call. The voice on the phone sounded frail, heavy with something more than age. Formality. Elegance. Professor Bless-ing had been expecting her call.

"I look forward to our meeting," he said. "And please, do not be late."

With beauty-pageant posture and a confident stride, the young woman leaving Blessing's studio—white, half Eden's age, fully made up, with her blond hair swept up into a bun—gave Eden a pinched smile as she swept past her toward the front door with a red silk scarf flowing and flowery perfume wafting in her breezy wake. A full twenty minutes later, Blessing called Eden into his music room.

High ceilings were crossed with thick wooden beams. Dark wood-paneled walls held oil-painted canvases—portraits and land-scapes—and above an enormous fireplace, a woven tapestry of deep reds and browns featuring a man on horseback with a landscape in the distance. Two red velvet loveseats faced each other and hundreds of hardcover books and records lined one wall on floor-to-ceiling shelves. Along another was a huge grand piano with a mirrored black lacquer finish. Eden would not have thought such rooms existed behind the grim, brick exterior of the buildings along the avenue had she not re-membered seeing Aunt Baby's place in New Orleans when she was a young girl. It may not have been so similar, but the feeling was the same.

Blessing sat at the piano; his narrow shoulders hunched over the keyboard as if it were a child he wanted to protect. *This guy is odd*, she thought. He was thin, hollow-cheeked, and balding, with wavy, salt and pepper hair combed back from the crown of his head. How old was he? Seventy? Eighty? She couldn't tell. At one time, she thought, he might have been a handsome man with his sharply cut cheekbones, deep, wide-set eyes, and a square jaw flecked with gray stubble. She could tell by the slope of his neck and shoulders at the piano that if he stood up, he would never be able to straighten his back.

He hadn't asked her name, or even said hello. Not that he didn't know her name. Of course, he did. He must know it. But he seemed so detached, she was taken aback. With his head down, he stroked the keys, nodded occasionally, his eyes closed as he fingered a simple melody. After the opening bars, Blessing's quick finger-dance across the keyboard produced a shimmer of sound so light and fast that she could barely see where he made contact with the keys. He played for several minutes as if she weren't there, and when he finally finished, he looked up at her.

"Mozart," he said. "We'll get to that later. Maybe. For now, let's warm up a little. Stand up straight, don't slouch. Sing this on the syllable, 'Ahhhh...'"

He played four notes with his right hand, then waited, and gestured with his left as if inviting her to enter into a room. "No!" he said, almost as soon as she opened her mouth. "Sing from *here*." He pointed to a part of her face that she could not imagine singing from since it was not her mouth. "Focus your energy there."

He played three more notes on the piano, then a fourth, asking her to repeat each tone, loudly, softly, and in between. He had her go up a scale as high as she could, then down as low as her voice would take her.

He looked up when she reached a C above the staff, slightly raised his eyebrows, made a small *hmmm* in his throat, then returned his focus to the keyboard. This scale thing went on for a while, and Eden, bored and restless, wanted to sing and show him what she could do. Finally, she spoke up.

"Um…like, I didn't really prepare nothing—anything to sing, but I could sing something I used to sing in church."

He nodded for her to begin.

She began "How Great Thou Art," the song she had sung in New Orleans at the Fifteenth Annual Women's Day Service at Blessed Redeemer. She had no idea what key it was in, but by the second verse, Blessing picked up the melody and played the accompaniment as if it were a song he'd written himself.

She finished on a high note, sustained it for a good time, proud of herself. She held onto the tone without a crack. A solid finish, surely he was impressed. He said nothing for a moment. After an uncomfortable silence, he queried her. How much did she know? Any European languages? Had she ever studied vocal production? Ever had a real voice lesson before? No? What had she sung beside the church songs? Did she know anything about tone production? The soft palate? Vocal placement? Head voice? Chest voice? Breath control, diaphragm support? Singing in the mask? Did any of this sound familiar? No?

They did slow scales again, note by note. He made some suggestions to her, things to "think about" as she traveled to the top of her range. After an hour, he smiled politely, his eyes not quite meeting hers. "I think that will be all for today," he said and nodded in a way that suggested there was nothing more he needed to know.

"Yes, sir," she said, but she wanted to tell him she knew some other songs. What just happened? She didn't even get a chance to really sing. She gathered her things.

Walking through the foyer, she remembered she wanted to ask to use the restroom before heading for the subway. She turned back. But from behind the door she'd just exited, she heard a conversation and paused. The professor's voice first, then the woman's.

"She's had no training…she doesn't know anything…No language skills besides English, which she doesn't even speak very well…Her voice is a mess…uneven throughout, no tone, breaks everywhere… Sings through her nose most of the time…forces everything, vowels flat and consonants swallowed…I can't believe…just doing a favor for a friend…talented, there's a voice there, but…and she smokes, too?! And she wants to be a real singer?"

The woman said, "*Sherbet*! She thought I was asking her if she'd brought…I can't even say it with a straight face! And did you see what she was wearing? I'm sorry, I just don't see it."

Eden blinked tears from her eyes, steadied herself with a hand against the door, and headed home.

CHAPTER 18

New Orleans, 1922

"It's a beautiful day, after all the rain." Catherine opened the curtains to let in the sun, then pulled back Celia's bedspread. "Did you hear it? It poured last night!" Catherine went back into the kitchen and returned with a cup of chicory coffee on a silver tray.

"Did it?" Celia smiled, stretched her arms. "Good. We needed a good rain." Celia didn't recall. She only remembered the dreams that had come again.

They always began after sunset, the dreams: Celia was out, walking. In one version, she was at the river and heard the fire, waves of flame crackling like giant sheets of stiff parchment. Walking toward the burning building, she heard voices. *Stop! You! Don't take another step!* She froze in her tracks. The two men approached her, grabbing her arm. *Come with me,* the taller one said.

But in another version of the dream, she was already at the corner of Bourbon and Toulouse. First as a flicker, then as a deluge of orange heat, flames drowned years of history. Moments later at the police station, the white, mustached men in black and gray questioned her. *Did you set the fire? Did you?*

In her dream, as in real life, she'd been asked that question and hadn't answered. But she'd already decided the answer would go with her, sooner rather than later, to her grave.

When Catherine returned with a china plate of steamed apples, toast, and ham, Celia sat up. She took a bite of toast, then called to Catherine. "Can you bring me the newspaper?"

Sick as she was now, she still wanted to keep up with the go-ings-on in the city. Four years since the War ended, new energy in the city surged and took hold. There were buildings along the docks and more traffic now on the river. The first classes of Catholic students were about to graduate from Xavier University—black students! New cottages were sprouting up on land near the lake. Progress everywhere. The city was taking its place in the modern world.

There were other signs too, she had read. Talking pictures. Jazz, with its bump and sass. It burst forth from the city to roam the world as riverboats headed north on the Mississippi bucked with that new sound. Buddy Bolden. Louis Armstrong. A sound of her own people.

Yes, there was music everywhere, but none from the opera house. The land where it sat was still empty, the air still mute. It was as if a part of the city had died.

She read about a new French café opening and thought of Mae-stro, her former lover, the great Henri Benoit. She had not seen him in years, and the betrayal still hurt. But she was grateful for Catherine, and Celia could now think of him without wincing, kindly, even. She recalled the thick, dark hair, blue eyes, and square jawline, the power of his arms when he lifted her. What had become of him? She'd heard he'd moved back to France after the fire that burned down his real mistress, the opera house itself. And that his wife had died. Pity.

But Celia could not muster sympathy. His reneged promise to put her on the great opera stage lingered in her head like the memory of the smoke that curled through the Quarter the night the same stage burned to the ground.

If only he had allowed her to sing the role of Carmen, as she was meant to, everything else would have been different.

"I hope Maestro is doing right by you." Celia took a small bite of an apple. "I hope he is paying you enough to make up for my incorrigible moods."

"Ma'am, it is my pleasure. And you are no trouble at all."

Celia took the cup and drank the coffee long and slow. "The morning paper? I don't see it here. Where is it?"

Catherine turned. "Oh, well, I didn't...I must have forgotten it."

When she returned with the paper, Celia looked through the pages, then looked up at Catherine. "There seems to be part of it missing. Is there something you don't want me to see?"

"I'll bring it," Catherine said.

She returned with four pages of the first section of the *Times-Picayune* and set them on Celia's tray. Celia gave her a cursory look. "Don't tell me," she said, smiling sardonically. "They have given me a horrible review, even though I haven't sung a note in public in years!"

Catherine's fingers kneaded the space between her eyebrows. "It doesn't mean anything," she said. "It's just a simple mistake."

"What do you mean?"

Celia turned the first page of the section. Blood drained from her face.

"The Black Donatella Dies." The headline blasted like a gunshot. Below it was the image of a woman with dark, wavy hair parted in the center, pulled back, and secured into a small bun at the nape of her neck.

Bile rose in Celia's throat, and her head went light. *Who was this woman?* This was more than a case of mistaken identity. It was an outrage. She, and no one else, lay claim to the title of The Black Donatella.

She read the story. Whoever she was, the woman had the same brown skin as Celia, but otherwise looked nothing like her. The article described her as a soprano, hailing from Newport, Rhode Island, and having, the writer wrote, "a voice like a goddess," a line Celia recognized from many of her own reviews, including the most recent one in *The New York Age*.

It went on:

Often referred to as "The Black Donatella," after The Great Adeline Donatella, the dusky diva sang for queens and kings, and at the White House for four US presidents, including President Theodore Roosevelt...

She put a hand to her throbbing forehead as she continued to read. She looked for a name and toward the end of the article, found it. The woman they were calling The Black Donatella was named Florence Wellsap Burton. She remembered the name, then the face.

It was the same girl. Years ago, Celia had sung at Remington Civic Hall in Massachusetts, where a young girl, about ten years younger than Celia, stood in line to meet her afterward. Gushing with admiration and fawning praise, the girl smiled shyly. She was also a singer. Would Madame be so kind as to accept an invitation to hear her sing the following Friday night at the Charles Street AME Church in Boston? Curious and not busy, Celia went. The girl had a modest talent—a small voice with a limited range—and Celia was surprised to learn later that she'd had a fairly successful career. Nothing exceptional, though. Nothing like hers.

Nothing that should qualify her to be confused with me, or her mediocre career with mine.

The Black Donatella. This woman, Florence, had died, but The Black Donatella still lived. She had always despised the name, and now, she was defending her claim to it. If they had only used her name—Celia, the name her mother gave her—in all those articles and reviews over the years! This would never have happened.

"Ma'am, are you all right?"

Catherine stood by the door. Celia had heaved the paper across the room and was struggling to get out of the bed.

"Am I all right? Am I all right?" She wrestled her pale feet out of the tangle of covers, her voice pitched high and shrill. "I have just read my own obituary! Did you read this? Apparently, I have recently passed away!" She tossed the covers back and tried to scoot toward the edge of the bed.

"This must be corrected at once! Who is the writer? Find him and tell him! *I* am The Black Donatella! I am alive! The Black Donatella is alive!"

Catherine was quick, but not quick enough. Pain shot up Celia's hip as she tried to put both feet on the floor. She fell onto the hardwood near the fireplace with a thud. She wailed.

"Ma'am! Please, don't move! Let me help you!"

Celia lay still for a moment, then allowed her nurse to help her back to bed. Catherine reached at once for the bottle, found her cup, and poured the green liquid into it.

"Here. Drink," she said.

After two sips of the absinthe, Celia calmed down, leaning her head against the pillow. Catherine shook her head. The doctor had warned her there might be times like this.

Catherine took the tray from the bed and removed the offending newspaper article. She surveyed the room; the chamber pot was emptied, the floor swept. In the hallway, she stopped to listen at the door of her mistress. Hearing her steady breathing and the occasional deep snore, she was satisfied: Celia was asleep.

She slipped quietly into the hallway and telephoned her daughter, a nursing student at the medical college. She held her voice to a whisper. "Yes, Miss Celia is sleeping now. No. No, it did not go well. I couldn't keep it from her. No. No, she did not see the other article. Thank God for small miracles."

That night, Catherine lay awake and alert for an hour, then got up to make another cup of tea. Hiding another mistaken obituary from the *Gazette*, the one that would surely have given her mistress palpitations, had not been difficult. Later, she would burn it when Madame was deep in her dreams and would not be alarmed by the odor.

It was dated the day before, and had Catherine not opened the newspaper to the center section, she might have missed it herself. She pulled it out of the drawer next to her bed and read it again: GREAT NEGRO SINGER DIES—ONCE QUESTIONED ABOUT OPERA HOUSE FIRE

There was no proof, of course. And Catherine dared not ask Madame about it. She'd heard the rumors. She read the words again, as she had many times already. Could she have done it?

She thought she heard stirring from Madame's bedroom and tiptoed back and opened the door wide enough to see the profile of deep slumber. Madame's body angled away from the door, her back to her.

The Great Black Donatella. Silver strands of wayward and matted hair lay against the white satin pillow. Years ago, robust and with an ample figure, she seemed as formidable as the ancient live oaks that hovered along River Road. Now, her body as limp as an oak leaf after a good rain, she seemed small.

Later, in her room, Catherine carefully unwrapped the bright red tignon from her head. She ran her fingers through the tight curls in her hair. The head wrap was a gift from her mother, a healer in the West African tradition, before she died. It was a reminder of Africa and the tribal dress of the Yoruba; even here in America, there was tradition to be honored and dignity to be found in it.

She lay the tignon on the table by her bedside. From her window overlooking Rue Conti lay the dim courtyard, the swaying leaves of the banana tree, its shadows splayed like fingers across the dark cobblestone path. It was a hot night and she opened the window slightly more to let the damp courtyard breezes through. She reached into the drawer by her bed, rummaged beneath the scrapbook, and found the gold pendant necklace. She held it in her hands and pressed it to her chest. It was the most beautiful thing she had ever seen. And it was hers. Or would be someday.

She had tried to do what Madame asked, but how could she tell her? It was best that she never learn that, so far, all Catherine's efforts proved futile. She'd written to the *New York Times* and other prominent newspapers in the city, and nothing had come of it. In fact, no paper, including the local *New Orleans Star*, was interested in the story of a black woman and singer who had outlived what fame she'd had.

She placed the necklace on the table by her bed and wondered if the story Madame had told her about it was really true. Extraordinary, if so. If true, she might become wealthy beyond her dreams. Real gold. But of course, she would never sell it. It was too beautiful, too precious. She would keep it, wear it her whole life as proudly as Madame had, then pass it on.

In the meantime, she vowed to herself she'd keep trying. Someday, Madame's story would be told.

CHAPTER 19

She might as well pick up—he was only going to keep calling.

"Finally," he said. "I've been trying to reach you for weeks."

It had only been thirteen days since the twenty-eighth, but Eden didn't correct him.

You don't forget the date of a disaster, those black-draped days on the calendar of emotional memory. The day her father died, or the day her boyfriend dumped her after she found out she was pregnant. Or the day the big storm came through. The day she understood irrevocable failure, the kind that made it difficult to hold her head upright. The most humiliating day of her life.

She listened quietly while Evan talked. "I spoke to Ernest after you sang for him…more impressed with you than you realize…a little tough on people, but that's just his way…the bigger the talent, the harder he is, the more he expects…"

She kept the phone at her ear while she ran water in the kitchen sink to wash the cereal bowls and waited for him to take a breath. She jumped in when he paused. "No. Thank you. I think I'll just stick with what I'm doing."

She looked at her watch; her shift began in forty minutes and she hadn't showered yet.

"And just what are you doing?"

"Excuse me?"

"I mean, you've got a million-dollar voice and you're working for $6.50 an hour, for God's sake."

Making a living the only way she knew how, that's what she was doing. Not putting all her eggs in a basket full of holes is what she was doing. Not listening to some guy who doesn't even know her try to tell her how to run her life. *You trying to help, but I don't see you trying to pay my rent*, she wanted to say.

Instead, she said, "I know when somebody likes me. And I know when they don't. You shoulda heard what they said about me, him and that lady, after I left. Why should I waste his time and mine?"

He sighed. "Look, never mind. I want to invite you over to see my new space. There's something important I want to show you."

He just wouldn't quit. "Well, my work schedule is…I don't know when I can get over there."

"What about tomorrow?"

"Got a double shift."

"Well, when?"

"Not sure. Like I said, I'm—"

"You can't spare an hour?" A pause. "Well, look, will you at least bring back my damn jacket?"

She remembered. The wind on the ferry, the chill on her arms. He had slipped his jacket over her shoulders. And then she'd run out of the church and worn it home, intending to return it to him, but got distracted.

"Your jacket. I'm so sorry. Really, I meant to give it back to you. Of course, I'll bring it back. Day after tomorrow, after work. I'm so sorry."

He laughed. "Don't trip. I was just messing with you. Honestly, I pretty much forgot it myself." He gave her the address. "Oh, and by the way, if you don't mind, there's something else I'd like you to bring."

The building, a massive brownstone on a corner in gentrified Clinton Hill in Brooklyn, was not what she'd expected. The front door opened to a foyer of peeled plaster walls, pockmarked, thick-paned glass, and a row of dingy, metal mailboxes. But as she ascended the stairs, each landing revealed the building's progress toward revitalization. By the fourth floor, odors of carpet mildew succumbed to aromas of fresh paint and floor varnish. Only a few units appeared occupied: a musical instrument repair shop, a re-upholsterer, a computer repair business, and Blankenship's Antiques and Collectibles.

From behind the door on the top floor rolled a stream of slow, melodic jazz, "This Bitter Earth." More than anybody, more than Ella or even Carmen McRae, her daddy loved what magic Dinah Washington could work with a torchy ballad. Dinah's voice sifted through the hallway and down the steps toward her like a jasmine-scented breeze. *Slick*, she thought. This Evan guy had her number and knew how to set a welcoming table. Had she told him about her father's adulation of Miss Dinah? She must have.

He met her at the door. "Glad you made it. Come on in, and excuse the mess."

Blankenship's was a rectangular loft space in the intermediate stages of renovation. High-ceilinged, light, and airy, it smelled slightly of sawdust and lemon-scented oil. Two ladders stood beneath a skylight. Paint cans sat atop rumpled drop cloths and faded bedsheets splotched with drippings of semi-gloss buff and tan, and a cordless drill and a color-swatch booklet sat in the middle of the wide-plank oak floors. Long shafts of sunlight angled in through the floor-to-ceiling windows. To Eden, the place had all the slickness of a TV sitcom set, the kind where young, underemployed New Yorkers mysteriously occupied spacious prime real estate.

"Sorry, I'm a little late," she said, setting her bag down. "Wow, nice. Cool."

There was very little furniture. Only a pair of old, English walnut desk chairs that sat near two showcase console tables of mahogany and leaded glass. At the western-facing windows was the view of the Warren D. Chessler Middle School and an oak and sycamore-lined park. Against the walls were tall bookcases lined with clothbound hardcovers, and in the middle of the room sat a vertical display case of odd, unrelated items: an ancient black Remington typewriter, a vase of patina-ed brass, a pewter lamp, an art deco hand mirror, and four green glass figurines.

If there had been any tension in their last conversation, it didn't show in Evan's greeting. "Sorry for the craziness," he said again. He moved about the space, his energy high and upbeat, like a boy showing off Christmas toys. "We just moved into this place a few days ago."

By "we" he meant he and his employer, Arnold Blankenship, a sixty-something recent retiree who inherited the antique business from his father twelve years ago.

"It's really cool-looking," she said, looking at the glass cases and shelves where more items—watches, wire-rimmed eyeglasses, rings, and antique mirrors—were on display. On one shelf were several egg-shaped dolls painted in bright reds and yellows.

"Oh, you like those," he said, picking up one of the larger eggs. "Russian nesting doll." He opened it to reveal another doll, which held another, and then another.

"Nice," she said, smiling at the final egg, no bigger than her thumb.

"It's from the twenties. They're pretty common, but collectors love them," he said. "Then there's this." He reached for a vase, red, purple, and green, sitting in a wire stand. He held it up to the light.

"Really old, rare, and valuable. Chinese. Ming Dynasty. I've had offers, but I'm holding out. Worth a couple hundred thousand. Easy."

Eden's mouth dropped open. "Wow."

"Here, check it out," he said, tossing it to her.

She gasped but caught it in both hands.

He laughed. "K-Mart," he said, "$12.95."

She breathed hard, her full hand clasping her chest. "You trying to kill me? Please. Don't do that again."

He took the vase from her, still laughing as his phone buzzed. "Oh, sorry, I gotta take this."

"Oh, hey, Mama," he said into his BlackBerry, then whispered to Eden, "Just make yourself at home. Look around if you want. I'll just be a minute."

A sense of humor. So, he's not so serious after all. She tried to ignore his conversation, but was thinking about the woman on the other end, his mother, and what he had told her about her. A singer, he mentioned, with a voice something like hers. But did she actually sing anywhere? She couldn't remember.

He turned the volume down on the CD player now bellowing another jazz ballad, something on piano, and disappeared with his phone into a smaller room of metal storage shelves. She looked out at the view of the park. She peeked behind a half-opened door. Trendy updates—a white bathroom with modern fixtures, a cool skylight, and light-colored re-finished floors—contrasted with the building's age. She peeked inside another door slightly opened and found a tiny bedroom with a twin-sized mattress flung across the floor, a makeshift nightstand of cinder blocks and plywood that held a pile of paperbacks and a laptop, and a two-drawer chest with a small TV on top. Was he living here?

She realized she actually didn't know very much about him. The books on the shelves caught her eye: Sun Tzu's *The Art of War*. Faulkner. Murakami. James Baldwin. A book called *A People's History of the United States*. And even a small volume of what looked like poetry written in what she thought was French. Were they his books? She picked up a book by Toni Morrison and thumbed through it. *Beloved*. A book her father loved. *Huh. Always meant to read this*, she thought, then put it back.

When he returned, he seemed different, a new tension surfaced in his eyes.

"Sorry," he said. "My mom. She moved up here a few years ago after my father died, to be closer to my sister and me. Arnelle, she's the oldest of us, lives over in Jersey—Morristown. After mama turned eighty-five, we've been talking about getting her into a place for seniors. She's OK for now, but we're looking at some possibilities down the line. Anyway, she's not even listening to us." He stopped, slightly embarrassed. "It's a long story. Anyway, thanks for coming over. I know you didn't want to."

Eden felt embarrassed and smiled. "Well, it wasn't that, really…"

He held up a hand. "Oh, I don't blame you. My helping you keeps blowing up in your face! Sorry, but I wanted you to come over and I almost gave up, till I realized I could play the shame card."

"'Scuse me?"

"My jacket."

She laughed. "Well, it worked."

"Sorry, uh, here, sit down," he said, pointing to the two wooden armchairs. "Want some coffee? A fresh pot's on the stove."

When she nodded, he walked toward a corner of the room to what passed for a kitchen—a counter area with a small sink, microwave, and vintage electric hotplate—and poured coffee from a glass carafe into two white mugs.

"So, you live here?" She took a sip.

He nodded. Blankenship, he said, was an old friend and fellow music lover he'd met during his early jazz-playing days in New York.

"I've been working for Arnold for years, but when my lease expired, I needed a place to stay. It's cool. I like being near work. I didn't know that much about the business, but I learned. Anyway, I think I got my love for it from my mother. Our house was full of all kinds of old things, furniture, dishes, jewelry. 'Antiques,' she called them. But some of it was junk. Her passion, after raising us. That, and of course, singing."

Singing. At the mention of the word, his eyes darkened. He explained that when he was a kid growing up in Nebraska, his mother sang soprano in the A. C. Bailey Choir of the Mount Pleasant Baptist Church. She had a high voice, shimmering, transparent.

"She could have been one of the great ones," he said. "Anyway, that's what I think." When she was still a young woman, she had the chance to go to music school. They'd just given birth to his older sister, Arnelle. His father said no.

It was the second time his mother had heard the word. Years before, when she was a talented twenty-something, she'd won an audition to the Mannes College of Music, and it had been her daddy who'd said it. Send his only daughter to that city? Not even if they could afford it, which they could not. He didn't know anything about New York except what he saw in reruns of *Naked City*. His family, the Robert Jeffersons of Bronzeville, Nebraska, were black, upstanding Baptists and didn't know white folks' music. As for opera, they'd never heard it, didn't know anything about it, and didn't want to.

But when she was grown, married, and heard about a regional audition for the Metropolitan Opera—the best opera company in the world!—his mother dared to dream again. But this time, her husband ruled her fate with a father's hand.

"Daddy didn't just talk her out of it, he forbade it. No wife of his was going to go off somewhere singing some kind of music he never heard of with folks he didn't know. And besides, there was nothing to be gained from that kind of risk except heartbreak. If she wanted to sing, then go ahead, sing. Mount Pleasant had the best gospel choir in town."

So, his mother taught school until she retired and had given up the idea of a singing career long ago. In fact, she even stopped singing in church.

"I miss her singing so much," he said. "Now, her mind is going, I think. Nothing real serious yet, but she never sings anymore. Doesn't remember a lot of the songs she used to sing around the house. Some of the classics, the ballads, the jazz tunes. It all just left her."

When he heard Eden absently humming or singing at Estelle's, it was like seeing light spill into a dark room.

"She used to do that, you know. She'd be washing dishes or doing laundry and a song would pop into her head, and she'd either sing or just hum if she didn't know the words. So, I'm sorry if I was a little..." His voice faded. "Speaking of remembering stuff, did you bring it?"

She was still lost in thought about the things he'd said about his mother. "Bring it? Oh, yeah," she said, reaching in her backpack for the jacket. "I didn't know if you wanted me to clean it or anything. I appreciate your letting me use it that day. Really, and I'm sorry I forgot."

"I couldn't care less about that jacket," he said. "Did you bring the other stuff?"

She'd almost forgotten. From her backpack, she pulled out the plastic Walmart bag, sagging with the weight inside. She took out the necklace and the scrapbook—she handled them delicately, as if suddenly aware of their value, and placed them on the glass of one of the console tables.

He held the necklace up to the skylight so the gold chain and pendant sparkled. "Yeah," he smiled. "This is it. This is the same one."

The same one?

From another box near the display table, he pulled out what looked like a recital program, frayed at its edges and yellowed with age. On the cover of the program was a portrait of a young black woman, her head in profile, her hair hanging in curls that drooped on her forehead just above her eyebrows; the rest of her hair was thickly coiled into a bun. Around her neck, she wore a necklace with a hanging pendant. Above the portrait were the words CELIA DEMILLE, SOPRANO. BECKSTEIN HALL, LONDON. 1901.

Eden's pulse raced. "Where did you get this?"

He'd found it while he was hanging out in London after the Gulf War in the mid-nineties. He'd seen it in a used book and record store on Charing Cross Road. *His mother would love it*, he'd thought.

But he didn't get the reaction he'd hoped for. His mother had looked at the rare, old program of the beautiful young singer and said, "Thank you, son." Then she opened a drawer near her bed and placed it inside.

He was at the very least a bit hurt, and at most, heartbroken. He'd been so proud, playing the good son. How many young men, pub-hopping and partying in London after a thirteen-month tour, were thoughtful enough to bring their mother something so special? But he might as well have given her a book of crossword puzzles. Once, and only once, when she didn't think he'd seen, she'd pulled it out of the drawer, opened and read it, her eyes glassy as she traced the lines of the young black woman's face. Regret, perhaps for her own life, darkened her eyes.

Eden's admiration for Evan grew. How long had she known this man? A few weeks? Months? Today, it seemed as if she'd known him most of her life.

"Anyway, when you told me about the woman, the name didn't ring a bell. And I didn't remember the necklace," he said. "How did you say you got it?"

She told him her Aunt Baby—Aunt Julia—in New Orleans found it in a neighborhood wrecked by the flooding after Hurricane Katrina.

He opened the scrapbook and turned the first few pages with care. "And this…wow," he said. "Do you know what you've got here?"

His excitement excited her. Maybe the trip home might prove more lucrative than her seven hundred dollars' worth of vengeful payback. She let her mind leap to the possibility of cash. "I mean, how much do you think all this is worth?"

He had no idea, he shrugged. He'd do a little research, but if selling it was on her mind, he could check with Arnold and see if he was interested.

"But you know, if I were you, I'd keep it a while."

Eden frowned. "But if it's real valuable…you know. I could use the money right now. And if I can sell this…"

"Still." He was looking through the articles. "This is pretty interesting stuff. There must be about three hundred press clippings here. Interviews, reviews. The story of her life. It's right here. Have you read all this?"

She was about a quarter of the way through it, she told him. Before bed each night, she'd found herself lost in it: the long interview pieces about her family, her father's time as a slave, moving his wife and daughter North after Emancipation. Her singing from the time she was a child. Then more details, from her first appearance in a recital up to her performance for President Harrison and her Boston debut.

"I think she kept everything ever written about her. It was almost like she was keeping a record just to make sure nobody forgot who she was."

"Finish reading it. Then we can talk about how much it's worth." He closed the book and put it back in the bag along with the necklace. "You said it was left behind, part of the wreckage. Are you sure it doesn't belong to somebody who might be looking for it?"

She hadn't given it any thought, she told him. Aunt Baby handed it to her as if it were hers to give.

He took a sip of tepid coffee, then gave her a long look. "So, why did you run out on me that day? At the cathedral?"

She tensed. She'd hope never to have to talk about that day again. The woman in yellow. The most beautiful, heartbreaking sound she'd ever heard. The sound that bore straight through to the truth only she knew.

"I don't know. That lady…" she shook her head. "She just sang so pretty. It felt like she was singing to me…no. *About* me. About all the mess I been through. Like she was singing my life." She flushed. "Sorry. I guess I was just thinking about how I could never learn to sing like that. Not in a million years."

She looked up at the skylight. It was an old trick. *Look up to keep your tears from falling.* She dared not blink. There was so much she wanted to tell him. *You see, it all started when…*But no, nobody wanted to hear her sad-ass tale. Maybe someday, if he ever asked. And even then, she wasn't sure how much she could tell. Because if she told it, she'd have to own it.

"Look, Eden. Ernest—Mr. Blessing—told me you've got something special. Raw, yes. Unfocused. But nobody is born with technique. It's about the talent, that instrument in your throat. That's half the battle." He leaned forward with his hands clasped. "Please. Just give it one more try."

What could she say? A vision of his mother—a woman she'd never seen—filled her head. Then her father. Her brother. Regrets. She had too many of those, a pile of regrets so high she feared it would topple over and bury her alive.

If she tried or if she didn't—what was the difference? What it all boiled down to was that one choice took your life one way, a different choice took it another.

She almost said no. But what if she could really learn to sing?

She held the program of Mme Celia DeMille, soprano, between her thumb and forefinger. Celia DeMille, the daughter of a slave.

"Mama doesn't remember anything about that program," he told her. "Keep it. It's yours."

"Really? Are you sure?"

He nodded.

She thanked him with a quiet smile, put the program in her backpack, and flung it across her shoulder. She headed for the door, then stopped.

"Sundays. Sunday evenings are good, like last time, if it's all right with Mr. Blessing. Or Mondays and Tuesdays after work." She reached for the door knob. "Maybe I can even find some Schubert to sing."

CHAPTER 20

She'd not been home two minutes before her phone rang.

Her brother, probably. She hadn't talked to him all day. But the voice on the phone was feminine, and unfamiliar. The area code was 504. New Orleans. And the woman's name didn't ring a bell.

"Sorry, I didn't catch the name?"

"Mildred. Mildred Fountaineau, calling you from New Orleans. A friend of your Aunt Julia's. Your Aunt Baby. She gave me your number."

Eden dropped the phone to her chest, her eyes welling up. *Aunt Baby's gone*, she thought. She braced herself.

"Hello? Hello? Are you there?"

"Yes, yes, I'm here."

"Like I said, I'm a friend of hers. Julia and I were close growing up. We still are."

Are. Present tense. Still alive, thank God.

Mildred said Aunt Baby had fallen and fractured her hip. No surgery, but she would need therapy and would need a walker, probably indefinitely. And even then, she would need to be watched; there was a chance of infection.

"She asked me to call you. She said she wants to see you."

Eden sighed her relief. "But is she OK?"

The woman chuckled. "Well. She's still Baby Claremont, if you know what I mean! Just as feisty as ever. The woman dragged herself from the yard into the house and dialed 911! I couldn't see doing that, and she's got twenty years on me. Doctor says these next few weeks are critical, though. So, can you come? The smile you'll put on her face will help with the healin'. She talks about you all the time."

Yes, she told Mildred. She'd ask for a few days off work. But scraping up money for the trip would be hard.

"Don't worry about that." Mildred didn't hesitate. "You know a Western Union office you can get to? Find a flight and I'll wire you the fare. Can you come by Friday? She gets out of the hospital then. I'll be helping her, but you know your Aunt Julia. The woman is a handful. It would help if someone else she's fond of was here, too."

"How did it happen?"

"Oh, you know, I'd been telling her not to dig around in that yard of hers. She had it in her mind to start a garden again, you know, how she used to have. She was coming back in the house trying to carry a bag of mulch and stepped on a loose brick. Down she went."

As she was talking, Eden remembered Aunt Baby mentioning Mildred, a home health nurse retired from a job at Charity. The woman who lived near the bridge. The woman whose house had floated off the slab and landed in the middle of the street.

The house where the box with the necklace and scrapbook had been found.

"Miss Fountaineau, Aunt Baby told me about your house," Eden said. "Are you OK?"

"Call me Mildred. Child, it was just awful, but I'ma be all right. Or as all right as anybody can be who went through all that mess. My house, well, I guess Julia—Baby—told you how it happened. The water just picked it up and carried it away, clean off the slab. Floated down the street."

"I know. I couldn't believe it. I'm so sorry."

"Thank you, child. Insurance folks about to drive me batty, but right now, I'm worried about Baby. I been in Houston, but for the time being, I'm staying with her. Let me know when you leave to come here."

"I will. Tell Aunt Baby I'll see her soon."

"We're not having this conversation again. You know you can't go. Why do you keep asking me?"

She'd known an argument was coming. Reginald Jr. balanced the two grocery sacks in one arm, fished in his pocket for the key, then opened the door of the building.

"You told me last time I could go next time."

She adjusted her sack of vegetables in the crook of one arm as she sighed. The boy's abrasive tone and snarky sarcasm vexed her.

"I didn't say no such thing. You've got school. And what about your job? How you gonna get away if you're working three nights a week till seven?"

The job thing. The fact that he was working now, after all, was a plus. They needed the money, and it pained her to admit that things had gotten easier since he took it on. Between her extra shifts at McDonald's and his messenger service work, they'd not only been able to pay the rent but they also had even found him a good deal on some almost-new boots at the Methodist thrift store.

"Aw, I can get off whenever I want to. It ain't no thing."

"And school? Don't you have testing coming up next week? Semester's almost over and you gonna run down to New Orleans for what, exactly? Hang with your crew, get your behind in some more trouble? I don't think so. You concentrate on those books and in one more year, after you graduate, you can do whatever you want."

He bounded up the apartment steps ahead of her, opened the door to their unit, and dropped the grocery bags on the kitchen counter.

"Don't slam that stuff down! There's bottles and stuff in there."

He huffed, threw himself on the futon, and put his backpack on the floor next to his Timberland-clad feet. He grabbed the remote control for the TV.

"You know you need to let me go, after what happened last month. You owe me."

"What do you mean, I 'owe' you?"

This was the first time they'd talked about the eviction. *Figures. He's just been holding that card, waiting to play it.*

"You know what I'm talking about. Didn't I get us outta that fix?"

She said nothing as she put the groceries in the refrigerator. The boy was right. She'd never really thanked him for stepping up the way he did, calling McGeavy and paying the rent with his own money. But she figured making one of his favorite meals—shrimp po'boys, the way they used to have them at home, fully dressed with shredded lettuce, pickles, a little red sauce—had been thanks enough. "I'm just going down to check on Aunt Baby. I'll be gone maybe two, three days. Tops."

And she might have let it go with that, except she felt she owed him more. He was no longer a kid whose tedious questioning of every decision could be dismissed with a turned head, a wave of the hand. "Because I said so" was no longer an appropriate reason for someone who'd found a way to get the rent paid and kept them living indoors.

"Look," she said, her voice thin and tired. "I'm really sorry. I know you want to go back home. I wish we could both go back there to live, go back to the way things used to be. But you know this is the way it has to be now. You just have to trust me."

She could see in his face that her apology completely disarmed him, as if it was the first time an adult had ever truly, sincerely apologized to him—for anything. And maybe it was.

"Well…" He trailed off, unsure. "I mean, I just think…I miss the place, you know."

She wanted to tell him more. *I'm sorry I couldn't do better by you. I'm sorry your father is gone. I'm sorry you didn't have a mother to raise you. I'm just sorry.*

Reginald Jr. crossed his feet at the ankles on the coffee table. The bag next to his feet landed on the floor with a clang.

Eden ran to pick up the bag. Her fault. She'd forgotten to put the necklace back in the top drawer of her nightstand. "Watch out! You might break it!"

Reginald Jr. leaned over and picked up the bag, pulling the necklace out. "Nothing broken." She took it from him and put it back in the bag.

Reginald leaned back again, crossing his arms across his chest. "That thing worth anything? Look like it might be worth something. We oughta sell it."

"We oughta not do nothing with it. It's mine. Aunt Baby gave it to me. It belonged to a famous singer. A black woman singer, a long time ago."

"Yeah? That woman in that book you been reading, right?" He pulled the necklace out of the bag again and held it around his neck. "Where'd you take it the other day?"

"To a friend who knows about old jewelry and stuff."

"Look like it might be real gold."

"How would you know? Everything yellow and shiny ain't gold."

"So, what did he say it was?"

"He didn't..."

Reginald Jr. stopped and leaned forward, his attention trained on the pendant. "Hey, look at this."

He held the disk-shaped pendant between his thumb and forefinger and inserted his thumbnail into a crease in the metal. It opened, like a locket.

Inside was a small scrap of linen, dirty and worn. And on it was writing, block letters forming a single word, in black ink.

"Lottie."

CHAPTER 21

Mildred Fountaineau, a heavy-thighed, box-figured woman of seventy or so, had the bright, intense eyes and energy of someone half her age. While Aunt Baby trudged through the rooms at a pace true to her ninety-plus years, Mildred's steps were quicker, only slightly hobbled by an arthritic knee. "Come on in." Her husky alto suggested years of cigarettes and late-night libations. And as if their last conversation had been five minutes ago instead of days ago, she took up where they had left off. "So, I've got great news, and I've got good news."

Aunt Baby's house was unrecognizable from Eden's last visit weeks ago. In the living room, drywall filled the space between studs, spackling tape and paste-smoothed seams. A finished space was emerging.

The great news: Aunt Baby's therapy had progressed to the point that she would be released from the hospital tomorrow, one day earlier than predicted by her doctor. The good news: new furniture, a sofa and a loveseat ordered a week ago, would be delivered in the morning.

"That'll put a smile for sure on Julia Claremont's face! Baby loves nothing more than new stuff. So, we'll be able to sit on real furniture in this room, instead of on these teensy little romper room chairs," Mildred said. "You came just in time."

The women sat on wooden folding chairs at the tiny pine table in Aunt Baby's near-finished yellow and white kitchen, drinking glasses of iced sweet tea, looking out the window as they talked about the city as if it were a relative recovering from heart surgery, facing an arduous rehab. The slow grind of progress after a beat-down by a once-in-a-century flood. The families who'd returned and those who hadn't. The ones who swore to return and those who swore never to. The folks who'd raised their hammers to their houses and their fists to the Almighty. The rip-off artists. The con-men. The companies who took money up front for work they would either half-do or never do. Everyone had a different story, but each story had a common thread—life was hard.

The struggle could have been harder for a woman like Mildred—retired from nursing, long-divorced, and living alone. But she was lucky. With a paid-in-full house passed down to her by her grandparents and paper-proof of ownership, she was one of the very few in her neighborhood with flood insurance. And with a cousin in the construction business and relatives who did roof tiling, flooring, and cement finishing, she was on her way back.

But still, there were countless headaches. The well-meaning young college volunteers from the University of Massachusetts or Florida State or Tennessee or North Carolina, "God bless 'em," who screamed and ran when they saw a mouse. Or the older volunteers from the churches in neighboring states who got dizzy on ladders and sick in the humid heat. And there were the insurance folks. Mildred swore there'd be a Second Coming before somebody from Gulf Coast Life & Casualty wrote her a check. But, "the Lord willing," in three months, her house would be finished, sitting in the same spot as before, only elevated five feet from the ground.

The conversation shifted to Aunt Baby, how she was really doing, and whether it was wise to let her live alone at her age. Eden had sent letters every week but hadn't talked to her since she'd left. Since the storm, her great-aunt was a challenge to communicate with; she did not suffer the unnecessary foolishness of technological advances, like a cell phone, and was always at the mercy of the US Post Office and her neighbors' land lines.

"But she's doing OK, better than OK for somebody her age," Mildred assured. "That is, until she fell." And even now, Mildred said, the old woman's spirits were high, just knowing her great-niece was coming.

After an early supper of Mildred's special shrimp étouffée and collard greens (the étouffée was spicier, the greens peppery and more tender than Aunt Baby's), Eden reached in her backpack to pull out the scrapbook and the necklace and placed them both on the table between them. Now was as good a time as any. The thought of giving up the possessions, now precious to her, saddened her. But the woman had a right to what came out of her own house.

"Miss Mildred, you know how Aunt Baby collects all kinds of stuff? This turned up in a box in the middle of Galvez Street, close to where you lived. Auntie thinks it came out of one of the houses there after the storm. Maybe even your place."

Mildred wiped her lips with a napkin and moved her plate aside. She took the necklace and held it up to the fading light of the window facing the street. Then, taking the scrapbook and turning the pages gingerly, she began to read, squinting.

She frowned, shook her head in disbelief. "Oh, Lord Jesus," she said. "This can't be."

Mildred ran her fingers lightly across the pages. She'd first heard about the famous singer when she was a child. Catherine Fountaineau, her grandmother, the woman who raised her, had worked as the singer's private nurse for years. The highest-paid colored performer in the country and one of the most famous singers in the world, she'd been told. Mildred's eyes misted at the recollection.

"Grandmama must have had this in one of those boxes up in the attic." She spoke in a low and hoarse whisper, holding the chain of the necklace in her fingers. "I just can't believe what I'm looking at. I never thought I would see this again as long as I lived. This woman, this singer, uh, Celia, Celia something…" She looked at Eden.

"DeMille."

"Yes! Yes, that was her name. Celia DeMille. Grandmama loved Miss Celia, but oh, the stories she told about her! Kings and queens falling at her feet! Thousands trying to get in to hear her perform! A voice that made grown men cry. Traveled the world and had houses all over the country. Pretty, too. Always dressed in the latest fashions. And the rumors—this wealthy man or that one, wrapped around her fingers. The woman was something else. But they wouldn't let her sing. Not with the white opera companies. Some folks said that drove her mad."

But she wasn't mad, not crazy mad, Mildred said. Resentful, yes. And sad, especially toward the end of her life. Catherine and Celia had been close, and Celia trusted her nurse to make sure her story was told. By the end, all she wanted was to be remembered for the great singer she was.

"Grandmama made a promise to her." Mildred's voice dropped. "A promise she couldn't keep."

Don't let the world forget me, Celia had pleaded to Catherine. If she was going to die poor and without recognition, then let it be with the hope that someday she would be assured her place in history.

Before she stopped singing, Mildred said, a reporter had promised to write a story about her for one of the big newspapers, the one all the white folks read. "She waited for that story like a child waits for Christmas. A big feature in a big New York paper, the *New York Times*. It would have made her even more famous, would have given her career a second chance."

But it never happened. "In the last few months of her life, when she couldn't sing anymore and knew she didn't have long, she made my grandmother promise her she would get the *Times* to make good on its promise someday," she said. "She didn't care how long it took. In exchange, she promised her this."

She held the necklace up. "It's even more special-looking than I remember. Fit for a queen. Grandmama showed it to me when I was about sixteen or so. But I don't remember it looking all shiny like this. What'd you do to it?"

"Just cleaned it up a little, me and a friend of mine. A little scrubbing, soap, and toothpaste, and it got all its shine back."

"You telling me. Shining like new money. Like gold."

It was clear now to Eden: this woman was the rightful owner. "Miss Mildred, if the necklace was your grandmother's, then I guess it belongs to you now. I have a friend who knows about stuff like this, and he thinks it might be valuable. The scrapbook, too. Whatever it's worth, it ought to be yours."

"You say Baby found it?"

Eden told her about the pile of trash near where Mildred's house had been. As if the storm had turned the house upside down, emptying long-buried contents of closets, cubbyholes, and attics into the street.

"Well…" Mildred put the necklace back inside the bag and pushed the bag toward Eden as if it emitted some toxic smell. She folded her hands across her chest, turning her head away. "I don't want nothing to do with the likes of that." Her voice was sharp, her hand waving dismissively.

"Excuse me?" Eden said.

Mildred ignored her, pointing toward the corner. "That your bag over there? Let's get you settled in your room."

And with that, Mildred got up, took Eden's bag, and rolled it out of the room.

Nothing to do with the "likes of that?" Eden followed Mildred to the back of the house and the room where she'd stayed before.

Mildred put Eden's overnight bag in a corner and Eden placed her backpack on the bed. Except for the strong scent of Lemon Pledge and new white curtains hanging where older ones had been, the room looked the same. A glass vase of daisies, fainting in the humid air, sat on a dresser of knotty pine.

"You know where everything is," Mildred said, taking out one of the drooping daisies. "Towels and washcloths in that chest by the hall, you need any extras. What time you like getting up? I'ma early riser myself. Baby should be released by about noon, they say, but I plan to be there by 11:30. Furniture coming at 9:00, so everything should work out fine, time-wise."

Eden couldn't let go of what Mildred said. "Miss Mildred, I don't understand. The necklace...what bothers you about it?"

Mildred crushed the drooping daisy in her hand and dropped it into a wire trash basket. She sighed. "Girl. There's a long story behind that necklace. I just think it's got the wrong kind of feeling behind it."

She turned to go back to the bedroom across the hall, then said, "Did you look inside the pendant? Was there anything in there?"

Eden told her about the name, Lottie, written on a small scrap of fabric and folded inside the locket.

Mildred nodded, her eyes closed. "She was a child. Just a four-teen-year-old girl."

"Who was she?"

Well, that was the long story, Mildred said. "You sure you want to know? It'll break your heart."

CHAPTER 22

Boston, Massachusetts, 1901

The man stood toward the back, near the oak double doors of the Methodist church on Charles Street. His too-large suit of dark blue wool drooped over his narrow shoulders, his arched cheekbones sculpted by the shadows and dim light. As Celia DeMille finished the final encore, "Swing Low, Sweet Chariot," a thunder of applause rose from the pews and the entire congregation of more than three hundred souls stood as one. The man in the dark blue suit, his head bowed, did not clap. When he looked up, Celia caught his eye. At the end, when some in the crowd lined up to greet her with lavish praise—first the white folks, then the Negroes who were allowed only in the back pews—he stood behind them, eyes fixed on her, his hat dangling on the ends of his fingertips.

When he reached her, he extended his big calloused hand. She was surprised at his humble touch, and the tears in his eyes.

"I ain't never before heard something so...so..." He could not continue. She reached her white-gloved hand to his wet cheek.

"Thank you for coming," she said. "And what is your name, sir?"

"Isaac, ma'am. Isaac Freeman." He bowed his head and let the tears fall. She paused to let him gather himself. He sighed deeply. When he was finally able to speak, he asked, "Would you, ma'am, Miss Celia, allow me to walk with you a spell?"

Each time she sang a concert in Boston, she retired afterward to a room arranged for her and dined alone. But this time, she felt compelled to walk with Mr. Isaac Freeman.

Boston was cool in the evenings of early October. The leaves had begun drying into deep rusts and golds, and as Isaac Freeman and the diva walked, the crisp music of oak and elm rustled amid the breezes from the river. The man was old, mid-eighties she guessed, his short, thick beard stark white against the deep brown of his skin. He seemed a gentle man, and she felt no harm would come to her. At thirty-two years old, she was fearless; she had already traveled the world. Earlier in the year, at the famous Beckstein Hall in London, she had sung for an enormous crowd. There was not one person there with color in their skin.

They walked beneath the branches of elms toward the colored rooming house a few blocks away, where she had stayed the last two nights. He had been in Boston many years, he told her, leaning on his hand-carved hickory cane and loping with an elder's gait, his hat now fixed squarely on his head. She told him she had been born here, but hadn't been back since her parents' deaths years ago.

A week ago, he told her, he had turned eighty. It had been more than forty years since he'd decided that the risk of death was a small price for even a chance to be free. "I done stole myself from the man what owned me," he said.

He looked toward the river as he began telling his story. A slave's life on the Denny plantation in northeastern Georgia was one of endless and thankless work, from the cock's crow till the fading of the night stars. He was alone now, but he had not always been. Even on the plantation, after the work was done, his evenings were sweetened by the smiles of the women he loved, his wife and young daughter.

But all that ended.

The plantation owner, Jacob Denny, was a young single man who owned Isaac and the land he worked. About to be married, Denny wanted a wedding gift for his soon-to-be bride.

William Hardaway, a neighbor, planter, and widower, was getting on in years. His back was weakened with bone pain and he anticipated a time when he might need the care of a strong young woman to attend to his ailments and look after his needs. He would not marry again. He'd had many good years with his dear Elizabeth, who had gone to God years before. He had no children. His slaves were all male field workers, his fortunes had dwindled, and he had no money to purchase a young woman to be his caretaker. He confided all this to Jacob Denny.

Denny listened with one eyebrow raised. It might be that they could help each other.

William Hardaway, it turned out, had in his possession something Jacob Denny wanted: a stunning antique gold pendant necklace that had been passed down to William Hardaway on his mother's side. Jacob Denny's fiancée had seen it hanging in a glass case when she and Jacob visited William's farm one Sunday after church. She had exclaimed over it and Jacob thought the necklace would be the perfect wedding gift. Would William be willing to part with it in exchange for a slave, someone to care for him in his declining years?

When the two men shook on the deal—one gold necklace for one young slave—the question was which slave should go. Jacob Denny had sixteen working his fields and in his house. But William Hardaway needed a particular type. A healthy young woman, strong, agreeable, and serious of purpose.

"He chose my only daughter, Lottie," Isaac said.

Isaac and his wife, Mary, were devastated, and young Lottie was fearful. But Isaac promised his daughter they would see each other again. Jacob, surely, would let him visit his daughter on the occasional Sunday, for the Hardaway land was not far—a half day's journey by foot. But months later, when Isaac was allowed to set out for

Hardaway's farm to see his girl, there was no one there. The farm, the house, its fields—empty with no sign of life.

Had the old man died? Had he moved to another state? Isaac returned to Denny's place and questioned his master.

He removed his hat and bowed his head as tears shredded his voice. "Marse Denny, sir, they gone! Ain't nobody there! My daughter...everybody. Do you know where they be?"

"I'm as surprised as you are," Denny shrugged.

Isaac hated to witness his wife's bloodless expression when he told her the news. Lottie was gone, and it was unlikely they would ever see her again. Years passed and Mary became ill and died.

"Her heart broke from us losing Lottie," Isaac told Celia. That was when he decided to take ownership of his body, his life, and his breath, consequences be damned. He had lost everything he had loved, and there was nothing left to lose.

It was early in 1860. Even in the Quarter, the air moved with the scent of a new age coming; there were rumblings of war, of abolition, and even talk of slaves running North and never returning. One heard tell of freedom paths through the woods and across the hills and waters, and a good man could find ways to outrun and outlast the patrollers with their rifles and their dogs.

On a hot Sunday in June, when the air was thick and damp and the full moon was as plump as a melon, Isaac set out on his path. From talk in the Quarter, he'd heard of a safe house across the fields and woods to the north and on the other side of the river. He also heard about people, some colored, some not, who would help those who sought to free themselves. When his best friend, Silas, a young man blessed with big fists, strong legs, and great foot speed, didn't show up in the field on a Monday or the next Tuesday, Isaac knew his friend was dead or just gone. Either way, he was free.

Sometime after, Isaac set off, but not before settling his score with Jacob Denny. He thought long and hard. "I had killing in my heart," Isaac told Celia, his eyes glistening in the streetlamp glow.

But he could not bring himself to kill a man. Denny had killed the life he'd had with his wife and daughter and, therefore, his spirit. But he could not return the favor. Instead, he waited until his master and wife were away in the nearby town. When night fell and the farm was quiet, he stole into the house and the dining room.

Mrs. Denny kept her family silver and jewelry in a wooden case near the sideboard, under lock and key. It wasn't hard to get into; Isaac had built the case himself and made the key.

He grabbed the necklace and took only what he could carry from the larder—apples, potatoes, cheeses, and bread. Then he slipped out of his master's house and into what fate awaited him.

He made his way out through the woods, beneath the broad black sky and into the moonlit Southern night. Running, walking, wading, and swimming as far as he could, he slept until the first shimmer of light seeped above the hills. When his stolen food ran out, he snatched wild berries from vines and stole apples and melons in orchards and patches where he could find them. In North Carolina, he hid out in a shed someone had told him was owned by a Quaker widow, a kindly sort who had freed her own slaves years ago. In a sweetgrass basket leaned against a wall, he found a steel jug of water, a loaf of fresh-baked bread, and six green pears.

In Virginia fields, he heard the barking of hounds and the rustle of grasses before he finally reached Little Bird River, where he joined a group of runaways bound for Canada, awaiting abolitionists to ferry them across the water. The rifle fire of a rabbit hunter in Maryland startled him so that he ran onto a jagged tree stump that drew blood from his leg. But on he went.

Boston. Even the name had a ring of dignity about it. When he entered its broom-swept streets, he knew he was home. He found work where he could, blacksmithing and barrel-making, and even apprenticed at a tailor's shop. At the AME church on Anderson Street, former slaves and abolitionist politicians welcomed him with open hearts and wide-spread arms. On New Year's Day, 1863, they all gathered at the Tremont Temple to cheer the president's proclamation. He was a free man now, although the feeling was bittersweet without Mary and Lottie. In all his years, he never married again. But he'd already decided—a free man, a man who owned his life, would need a second name. Isaac Freeman was born.

Isaac and Celia talked on and walked in the brisk night air, the gas streetlamps coating the dark cobblestone in a copper-like glow. Above, a harvest moon shone full and round in the wide sky. He relaxed into their conversation and asked about her singing. Her voice was a miracle, he said, and he had never known that "one of us," or any other human for that matter, could sound that way. "I guess you done been all over the world," he said. He wanted to hear about her travels, all the places he'd heard about, but would never see. She told him about the streets of Paris, full of music and fashion and the smells of sweet pastries and wine. In London, they crowded her recitals and demanded four encores and stomped their feet at her final song. But she dearly loved singing here, the place where she was born.

"Did you ever find her? Your daughter, Lottie?" Celia gave him a hopeful look.

He touched a finger to his forehead and sighed. "Never did." But he dreamed about her often, imagining her a free woman, married to a good man, mother to several bright-eyed children. Happy. And then his speech faltered, as it had before.

"When I saw you, I saw my Lottie," he said. "She was only fourteen when I last saw her, but you had a look about you that put me in mind of my girl."

As soon as he arrived in Boston, he was determined to learn to read and write. He built a smokehouse for a tiny, freckle-faced, red-haired woman who belonged to the abolitionist society and had a nephew whose wife taught former slaves to read. "I wanted to read the Bible," he told Celia. And there was one thing he wanted to write.

He reached in his vest pocket and pulled out the necklace, then held it up to the gas lamp at the front door of the rooming house.

When he opened the locket, he pulled out and unfolded a small piece of linen, yellowed with age. On it, he had written Lottie's name.

"I carry this with me wherever I go," he said. "First word I ever wrote. For a long time, it was the only word I knew how to write.

"When I took the necklace, it was out of spite. That man stole half my life when he sold my Lottie away, so I had to take me something back. This was all my daughter was to him. That necklace. That was all she was worth. I couldn't get my Lottie back, but I could take the thing that mattered more to that man than my baby's life.

"But when I run away from all that, something done changed." Now when he looked at the necklace, the bright gold edges of the disk that caught the gleam from the sun, he thought of Lottie, the golden light of her bright brown eyes, her first toothless baby smile, the way she laughed.

He folded the linen piece back in the locket, put the necklace back in his vest pocket, and patted it. "This here," he said. "This is my Lottie."

Celia blinked, swallowed hard. "I am so sorry about your daughter."

She thought about her own father. What had become of the men he had betrayed? Had they succumbed to the hounds and the rifles? What had been the price of his telling his master about the planned escape of three men at the next full moon? The master had rewarded her father with one Sunday off and new duty in the stables, no longer in the hot fields. No overseer's hot lash to blister his aching back. But what had been the price of his privilege? Her father never talked about it, except to say that he would take the burden of betrayal to his grave.

This man could have been one of those men. This man could have been betrayed by a man like her father.

When she said good night, she knew she would see him again. And she did.

Over the next six years, she sang in Boston four more times. Her reviews dripped with praise—"extraordinary," "sublime," "angelic"— and she made her way around the Northern cities and to Europe. But she always returned to Boston, and each time, at the end of the line of adoring well-wishers, stood Isaac Freeman.

She spotted him on a cold Sunday evening in March, six years after their first meeting. As usual, he offered to walk her home, and as usual, she obliged.

"I am not well," he told her, his voice now thin and frail and his back, once straight, now curved. His steps were slower. "I don't know how much longer I got."

She took his arm. "Is there anything I can do for you?"

He hesitated, looked away. "I want you to have this, a gift from me, and keep it with you." He handed her the necklace. "I don't have my Lottie to leave it to, and I know I never will. But I got you. Like I told you, you put me in mind of her. I just hope she grew up to be as fine a woman as you."

Celia's throat felt thick and her eyes full. "I cannot..."

Isaac took her hand, pressed the necklace in her palm, and closed her fingers around it. "Please, ma'am."

She returned to Boston many times, but she never saw Isaac Freeman again. In her next tour of England and Europe, she was invited back to sing in London at the famous Beckstein Hall, and this time, she wore the necklace with her gown. From then on, she never sang without it.

CHAPTER 23

"So, now you know. Or at least you know about as much as I do, as much as my grandmama told me." With a small groan of effort and a popping sound from her knee joints, Mildred eased herself up from the edge of Eden's bed.

Taking the necklace in both hands, Eden unclasped the locket and unfolded the roughened and worn piece of linen that bore Lottie's name.

"He wrote that hisself, Isaac did. Wanted the girl's name close to him, close to his heart. Believed fixing his mind on her name would keep her spirit alive, no matter what happened to her. That's why he had a fit to learn how to write it."

An hour had passed, and a long slant of late afternoon sun tinted the small bedroom in sepia light. Eden folded the square of fabric and placed it back inside the locket.

"I still don't understand, Miss Mildred, why you said what you did. I mean, it's just a necklace."

Like most everybody in Louisiana, Eden grew up with all of the tales—the spirits, the spells. The curses. The juju and gris-gris. It came with the territory, all part of being born in a city drunk on history and lore. Did Mildred Fountaineau buy into all that business about bad spirits, evil powers in ordinary things? Surely not.

Mildred's eyes narrowed. "Listen. That thing, that necklace, got the soul of a young girl all wrapped up in it. You ain't got to be voodoo crazy to believe there's evil in some things. When I think about that girl, sold away from her mama and daddy like that, and all because of that thing? I swear.

"Buying folks, selling folks. Separating a child from her people, her mama and daddy, just so somebody could have a necklace? Like blood and bone and soul don't matter if a man needs something pretty and shiny to impress his wife? No. I don't care what nobody says. It's just evil. That thing just reminds me of the evil that one person can do to another. But that's just me," she said.

Eden fell quiet, her words buried beneath jumbled thoughts. Outside the bedroom window, tall weeds climbed above uncut grass, but even in the waning light of evening, the orange flower of an angel trumpet shone a brilliant gold. Isaac Freeman's story, passed from Mildred's grandmother Catherine to Mildred and now to Eden, landed more softly in her mind. Maybe stealing that necklace from his master hadn't settled the score. But still, a man who had taken back his power could walk a little taller. If Isaac's daughter's life had been claimed with a necklace, then Isaac had reclaimed it.

Mildred said, "Now my grandmama, she thought it was the most beautiful thing she'd ever seen, since Miss Celia herself wore it. But Grandmama never had the heart to put it on. Didn't think she'd earned it, hadn't kept that promise. She wrote to all them big papers in New York. Even wrote to one paper in London, where she sang for the king. Couldn't find anybody, not one soul, to tell her story. She tried, she really did."

Over a year, at the rate of about one every six weeks, Catherine Fountaineau wrote eight long letters to the *New York Times*, to a man named Arthur Flanagan, and to every other important newspaper she could think of, Mildred said. But she never heard from any of them.

"She was just as good as that other one, the white one, Donna-whatever. Maybe better, or at least that's what some of the papers said. But beautiful as Miss Celia sang..." Mildred's words trailed into silence and her eyes glazed. "Well, you might find some folks around old enough to remember hearing 'bout her from old-timers in their families. But she shoulda been in all the history books. Folks should still be talking about her, to this day."

"Nobody made a recording of her?"

Mildred scoffed. "They could have. Would have, if they'da let her sing with the opera, like they promised. By the time those record companies decided there was money in catching black folks' voices on records, Miss Celia was long past her prime. They weren't just not interested—they didn't remember her. Somebody who sang at the White House, and for the king of England. Even one record of her, one song left after she died, woulda helped. Woulda proved how great she was!"

In her later years, Mildred said, Celia had taken to long walks by the river and in the neighborhood near where the opera house stood. She'd even been seen near the opera house the night of the fire that destroyed it.

"Believe it or not, there was a rumor that Miss Celia set that fire, put a curse on that building, mad 'cause they wouldn't let her sing there!" She let out a sarcastic cackle. "Can you imagine that? But, funny thing, that opera house never got rebuilt, even after all these years. Never found out what really caused the fire. Still a mystery. You ask me, the way they treated Miss Celia, woulda served them right if she'd lit a few matches and torched that sucker!"

Eden rubbed her fingers along the edges of the pendant as if for the first time.

Mildred left and came back to the room a minute later with two yellow and white striped washcloths and a towel.

"Here, use these. They brand-new. Bought them down at that Walmart they reopened after the storm, and forgot I had 'em. I'll be up by six, but you sleep long as you want. Got some housecleaning to do before Baby comes back. We'll need to get going around eleven to pick her up from the hospital," she said. She started to leave again, but turned back at the door.

"If that thing is worth some money, then help yourself, get all you can out of it. You and your brother, y'all need it. I know Baby been carrying a lot of guilt about you two. How she let y'all down."

Surprised that Aunt Baby had confessed her feelings of guilt to Mildred, Eden remembered Aunt Baby's words, her voice low with regret: "I wasn't there for y'all kids." She remembered her own initial disappointment with the box of meaningless materials: old papers, a scrapbook, rusted medals, and a necklace. They weren't so meaningless now.

"If you can get some money outta that thing, then maybe it'll turn out to be good for something. Something besides tearing apart a family, causing pain. Sell it if you want and keep that money. You need it, you and your brother, more than me."

CHAPTER 24

"Morning, child. You up early!"

Singing as she scrubbed, Mildred worked the rag mop in wide arcs across the kitchen floor. She wore a yellow smock that covered the girth of her torso and her fuzzy brown slippers scuffed the unwashed sections. From the tinny-voiced radio near the sink came the Sunrise Gospel Hour on station KXOR, a chorus of women's voices singing "In the Sweet Bye and Bye." Mildred hummed along a quarter tone below the pitch.

As far as Eden could tell, the brand-new laminate squares showed no need of cleaning, but she figured Mildred's hospital training left her with a penchant for sterility. "Yes, ma'am," Eden said. "Woke up an hour ago."

Eden stood and poured a half cup of coffee from the carafe that Mildred had placed on the counter. Taking a long sip, she slung her backpack across her shoulder. "I'm going out for a little bit, Miss Mildred," she announced. "I'll be back in a couple of hours, before noon. You need anything?"

Mildred grabbed the mop loops in both latex-gloved hands and wrung the water into a white plastic bucket. "Not as far as I recall. You wanna just meet me at the hospital?"

"No, I'll go with you. I'll be back long before time to leave."

She had to get out of the house. A few hours of fitful slumber left her nervous and anxious. Her heart pounding, forehead damp, she had woke and sat straight up. The details of the dream were gone, but the feeling she'd awakened with—an unsettling roiling in her chest—made her glad she couldn't remember it. There'd been some kind of music in it, but even the music hadn't calmed her.

So, she had to get out, get away. There was way too much to think about now, and getting her body moving always helped. She wanted to talk to her brother. She hated leaving him alone, again, and even though Mr. Wembly in 8C had agreed to check on him daily, answer his calls if needed, she still worried.

And Miss Mildred's story about Celia and the necklace, the sad tale of Isaac and the young daughter, sold away because of it. Terrible. But a necklace, evil? It was just a thing. An object. It could be whatever you wanted it to be. Isaac had looked at the necklace with its glittering golden light and was reminded of his daughter. Miss Celia had seen it as a precious gift from a special old friend. For Eden, it would be... what? She didn't know yet.

She walked the few blocks to St. Claude to wait for the 88. A long bus ride through town seemed a good idea. And, ironically enough, considering the still-wrecked state of the city, it might settle her jumping nerves. Or provide a distraction, at least. When the bus came, she headed for a window seat in the back.

Within a few minutes, she'd settled into the ride, no destination in mind. Oddly, the strong coffee had relaxed her. In the back, near her, sat a young sandy-haired, bespectacled man in his twenties wearing a tool belt and a VOLUNTEER badge. Thank God for people like him, who'd come from all parts of the country to help get the city back on its feet. He leaned toward her.

"Excuse me, miss, does this bus go to the French Quarter?"

Eden nodded, smiling, thinking he must have been with one of the college volunteer groups. "Yes, it does. Sort of. You can get off after Rampart Street and walk from there. It's just a few more blocks."

He smiled, thanked her, and sat back in his seat. *A good idea*, she thought. She would get off there, too, and walk through the Quarter, clear her head. No matter the discouraging sights along the way—the trash heaps and blue-tarpaulined rooftops, the plywood-covered windows, and the sheer absence of residents—the unscathed French Quarter built on the city's highest ground would help her forget, momentarily, the struggles of the city beyond it.

So, she rode on, blinking when bright shafts of sunlight striped the aisles through the dust-filmed window as the bus eased past neighborhoods just waking. The few active businesses unshuttered their windows and unlocked their doors, hopeful about the prospects of revival. Along St. Claude Avenue, a hill of debris towered at the entrance of Rodale's Auto Parts Store, and Lucky's Barbecue Emporium and Church's Chicken were still boarded up. Ebony Bliss Hair and Nails, where she'd once spent five hours getting her hair braided for high school graduation, still looked blank, mold blooming on the clapboard siding. The white-bearded old man in denim overalls, whose name she never knew, raked trash from the sidewalk in front of Centano's Lube and Oil just as he had done daily for as long as Eden could remember, even though the place was closed. A high water mark stretched like a dingy waistband across its doors. Even St. Roch Market, patched with plywood and sporting a blue tarpaulin roof, was a long way from a grand re-opening.

She took it all in, these gestures of normalcy in an abnormal world, wondering how long it would take a city that once brimmed with life to come back to it. Broken New Orleans was on the mend, if some of the pieces were still scattered and lost.

When the bus reached Rampart and St. Peter, she got off; the young volunteer ahead of her walked with one of those hotel maps of the French Quarter in hand. Still, with no purpose in mind, she walked in the direction of the river. Jackson Square was ghostly quiet in front of the towering spires of St. Louis Cathedral; in pre-storm New Orleans, painters and tarot card readers would have crowded the square full of bright-colored canvases of wrought iron balconies dripping spring blooms, while headscarfed women sat at card tables predicting the fortunes of young and old. Now, only a few milled about with a straggle of artists set up here and there.

She walked on, reveling in the early hours of morning in the Quarter, the streets glistening from the wash-down of street-cleaning trucks, the shopkeepers on Royal dusting antiques and readying their wares. She turned at Bourbon Street.

Ordinarily she bypassed the tourist haunts. But she was a little hungry, and the thought of Café DuMonde's sweet beignets and chicory coffee, unmatched by anything in New York so far, made her feel downright giddy. At the café, she slipped past the long line snaking around the exterior and stepped inside to the takeout counter. A man with thick shoulders and luminous blue-black skin smiled as he took her order.

"Have a blessed day, ma'am." In less than a minute, he handed her the sack of beignets and a café au lait. "You, too," she smiled back, then headed toward the levee and the river.

She wasn't sure why she wanted to go to the water since there was plenty of the same river near Aunt Baby's house. There, placid waves hummed muted hymns, nuzzled the edges of the earthen levee, quiet as a prayer. But here near the Quarter, a different beast—bold, noisy with cruise ships and riverboats—rolled toward the Gulf. A few people walked along the levee or sat on the benches with coffee and newspaper. On the water, a massive barge glided toward the bridge. She placed her coffee cup, beignet sack, and backpack on a bench, then squatted to pick up a rock near the water's edge. She flung it across the water, watched it skip the surface twice before it disappeared.

"You've got to spin it side-arm. Like this." Her father had taught her well. As the steamship Natchez powered across the river toward

Algiers, his face sharpened in her mind. A flash flood of memory. The engine moans of the steel hulk, the melodic toots of the calliope. The mutter of waves. The fading orb of gold slipping into the horizon as her father skipped rocks across the river, gabbing about his marching band days. Or effusing nonstop about the night Count Basie came to town. Or the time he saw Miles Davis coming out of the Peabody in downtown Memphis. "Standing close to him as I am to you. 'Good morning!' I said, and he nodded, looked me right in the eye!" Her daddy could tell a good story, and that was one of the things she had loved most about their outings along the levee. When the steamship calliope began, he'd stopped, cupped a hand to his ear, and cocked his head. "Hear that? What's the name of it? Come on! You know that song, don't you?"

This morning, the first three notes from the calliope dimmed as the ship surged ahead, and sounded newly familiar, a remnant of something she knew. She tried to hum along, but the tune in her head, while similar, was not the same song the calliope bellowed out. Still, those first three notes—*da-da-dum*—how did it go? It irritated her, not being able to recall it. After a moment, she remembered; the woman in the yellow dress in the church. It was the first three notes of one of her songs. And wasn't it the same music as in her dream?

Scraps of last night's dream clung to her like a sticky film and now pieced together in her mind. There was a woman. Yes, a woman, tall and lean, but large-boned and dark-skinned, with straight black hair. And she was singing, something high, silvery. The woman in the church in New York? No, it couldn't have been. The woman in the dream was not in yellow like the church singer but was dressed in an eggshell gown of fine old lace, her hair pinned back in a style of women seen in history books and old paintings. She wore long white gloves and a bright, gold pendant necklace hung around her neck.

The dream-singer's voice rang with the power of the woman in the church. But the face was unmistakably Celia DeMille's.

Two women in one body, two women with one voice. It was rare that she'd remember a complete song after only one hearing. But the tune she'd heard that day in St. John's Cathedral now sprang whole, from beginning to end, from some unlocked vault of memory. Pretty. Catching. She hummed it softly above waves stirred by the rustle of wind. Celia had loved this river. In the interviews and articles in the scrapbook, she recounted walks along the water, thinking, singing. "Sometimes," she had said to one reporter, "the river sang back to me. It gave me peace."

Still humming, Eden walked farther along the levee. So much had changed in this city over the past year, the past century. Buildings rose, multiplied, spread to fill in the land. Some endured, some didn't, their fates shaped by fire or flood or some grand urban plan. Where swamps once swallowed earth, whole neighborhoods emerged. Hurricanes swept through. Floods raged. Dirt streets succumbed to cobblestone, then cement. Bridges and overpasses arched over the city like sprawling webs of steel. Entire populations grew, lived their lives, and were gone. Then they grew again.

So much change, Eden thought, *but not this river.* The same Mississippi that Celia DeMille had walked along, sang to nearly a century ago, remained. The same river she had walked toward that night of the fire, according to Mildred's passed-down story. Eden stood on the high point of the levee and watched a small boat disappear in the distance. *Was it here? Was this where you walked?*

She reached down, chose one more rock to skip across the water, then headed back toward Rampart Street and the bus stop. She'd only walked a few minutes when she noticed it: a feeling like an eerie presence.

She stopped walking at the corner of Bourbon and Toulouse. There was nothing special about the location, the juncture where rowdy, stumbling Bourbon Streeters met French Quarter strollers; a drunken bachelor party spilled over onto a parade of wide-eyed tourists. Before her was a modern, elegant faux-Victorian hotel fronted with bright flags and blue awnings, modernized with glass double doors, contrasting sharply with the nearby buildings. The three-hundred-year-old

Creole cottages and carriage houses along Toulouse, the Spanish-style wrought-iron balconies of Bourbon, were relics of a bygone age. But there was something oddly familiar here. The hotel itself gave nothing away, showed no sign of history, but hinted at a ghost of a past that lay beneath it.

She must have passed this spot a thousand times on her way to the Hotel Monteleone or the Royal Sonesta, where she'd worked. Now, she almost shuddered at the feeling that someone or something was standing behind her. She heard a high voice like spinning silver. She turned in the direction of the sound: No one there. She took a deep breath and sighed. *Weird,* she thought.

The voice sounded again. This time, she turned around completely. It was not a woman, but a man across the street, singing in a beautiful high soprano. He swept the street with a straw broom in front of one of the blue-shuttered Creole cottages. He was rail-thin and very old, with withered, dark skin. A worn hat of faded yellow straw cocked sidewise on his head. His back curved like a comma. His voice pitched higher now in a warbly falsetto. *Like Mildred,* Eden thought, *singing to match the rhythm of his scrubbing to make the time go by faster. Or like me. Singing because he liked to sing.* How nice to be in a place again where nobody cares if you sing while you do your work.

The voice startled her like a shoulder tap: *Pay attention.* Something had happened here. She turned again and realized where she was. It might have happened right here, in this spot, nearly a century ago. She looked up again at the hotel. She had seen it before, or felt she had. But not like this. It looked familiar for a different reason.

She looked across the street and the singing man was gone. But the blue-shuttered cottage—she knew now where she had seen it: an old photograph of this neighborhood, a black and white postcard in Celia DeMille's scrapbook. And right across the street was the carved-out curb for the horse-drawn carriages of the patrons dressed in their finery, and just above the curb was the rounded-out shape of the corner of the building with its tiered balconies.

She stood here, Eden thought. Mildred told her Celia had been seen walking near the opera house the night of the fire, and told her about the rumors. A crazy woman, looking for vengeance. As she looked up at the modern building that had replaced what was once the jewel of the city, the greatest opera house in America, Eden felt a rippling sensation in her gut.

Celia DeMille had stood here and watched the beautiful, grand opera building burn to the ground, and her dreams with it.

CHAPTER 25

It was now called The Inn. Neutral pastels, and salmon and soft rust tones dominated the modestly decorated interior of the lobby, its understated furnishings bowing to tradition with a nod to contemporary elegance. Abstract paintings in primary colors lined a long wall behind mid-century loveseats cushioned in textured wool. Along another wall stood the front desk, a low, horizontal mass of modern oak, and along another was a row of black and white photographs.

A brass wall plaque read: ON THIS SITE STOOD THE FRENCH OPERA HOUSE, 1859–1919. The photographs, apparently the only record of the Greek Revival colonnaded structure, drew her gaze. Grandiose and stately, the stone and brick theater presided over neighboring shops and businesses like a monarch over a small kingdom. Inside, tiers of horseshoe-curved balconies ringed the space, giving it the look of a hollowed-out wedding cake. Columns stood on either side of the grand stage.

One photo showed the theater packed full of nattily coifed and groomed patrons sitting shoulder to shoulder in their evening wear, men in tuxedoes, women in petticoated gowns, occupying every seat in every box from the orchestra floor to the high balcony.

Another showed a gloomier sight: the opera house engulfed in a blaze. The fire, bleach-white again the black sky; the flames fanning out in the high wind. In another, it was gutted to a shell of smoked-charred brick and plaster, a jack-o-lantern of windowless frames and toppled columns and piles of debris while giant sprays of water from fire truck hoses arced futilely toward the remains.

Another photo caught Eden's eye. A thin white woman dressed in a costume so voluminous and thick it made her look upholstered. Her small head tilted beneath the weight of a heavily flowered bonnet, she offered the camera a wan smile of aristocratic boredom. The woman's hair was swept up in a confection of curls, and her skin, even in the black-and-white photo, looked pasty. Clearly, she was a singer or performer of some type. Beneath the photo was the caption, ADELINE DONATELLA, THE WORLD'S GREATEST SINGER, A STAR OF THE NEW ORLEANS FRENCH OPERA.

Next to the portrait was a painting with the caption, MME DONATELLA'S HOUSE, 631 ROYAL STREET, NEW ORLEANS.

So, this woman, Adeline Donatella, lived here in New Orleans? Donatella's elegant, yellow cottage on Royal Street exuded wealth, lavish even by nineteenth-century French Quarter standards: wrought iron settees on dark cobblestone and a tropical courtyard with palms, yucca, banana trees, hibiscus in full bloom led to stairs and a wide balcony. So, this was the woman the whole world compared to Celia? Her own name wasn't good enough? She had to be "The Black Donatella?"

"Amazing, huh? This hotel used to be an opera house, the best in the country at the time. Such a shame about the fire."

She nearly jumped. She was so absorbed in the photos, she hadn't noticed the man standing behind her.

He apologized for having startled her, then introduced himself as Walter, a journalist in town doing research. He looked to be in his forties and had blond hair and gray eyes. He was an opera buff and knew about this spot, where the old opera house once stood before it was destroyed by fire.

"Shame, isn't it? Beautiful, to look at these old photos of it."

Eden was interested. "Do you know how it burned?"

Walter told her he'd done a little research on nineteenth-century opera houses, this one in particular, and that how the fire started was never discovered.

"It's not unusual," he said. "Buildings like this, back in those days, were always burning, for one reason or another. Flammable building materials. No sprinkler systems. No sophisticated alarms. With this one, it's possible the fire might have started in the kitchen of the restaurant, on the first floor. That would be the most likely answer. But also, the opera house wasn't doing well financially. It was put in receivership a couple years before the fire. Losing money. So, arson, to collect insurance, couldn't be ruled out. And it was a lot harder to prove in those days."

Eden nodded and walked back to look at the photo of the intact building. "Well, you're right. It was really pretty." She walked along the row of photos and stopped again at the one of Adeline Donatella, dressed in a costume that, even in black and white, was the most elaborate gown Eden had ever seen. Much grander than anything worn by Celia DeMille in the scrapbook photographs.

"So, you know about her?" Walter said. "Adeline Donatella? Lived right over on Royal Street in the early part of the twentieth century. A true genius, they said. Sang all over the world. They say she was one of the great Carmens. You know, the opera about the gypsy cigarette girl that got murdered by her lover? In fact, Donatella was maybe the greatest singer in the world during her time."

Or maybe not, Eden thought.

"There was this singer, Celia DeMille," Eden said. "Ever hear of her?" He frowned. "No, don't believe I've heard of her. Funny, you asked about the fire, though. There was actually a rumor that some disgruntled singer, somebody who got passed over for a role, might have set the fire herself. Or an even better rumor has it that she put a curse on the place! This being New Orleans and all. It fits!" he laughed.

Eden smiled as politely as she could manage. "Well, I've got to get back. Nice talking to you, uh…"

"Walter," he said. "Or just Walt."

"Eden." They shook hands.

"Look, I hope you don't mind my asking you this, but are you from here?"

He was a travel writer by profession, he told her. His newspaper back east was doing a series of articles about the first anniversary of Hurricane Katrina, coming up in a few months. Would she mind if he gave her a call in a month or so? He was organizing interviews with locals who had a story to tell.

"There's going to be a lot of us down here, I'm afraid," he said. "Every paper in the country. Looking for stories."

She told him she didn't think she'd be available; she was from here, but no longer lived here. And she wouldn't be in town then. She added, "I actually left before the storm. So, I wasn't here during all the flooding and everything. I don't think I'd be much help to you."

He told her she wouldn't have to be here in New Orleans, and even though she wasn't in town during the storm, he still might be able to use her for some background material, about life in the city before and how it had changed in the last year.

"Just think about it, and if you change your mind, please call me," he told her, and handed her his card.

"I will think about it. Thank you."

The day had grown hotter and the walk back along Rampart to the bus stop seemed longer. When the 88 arrived, she climbed the steps and again headed to the rear of the nearly empty bus.

Celia was still rooted in her mind. Her greatest rival, living here in the same city. She must have heard Donatella sing in the opera house, the place that refused her. Must have sat up in the colored section of the balcony witnessing the success of the woman in whose shadow she lived. Maybe the two women even passed each other at the market. Two divas, both great artists. One, world-famous, successful, and wealthy. The other, her fame short-lived, and she died poor and forgotten. No wonder Celia took those long walks by the river.

A sadness weighed on Eden at the thought of Celia's unfulfilled dream. What if she could have sung at that opera house? What if it had never burned? And what about those rumors? Did she have anything to do with that fire?

The card Walter had given her was still in the pocket of her jeans. When the bus pulled away from the stop, she reached for it and read it before putting it in her backpack. It read: WALTER MEYERHOLTZ, STAFF WRITER, THE *NEW YORK TIMES*.

"Hey! You back already?"

When Eden got off the bus, she had not walked more than thirty feet when she heard the voice and the sound of a truck horn. Randy Marvais leaned out of the driver's side window of a blue Ford pickup, its door panel emblazoned with a sign: MARVAIS & SON'S HAULING. He slowed to a crawl to keep pace with her walking. In the bed of his truck were piled scrap wood, flooring, metal scraps, a worn sofa, and two old refrigerators.

Randy parked the truck along a curb, got out, and leaned against the door, his sleeveless tank showing off the biceps and abs of a man on good terms with labor. He grinned, working a toothpick between his straight, pearl-white teeth. The gold grill he had worn before was gone.

Remembering what she'd taken from him during their last encounter, Eden felt merely annoyed. He was the last person she'd wanted to see.

"You back to stay this time?"

She held her hand up to her forehead. "Hey."

Even with his billed cap turned backward, she could tell that his dreadlocks, once his pride and joy, were completely shorn, giving him a clean-cut, almost collegiate, look. *Better looking now*, she thought. He seemed at least five years younger.

"So, like, what up? Everything cool with your people? What you doing back here?"

She told him about her aunt falling and breaking her hip. She wondered when he would bring up the money she took from him. But his next words surprised her.

"How your little brother doing? Up there in New York. He keeping his head down? Staying out of stuff?"

"Yeah," she said. "In school and everything. Got one more year."

She glanced at the sign on his truck. "Didn't know you had a son."

He looked at the sign, shrugged. "Yeah, he ain't but three. Live with his mama in Tulsa, but we not together. Anyway, had to name my business something, and Marvais and Son sound like a real company."

Why did her heart flutter at this news? He had a child. They'd had a child, too. In the brief time she had spent with him during her last trip, she'd seen no evidence of his fatherhood: no photos of a teething toddler taped to a refrigerator door, no rubber ducks in the bathroom, no stuffed toys stashed beneath the bed. Yet somebody called him daddy. Whoever the woman was, the baby-mama, she had done what Eden had refused to do: she had brought a child into the world.

"Well, that's real nice," she said, and looked away. "I gotta be getting back, see about Aunt Baby."

He opened the door to climb back into the truck. "You know, I was gonna give you that money. You didn't have to go and take it from me like that. Like you don't trust me or something."

Like I should, she thought. "I don't know what you're talking about."

He was silent a moment, then he gave her a slow, sly nod. "Yeah, OK, baby. Whatever."

She'd already started to walk away. "See you later."

He started the engine and began to slowly pull off as she began walking, then stopped his truck again and leaned out the window.

"Tell your little brother if he know what's good for him, he won't show his face here for a while."

"What do you mean?"

"You ain't heard?"

"Heard what?"

"Cops picked up two of them dudes was with your brother that night. Can you believe they still in town? Stupid. Wouldn't be surprised if they looking for your brother, too."

A shiver crawled up her spine. Randy was much older than the guys her brother hung out with before the flood, but he was the kind who knew the streets like a farmer knows his fields. He kept his ear to the ground, his finger to the wind. When something big was about to go down, he passed the word: "Don't go to that party at the rec center Friday," or, "I heard some things—stay away from the QuikTrip by the school after the game this Sunday." His predictions usually bore out on the evening news. He kept his instincts sharp and his antennae poised for signals of trouble. It was a trait she wished her brother had.

"What'd you hear?"

"Just that." Randy looked at his watch. "Customers waiting. Gotta get to these folks before noon. Set to make some big money today. Listen, a lot of stuff that went down right before the storm, well, they catching up to it now. For some folks, anyway. I'm just sayin'."

"Well, my brother didn't have nothing to do with that mess," she said, her tone unconvincing, even to her.

"OK." He smiled, shrugged. "You say so."

He turned his cap around, the bill facing the front. He was about to accelerate when he gave her one last appraising wink.

"Looking good, girl. Still. Like your hair. By the way, your auntie, she need any trash hauled? Tell her I'ma give her a special deal. Friends and family, you know."

CHAPTER 26

No accident or doctor's words were enough to keep Aunt Baby from returning to routine. Unaided by a cane, walker, or helping hand, she went to her garden twice and hobbled around her kitchen, checking on the pot of leftover gumbo Mildred had placed on the stove, occasionally sneaking in extra shrimp, sausage, and pepper until it suited her taste.

But to Eden's eyes, the fall had taken its toll. Maybe it was the lack of makeup or the too-thick, jet-black, curly wig, which looked as false as a clown's nose, but for the first time, Aunt Baby had begun to look her age, or as old as Eden suspected she must be. Her eyes, faded by glaucoma, looked more gray than brown. Her shoulders, thinned by bone loss, seemed even more sharply angled beneath her too-large wrap dress.

Whatever strength had faded from her body was redoubled in her sharp mind and stubborn will. "No, baby, over here, on this wall." Aunt Baby stretched a finger toward a white wall with French windows. The furniture delivery had been delayed by several hours, giving Aunt Baby time to add three more items to her list: a loveseat, brass floor lamp, and a sixty-inch flat-screen TV. By late afternoon, the new cinnamon velour sofa had been moved twice already, and its overstuffed pillows were stacked on the hardwood floor near the cream-colored loveseat and ottoman. She stood in one corner of the living room while Eden, Mildred, and a baby-faced delivery boy named James launched into a second hour of furniture arranging.

"No. No, that ain't working for me. Put it back over on this here wall like it was before. And those two lamps, yeah, that one and the new one. Put them over near that side table 'til I decide what to do with them."

James removed his billed LSU Tigers cap, pulled out a white handkerchief, and wiped sweat from his forehead. Mildred put both hands on her hips and shook her head as she sucked her teeth. "I'ma stand right here for a few minutes," she said. "Let me know when you make up your mind. After that, I'll give you two minutes to change it again. Then I'll move."

Eden flopped down on the loveseat and let out an exhausted sigh. Baby shuffled her walker toward the loveseat where Eden sat. "Y'all youngsters ain't worth a dime. I'm the one who just got out the hospital! An eighty-something-year-old woman got more energy than all of you."

Eighty-something? Mildred threw a glance to Eden, as if saying, "Do you believe what she just said?" Eden returned a silent response. "Let's just let that one go." If a little self-delusion made a woman well past ninety feel young, then God bless her.

Another hour later, the living room looked fit for living. Floor-to-ceiling silk curtains in a soft avocado hue hung over the windows facing Douglas Street. A massive flat-screen TV dominated the wall opposite the new sofa. The former dining surface—a metal folding table that Baby had found on a curb—had been banished to the side porch and replaced by a teak dining table that Baby had found at a clearance sale at Sears. By the time the furniture was arranged, the stock pot of gumbo nearly empty, and the dishes cleared, it was almost 9:00. Eden, Aunt Baby, Mildred, and even James—having been seduced by the smiles of fawning women and the aroma from the cast iron pot—sat in the newly appointed living room.

Aunt Baby let out a sigh. "Long day, tomorrow. Eden, before you leave town, I want you to go with me to the store, pick up a few things for the kitchen."

Eden held back a sigh. "Yes, ma'am."

"Lord, it's hot in here," Aunt Baby said. In a single motion, she whipped off her curly black wig and fanned herself with it. She scratched at the tight balls of bobby-pinned hair pressed against her scalp.

"What?" Aunt Baby said at Eden's wide eyes and dropped jaw.

"Nothing," Eden said, and James, apparently no stranger to the eccentricities of old age or odd relatives, didn't blink. He mentioned something about early morning deliveries, thanked the women for dinner, and explained the TV remote control once more to Aunt Baby while Eden began to nod off. When he was gone, Mildred yawned, putting a hand to her mouth. "I'm beat. Glad you back, Baby," she told Aunt Baby, and gave her a quick hug as she left for her room.

Eden and Aunt Baby sat longer, watching news on the new TV, flipping the remote control from one station to another, hypnotized by the bold, sharp colors and electronic dazzle of the oversized screen. Eden told her about her morning, her walk to the river, and her visit to the place where the opera house had been, leaving out the part about running into Randy and the warning about her brother. For the time being, she dismissed the whole thing as Randy's mean-spirited vengeance, his jaws all tight from her taking money from his stash. Nothing to worry about—probably. Instead, she told Aunt Baby how preoccupied she'd been with the scrapbook and the box of jewelry and medals.

Eden looked down at her hands, then up at Aunt Baby, a thoughtful, wistful shine in her eyes. "It's like this woman…this singer…I can't stop thinking about her. I even dream about her. And now that story Miss Mildred told me, about the slave's daughter and everything, and that necklace. It's just…It gives me goosebumps."

At Aunt Baby's puzzled look, Eden launched into the story Mildred told her. Aunt Baby listened attentively, then gave her a wizened, knowing nod. "You see, there? I knew something good would come out of you coming down to see me. That necklace, where is it now?"

"In my suitcase."

"When you get back, go find out how much it's worth. Then put it in a safe place. Get you a safe deposit box or something. Might be worth a whole lot, old as it is, especially if it's got some gold in it. Take it to a jeweler. See how much you can get for it. Then put that money in the bank. That'd be the best thing you could do for yourself. You and your brother."

Sell it? The thought tied her gut into a queasy knot. How often had she taken it out of the plastic Walmart bag and held it up to the light just to see light dance against the metal? She'd worn it a few times to the grocery store, and felt a little bit silly, but also a little bit special. Everything she'd ever owned paled in comparison. It was the only thing she had in her whole life that made her feel…worthy? Special? *Interesting.* That was it. When she put on the necklace, she no longer felt ordinary.

It also made her think about Celia, Miss Celia, as she had come to think of her. When she wore it, she swore she felt the whole weight of that woman's life, but it was a weight that made Eden's life lighter. Like everything would in the end be OK, like she and her brother would, someday, be just fine. Compared to Celia, she knew nothing of hardship. Even in her darkest times, Eden found reason to be grateful: she was not a black woman living in America just after slavery.

Standing in front of the plastic-trimmed dresser mirror in her bedroom, hands clasped beneath her breasts the way she'd seen singers do, she turned left and right as the gold flickered with each angle. Sometimes she'd sing the scale that Ernest Blessing had taken her through, from middle C up to the one high above the staff, low and soft, and then at the top of her voice, and spread her arms wide. And in her head, she heard applause, roaring and ringing in her ears. She felt the will of Isaac Freeman, stealing freedom. The boldness and genius of Celia DeMille. It was as if it all had all sifted down the long chute of history to land in the lap of Eden Malveaux.

Eden let out a sleepy yawn, open-mouthed and audible. But Aunt Baby made it clear she intended to be up for a while and wanted company.

She reached down for the two fingers of neat scotch in a Mason jar near her and pressed her backside deeper into the new sofa pillows. Eden longed for bed, but felt obliged. The woman had summoned her here and had paid for her company.

Aunt Baby held up her glass. "Eighteen-year-old scotch, single malt. You ever tasted it? Smooth as silk. Brought it back from England years ago. I hate to drink alone. Not that it ever stops me."

Sensing her cue, Eden got up to find a water glass and poured herself a quarter inch of the scotch. Not terrible. She wouldn't exactly call it smooth, not at all like the fruity zinfandel she sipped on the fire escape in New York, but silky, decent. They talked about the city, what Eden had seen of it. Volunteers with strange accents—Boston, France, and other distant ports—milling in and out of the Rite Aids, Walmarts, and restaurants that boasted a "Better-than-ever!" return to business. On Aunt Baby's block, three more neighbors had returned. But progress was deadly slow. "But we're here," Aunt Baby said. "Not going nowhere else, not in this world."

Eden yawned again. "Right. Well, I guess I'll be heading to bed."

Aunt Baby ignored her. "Sure miss Reginald, your daddy, even after all this time. I imagine you do, too."

Where did that come from? A beat passed before Eden spoke. "Yes, ma'am. I sure do."

"You know, your daddy and me, we fell out a long time ago. He ever tell you why?"

In a flash, Eden was twelve years old again, in her daddy's car parked outside Aunt Baby's house that October night. Sure, she'd gone to visit without permission, but what was the big deal? The woman was her great-aunt, his aunt, wasn't she? "Stay here in the car," he'd told her. Even now, she remembered how her father's deep baritone had cut the thick quiet like a jagged blade. Then, minutes later, the sound of a woman's high-pitched ranting and her father's desperate tears. He'd staggered back to the car, stone-faced and pale. Bewildered, she'd cowered beneath his rage. "You are not to set foot in that house again," he'd said.

Eden's heart pounded. "What? No. No, ma'am. He never told me."

Aunt Baby nodded, took another drink. "It's time you knew," she said. "It's time you knew what happened."

Aunt Baby hobbled up from her seat, poured herself another finger of scotch, and headed outside, as if whatever truth she was about to unleash required strong liquor and open air. Eden followed, carrying both drinks out to the front steps of the camelback shotgun that faced the levee, where she and her aunt had sat countless times before when Eden was small and her mother and father were both alive. In this corner of the city, the thick air sagged, muggy afternoons slid into sultry nights, soundless except for the lapping of water against the packed earth, dark except for a strip of moon-glade, a silver necklace of light strewn across the surface of the Mississippi.

The house was so near the levee, they could almost feel the motion of the current, the moist bands of river air a whisper's breath on the skin. At night, the water, ink-black and shimmery, calmed the mind. Daily calamities dissolved into lullabies of lapping waves, swallowed by the force and depth of a river as old as the continent across which it flowed. Eden eased a hand on Aunt Baby's back as the old woman lowered herself to the red brick steps. Aunt Baby perched her cane against a step and took another sip of scotch.

"I sure didn't mean for it to happen," she said. "How many times did I wish I could have that night back."

"What do you mean?"

Aunt Baby closed her eyes and leaned her head back. "I mean, I'm the one. Just as sure as I'm sitting here right now by this river. I'm the one."

"You're the one what?"

"I'm the reason she's gone. I'm the one caused your mama to die."

CHAPTER 27

He was a big, powerhouse of a man, your daddy, when he was young. Do you remember? Big shoulders, back arrow straight. Stood a head taller than your mama, even with her high-heeled shoes on. Your daddy could walk into a room, pretty as a prince, and folks would turn to look. Couldn't help themselves. Especially the ladies! Had that smooth skin, shiny hair. That wide grin with those even teeth. Thick eyebrows, long lashes like a girl's. And could sing, too! Sang like David Ruffin, that tall drink of water that sang lead with The Temptations on "My Girl." But you don't know nothing about that.

He was my only sister's only child, so when he went off to fight in Vietnam, baby-faced with his mama's milk still on his breath, we held ours till he got back.

But then what did he do? Signed up for a second tour! Said he couldn't just leave his buddies over there. Had to go see about 'em. Thirteen more months! His mama wanted to choke him. His daddy too, but Clarence didn't say much—it was Everline, your grandmama, who did a whole bunch of crying and moaning. But I loved that boy just like they did. Maybe even more. He just as well could have been my child.

It changed him, that war. Not that first tour, but the second. After that first one, sure, he had that look in his eyes, the look of a new man. Chest all puffed out like he could set the world on fire and nobody could tell him nothing because he was a man now. He'd found his meaning. Fighter. Protector. That first time put the steel in his spine that wasn't there before.

But when he came back the second time…well, I don't know what happened. Something he'd seen, but never talked about. Grief, maybe. Maybe he lost somebody, or something he knew he could never get back. Or maybe he just realized how foolish it all was, all that fighting and killing and dying. Anyway, he came back and it seemed all the light had gone out of his eyes. All that young-man light turned to shadow. He moped around, musta been a good year before he came back to himself.

Music. That's what got him going again. That, and your mama. First came the music, though. After that year, first thing he did, went up to the attic in Clarence's house and dusted off that trombone his daddy bought him in high school, and started playing in that group, that Fairview Marching Band that Brother Danny Barker and them put together at the Baptist Church.

Like most of those boys that came home from those jungles, he'd been wanting to get back to a city, so he started clubbing, partying all night long. Guess he figured he could forget what he needed to forget with some booty-shaking music, some whiskey, and pretty women. You know how men are. But I guess somebody told him if he wanted a good woman, not one of these young silly fools, but a good one with some good sense, he'd better head over to the church.

So, he did. Slapped some of that English Leather on his face, dressed to the nines every Sunday morning. Avondale was hiring, so he had got him a pipe-fitter job down at the shipyard, making good money. Even bought hisself a Deuce-and-a-Quarter, secondhand, of course.

Your daddy was proper-speaking, articulate-like, don't know where he got that from—not from Clarence and Everline. Talked like a teacher. Always correcting my speech, even when he was little. "Auntie, don't say that, say this." Two things got his neck out of joint: racist talk and bad grammar, and don't let them come out the same mouth! One time, a white man, foreman down at the shipyard, told him, "You got to be the most up-pity-est Nigra I ever seen." Your daddy said, "believe you mean most uppity, not most uppity-est. If you'd paid attention in school, you would know two superlatives don't belong together in the same sentence." I'll never forget it. The man gave him a proper reply—a fist across your daddy's face! That was the only fight he had, so far as I know. Or at least the only one outside a Vietnam jungle.

When he started singing baritone in the choir, well, you shoulda seen that thick circle of sisters buzzing around your daddy, like they was flies and your daddy was a plate of ribs at a picnic! A handsome single black man in a midnight blue Buick Electra 225? Tall, too? And just back from fighting a war, with no woman, no babies, and no plans? Shoot. Believe me, those sisters had plans for him. From day one.

Talise wasn't one of those round-the-way girls he'd took up with right after. She was a dainty little thing, quiet, shy. Fragile, I would call her. Something about her that was...what am I trying to say? Breakable. You could just see it. Something about her that just seemed like she could easily break.

Of course, your daddy fell for her. She kinda reminded me of a old-time Hollywood actress, like maybe Diana Sands, but I don't suspect you know nothing about her. Talise didn't line up for him like the others did—she stood off to the side in the shadow. He found her. I must say, she had a smile that could melt steel, even the steel in a soldier's spine. So, maybe it was her smile that reeled him in, slipping around the hooks and claws of all them other girls. Anyway, it wasn't long before they were...what they call it? A item.

I think about what it was between your daddy and Talise. Now, your daddy—he was a sergeant in the marines, in charge of a lot of men. Never talked about the buddies he had over there, the ones he went back to be with. Maybe they didn't make it back, I don't know. I had a feeling something went down over there in Vietnam, something that made him feel like he fell short. Anyway, Talise, well, she was somebody who looked like she needed protecting, and Reginald, he was the one to do it.

They made the cutest couple at the wedding, him looking every bit *a soldier, her as pretty as a brand-new rose. Coupla years later, you was born. My nephew acted like he was the first man in history to father a child! You'da thought he was the one who carried you in his belly for nine months. For three months, he wouldn't let nobody touch you lest they wash they hands first! Couldn't take his eyes off you. Yessir. If that war took the light from his eyes, you put it back in.*

And what was I doing all this time? Half of it, I don't even remember. All I know was, I wanted to be free. Didn't want to be tied down to nobody and nothing. And I wasn't.

I traveled the world. It was a damn good time to be a woman like me, a woman who wanted her own life. I had a good figure, good bones. I wore tight hip-huggers, halter tops, and big hoop earrings. Had me a Afro out to here! Or sometimes, when the man was rich enough and the occasion called for it, I wore furs and silk. Like I said before, I was a fox, and a free one at that! Didn't burn my bra, but at no time could I tell you where it was. Once I saw how men looked at me, baby, you best believe I played that card. Those young white girls in the movies didn't have nothing on me—I did as I pleased, when and where and with who I pleased. I worked here and there, enough to make my way, but mostly I lived off of successful men. Oh, I know folks said things about me and what I was doing. Half of 'em wasn't true. But truth to tell, half of 'em was. And that was plenty.

Well, as you know, your granddaddy and grandmama Clarence and Everline, they divorced, and a few years later, your grandmama, she died. I miss her, my sister, to this very day.

I was gone a few months after your grandmama passed, can't remember where, when Reginald phoned me that your mama, Talise, was sick and they didn't know what it was. She'd just pass out on the floor, eyes rolled all back in her head. Seizures, they said. Took a while to figure it out, but there wasn't no cure. Doctor changed her diet and prescribed something, but the bottom line was she needed looking after, needed to be careful about where she went, what she ate, how much sleep she got, how hot or cold it was. She needed to be watched.

And Reginald did all that. Then years passed and everything looked

OK. Talise seemed to be doing all right. Then came a time when Reginald had to go out of town, check on one of his Marine Corps buddies who'd had a heart attack in Georgia. I was just back from Lyon, over in France. Had just got divorced from my second husband, Jordan, and I was in New Orleans, cooling my heels, so to speak. Had me a little small place over a laundromat over by City Park. Talise hadn't had a seizure in years, but he was careful with her, just the same.

I don't recall how old you were, but it was the summer you went away to Blue Bird camp at that place up near Natchitoches, your first trip away from home. When he had to leave for a few days to go to Valdosta, he asked me if I would stay with your mama. I said, sure, I would.

He didn't know about my habit. Hell, I did my best to hide it. But I wasn't in no shape to take care of myself, let alone another human being.

At first, he was gone only four days. Called every day. We got along fine, me and Talise. She soft-scrambled eggs for breakfast and I pressed and curled her hair. At nights, we'd play gin rummy or watch the Johnny Carson Show, *snacking on buttered popcorn, Schweppe's ginger ale for her, Jack Daniels for me. But then his buddy, turns out, had to have surgery. Reginald stayed there in Valdosta, asked if I could stay longer with Talise. I said that'd be OK. I didn't have nothing else to do. At least, not until he came along.*

Tommy Mercer. He was a man I always had a warm spot for. If you ever saw him, you'd know what I mean. Jazz musician. Worked as a plumber till he got a job playing with Count Basie's band. Hell of a drummer. Good-looking was only half of it. You know I liked tall men, but Tommy wasn't but a coupla inches taller than me, and wasn't even the handsomest man. Still, he had something, that thing you just can't put your finger on. Style. Confidence, maybe, or charm, that made my legs go weak and my brain go soft. Smooth, that's what he was, had that sexy smile that could coax you into a burning house! Wore those nice gaberdine suits and those stingy brim hats with a feather in the band, and you know how I loved a man who knew how to wear a hat! We'd had a thing, a while back. I shoulda known better. The man was trouble on two legs looking for an open door. He phoned, said he was in New Orleans for a hot minute. Had a night off, talkin' 'bout did I want to go check out Lionel Hampton's band over at the Saenger. Stupid me. I went. Things got ugly after that.

Long story, short, I told Talise I was going out for the evening, and she seemed fine with that. He sent a cab for me and I left and went to Tommy's—he had a room at the Butterfield Inn out on the highway past the parish line. We didn't never make it to Lionel Hampton's show. I stayed three nights. I had been clean, sober, sort of, since I got back from France. Planned on keeping it that way. But there I was, back in the devil's den.

It wasn't something I planned, and like I said, I can't tell you how many times I wished I could take back that night I left Talise. Finally, I came to my senses. But by the time I got myself straight and back to Talise, she'd already been taken to the hospital. One of her girlfriends from church kept calling and couldn't get her, decided to go over to her house. Don't know how long she'd been on the floor—non-responsive, they said—before they got her over to the emergency room at Charity.

I rushed over there, could hardly breathe, thinking on the way, Lord, please… Well, she survived that one, no thanks to me. When your daddy got back, he liked to had a fit. Talise pulled through, but she just wasn't the same. It was like it just took too much out of her. I felt so bad, I can't tell you. I couldn't even bring myself to ask your daddy to forgive me. I wouldn't have, if I'da been him. We didn't speak after that. He went his way, I went mine.

Talise was all right for a while. But she had two more seizures that year, and it was that last one that she didn't come back from.

Anyway, the years passed. Your daddy and I were like strangers.

I will never forget that night you wandered over to my house. How old were you? Twelve? Thirteen? Eyes all wide, curious. You reminded me of myself when I was your age. Seem like you were just itching to see what was happening in the world, and how you might fit into it. Didn't surprise me a bit when your daddy showed up, mad as a hatter, calling me every-thing but a child of God. I had a feeling I shoulda sent you home, but I didn't. I could see so much of your daddy in you, I guess I just wanted a piece of that memory, whatever tiny little bit I could get.

And then you sang something, do you remember? I put on a record, don't remember what it was, but something your daddy liked, something by…who was it? Sarah Vaughan, I think. You sang along with it—Lord, that voice of yours!—and I swear, it was like I had my nephew back, my sister's baby boy. If I'd lost Reginald, at least I had some of him back, through you.

I'm telling you all this because it's time. I don't want to leave this earth with that on me, that unfinished piece of business. I wanted you to know the truth.

Your daddy was a good man, a damn good one. Took care of his own: you, your mama, your step-mama, your brother, even me. Yes, that's right. Your daddy was always good to me. What happened between us was my fault and I don't want you to think for a minute that I didn't know that. He had every right to treat me the way he did after everything went down.

Damn near broke my heart when he passed. I remember it so well. I knew he was sick all that time, but I couldn't bring myself to go. We hadn't spoke, like I said, in years. Finally, I just got up the nerve. I decided, even with all that bad blood between us, I was gonna go see him before he got away from me.

And am I glad I did. You were working that day in the Quarter and the hospice nurse let me in. I went into his bedroom to see him and I knew right away it wouldn't be long. But your daddy wanted to talk. He smiled, seemed like he was…not just happy, relieved to see me. Like he'd been waiting for me. You know what he talked about? You. How pretty you sang. How he had hopes for you. Your brother too, but mostly you, I guess because he believed his son would be all right with you looking after him. But who would look after you? It was you he hoped for, prayed for. Hoped that singing would open up your life, prayed it would take you away from what you knew, and to places you'd never dreamed you'd go.

I'm also telling you because I want you to know what it took me all this time to figure out. Took me all these years to learn to just let the past go.

Just telling you all this now—and by the way, you the first person I told all this to—makes me feel like some kinda heavy weight been lifted from my chest, and I can breathe again. I don't want you to be as old as I was before I learned what I learned. Leave the past, just let it go. Forgive yourself the way you might forgive somebody you love. I was who I was, I did what I did, and there's a time when you gotta move on. I wish somebody hadda told me that when I was your age.

I didn't tell you all that to upset you! Oh, Lord! Why you crying, baby?

CHAPTER 28

Words spilled; tears fell. And once she began, Eden couldn't stop. Aunt Baby listened, leaning forward, pulling at the tangled yarn of memory and truth. Eden wanted to tell her great-aunt everything, so she started at the beginning.

Talise Malveaux. It was true: her mother had been a pretty woman. Sweet, quiet. Always kind. Eden didn't know who Diana Sands was, but yes, movie star beauty, that was her memory of Talise. Thick, curly brown hair, swept up around her forehead. Deep dimples, bright, wide eyes. Her skirts, wide swirls of periwinkle blue, her favorite color. And smelling of something sweet and flowery—jasmine, lemon. Something like that.

"The fits." That's what they had called them. Only once had Eden seen it happen, her mother stretched out on the black and white polka-dotted rug in front of the living room TV, her hands reaching for something unseen, her eyes unfocused and showing mostly white. Eden's father told her, "Your mama is sick."

But Eden didn't know what that meant. And when Talise was finally gone, her absence, so final and unrelenting, was as present as a life itself.

Two years passed, father and daughter leaning on each other, each a light in the other's cave. But from the first minute Eden saw Ethel Kinsley, her father's new wife-to-be, she knew the difference the woman would bring to their lives would be a difference she could not bear. Nothing had been calculated, but things happened, first one thing, then another, until Ethel was gone.

"I didn't know why I...I just wanted to..." Eden looked away, shook her head, and then sat up straight, catching a tear on the tip of her finger.

After Talise, their teamwork—father and daughter managing the minutia of breakfast, dinner, homework, dishwashing, and house-cleaning—had been her joy, her way of setting the world upright again.

"So, I did...it wasn't on purpose. I didn't realize she would just up and leave like that and never come back."

Her father had instructed Eden to pick up the medicine from the drug counter at the pharmacy two blocks away. "Take it to Ethel's bed," where she spent most days.

"The blues," he'd told her. It was humid that summer morning. From the lace-curtained kitchen window, sun streaked across her father's creased brow as he searched his mind for an explanation. Eden spooned herself a mouthful of oatmeal while her father poured his coffee and added one lump of sugar.

"Sometimes," he said quietly, "women give birth and just when they should be feeling the greatest joy, they have the opposite feeling." But a bout of post-baby blues was nothing to worry about. Ethel would snap out of it soon and be back to her old self. The medicine would help.

Meanwhile, Eden washed dishes, made beds, and retrieved nearly burned pot roast or over-baked chicken from the oven as mute, blank-eyed Ethel stared at a television screen whose dancing images had no effect. She slept most days and all night, ignoring Reginald Jr.'s wailing; her own child's crying was unrecognizable. It was Eden who hoisted the baby boy up on her shoulder. It was Eden who changed

Pampers and warmed milk and tested the temperature with a drop or two on the back of her hand before feeding him.

And it was Eden who had forgotten to go to the drug store. Just forgotten, innocently, the way you forget to lock a door or hang up a coat.

She had forgotten. Hadn't she? Or had she, willfully, without a thought to consequence, ignored her father's request, the one thing he'd asked of her? "Be sure to stop at the pharmacy after school. It should be ready tomorrow. You'll see. It will help."

A week passed before she remembered she hadn't made it to the pharmacy. Her father, pulling double shifts at the shipyard, assumed his daughter, unfailing in her obedience, had done what she was told to do.

"It wasn't on purpose. Really. I just forgot."

So, when Ethel's gray houndstooth coat, black patent leather purse, and the fourteen ten-dollar bills kept in the blue Tupperware bin in the cabinet above the kitchen sink went missing, it seemed a little odd. Ethel's departure on the noon Greyhound, leaving only a note scribbled on the back of the electric bill envelope—*Took the bus to see my sick Aunt Elnora in Pine Bluff*—somehow made no sense. The only aunt she'd ever talked about had died, she'd said, years ago. When Eden's father came home, he questioned her. "What happened? She's gone? Where? What did she tell you?"

Later, when it was clear that there was no sick aunt in Pine Bluff, her father called the police.

There was nothing to be done. Her father tried for months to find her. But she was a grown woman who decided to leave. Not missing, just gone.

Eden looked across the water when a tugboat on the river made a low sound. She turned up the glass of scotch to her mouth and drained it.

Both women were silent for a moment, then Aunt Baby said,

"Ummphf. Is that what's been troubling you so? You think your step-mama left and never came back because of something you didn't do?"

Eden shrugged, turning away as more tears fell. "I let him down. He wanted to be a grandfather. When I got pregnant, I couldn't go through with it. And then, Miss Ethel and the medicine. He trusted me and I failed him. Again. It was my fault. His son, my baby brother, grew up without his mama." Aunt Baby reached a hand up to Eden's shoulder and rested it there. "Oh, child. I could tell something wasn't right with you. I could tell it every time I saw you, every time since the day your daddy died. You been carrying something. What did he say to you at the end? What was the last words he spoke?"

Eden remembered aloud—she'd bent her head low to hear him, his voice hoarse but whisper-soft. His eyes locked on hers, his hand gripping her arm. And his strained words, "There's some..." was the last sound she ever heard him make.

"He never got the whole sentence out. I've racked my brain ever since then, wondering, *What was he trying to tell me?* All this time, I've wondered if what he wanted to say to me coulda made anything different for me, any easier for us."

Aunt Baby shifted her hips against the step. "Let me tell you something," she said. "When your daddy was sick and I went to see him, I didn't know what to expect. But whatever happened, I was ready to accept it. I didn't know if he would even let me come in the house. But as soon as I took a seat next to his bed and saw him smile, I knew I did the right thing. I'd held on to so much for so long. Your daddy taught me to let it all go. Because he had. He reached across and took my hand and squeezed it. I knew he didn't have much strength, so I squeezed back hard so he wouldn't have to. I bent low to hear him so he wouldn't have to talk loud.

"The one thing I want to tell you is what he said to me. Do you know what that something was? Just three words. And I believe they were the same three words he would have said to you, if he could have.

I'm sure of it. He was telling me he knew. He understood I did the best I could, I did the best I knew how to do. Until I knew better.

"Just three words, in a whisper." She sighed. "That's what set me free."

PART III

CHAPTER 29

She arrived twenty-eight minutes early. It was one of those rare days in the city when the machinery of New York transit hummed; trains arrived in stations and departed from platforms with clock-like precision, their connections as synchronized as a Broadway chorus line.

A stickler for punctuality, Ernest Blessing promised her one hour, no more and no less. For free voice lessons donated to a promising talent, the least she could do was abide by his rules.

She could have sat in the foyer and waited, as she had done before their first meeting. But today, her mood was too buoyant for the dark, windowless hallway of embossed, fading wallpaper; it was warm, a beautiful sky-blue day, a day to be outside. Sitting at an outdoor table at the Chesterfield Café a half block away, she sipped a hibiscus iced tea.

Twenty minutes before the hour. Giving in to reflex, she dug a hand into the side pocket of her purse. Nothing, of course. It had been empty for three weeks. God knows, of everything he'd asked her to do—listen to the German language tapes, practice the scales he'd taught her, and play the CD of the new song enough times to memorize the whole thing, including when and where she would breathe—the quitting smoking part was the hardest. What had he said to her?

"Either smoke, or sing. Take your pick. But if you have even one cigarette between now and the next lesson, don't even bother to come back. Ever. And don't think I won't know."

A walk around the block. It would clear her mind, shift her thoughts from the nicotine craving, give her more time to run the opening eight bars of the Mozart once more through her head. And then, there was this new city to see.

Since returning to New York a month ago, everything had changed, or at least it seemed that way. Now, her mind felt sharper, the air around her lighter, her eyes clearer, the better to see what had been there all along. The cut-out rectangles of sky between bank towers and hotel rooftops, once pale compared to the wide swaths of Louisiana blue that seemed to go on forever, now blazed an electric hue to rival anything in her memory. And since she arrived months ago, reeling from the storm and displacement, she hadn't noticed that there was great street food all over this town, the warmish air spicy with scents to make your mouth water. Not so much the Creole gumbos or Cajun jambalayas of home (she'd yet to find that here), but the Mediterranean falafels and lamb-filled gyros searing on portable grills on 66th, the garlicky sausages from the kitchens of the Italian delis, and the sweet fried plantains from the Cuban restaurant at 52nd sent a waft of aromas thick enough to taste.

Then there was the music—everywhere she turned.

Of course, at home, there had always been amazing music, before and after Katrina. The genius tenor sax player riffing "Sleepy Time Down South" near the Café DuMonde. The strutting brass bands, showboating for the tourists in Jackson Square. *This is what we didn't lose. This is what no storm can wash away*, their horns announced. Music, always the city's lifeblood, now pumped its beating heart.

But in New York City, the music took her to unfamiliar landscapes. Walking along the periphery of Central Park at dusk, she'd heard the strains of an orchestra—trumpets, trombones, clarinets, strings—and it transported her across oceans and borders to places she could never have imagined outside her limited world of TV movies and the odd exotic dream. Near the bus stop, five men playing clarinets, a fiddle, a trumpet, and a bass—when she'd asked, they'd called themselves a Klezmer band—made her think of subtitled films set in old-timey Europe. Once, in the depths of the Columbus Circle subway tunnel, she'd been awestruck by a duo of two young violinists, their dazzling scales bouncing off subway tiles, darting back and forth between them, something by J. S. Bach, according to the cover of the music book. She dropped two of her hard-earned tip dollars into their plastic bucket before she'd even realized she'd opened her purse.

It wasn't as if she'd never heard classical music before. There'd been yearly trips to the symphony during school, where an orchestra on a stage far below her balcony seat ground out Mozart and Beethoven. But here, it was within stumbling distance. She knew what it was like to collect your pay from the change purses of strangers. With a real job, boosting somebody else's stash made her feel powerful, grateful, and for the first time in ages, generous.

The "real job" was something she couldn't imagine a year ago, and even when it was offered to her, she scarcely believed it. She'd quit her McDonald's job when she was sure she didn't need it anymore. It had taken her two auditions with David Kim, and hours of memorizing, by rote, six songs—two show tunes, a short aria by Menotti, two spirituals, and a German art song. All that, and a promise from Kim that she could sing near the front of Maestro's dining room and not near the seventy-third-floor windows.

On her first night, her hands shook so violently, she had to pin them behind her back. The fourth night, after her "You'll Never Walk Alone" left a table of six swooning, the one-hundred-dollar tip left her stunned and stuttering effusive, incoherent thanks.

She was walking differently now, literally. Blessing had been giving her grief about her posture and bearing. "Pull those shoulders back! Why do you walk with them all hunched in and your head down? If you don't have pride in who you are, then you must pretend." It made a difference in the singing, he claimed. The man had a point. Clearer lungs and wide-spread shoulders made her high tones ring bell-like above the staff. And who knew? A new heft boosted her volume while a new spark lit her top octave. Intakes of breath came easier and stayed longer. Now, after only a month, even when she wasn't singing, she found herself standing as if she were; if she felt the creeping onset of a lazy slouch, she'd snap back her shoulders, as if Blessing's own hands had reached around to grab them.

Her head high and shoulders square, she made the final turn around the block, singing the first line of the Menotti aria. This morning in the shower, her voice booming above the spray, she had worked out some of the phrasing. And still singing while she poured instant pancake batter onto the griddle, she caught her brother's approving half-smile before he turned up a glass of orange juice.

"Somebody feeling good today," he said.

Yes, she was. The music lessons, the job, the money—they changed everything. But ever since that talk with Aunt Baby, she'd felt as if a boulder had been lifted from her back.

Three words: *I forgive you.*

If she wasn't convinced that Aunt Baby was right about her father's final words, she at least believed it was possible. Reginald Malveaux, Sr. was a proud man, but a forgiving one. Whether he spoke his forgiveness in his final moments with his daughter no longer mattered. Of course he had forgiven her. She could not believe that for all these years she had doubted that simple, irrevocable truth.

So, she packed those words with her and took them back to New York, along with the last thing Aunt Baby said.

"It was you he hoped for, prayed for. Hoped that singing would open up your life, prayed it would take you away from what you knew, and to places you'd never dreamed you'd go."

Nothing could have meant more to her. And nothing could have put her more squarely on a path that led to Ernest Blessing.

When she knocked on his door, precisely at 2 p.m., he gave her the closest thing to a smile she had seen.

"Ah, you are prompt," he told her, opening the door to the music studio. "Let's get to work."

It was the most humiliating experience of her life.

What had she gotten herself into? She'd spent hours practicing the scales, the breathing exercises, and the Mozart. Blessing lit into her from the moment she opened her mouth.

"No, no, listen," he said, tapping on a black piano key. "Listen to the B-flat. Find it, the center of the pitch. Did you use the pitch pipe I gave you? Here, now. Once again, up the scale, there should be no break. And remember what I...no, no. Legato there! Sustain the tone throughout! Support it, from the diaphragm! Put your hand on your belly, not there, yes, there! Now, in! Did you do the crying exercises I gave you? To smooth the transition from the chest voice to the head voice? Did you do it? Clearly, not."

"Well, I thought I..."

"Your muscles are not relaxed. You cannot sing if you have tension in your neck and throat! And you're still taking your chest voice up way too high! Did you warm up slowly today before you came? You couldn't have."

Eden said, "I did. I did warm up. I practiced. I thought I was doing what you said."

"And just because the eighth notes are short doesn't mean they don't have to be in tune! Begin again. And one and two and three and four..."

They worked for another ten minutes. Finally, Blessing stopped. "You are not prepared. This lesson is over."

Eden was dumbfounded. "Uh, what? Over?"

"Over. Don't come back unless you are prepared."

She headed home, breathless, through a fog of tears. She would call Blessing. She should have known better; she was hopeless. Rehearsing her speech in the bathroom, she told her reflection, "Thank you, but I just can't do it. I just can't. Sorry for all your trouble."

But days later, when she recovered from the downward pull of self-deprecation and dejection, she took out the pitch pipe, the tape recorder where she'd captured the exercises Blessing had given her. *Why had he been so mean?* She decided that rather than think about that, she'd get busy. Forty minutes each morning, and an hour each night before bed. When her brother rushed into her bedroom as she was doing the crying technique, wondering if she was OK—"You sound like some cat or something!"—she figured she was doing it right.

The next lesson went so much better, she wondered if Blessing was paying attention. He listened to her scales and exercises and didn't complain once. When she finished the spiritual, ending on the high C with a fading pianissimo, he looked at her and nodded.

"That's enough for now. Sit for a minute. Let's talk."

She followed him into another room with large windows and high, wood-beamed ceilings, lined with books. Walking behind him and watching him walk, his back not quite straight, his sluggish gait favoring his right leg, she thought he seemed frail, but in an almost indestructible way, like Aunt Baby. Clearly, he had once been a taller man, robust—handsome, even. With his nut-brown skin glowing in the lamplight of the study, he reminded her of pictures she'd once seen of an Ethiopian emperor. In their lessons, he'd never told her much about himself, but she noted his tastes; he favored dark colors—browns and blues—for his walls and for his suits. His thick eyeglass lenses suggested a life-long love of reading, like her father. His white shirts buckled with too much starch, and he drank strong oolong tea from pots as weighty as doorstops.

From somewhere in the apartment, a tea kettle whistled—two tones in harmony—and he disappeared into what had to be a kitchen. From a small iron pot on the tray of a low coffee table, he poured tea into two cups and handed her one, then gestured for her to sit in a leather armchair opposite him.

He wanted to know just what it was that she wanted. When she looked puzzled, he explained, "From your singing. What do you want from it? Why are we doing all this?"

She took a breath, thinking. "Uh, I don't know...I mean. Um, because...I want to get better at it? 'Cause, you know, I just want to see how good...how well I can do?"

His thinning brows furrowed. "You're asking me? Or are you telling me?"

She smiled, a little embarrassed. How many times had her father warned her about making declarative sentences sound like questions?

"Sorry. Yes, sir. I want to see how much better I can get. I mean, I've always sung. But, um...I've never thought about singing *this* kind of music. The more I hear, the more I like it. And the music is real pretty, and I guess I like the way I sound now. Since I've been working with you, sir."

He nodded, took a sip of tea. "And then what?"

"Beg your pardon?"

"I mean, after you see how much better you can become, what then? What will you do?"

She pondered this. The man was asking a fair question to which she had not given a second's thought. The music lessons had gotten her out of that horrible McDonald's uniform and put more money in her purse, but to hope for more? It seemed greedy. She was satisfied. When, before now, had she ever loved arriving at work? Getting dressed for it, putting on the slim, dark skirts, the flattering, close-fitting tops, the deep red thrift-store pumps that looked almost brand-new. The makeup. She had a job where she could do what she knew— waiting tables—and what she loved—singing—and look good doing it. What more was there to hope for?

"Uh, well, things are going pretty good at the restaurant. At Maestro's. Seem like they like me there. If I could, you know, stay there for a while, it'd be great."

"I see." He tapped his fingernails on the arm of his chair. "Well, your lessons are going better than I expected. However…"

Better than he expected? Eden thought. *After that last lesson?*

And then he released a litany of her faults. Her placement was inconsistent, her vowels still somewhat flat, and her consonants mushy. The German tapes were helping with her pronunciations in the song she had chosen, but the language might be a bridge too far for someone who clearly found her native tongue a struggle. Nonetheless, her breath control, while not good, was better; she was finding tone and beginning to understand the skill in sustaining the legato line. But her grammar, her diction…Language was part of being a singer. "You have to make it organic," he told her. "You have to want to speak correctly." She offered a resigned nod.

"My father," she said. "He was always on me—like you are, sir—about how I talk, and everything." She told him about the time her father looked bug-eyed after she'd used a word that didn't exist. "There's no such word as 'conversate!'" he'd nearly screamed at her. "He made me write fifty different sentences using the right word, 'converse.'" It had taken her two hours.

Blessing smiled and asked her what her father did for a living. When she told him, she could see that he was interested. He slowly sipped tea as she talked. She told him how her father had been a shipyard worker, that he loved music and loved to read, and sang in the church choir. He'd died fairly young, and left her with a younger brother to raise alone. When she mentioned the storm, the evacuation, the cities she and her brother had traveled to before they ended up in New York, she saw sympathy in his eyes.

"I…I had no idea," he said. "Your friend, Evan, never mentioned this to me. He said you were from the South, but I didn't know…"

"Yes, sir," she said. "I was born and raised in New Orleans."

"Well, that's interesting," he said. "I have been in New York most of my life, but I was born, like my mother and father, in Hattiesburg, Mississippi. Not far away from New Orleans."

Mississippi? She had never figured him for a southerner.

"A shame about what happened in New Orleans." He shook his head. "Such history. But those people, those politicians…" he stopped, looked up at her. "I sincerely hope that you and your brother are faring well here."

She gave him her stock answer: "We're OK. It's been hard, we're getting by."

Unlike almost everyone else who mentioned the storm to her, he seemed satisfied with her answer and did not elaborate. There was no *Where were you when it happened?* Or *Is it as bad as they say?* She appreciated that. Instead, he said, "Well, let me tell you why I wanted us to have this chat."

He put his teacup down, folded his hands in his lap, and crossed one long leg over the other. His suit was old-looking: out of style, a little shiny, made with a dark gray fabric with knife creases and bagging around his thin legs. But his black shoes, an old wing-tip style like her father had worn, held the shine of mirrored glass.

"I have always loved the human voice," he began. "But I haven't always been a vocal coach."

He came to New York from Mississippi in 1962 to study piano, he said. He was good enough for a concert career, but for a black man, that was out of the question, even if he had the financial backing, which he did not. So, he became a coach and accompanist, working with some of the greatest singers in the country—from Broadway to the Metropolitan Opera—as they prepared for recitals, shows, and performances around the world.

"I say this, not with pride, but with confidence. I am recognized as one of the three or four most effective coach/accompanists in this city," he said. "So I didn't take you on so that you could continue to sing show tunes in restaurants while prime rib and filet mignon are being plated in the kitchen. I prepare my students for something greater than that." He leaned back in his chair. "I have told you what is lacking in you," he said. "Now, let me tell you what is not."

What she had, he said, was the absolute most important thing. "In the vast carousel of attributes every great singer needs, voice is the lion's share," he said. "You have one of the purest, most naturally beautiful vocal instruments I have ever heard."

But, he added, not every singer gifted with it can learn to use it properly, to fulfill its greatest potential.

"After that first lesson, I would never have believed you would have come so far in this time," he told her. "Your voice, while impressive, is extremely raw. You had no technique, of course. You don't speak well. And frankly, there is nothing about you that suggested you would be a good candidate for the kind of work we are doing.

"But your friend Mr. Smallwood called and asked me to give you another hearing. When you came back, not much had changed in your voice, but there was something in your eyes, some need, some desire that hadn't been there before.

"You have worked hard. But if all you desire is to be a singing waitress, please tell me. We will end our association now. You have already learned enough to, shall we say, sing over someone's supper. But if you see something greater for yourself, we can continue."

She didn't know what to say. She thought of the woman in yellow in the cathedral, the voice that filled it up, pouring into every space like an invading sun. The voice that seemed to come from the core of the earth.

"Yeah—I mean, yes. I'd like to learn as much as I can. I'd like to be a singer, for real."

All right, he said. If she was committed to becoming better, then she should consider the next step: there was an audition coming up that might interest her. The Fedak Family Memorial Scholarship Foundation was designed to help promising young artists like her, with more talent than means to explore it.

"They are an angel organization," he explained. "The competition is coming up in a few weeks. The winner will win a full scholarship to the Manhattan School of Music, plus a modest stipend for living expenses."

He changed his sitting position, leaning slightly toward her. "This family is a big patron of the arts, and of singing, in particular. Ellen Fedak—she's the head of the organization—is descended from a family of Polish immigrants who came to the states through Ellis Island in the 1920s. Her mother was a singer. But when the family came to America, they made a fortune in manufacturing housewares. They've made a point of traveling around the country to find people who have unusual talent, but no means to develop it."

"A month ago, I would have said there is no way, but I now believe you could be ready for it."

She stared. *Was he crazy? Study at the Manhattan School of Music?* Not that she'd ever heard of the place, but it was in New York, so it had to be fancy. Not possible. Even if this scholarship paid for everything, how would she eat? And there was her brother to support. And that word, "stipend." What did that even mean?

Her brother. In a year, he'd be graduated, able to get a real job. Who knew what he would do? Go back to New Orleans, probably, even though that might spell disaster for him. Still, he'd be grown, no longer her responsibility. It would be time to let him go to live his own life.

But her biggest concern was not how she would live off whatever funds the scholarship provided. She would be in a place with people who were more…what? Educated? Cultured? Smart? All that. She already knew she'd be as welcome as a cockroach at a banquet, as Aunt Baby would say.

The Schubert song she'd chosen, "Nacht und Träume," or in English, "Night and Dream," would work, he told her. It was a tough one and required a lot of control. "And it's in German. Difficult for someone just learning the language. There are easier songs. What is it about that particular one?"

She looked down and laced her fingers together in her lap. *Did you bring any Schubert?* She hadn't seen the woman who'd answered his door since that day, and later learned she was a former student visiting

Blessing and temporarily helping out. Eden hoped she never saw her again. But in a way, the woman had helped her. It was weeks before she'd realized the haunting music the woman sang at the cathedral, the first song on the program of Miss Celia's concert at Beckstein Hall in London, the music in her dream, had been that song by Schubert. Then at the river, the first notes from the calliope on the riverboat were the opening notes of the song.

A series of coincidences. It happens. But everywhere, it seemed, the damn song kept showing up. But for Blessing, she offered the simplest explanation. "I heard this lady singing it in a church, and I liked it. And then I saw it on a program by this famous singer who lived a long time ago—like a hundred years. A black lady."

Eden fingered the edges of the locket around her neck. She told him about her great-aunt, sifting through the neighborhood rubble left behind in the destruction, finding a box with the necklace and scrapbook belonging to a singer.

"This singer, she was real famous, I guess. She sang at the White House like a bunch of times and even for the king of England. She sang all over. Anyway, I been reading about her, this woman—Celia DeMille is her name—in the scrapbook, and—"

"Excuse me, what did you say her name is?"

"Her name is Celia DeMille."

"Celia DeMille? And this necklace you're wearing belonged to her? And you have her scrapbook?"

She smiled. "Yes, sir."

Blessing's eyes filled with tears. He turned his face toward the window, paused a moment and removed his glasses. With a handkerchief, he wiped his eyes.

"Oh, my dear," he said. "Oh, my dear."

CHAPTER 30

With the summer nearing and the nights warming, the rooftop patio
of Maestro's Bistro and Bar was open and packed with diners decked
out in silks and linens. Subtle whiffs of Chanel and Jean Patou battled
in the open air. Giant pots of ferns and yucca plants flanked glass-
topped tables and heavy wrought iron chairs. Servers balancing plates
wove their way between them. Earlier, inside the main room after
serving a table for four, Eden had held her lyric soprano to a modest
mezzo-forte, floating it just above the din. But even before the second
verse of "Send in the Clowns," customers from the bar at the front to
the windows in the back had sighed, dreamy-eyed and wistful. That
song alone helped turn what was already a good tip night into a spec-
tacular one. When her shift ended at eight, she joined Marianne and
Evan at an outdoor table near a row of clay-potted dracaenas.

It had been Evan's idea. The three had not been together since
their evening at Divine Grind months ago, and with the mercurial
rains of late spring giving way to warm, dry breezes of summer, it was
a good night for belated toasts: Marianne had quit her job at Estelle's
and had been accepted into a nursing school in Virginia, and Eden's
month-old job at Maestro's and recent news—a chance at a music

scholarship—demanded a celebratory drink or two. A bottle of Moët et Chandon chilled in a bucket at the corner of their table.

"Not exactly Estelle's, huh?" Evan said, turning to look at the view of Central Park below—the clots of leafy treetops, the lakes and swirling paths—and the dusky skyline beyond, a faded gray outline of brick and steel towers as abstract in the evening light as a child's finger-painting. The view, Eden had to admit after a nervous backward glance, was impressive. To ease her fear of heights, Evan ordered her a strong old-fashioned. "This will help," he said. He wasn't wrong, but she still turned her chair with her back to the view.

"OK, I'm out here," she told Evan as he poured champagne, first into Marianne's glass, then into Eden's. "But when I get up from here, I'm not walking anywhere except back inside."

Evan said, "Let me remind you about the first day you came to this place. Remember? Just the idea of singing up here freaked you out. Now look at you. Fearless. Getting your diva on every night, singing like a pro, and raking in the tips." He smiled. "For somebody who can stand up and sing like that, an hour on a seventy-third-floor patio should be a piece of cake."

"It's different, singing," Eden said. "My daddy always said it came natural. To him, and to me. He always said you can learn how to sing, but you can't learn to have a good voice."

"Yeah, and some folks can't learn either," said Marianne. "Tone deafness is a strong tradition in my family. Everything we try to sing sounds like the Pledge of Allegiance. I couldn't carry a tune if you poured it into that ice bucket."

Evan smiled. "I doubt that. They say true tone deafness is extremely rare."

"Trust me," Marianne said. "Tone deaf with a capital D. And please, don't make me prove it." She took a long drink to empty her glass and reached for the champagne bottle. "Well, this is the place to be if you're a woman on the hunt, or even if you're not. Don't look now," she said, winking at Eden. "But all of a sudden, it's raining men."

Eden looked toward the door. Three tall, impeccably groomed men in expensive-looking close-cut suits entered and stood at the bar, surveying the scene. Marianne recognized the white one, blond with a beard; a late-round NBA draft pick from years ago.

Evan's glance caught Eden's eyes, looking at the men, then down at her plate. He fixed his face in a sarcastic half-smile.

"Yeah, well. If you like that type."

Marianne scoffed. "What? Tall? Good-looking, well-built, and reeking of money? Why would anybody want that? Now, ugly, short, and broke?" She patted her chest. "Be still my heart."

Eden laughed out loud, and with a resigned head shake, so did Evan.

A young, olive-skinned waiter named Ivan, with a tattoo of a zebra on his forearm and four stud earrings in each ear, arrived at their table, and they all ordered tiramisu for dessert. Mysteriously, another bottle of champagne appeared in the bucket. In a corner near the glass doors to the restaurant, a small jazz trio set up: an upright bass, drum set, and a portable electric piano. They rolled out an upbeat "Girl from Ipanema" as an older couple with more tequila-fueled nerve than dance skills found a small space for an old-school two-step.

A half-hour later, jacked on sugar and buzzed on champagne, their laughter louder and strident, they downed more drinks. The talking grew louder with the music, and the more they drank, the more they laughed, their boisterous joy dissolving into the chatter in the room like voices joining a chorus. They reveled in the rare treat of friends drinking and eating together in the open air on a warm, star-speckled New York night.

"This is a good fit for you, girl," Marianne said. "And my God, you sound unbelievable. Even from where we were sitting at the bar. Made me realize I'd never really heard you sing. Not like that. Can't believe you've been hiding that all this time."

"Thanks, girl. Can't believe I'm working here. I keep pinching myself."

Evan held up his glass. "To a star in the making." And with a look to Eden, then Marianne, he said, "In fact, a toast to two fierce women. One who wants to heal the body while the other feeds the soul."

They clicked glasses and sipped. An hour later, when patrons began to leave, the band notched its groove down to lazy ballads, "Mood Indigo" followed by "Girl Talk." Low-pitched conversation underscored last-round sounds of clinking crystal and busboys stacking plates. Evan ordered cappuccinos, and the conversation changed to the competition and Eden's last lesson with Ernest Blessing.

She would sing two songs—a required piece for her voice type, "Deh vieni non tardar," from *The Marriage of Figaro,* which she would sing in Italian, and one of her own choice, the Schubert song. The same one, she told them, that she'd heard the soprano sing in the church, and the same one sung by Celia DeMille, according to the concert program from Evan, at London's Beckstein Hall.

When she told them about Ernest Blessing's reaction to the diva's necklace, Marianne sat back, frowning.

"Really? He cried? From what you said about him, he doesn't seem like the emotional type. The way he talks to you. I had an econ teacher like that once. Sounds like a little bit of a hard-ass."

The tears had surprised her, too, she told them. But when he told her the story, she understood there was more to him than she realized.

"So he knew about Celia?" Evan asked.

"Yeah. Was there some kind of connection or something?" Marianne said.

"You could say that," Eden said.

Sitting back with both hands in her lap, Eden began to recite Ernest's story as best she could. "So Ernest Blessing's grandfather, Ephraim, was a sharecropper in Mississippi."

As a young man working his father's farm, Ephraim Ezekiel Blessing sang in a big, lusty tenor that rang through the rows of workers in the cotton fields. The sweeter he sang, the easier the picking. The other field workers always joined in; the music eased the weight of cotton sacks, salved fingers, and palms against the burning prick of thorns. Whether from friend or kin in New Orleans and beyond, every colored person on the farm had heard of Celia DeMille, the woman who sang for presidents and kings, dressed like a queen, and traveled the world. "She got a voice that make the angels cry," they had heard. When it was announced she would be singing in New Orleans, Ephraim Blessing made up his mind. He got permission from his father, saved his money, and walked day and night until he reached the city.

Dusty, dirty, exhausted, and hungry, he finally reached St. Charles Avenue in New Orleans, thrilled at the sight of the big white hall where she and her group, The Black Donatella's Troubadours, would perform. But by the time he arrived, the section upstairs marked COLOREDS ONLY was full. He spotted a seat in the white section but was strong-armed away by a brawny white man in a cream-colored three-piece suit. An old live oak tree stood near the building on the grounds. A high, thick branch curved like a sickle put him in mind of a makeshift balcony seat, and after climbing the tree, Ephraim balanced himself, peering into the opened side window of the hall. Even from his awkward perch, she was the most beautiful sight he had seen, dressed in a white gown fit for royalty. Her final, high B-flat was an arrow that pierced his heart. When he got back home, he vowed he would someday join her company. Eleven months later, with a homemade knapsack and twice-resoled shoes, he again walked the long miles to New Orleans, found Celia and her company, and asked to sing for her. He was hired on the spot.

But weeks later, when Celia's husband and manager disappeared with the company's money, it was a death blow to The Troubadours. Already in deep waters financially, they toured a few weeks on a shoestring and a promise of pay, but disbanded a few weeks after Ephraim joined the company. For Ephraim, the journey back to the farm in Mississippi felt miles longer, saddled with the burden of a broken spirit, but he resumed his life as a sharecropper's son, singing in the fields, remembering. It had been the greatest few weeks of his life. His last chance to realize his dream to sing on the great stages of the world. And for a brief time, he had sung with one of the world's greatest artists. As the years wore on and he grew older, the memory of that time always forced a smile, a bright glimmer of light in his aging eyes.

Eden paused, looked down at her drink, then took a sip of wine as the four patrons at the next table paid their bill and got up to leave. The air was cooler now; a strong breeze blew across the patio up from the streets and the park below. The band finished their last set with "A Nightingale Sang in Berkeley Square," then packed their instruments. They were the only remaining customers.

"That's quite a story," Marianne said. "A sad one."

Evan nodded soberly. "Depends on how you look at it. Old Ephraim had his moment. Took a risk and it got him an experience he could carry to the end of his days. I'd planned to tell you this later, but I may as well tell you now…Celia DeMille's necklace," he said, nodding toward the gold pendant hanging just below Eden's clavicle. "You might want to be careful when and where you wear it."

He had done some research. The photo he'd taken of the locket revealed a stamp that confirmed what he thought about its origin. His partner, Arnold Blankenship, had agreed: ordinarily, a necklace from one of England's oldest jewelers, Rundell, Bridge, and Rundell, would bring about £900, or about $1,800.

"But if this was really owned by royalty, Robert Hardaway—an earl—in the early nineteenth century…well, it could be worth more. A whole lot more."

Evan was still researching the history. But it might have been purchased as a wedding or birthday gift to someone, then passed down the line in the Hardaway family. It ended up with James Hardaway before he set sail for America to seek his fortune as a planter.

"So, your great-aunt's friend—Mildred, did you say her name was? The story she told you holds up. And there's a lot more value in it, if it can be authenticated by the craftsman as the original locket. If you trust me with it, I'd like to take it, do some more research, and maybe even see what it would cost to insure it."

Eden wasn't sure. She trusted him, but she'd grown so attached to the necklace, it was a talisman now, tethering her to the woman whose life had become her obsession. She couldn't have cared less if it were made by a famous English jeweler; to Eden, it was invaluable, and personal.

But she said, "Of course, yeah, I trust you." She looked down, stroked the chain, then rubbed the locket between her forefinger and thumb. "I guess it wouldn't hurt to see what it's worth."

"Great. I can get it from you later. I promise I'll take good care of it. And our company is insured for whatever's in our possession. But please, be careful with it."

They got up to leave, the last patrons in the restaurant. "I need to go to the girls'," Eden said to her friends. "I'll meet you at the elevator."

When she came out of the ladies' room, Eden headed toward the elevator, but stopped. She sneaked a peek over the edge of the high, glass wall that separated the seventy-third-floor patio from the rest of Manhattan.

She took a long deep breath and leaned over, steadying herself against the rail. At the view, her mouth opened with an audible sigh of awe. To her surprise, she felt no jumping nerves, no thumping in her chest. She looked as far as she could to see where land, trees, and buildings bled into gray-black sky. It was, in fact, breathtaking, the air this high above the street so clean and pure. Inhaling again, she felt a rush of power. Maybe it had to do with being born below sea level, but as she viewed the boundless world that lay before her, she questioned her fear of being up so high. *No big deal*, she thought. *The higher you climb, the more there is to see. The bigger the map of your world.*

Back on the street, the friends said goodbye. Evan headed toward the subway back to Brooklyn and the two women hailed a taxi.

"So, I guess I won't see you for a while," Marianne said. "We'll have to plan a visit later in the year, after my exams. Maybe at Christmas."

As their cab pulled away from the curb in a tire-squealing, hard-swerving U-turn, Marianne leaned into the curve and shook her head. "There are a few things about New York I don't think I'll miss."

Eden laughed. *Funny*, she thought. *I'm just getting used to the place.* "You've got to come back to New York at Christmas," Eden said. "I hear it's fantastic. Last year, I was still in shock. I was in such a funk those first few months, I felt like I missed the whole thing."

Marianne gave her a cursory look. "Sweetie, by the time I see you again, you just might be famous. Funny how both our lives are about to change at the same time. And speaking of missing out, what's up with Mr. Smallwood? He got a friend we don't know about?"

"Don't know. Haven't really thought about that."

"Oh, please. Save that for somebody else. A single man—not bad looking, I must say—running around loose, does not remain unattached for very long. I'm just saying, it's been a while for you. Actually, for both of us."

"Yeah, right, you interested in him?"

"Me? I'm leaving town and headed into the world of blood and bedpans. Don't get me wrong. I've always wanted to be a nurse and I'm truly happy about this. But the next man I interact with on a one-to-one will probably need his diaper changed. No, that's the furthest thing from my mind. Besides, been there, done that. Might do it again, but not soon. You, on the other hand, need to get off your duff and start living again."

Eden smiled, looked out the taxi window as the driver made a left turn, then honked at a motorcyclist.

"And if I get this scholarship to go to a music school, I'll be in the same situation as you."

"I don't think there'll be any twelve-hour shifts or 3:00 a.m. emergencies in the conservatory. No, I suspect you'll have some time to be a woman again. It's none of my business, but he is a nice guy, clearly likes you. Single, too, or did I already say that? And now that your brother is about to graduate—"

"He's got one more year."

"Right. How's he doing, by the way? Still doing messenger work?"

"Yeah, too much. He's coming home later and later. But he's OK."

"Sounds like he's getting ready to fly, find his own way. His last year in school—you'd be surprised how fast that time will go. Your nest will be so empty, you won't know what hit it. Just saying, Evan's a good guy. You could do worse. And like I said, he likes you."

"Yeah, he's cool. He's a good friend," Eden said.

Marianne scoffed, shook her head. "Not what I'm talking about. You're not seeing the signs? Thank God, you're not driving."

The taxi driver made a turn onto Eden's street.

"This is it, my friend," Marianne said.

Eden felt a bulge in her throat. "I guess it is. Listen, girl, I can't thank you enough…"

"Don't you dare say goodbye," Marianne said. "I'll see you soon."

When the taxi pulled up to her apartment, Eden got out and climbed the steps, her head still light, full of night air and laughter, music and champagne, and the view from high atop the tallest building she had ever been inside. She changed into her cotton robe and headed to the fire escape. It was late, but a perfect night to watch the stars, sip chamomile tea, and read from the book of Madame DeMille. By now, she hardly missed her late-night cigarette.

Tomorrow, she would set up a time to give Evan the necklace, the scrapbook, and other materials. The possibility of seeing him again soon gave her a small rush of joy. She had lied to Marianne just now. There *had* been a sign. A moment, fleeting but unmistakable: a small beam of light from across the table, aimed directly at her, from Evan Smallwood's eyes.

CHAPTER 31

14 April, 1928

Dearest Catherine,

My letters to you have returned to me, indicating that the old address I have for you is incorrect. Apparently, you have changed your place of residence since I came here from New Orleans. I will continue to write to you, and in the meantime will try to find an accurate address for your whereabouts. When I find it, I will send all the letters I am writing now.

There has been an unexpected comfort in returning here to Boston, my place of birth, to spend my final days. I am grateful every day for the generosity of the anonymous patron who insisted I be brought to the finest hospital here for final care. I will never know for certain who is responsible—my suspicion may never be confirmed. Every Monday at 8 a.m., flowers arrive, with no note.

They take excellent care of me here; the meals are more than adequate and the care is compassionate. But here, I do not have a companion as dear to me as you were. I miss that. I think of you fondly and will forever be grateful to you for your kind care.

There is one thing I must tell you. I have referred to the great fire of 1919 that took our beloved opera house, but I never spoke to you about that night. Perhaps it was too painful for me to speak about during those days in New Orleans. But even now, every day, I think about that night. I can now say that I was at the brink of madness, walking to the river as I did with such a plan, to end my life there. That night, the river I loved so dearly had seemed my only friend.

But when I saw the fire drowning my beloved opera house, I was drawn to it like a moth to a candle flame. I think of the irony; it may have been that fire that saved my life, diverting me from the river.

I did not set the fire, of course. Although, in my mind, I felt I had reason to, as it symbolized my greatest betrayal. In a way, I was glad to see it burn. When they asked me if I set it, I almost said yes.

If I had said yes, the world would know my name. They would remember my glorious career. Celia DeMille, who sang for presidents, royal courts in England and the Continent. Terrible isn't it? To want so desperately to be remembered?

Alas, I could not admit to what I did not do. Instead, I passed my reviews, letters, articles, and photographs, the book of my life, to you, with one hope: that someday someone would include my name among those whose great voices rise from the cavern of history.

My dearest one, I know how hard you have tried, but do not trouble yourself further. Perhaps I was merely born too soon for the attentions and respect of those who love the art of song. Perhaps the colors in my voice are not enough to distract some from the color of my face. But singing is all I have ever wanted to do, and because I have been able to do that, I will go to my reward with great gratitude to the one who gave me life and voice.

As for my legacy, I have faith that it will not die. Someday, I believe the world will know my song. My voice will rise from the earth and the rivers will call out my name.

The red birds are singing outside my window this morning. I sing with them, and we are one great choir. There is a small river nearby that reminds me of home, and sometimes at night, through my open window, I can feel its gentle pull. These days, this is the music that gives me great joy.

Yours always,

Mme C. DeMille

"So, that's it." When Eden finished reading the letter aloud as he had asked, she put it away and waited for Blessing to speak. When he said nothing for half a minute, she said, "Well, I just wanted to share that with you, sir. It's the only letter in the scrapbook, and the only thing I could find that she wrote herself, so I thought, you know, you might be interested."

On the table between them lay the open scrapbook of reviews, and three photographs were spread across the pages. He held up a quieting hand to her while he rubbed his forehead with his thumb and forefinger. "It is..." he paused. When he spoke again, his voice broke. "Extraordinary."

They sat in his walnut-paneled study, him at his roll-top desk and Eden across from him in the red leather armchair. It was Sunday afternoon, a full hour after her lesson ended. A ceiling fan whirred above them.

"They refused her," he said, staring out the window where the late sun streamed in. "They never allowed her to sing with the white opera companies. Even though her reviewers placed her among the greatest singers in the world."

Ernest Blessing removed his glasses, wiped the lenses with a handkerchief, and put them back on his face. He looked at her, then got up and went to the oak bookshelves, where he reached up to remove a leather portfolio.

"I want you to see something," he said. From the pages, he produced a scalloped edge black and white photograph: a black man who looked to be about fifty, his bushy mane whitish at the temples, his chin square and face unsmiling, and his icy stare fixed on the camera's lens.

"This is him," Blessing said. "This is my grandfather, Ephraim."

He wore a starched white shirt and had a proud bearing that belied his humble dress, the frayed fabric of his jacket, and the wear and stain of his collar.

Blessing never heard him sing, he told her, but everyone—his father, his uncles—swore to a tenor voice so big and powerful that even the mules in the fields cocked their heads to listen. Often, he talked about his time as one of The Black Donatella's Troubadours, his eyes glazed and distant. "He was with them a total of twenty-eight days. In four weeks, they traveled by train throughout the Southwest, to Texas and Arizona and on to California. The troubles they endured—a black company traveling throughout the South! Finding food and lodging, the poor condition of colored railroad cars. Safety issues, rumors of Klansmen about. The indignities, the abuses. You can't imagine. It was 1915."

He paused a moment, as if trying to remember them himself. Then said, "Madame DeMille was at the peak of her powers. He said when she sang, the strongest of men dabbed at their cheeks, their heads bowed. Even white men! He talked about it so many times, and each time it was so real to me, as if I could view the whole experience through his eyes.

"When Madame DeMille brought the company together backstage for the last time, there had been rumors, he said, long before he arrived. Already, the crowds had begun to thin. Pay was late, often as much as a week or two, and a missed meal was not uncommon. But he said it was the greatest experience of his life.

"When the company disbanded and he returned to the farm, he went back to sharecropping with his father. He met Sarah Bell, my grandmother, married her, and had four children, the youngest of which was my father. I know he must have thought many times about what might have been. He might have had a career as a singer himself, had things been different. But I think he was grateful to have had such a brush with greatness, brief as it was. He was not a man to harbor regrets. I'd like to think that, despite everything, he was a happy man."

Blessing smiled. "The fact that you came to me with...all of this,

this connection, not only to my grandfather's fondest memories of the greatest time of his life but also to this great singer, well, it's...remarkable." His words trailed. "Clearly, from the letter, she wanted to be remembered as more than a historical footnote. She wanted her name, her legacy, to outlive her."

He stood and put the photograph of Ephraim back inside the leather portfolio. "And so, a responsibility has fallen to you, young lady. Tell me. What will you do with all these things?"

She told him she wasn't sure, but that Evan had offered to have the materials appraised and advised her to insure them, if she could afford it. Or she could donate it to a university archival collection, maybe one of the historically black colleges.

"That sounds like good advice," he said.

She nodded. It made sense to her, too. The smart thing to do, the practical thing. But when she thought of parting with it, especially the necklace, she felt heartbroken.

As if reading her mind, he said, "You know, all of these things are valuable artifacts of history. One could call it truly fortuitous that this great singer's effects found their way to you, that you would be the one to inherit this, so to speak, under the most extraordinary circumstances. It should inspire you. But of course, what you do with them is your decision."

"Yes, sir."

"Well, then." He looked at his watch. "I think that will be all for today. What time spot did they give you for next Wednesday?"

"I sing at one, right after lunch, sir."

"Good. They'll be rested, no longer hungry, but not tired yet. Good luck."

"But...I don't get another lesson before I sing?"

"For what? You are as ready as you are going to be. It's up to you now. Just sing the way you sang today for me. Just sing the music as beautifully as I know you can."

Eden nodded and turned toward the door. "What do you think my chances are?"

"Of what?"

"Of winning."

He chuckled, removed his glasses. "You only need to be concerned about your chances of doing your very best."

He buttoned his jacket and walked toward the door. "Look, this is all brand-new to you and the competition is…well, tough. There will be dozens of hopeful singers, most with more experience and training than you. Honestly, your chances of winning are not particularly good. But this is just the beginning."

She shrugged her shoulders. "I wish you'da told me that earlier." She gathered the scrapbook, photos, and the letter and put them in her backpack. "I wouldn'ta gone to all this trouble, just to be let down."

"Wait a minute," he said, taking his hand off the doorknob. He cleared his throat. "My father told me he once asked his father what was he thinking, walking day and night across an entire state to try to sing with one of the most famous singers in the world. It was a fool's errand. No one in the state of Louisiana knew who Ephraim was. They surely didn't know if he could sing. As fate would have it, he arrived in New Orleans three days after the lead tenor of the company fell ill and had to withdraw before an upcoming performance in Texas.

"He was a sharecropper, an untrained singer, an uneducated farmer from Mississippi, Ephraim was. And he was black. He took a sack with enough food for two meals and carried little more than the clothes on his back. He caught bad weather, not unusual for spring in Mississippi and Louisiana, but he made it through. What were his chances of even making it to New Orleans on foot in one piece? Probably not great. Landing a job singing with the company? Maybe one in a thousand.

"So, go. Sing. Sometimes there is only one decision that matters, one that can make all the difference in the world."

"What's that?"

"The one where you decide to show up."

CHAPTER 32

Eden emptied the contents of the mayonnaise jar, carefully counted the fives, tens, and ones, then spilled the coins onto her kitchen counter. Not too bad, if she budgeted carefully. She could make it work.

When Reginald Jr. turned seventeen a week ago, she'd asked him what he wanted. The answer—"big pot-a gumbo"—surprised and pleased her. She'd wanted it herself since she'd left Aunt Baby's. The fixings were costly, even back home. But here? This city was crazy expensive. Twenty-count-per-pound shrimp cost an arm and a leg, even at Fairway's sale price, and for what she'd have to pay for fresh oysters and decent andouille sausage, she could buy herself a dress from Target and some new shoes. At least the seasoning part was taken care of. Months ago, in sympathy for her hard times, Andre, one of the cooks from Estelle's, had shown up at the end of her McDonald's shift with a surprise—a bag of special "secret" Creole spice blend, "light-fingered" from the restaurant pantry. In her cupboard, oil, flour, rice, salt, and a small tin of cayenne were all she had on hand. But once the idea got stuck in her mind, she would not be dissuaded. Come hell or high water, Sunday dinner would be gumbo and whatever else she could scrape together. She'd buy all the rest of the ingredients, even if it meant dipping deep into her saved-up stash of Maestro's tips.

It was time to celebrate. These days, she woke in bed on sunlit mornings, flung her arms wide in a cat-stretch, her relief and contentment evident in a long, exhaled sigh. They'd made it this far, here in the city almost a year. She had a good job and an audition to a music school coming up. School was out, and Reginald Jr. had managed to stay out of trouble. He'd made it through a year of classes without further incidents, and while his grades weren't great, all things considered, they were better than she'd dared to hope for. With any luck at all, he'd graduate next year.

They were whole, healthy, safe, and had landed on the other side of chaos and displacement. They were on high, dry ground, and the rent was paid. For once, they were slightly ahead of the game.

And she was singing. Not just singing, but singing better. Even her brother noticed.

"You sound really different now," he told her a week ago.

"Different how?"

"I don't know. Different...like powerful. Pretty. Like those ladies on TV. You sound like somebody famous. Or somebody who oughta be."

When was the last time she'd kissed her little brother? He may have been seven or so, and asleep in his bed. She grabbed him now and planted a kiss on the very top of his head.

So, with no regrets, Eden blew most of her last week's tip money—money she'd planned to spend on a hair appointment before her audition—on ingredients for her brother's favorite meal: dark roux gumbo, cornbread, and even some fresh collards she found for half-price at the green market on the corner of 110th.

Sometimes, missing home, her longing for Louisiana showed up as a restless jangle of nerves just beneath her skin, or a slow ache unwinding from some small corner in her gut. And sometimes it showed up as a deep hunger for the flavors of the place. An open restaurant door might release the steamy, sweet odor of gumbo filé, celery, and onions sautéing in oil. An opened door to an apartment in her building might let fly the seasoned vapors of smothered catfish. It brought tears to her eyes. If she couldn't be at home, at least she could smell it, taste it. Today, the apartment kitchen held the familiar steamy scents, savory triggers of the New Orleans of her childhood, a memory that now bloomed from the vision of her brother.

Sinking into the too-small folding chair and tucking impossibly long legs beneath the small wooden table they'd lugged home months ago from a sidewalk trash pile, he was a sight. Frighteningly close to manhood, Reginald Jr. looked more and more like the father she remembered, the one he'd barely met. How could he have grown this much since they'd arrived in New York? Sharpened facial bones, wide shoulders, a peach-fuzzed chin, and long knees now chafing the underside of the table top defined the man-child before her, marking the passing time like a ticking clock. If she had missed these signs of encroaching manhood, what else had he done while she wasn't looking?

"It's some cherry Kool-Aid in the fridge," she said. "Fix yourself a glass." Lifting the pot lid, she stirred the dark liquid, thick with large shrimp, oysters, and sausage, as a cloud of spicy steam escaped. She set the table and regretted not having done this before. For months, like passing boats in a shared sea, they'd been tacking around each other, each staying out of the other's way. It was time they ate like family, the way she, her father, and her mother had before Reginald Jr. was born.

She had to admit, the aroma of the gumbo was on point, even though she could only afford a pound of the shrimp and she'd had to substitute the gumbo filé she preferred with Andre's blend, which wasn't too bad for a New Yorker's version. But it looked and smelled like her father's, maybe better. Savory and peppery with just a hint of heat. The dark caramel of the roux was perfect, the texture somewhere between soup-thin and stew-thick. Reginald Jr. had a habit of bouncing his knee when he ate something that suited him, and she waited for it.

"Salt over there on the stove if you need it," she said. "Pepper, too."

"Naw, it's all 'ight."

At least that was what she thought he'd said, as his words came out, as they often did lately, in monosyllabic grunts. He didn't rave the way he would have when he was thirteen, too cool now to admit anything was greater than "all 'ight." She settled for the validation of a slightly bouncing knee.

"Slow down," she said. "The gumbo ain't going nowhere."

"Hungry," he said, stirring gumbo into the mound of rice and taking another huge mouthful.

She smiled, sighed. This was good. Eating a meal together, for a change.

"Thought you were going to get a haircut yesterday," she said.

"What? Naw. I like it this way."

Really? Two weeks' worth of new growth crept beyond his razor-trimmed hairline. *OK, whatever.*

"So anyway, I got some news." Eden stirred the rice and gumbo in her bowl and told him about the audition coming up for the music school. She probably wouldn't win it, but if she did, things would be different. She'd be going to school part-time and working part-time. She'd already worked it out with the restaurant, just in case.

And by the way, he was right about the necklace. Turns out, it did have some value, according to her friend, Evan. How much, they didn't know yet, but she explained he was still working on the appraisal.

His interest piqued, he looked up to meet her glance. "So, how much we talking about?" he asked. "We oughta sell it."

She put her spoon down. "We? First of all, I'll be the one making that decision. And anyway, it might be the best thing for it to be in a museum or something, or maybe some university. You know, it belonged to—"

"Yeah. I know. You told me. That lady singer way back. So, worth more than a grand, you think? Or two?"

"Got no idea. And not just some lady singer. She was really famous. At least back then she was."

"Well, if it's that big and it got some gold in it…just saying." He poured more gumbo into the well that he made in his mound of rice. "Where's it at, now?"

"At my friend's. You heard me talk about him. He used to hang out at Estelle's. He got me the gig at Maestro's."

"So, you just gave him the necklace? How you know you can trust him?"

"He's a antique dealer. Thought I told you that."

He shrugged. "So, I got some news too."

He was going to New Orleans for the summer. Now that school was out, he and a buddy whose older cousin lived in the city had decided to drive down for a birthday party his friend was invited to.

"Oh, no. No. We talked about this." Eden pressed both palms flat on the table as if to steady herself. "I already done told you. You enrolled in that summer school program at the Y for six weeks so you can get your math grade up. And besides, I told you it ain't safe for you to go down there."

She'd blown off Randy's warning, but she needed leverage and now was the time to play that card. She told Reginald Jr. about the two guys who had been picked up by the cops in New Orleans. Two of his best friends who were at the scene of the convenience store robbery where the manager was shot. Not fatally, thank God, but the case was still open, flood or no flood. "They'll be looking for you," she told him. "They'll tell them you were with them."

He laughed. "They ain't gonna tell nobody nothing. Nobody does. You get caught, it's on you. You deal with it. But you don't snitch nothing to no cops about nobody in your crew. Everybody know that. Besides, like I told you, I wasn't there when everything happened, when the whole deal went down."

She shook her head; she wasn't interested in hearing about some street code, his flimsy assurance of protection. "Don't matter," she said. "You ain't going to New Orleans."

He gave her a half-mocking look—raised eyebrows, a sideways

smirk. "I ain't asking," he told her. He took a large bite of the corn-bread. "And you ain't my mama."

With that, he got up and took his plate and bowl to the stove and dipped more gumbo from the pot.

You ain't my mama? Eden put down her spoon and stared at her bowl. When had he decided he was man enough to spit in the face of the woman who'd changed his diapers and held him when he was afraid to look under the bed? A vestige of guilt bubbled up from some hidden place. *He is right,* she thought. *I'm not his mama. And where was the mama he'd needed all these years? What if I hadn't...?*

She blinked the thought away; Aunt Baby's advice to unshackle herself from the past took practice, and she was new at it. The present demanded her full attention. True, she was not his mother. But she was all he had. And here it was, the time when she might no longer be able to convince him that she was the next best thing.

She pulled off a corner of cornbread, chewed it thoughtfully, de-ciding how to play this. *OK. If he was going to go, I at least have the right to know more about what his plans were.*

"Saying you going down for this party…How long you planning on staying?"

"Don't know. Probably stay down there. For good."

"What? Stay where? And not finish school?"

"Didn't say that. They got schools there."

"You can't do that, just enroll yourself in school. And anyway, half the schools aren't reopened yet since the storm, including yours."

"Well, ok, then, I'll just work and get my GED."

"That's crazy. Why quit, when you only got a year to go here?"

Now he stared into his bowl and spoke quietly. "Because I don't wanna stay here another year. I wanna go home."

She leaned forward toward him, her calm gaze commanding his. "Look. I know you don't remember him. You were only three. But Daddy told me to take care of you. I'm just trying to do what he would have wanted for you. I wish you knew how much he loved you."

"Yeah, you always say that. How come you never talk about him?"

"I've told you all about him. How much you look like him. How little things you do remind me of him."

And she had, hadn't she? She'd always tried to make their father as real for him as he was for her.

He shook his head. "Seem like I don't know nothing about him. Not really. And what about my mama? What happened to her? How come she didn't come back? Daddy died, but where is she?"

Eden took a breath as deep as she could muster and let out a slow sigh. *Where, indeed.*

Just before the storm, she had thought about it. She'd actually gone so far as to look into it. They had folks who could track down your kinfolks for you using your DNA.

She'd convinced herself that Reginald might benefit somehow from knowing his mother, wherever she was. Her brother was doing poorly in school, hanging out with people she didn't even want him talking to, let alone running with. She didn't know what to do, and there was no one to turn to for advice. Her father was gone. Aunt Baby was off in Europe or wherever, doing whatever.

If Ethel Kinsley were alive, she had thought, it might be worth a try. Maybe she'd gotten her life together. Maybe she wanted to know her son now, but felt too much guilt. Maybe she could at least let the boy know he had a mother, somewhere. And didn't he deserve to know?

But she'd decided to wait. When the time was right, she would ask her brother if finding his mother was something he wanted.

It was days before the storm when Reginald Jr. had been briefly questioned by a police officer. He had not been charged with a crime, but two of his buddies were determined as persons of interest in the convenience store incident. Just before the storm hit and the whole city flooded, she and Reginald Jr. boarded a bus for Houston. She put Ethel Kinsley out of her mind.

Now, Reginald Jr. sat before her, seventeen years old. She had done the best she could by him. But maybe there was more. Through the years, she'd given him vague reasons for his mother's leaving—depression, mental problems—but the boy needed to know the truth, all of it, including the role Eden herself may have played.

And if he wanted to find his mother, she'd do everything she could to help him.

She waited until he'd finished the last of his gumbo before she began.

"I'll tell you what happened." she began. "I'll tell you everything I know about your mother."

It took almost an hour. When she finished, he stared at the window, quietly, his face unreadable. He did not blink for what seemed like an unnaturally long time. Then he got up from the table, put his plate and bowl in the sink, and left.

CHAPTER 33

He pulled up the collar of his jacket and headed down the street toward the IRT—past his own building and on past the row of tall, gray and brown tenement towers, darting upward like fence slats blanking out the blue of the early evening sky. *Maybe that's why rich folks build them like that,* he thought, *so when poor folks look up, they don't see those blue skies that get you to thinking, get you to dreaming.* Instead, they see tower after tower of bricks, glass, and plaster, walls blocking out the dream of whatever might be better on the other side. But the walls in his mind were just as high, just as thick and hard, and his crazy thoughts kept ricocheting off one, crashing into another.

Shoulders clenched up and head ducked down, he dug his hands deep into the pockets of his jeans. The barbershop window threw back his reflection—a tall, skinny kid with wild hair, a high fade edging over his razor line—and he floated the idea that maybe he did need a trim. *Tomorrow. Maybe.* If he could spare the cash. When he reached the Korean nail salon and the Asian-owned beauty supply store, he turned the corner.

On the street in front of him, a young blond woman in shorts and sneakers talked on a cell phone while she pushed a baby stroller.

"'Scuse me," he said, taking long, quick strides around her, feeling more impatient and antsy than hurried. He needed space, air. Moving, feeling his boots pound hard against the pavement helped. It was all too much. Too much to think about all at once.

This whole thing with his mama. He didn't even know where the anger came from, except it must have been in the back of his mind for a while. But his words were out of his mouth before he realized what he was saying.

You ain't my mama.

That was cold. Almost before the words landed, he saw the hurt in her eyes, knotting the space above her brows. He'd wanted to snatch the words back from the air.

He hadn't thought about his mother in forever. He'd listened, slightly stunned. Sure, his sister was only a kid then…but still, it didn't sound like her. Hating on the woman, his mother, like that. Playing tricks, the thing with her pills, maybe even making her feel like she had to leave. But you can't blame a kid for that. Kids sometimes act mean, do stupid shit all the time.

She left, just walked out not too long after he was born. Mental problems. That had been the story all these years, and he hadn't questioned it. But that was so long ago. Did it even matter now?

He was only a baby, barely walking. And barely talking full sentences when their father died. His only memory—riding high, legs dangling over his broad shoulders, singing, laughing, and pounding his daddy's head with little drummer hands. He must have been two and a half. That was all he remembered of Reginald Sr. Every other image of him was borrowed from a Polaroid, his father with two marine buddies, that picture Eden had salvaged before the storm. He didn't obsess over it since not having a daddy wasn't all that unusual. Half his buddies back home had daddies who left home or never lived there in the first place, stayed across town, across the country, or in jail—those that had daddies at all.

But his mama? Almost everybody seemed to have one of those,

no matter what shape she was in or where she was. Even in his world, mamas didn't just up and walk out.

Twenty-five minutes of walking. He passed the hospital, the Y, a row of small markets and Indian and Salvadoran restaurants beneath a cloudless sky dimming to dusty rose. Dreadlocked vendors with thick accents manned the sidewalk, their portable tables crowded with scarves, gelés, hand-made ebony figures, and beaded jewelry. Just after the Puerto Rican grocery, he passed an older man in a wheelchair, selling single stemmed roses. "Here, brother! Look here! Nice for your lady, huh?" From somewhere near, the smell of grilling lamb tinged the air. He wasn't hungry, not really. He'd eaten his fill of the gumbo and had to admit, it was dope. But he needed something more. A beer, maybe. Yeah. A brew would taste really good right now.

Not that he was a big beer drinker, not like some he knew. But in New Orleans, he could have gotten his hands on an Abita or a forty of malt liquor so easy. Here, these folks didn't play that. If you weren't legal, you better know somebody who is. He decided on the next best thing. The weather was getting hotter now, and he'd give anything for one of those Sno-Balls from Artesia's on Elysian Fields back home. Dang, he missed those Sno-Balls. They didn't have them here, but a popsicle, cool and sweet—that would work.

The Shop-Wise Market less than a block away, a little store—bodegas or whatever they called them up here—kept its cold case behind the cereal aisle. For the strawberry Icee-Pop, he handed the plump, middle-aged woman in a headscarf and yellow tunic at the front cash register two dollars and change, then licked the frozen pop, so frosty it grabbed his tongue like tape. He bit off the top quarter, let it dissolve in his mouth. Sweet.

You ain't my mama. The words somersaulted in his head. She was about his age when she had to be both mama and daddy, something he couldn't imagine. If she wasn't his mama, it wasn't like she hadn't tried. Maybe not so much in the things she did that he took for granted, but in the things she had neither time nor energy to do. Going out on a date, for starters, or hanging out with her girlfriends. Or getting her nails done, or whatever women did. Staying a step or two ahead of him, making sure he had breakfast, clean underwear, lunch money, and good manners. It could suck the energy out of anybody. Even he could see that.

Most of the time, a real mama couldn't have been any more real. When he was about seven and stole a Hot Wheels Corvette from a bin of toys at the Walmart in Metairie, she'd grabbed his arm and squeezed until he stuttered a sobbing, slobbering apology to an indifferent store clerk. *You think the world revolves around you?* was a refrain he practically heard in his sleep. No, he didn't think that, but he couldn't help it if she kept acting like it did. So many times, especially lately, he'd wanted to tell her, "Quit worrying about me. Do your life." Because when the time came, he was damn sure going to do his.

The rent thing. He hadn't meant for it to be a big deal. Just do his part, dig them out of that hole, and get a little extra cash. He didn't want trouble. Not again. Not like in New Orleans. That night was crazy. He had lied to Eden. That night, he had been in the car when he heard the shots. And what kind of fool had he been not to know that Black Jack had a gun? The dude with his crazy ass was always talking about what he was gonna do with one, if he got half the chance. What surprised him for real was when he pointed that thing dead straight at him, daring him to try to bounce before the car started up. The shots he'd heard from inside the store still rang in his head. When they sped away, he'd held his breath and prayed for a red light because only a moron would risk running it and getting pulled over, or worse, maybe hitting somebody. When the car stopped at the intersection, he opened the door, jumped out, hauled ass, and never looked back.

Two days later, he and Eden were on a bus to Houston.

Now in New York, things had gone bust again. He hated his school. It had taken her too long to find a gig and the rent was overdue. They needed money, so what was he supposed to do? Sit by and do nothing? This whole city was crazy with ways to get paid if you needed to, if you were willing, just a little, to step outside the lines. Just spot a busy corner by the projects—any of them—and a brother could hook you up. Five-0 might roll by every now and then, but in between, you could make decent money. There was always somebody tapping one of the warehouses or a delivery truck, and brand-new iPods, cameras, and DVD players still in the case equaled good, quick cash. Every corner near the projects had something going. If you didn't make some money, you just weren't trying.

But his last time out, he'd gotten robbed himself. A stack of iPods, some portable DVD players, and a couple of Sony digital cameras—his whole stash right out of his backpack—gone. Not to mention the twenty or so joints he hadn't yet sold. So not only did he not make money, now he owed it.

He told his supplier he was good for it. He just needed a couple of days to scrape together the money. He'd fix it. Soon, he promised. It wasn't a big deal, not really. He had a couple of ideas.

An hour on the street and it was already getting dark. Hard to believe, but just now, he was hungry again. The gumbo might still be warm. It seemed like, lately, he was hungry all the time, no matter how much he ate. From some open window way above, he heard live music, a piano, and a woman with a low voice, deep and pretty, singing blues or something, and he thought of Eden. Since that whole eviction scene, he swore she looked at him differently. And tonight was the first time he felt like she'd talked to him like he was grown. Trusting him with the truth, showing herself to him, faults and all.

If she blamed herself all these years for his mama not being in his life, she was crazy. There was no way he'd hang that on a fourteen-year-old girl, or however old she was then. But tonight, before he went to sleep, he could think about what he'd really heard her saying to him. *My mama alive, maybe. Out there, somewhere.*

By the time he reached the building, the sky was completely dark; a full moon rimmed in a milky halo and framed between two high rises across the street. He pulled the note card from his pocket, checked the address again. This was it, 514. A brown brick building, second one from the corner, with a wrought iron gate and a five-step stoop painted gray. He fingered the small wad of bills in his pocket. It wasn't much, compared to what he owed. But maybe it was enough to show the dude that he was a man of his word—a good faith deposit. He'd get the money, all of it. He was a man who could be trusted to pay up. He just needed a little more time.

He climbed the steps and rang the buzzer for the intercom. The street was dark and quiet, except for the honking horn of a taxi double-parked a few doors down. Maybe it was the night air, but he felt better. Summer was coming. Everything would be OK. He'd find all the money he needed, no problem. Things would get better. Eden was singing again, getting into a music school—good for her. And in a couple of weeks or so, he'd be back home in New Orleans, where he belonged.

CHAPTER 34

The rush-hour rumble and clatter of the A train car, the low-pitched drone of wheels grinding against the track. The jerky heave and metallic clanking of the train entering and departing the stations. The subway's rhythms and heavy pulse comforted her. In the crowded aisle, the standing passengers gripped rails and poles, stumbling with the car's random jolts.

The trains weren't always this quiet; there were often conversations between people who knew each other. But it was that Southern thing, that brief and random welcoming of passing strangers into one's orbit, that she missed. Eye contact, a smile, a nod. A "How you doin', baby?" or "Have a blessed day." She suspected that was one of the things her brother missed, too. "It's just so different up here," she'd heard him say more times than she could count. And that was one of the reasons why he wanted to go back home.

Recovering from their heated face-off at dinner had taken her a minute. His abrupt exit made her wonder if he was going out for an hour or for good. She was relieved when he returned shortly after nightfall, his eyes anxious, the crease in his unblemished forehead deepened.

He hadn't wanted to talk about his mama; something else was off. She knew because he ignored the half-full pot of still-warm gumbo.

He struggled with this city; she knew that. When her fretting over him had shifted from life-and-death nightmares to his simple joylessness—when exactly was the last time he'd smiled?—she'd begun to see his point. He hadn't found his place here, and nothing she said could convince him that returning to New Orleans was anything short of bolting backward through the gates of a personal hell. But too soon, for better or worse, he would be out of her reach.

Almost grown now, and he just didn't get it. When she was about his age, hadn't she found herself with a young boy to raise? Eighteen, and she'd jumped into that deep well of duty with both feet. But that was different. Girls, they said, naturally maternal and more mature, could most often rise to responsibility. Besides, she'd had the added benefit of her father's wisdom for eighteen years. And God knows, she had tried, done her best.

Everything her father had taught her, at least most of what she could remember, she'd passed on to her brother. But who was she kidding? He'd learned more about life from the street, his buddies, school, TV, movies, and videos than she could have taught him in a hundred years.

Until this morning, as she rummaged through his drawer in search of a lost gym sock, she'd thought his biggest mistakes were getting into the wrong cars at the wrong time. But the brand-new iPod tucked in the missing sock made something flip over in her gut. *He bought it*, she told herself. *He bought it. Surely.* He was making his own money now, right? That's what he told her, when she'd confronted him.

"And anyway, what you doing in my underwear drawer? Can't I get some privacy?" he'd snapped, his tone more accusatory than defensive.

But if he hadn't stolen it, why was he hiding it? Why hadn't she seen it before?

So, the old fears returned. *What was he doing and who with?* But she was not his mama, as he had pointed out, as if that would have made any difference.

Montague Street, Evan had said. She'd told him she'd be there by eight. When she got off the train at Court Street and walked deeper into Brooklyn Heights, she felt the change even before she arrived at the dark oak door of The St. Georges Café. The streets were quieter, the night clear and cool, the air light, and this undiscovered part of Brooklyn had a casual vibe that made her feel unhurried. Above her, a deep indigo sky peeked between the patchy lacework of budding ash branches and maple leaves. Along the way, ancient churches of red brick and stone squatted on corners like anchored ships. Specialty shops and ethnic cafés lined the streets, shaded by green and red-striped awnings. Sidewalk markets held bins and baskets of imported avocados and limes, and brownstone window boxes spilled blood-red roses and pink azalea blooms. Un-congested avenues and navigable sidewalks proposed a laid-back and low-rise version of the city; if Manhattan made you pick up your pace, this neighborhood invited you to slow it down and look around.

When she found the sign and the address, she walked up the four steps to the brass-handled door. From the other side drifted a breeze of slow, easy jazz— a lyrical ballad with piano and drum set and upright bass—and the muted scents of alcohol and incense. Inside, sparse furnishings featured a six-stool bar of dark wood along the east wall while bench-seat booths lined the opposite wall and a few wooden tables filled the center. Deep in the back on a foot-high wooden bandstand, a quartet of musicians—a rhythm trio with a singer—seemed to be finishing a set. Eden recognized the song, a blues-tinged "Somewhere over the Rainbow," a song she'd loved since she was old enough to read.

A young black woman in her twenties, both hands at her sides, swayed on the bandstand with her eyes closed. Her light soprano spun from glittery, red-trimmed lips. Her slight, athletic figure was sheathed in a thigh-high dress of stretchy black fabric. The bass player, slender, bald with a graying beard and looking much older, sat astride a bar stool, one foot on the floor and another on the stool's low rung, his bass hugging his torso like an ample-waisted woman. The drummer, a wiry, dapper-dressed man looking even older, sported a white open-collar shirt and navy blue suit.

The group played another tune without the singer, this one a bright, bouncy piece. Standing back near the door, Eden observed the scene: Evan at the piano, clearly the leader, his shoulders leaning in, his head in profile. He nodded to the bassist, a flicker of a smile crossing Evan's face and then retreating with a change of chord and mood. At the song's bridge, the tempo quickened, the musicians playing off each other, tossing fragments of tune or snatches of rhythm circling from piano to bass to drum and back again like snappy repartee. Her gaze locked on to Evan, relaxed, at ease in his world. *How different he looked*, she thought, *from this angle and distance.*

They changed tunes, the new one more upbeat, catchy, the bassist thumping strings and slapping wood, the drummer's quick wrists grooving a lightning patter of sticks on high-hat cymbals. Evan sat up, his head bobbing and wagging with the new pace. A broad smile crossed his face when he looked up and recognized Eden.

She smiled back. In this dimly lit space, with his hair cut and beard trimmed, he looked different, younger. His looks weren't classically handsome, though he was good-looking. Since the first day she'd met him at Estelle's, he'd been a champion for her, a man who had proven himself the soul of dependability and trust. That had never changed. But when she looked at him now, she felt something else. A shifting in her heart.

It might have been because of her brother leaving soon, this shift. Letting go of one thing, making space for another. When she was five and learning to roller skate, her father had unclenched her tiny hand from his: "If you want to do this, you have to let go of me." Truth was, a change for Eden Malveaux was already at hand. She could feel it. But skate the big rink alone? It would be so nice to have somebody

watching her back. Somebody at her side, or even out in front sometimes, leading the way.

When the musicians finished the song, a smattering of applause
and whistles rose from the small crowd. Eden was about to walk toward the bandstand to meet Evan, but the woman singer approached
him and flung both arms around his neck, pulling him into a giant
hug. Then she kissed him.

Eden blinked. A cheek-kiss, but still. It wasn't a gesture she could
easily place. Unless she'd misread it, there was something else there. A
possessiveness, a territorial marking. Eden nodded to herself, affirm-
ing the thought, ignoring her nerves. *A girlfriend—had to be. And why
not?* The man had a right to his own life. But the fact that he might not
be available to her had not crossed her mind any more than the notion
that she might want him to be.

"Eden!"

He beckoned her to the bandstand, still smiling. "This is Eden,"
he said, introducing her. But Eden was distracted. *She's way too young
for you.* When he introduced her to the singer, Eden betrayed her sarcasm and jealousy with the broadest smile she could muster.

"So, Eden, this is…"

She didn't hear the name, instead watched the play before her.
She wondered how long this had been going on, at what stage it was.
When she heard her own name again, she tuned back in.

"…Studying classical singing. She has a wonderful soprano voice."

The young woman's eyebrows raised above her heavily mascara-ed
eyes. "Oh, wow," the girl said. "I love classical stuff. Wish I could do
it. Why don't you sing something? This place is pretty casual, and you
came on the right night. Kind of an open mic thing."

"Oh, well…" Eden met the woman's gaze. The girl seemed nice
enough, pert, bubbly, petite, with a geometric Afro tapered on the
sides, saucer-sized hoop earrings, and a wide, thin smile. *What did he
call her? Denise? Diane?*

"Uh…Eden, well, she just got here," Evan said. "Why don't we get her a drink first?"

"Sure thing. Take your time. Nice to meet you, Eden."

The woman walked away. Evan led Eden to a booth near the door.

"So, Danielle's dad, our bass player, owns this place. She's a former student from when I taught night classes in English Lit at CCNY. I didn't even know she sang until a couple of years ago. She's good, huh?"

"Yeah, she's got a really pretty voice." *A student? Really?* "You guys sound great. Really."

"Thanks." He grinned and lightly tapped his fingers on the table. "I love these old heads. Traditional, straight-ahead stuff, you know? These guys have got mad respect for the masters. Trane. Dizzy. I love it! They're way better than me, but they humor me, letting me play with them. I try like hell to keep up."

She nodded, thinking about her father's old vinyls and wondering whatever happened to them. "Sounds like you're keeping up pretty good."

When a waiter showed up with two glasses—one bourbon and one Merlot—Evan said, "So. I asked you to come because I got a little idea for you."

"OK."

Evan shook the ice in his bourbon and took a sip. "You're singing that Schubert song, right? 'Night and Dream?' I found the piano accompaniment to it in my mom's stash of old music! It's not too hard, the piano part, I mean. I'm not great, but I can lay down a few of the chords. Or if you want, you can sing it a cappella."

"Sing that? Here?"

"Why not? You can break in your audition stuff before you face a bunch of scary judges. These guys here?" He gestured a hand toward the back booths. "Everybody here is on their third, fourth drink. Trust me, a little liquor in the listener and all they hear is genius. You can't fail! They'll love you. Then tomorrow, they might not remember you, or that they were here. So, nothing to lose." He laughed.

"Let me think about it," Eden said.

He reached for a leather briefcase he'd brought over from the piano. "Well, OK. While you're thinking about it." From the case, he pulled out the necklace and scrapbook, which he'd transferred from the plastic Walmart bag to a cotton tote.

He'd only spent the last couple of days working on it, he told her. But already, he'd learned from talking to a couple of dealers in antique jewelry that the eighteen-karat gold necklace was indeed crafted by the artisans he'd identified earlier: Rundell, Bridge, and Rundell, British goldsmiths to royalty such as George IV and Queen Victoria. Between three and five thousand in value, he estimated based on his research, and it might bring even more at auction. It was a fairly rare piece, definitely a special order, made for somebody important—an earl, maybe—in the mid-nineteenth century.

He leaned back in his seat. "But the story you told me—about the young girl? Her father? And of course, the singer, Celia. Well, if it's all validated, that makes it even more interesting for collectors. And maybe more valuable."

More research was needed, of course, and he would help her find a good appraiser. She thanked him. She'd do it, just as soon as her audition was over.

"I need the necklace now," she said. "I can't sing without it."

She was serious. She'd worn it to every lesson she'd had with Blessing, and even in the few days it had been with Evan, she'd missed it. It was for good luck, she told him. But it was more than that. Without it, Eden was shy, directionless; with it, she was Celia DeMille. The whole world was unlocked and waiting. Or it felt that way.

Evan listened, rapt.

"And then there are these dreams I've been having," she said.

In the most recent, she had entered a great hall, a church maybe, to hear or see something of monumental importance. There were ushers, white-gloved, young ladies in white dresses like the ones girls wore to Sunday morning church services back home. The hall was packed, so she found a seat near the back. A tall, willowy usher approached her, hand outstretched. *Come with me.* Eden shook her head. *No, thank you.* The back pew was fine. But the usher insisted, reaching again for her hand. *This is where you belong.* The woman led her down to the first row, where a seat had appeared in the center.

When Eden sat, she turned back to look at the usher, now dressed in a long gown of antique white lace, a silver tiara crowning her swirl of black curls. When the young woman turned, she wore the face of Celia DeMille.

"OK. Then what happened?"

"Well, I looked up at the stage. And a woman was singing. It was…me."

Eden looked down at the backs of her hands, spread across the table. "Crazy, huh?" she said. Then she laughed, a timid, awkward giggle. "It's like this woman, she's my, you know, muse, or something. My spirit animal, or whatever they call it." After a moment, she added. "I know. You think I'm nuts."

Evan put his hands on the table, lacing his fingers.

"What?" She gave him a questioning glance.

He took a breath and paused a moment. "Look. I talked to Blessing. He told me not to tell you this—he thought it would put pressure on you. He told me you are the most talented singer he has come across in years. He said a voice like yours is truly rare. It has all the sweetness and color of a lyric soprano, and at the same time, the power and volume of one of the great dramatic sopranos. Most voices are either one way or the other. But yours is a voice you don't find that often. He said you could go far…sing major roles in an opera company…if you wanted to."

And her range, he added, was nothing short of extraordinary. But history was full of might-have-beens. Singers who had the talent to be great, but not the grit. Either they didn't really want it badly enough, or if they wanted it, were afraid of putting out what it would take to get it. Or they were willing to do the work, but something else stood in their way.

Eden massaged her forehead with two fingers, then sat back, and looked toward the ceiling. "I don't know. I feel like….like I'm losing my mind. I can't even think about that right now, I've got so much going on in my head."

Eden put the necklace around her neck and clasped it, then fingered the braided metal around the disk with her thumb and three fingers.

"So, I put this thing on," she said, her eyes wistful, her voice softer now. "I think about her, or maybe I am her. And I feel good. Better than good."

Evan said nothing for a moment, then signaled a waitress and ordered another round. The second Merlot triggered in Eden a mild impulse to giggle, calm down, then loosen her tongue to the point of unabashed truth-telling. Or it could have been her confession last night to her brother. First Aunt Baby, then Reginald Jr., now Evan.

She sighed, took a long sip, leaned her head back against the leather seat, and directed her eyes toward the ceiling. Evan's expression, his open heart visible in his eyes, promised safety and privacy in the space between them. It was high time Evan Smallwood knew who she was, really, and anyway, what was there to lose? She started with the night her father died, and once she began, the rest flooded forth.

She backpedaled to childhood moments. Summers in New Orleans. The scent of her mother's L'air du Temps on Sunday mornings, the smell of her Revlon dusting powder, and the Crimson Sunset tinge of her lips as she readied herself for Sunday school. Skipping stones with her father and watching the paddles of the Creole Queen churn white foam onto the belly of the Mississippi as it slogged toward the bridge. The sanctified Johnson sisters' shouts of amen and hallelujah for her gospel solos after the Sunday sermons. All the mess between her Aunt Baby and her daddy. A pregnancy, an abortion, a baby brother to raise. She told everything. She half expected some kind of judgment, or worse, pity. But even Eden's betrayal of her stepmother prompted a look of unexpected understanding. When she described the ordeal of the storm and flood, Evan reached out to touch her arm before she was even aware of her tears and trembling hand.

They were both quiet for a moment.

"I'm sorry," she said, embarrassed. "For dumping all that on you."

Shrugging, he said, "All that, and here you are. Stronger, better than ever."

She averted his gaze, looking toward the bar. "Sometimes it's almost too much, I don't know which way is up. One minute, I think we're doing better, we're making it, and then…" Her voice trailed.

"You know, your brother's gonna leave you someday. He's gonna go and live his own life."

She blinked twice, her voice in a whisper. "I know that."

"And you're gonna have to live yours."

"Yeah."

Tell him, she told herself. *Just tell him.* "So, um…here's the thing. I resented him, my brother. I didn't want him to be born. And I hated that woman, my stepmother, coming into our lives. And I had to take care of him when she left. And I hated it. And then daddy died, and I promised…"

A sigh rose from an unrecognizable place in her. The things we never say aloud. *How could she have wished her brother had never been born?*

Eden took a sip of wine, her hand still trembling slightly. When she placed her hand back on the table, Evan covered it with his. He looked, unblinking, at her.

"I mean…it's not…I love my brother. I do." she said.

"I know," he said. "I know you do."

A full minute passed, filled with the noises of conversations and recorded piano jazz from the box speakers hanging from the ceiling. They were silent, his hand still resting on hers.

"You know what?" he said. "Now would be a great time for you to sing."

The heat of his hand unnerved her, but calmed the tremble. Then she thought of the young woman singer and fought the urge to pull it back. "Not sure I can sing right now. I'm a mess. In case you can't tell."

He smiled. "Years ago, when my father died, I was a wreck, I was so depressed. My marriage had failed. No kids. I was out of the service a while, but still didn't know what I really wanted to do. I took a construction job, just to keep busy. The first week, fell off a ladder and got injured. Lower back. Wasn't terrible, in fact, I put off the surgery until a few months ago, right before we met.

"So, I quit working. Lived on disability, knocked around, you know, doing this and that. Taught a few night classes in literature, hung with my buddies, played music in dives so thick with stale beer and smoke you could hardly breathe. I was…unsettled. After he died, I thought, *Life goes by fast. I better figure this out.* A few months later, my mom sat me down. 'Baby,' she said. 'I missed my chance. My chance at doing something I loved.' She didn't want that to happen to me. She asked me, 'What do you want to do the rest of your life?'

"I had no clue. I'd fooled around with piano, but I wasn't that good and never thought of it as anything but fun. I honestly didn't know. Then she said, 'I don't have any regrets, raising you and your sisters. But you all grew up and left! And what if I could have sung?'" He sat back and took a long sip of his drink. "So, I thought about it a while. What did I like to do, really? I'd always liked to restore stuff, you know, take old things, fix 'em up, make them pretty again. Furniture, old clocks, watches, stuff like that. My mom said, 'Well, do that.'"

Eden nodded. "So, you did."

"I thought she was crazy. Make a living tinkering with stuff? But then I met Arnold. Got a job in his shop. People bring things in, old, broken, sometimes in pieces. But good stuff. Interesting. First piece I fixed was a gold pocket watch. Scratched up, black with tarnish. Took me weeks, putting it back together, making it shine and keep time. Found out later it once belonged to Dwight Eisenhower. Can you believe it? Anyway, Arnold sold it at auction for a nice piece of change.

That's how it started. Then he would send me out to estate sales or auctions or whatever. I loved it. I fell in love with all the old, dusty, broke-down things most people these days would throw away.

"Funny, nobody wants to fix anything anymore. Just throw it out. But sometimes the stuff that doesn't get tossed, that makes it to the next decade or next century, could be really special, hooks you up with the past. Lots of history or cool stories behind them, like your necklace. I know this might sound a little, you know, precious, but you gotta respect something special enough to survive all those years, generations, even. Sometimes there's a reason why stuff from the past makes it through.

"But you don't need it to be able to sing," he said. "Yeah, the necklace is cool, and if you think there's power in it, then good. But *that voice* you got. That's the *real* treasure. You've got honest-to-God gold in you, and I don't think you know it." He smiled. "Maybe that locket found you for a reason."

Eden laughed. "Well! No pressure there."

He stood up. "Relax. One step at a time. Right now, we're only talking about your singing a pretty song in front of a bunch of folks so lit they might not be able to find their way home." He tucked the piano music under his arm and extended his hand to her. "Not to get all New Orleans on you, but if that thing has got some juju in it, let's put it to work."

CHAPTER 35

After she sang and the bar closed down, it was late. Evan insisted on taking the subway uptown with Eden back to her apartment. She told him she'd be fine alone, but he wouldn't hear of it.

The earlier night's wind had settled, the breezeless air a little warmer, the black sky between the branches pitted with stars. A calm settled over Eden as the two walked toward the subway. She remembered the last time she had been out in the evening with a man. Doyle Dugan's face sprang to mind. How different the two nights, how different the two men. With Evan, she had never felt safer.

She had sung the Schubert song exactly the way she wanted to, the way Ernest Blessing taught her.

"Who are you?" Blessing had once asked her.

"What do you mean?"

"You must act the music, be the character," he had told her. "Whether you are singing Mozart or Sondheim or Gladys Knight. Your eyes, your hands, your body. Who are you? What are you saying?

"'Night and Dream' is about longing," he had said. "Wishing that beautiful dream, that thing you've longed for, not to disappear with the morning sun. Think of a dream of yours, a dream that you desperately want to be real. When morning and daylight snap you back into the world, your dream still clings to you, somewhere. Buried but still there."

A dream she wanted to be real? To linger past the night into the light of day? There were so many, now. Keeping her brother safe, seeing him grow into a man to make her daddy proud. Pouring everything she learned, every song she loved into waiting ears, singing with the power of Celia DeMille.

But lately, when the face of the diva appeared in her sleep, another dream took shape. Not for herself, but for the woman whose life had changed hers.

In the café, the music had flowed effortlessly. When she let go of the last breath, let the last silvered tone dissolve in the smoky air of the dark room, there had been a sacred silence, seconds long. Then, the club had erupted in applause. And every customer in the club—all eleven of them—stood and cheered.

It was nearly midnight when she and Evan reached the door of her building.

"Thank you," she said. "For everything. The people were great. You were right."

Hands in his pockets, Evan nodded. "Yeah. Good crowd, right? Good crowd and good music. Doesn't matter, Mozart, Schubert, or Ella. It's like the Duke said, 'There's only two kinds of music—'"

"Good, and the other kind."

Evan laughed. "What do you know about Ellington? You're way too young."

"My daddy," she said, smiling. "If it had anything to do with jazz, he knew it."

"Ah. Right." He gave her an acknowledging smile. "The club can get pretty noisy. All the times I've been playing here, I've never heard it so quiet. It was like you could hear folks listening to you. That's special." He cleared his throat. "What I mean to say is, well, you made 'em listen."

Eden smiled. "Yeah, I guess I did."

"Well, if you're going to sing for your future in a couple of days, you'd better get some sleep. If I were you, I'd turn in right away."

"Yeah," she said. "Guess so. Well, OK. Good night."

He nodded. "Look. That girl. The one singing with us. She's not… we're not, you know…there's nothing, I mean, she's a friend. Not even that, really. She's the daughter of an old friend."

Why was he telling her this? "Uh…OK."

"I just wanted you to know that." He reached for her shoulders. "Good luck," he said. "You're gonna kill it."

He leaned his head toward her and waited. It was a question, giving her space and time to retreat. When she didn't, and instead turned her face to meet his, his lips softly landed on hers, briefly. Then he smiled and pulled away.

Before she could speak, he was halfway down the steps.

Before getting ready for bed, Eden stared at her reflection in the bathroom mirror, touched her cheek, and said aloud, "Girl, who are you?"

The mirror threw back an intriguing stranger, not the girl who fled New Orleans for New York almost a year ago. That woman, flying by the thin seat of frayed pants with no plan except the one she made up as she went along, had no goal other than to keep herself and her brother alive, healthy, and well-fed. That woman had slowly faded to blankness, a snapshot left too long in the sun. Yet this new one looked hazy, unformed, an image floating through a cloud of steam. She stroked the necklace, then took it off and placed it on top of a cabinet near the sink.

Even though Ernest Blessing had said her chances of winning the Ellen Fedak Foundation Scholarship Award were not great, it was his words afterward that made her blood race. "You are one of the most naturally talented singers I have come across in years." She'd sung well tonight; she had a shot at this.

"Show up," he'd said. "You never know—anything was possible."

So many things had changed. Evan Smallwood, in fact, had shown up from nowhere, it seemed. Who knew? Proof of what was possible.

If the singing had been all of it, it would have been, easily, one of the best nights of her life. But from the time she said good night to him and headed upstairs, she could think of little else but the chafe of facial hair against her cheek and the mint scent of shaving lotion, the smile that flecked copper eyes with gold.

She brushed her teeth and turned off the bathroom light.

"What do you want? Really?" Evan had asked her. "And don't start the sentence with 'my brother.' What do you want for you?"

She'd sighed and said, "I'm trying to figure all that out."

By the time he had kissed her, she had decided. *This. I want all this.*

CHAPTER 36

RENOWNED COLORED SINGER DIES

A small gathering of fifty or more friends, acquaintances, and admirers of Celia DeMille gathered at the Fondant Street AME Church on Wednesday to pay final tribute to the Negro classical vocalist who sang throughout Europe in the 1890s and early 1900s, and for four US presidents.

Madame DeMille, a native of Boston and known as "The Black Donatella" (a sobriquet inspired by the world-renowned Adeline Donatella), succumbed to a long illness at the Marshall Friedlander Convalescent Home in Boston, Thursday, May 7. She was sixty years old.

Barred from performing with the world's great opera companies who did not hire black singers, Madame DeMille created The Black Donatella's Troubadours's traveling minstrel show based in New Orleans, LA as a showcase for her talent. Comprised of singers, comedians, dancers, and other performers, they entertained audiences across the United States before being forced into bankruptcy.

from The New England Afro-American

A small gathering of fifty or more friends? That's all?

Another article an inch long with a small headline began, FANS OF GREAT COLORED DIVA DISMAYED AT HER BURIAL IN A POTTER'S FIELD IN…

"Potter's Field." It didn't take a genius to figure out what that meant. An unmarked grave.

Eden sat in bed the morning of her audition, turned the last page of her scrapbook, and closed it. She held a hand on her chest, her eyes full and brimming.

She hadn't expected to feel this way when she reached the end of the story of Celia DeMille. Catherine, or someone else, had tucked in the last two articles between the final page and the leather back cover. It was the second notice of her death that Eden had seen in the scrapbook. The first was clearly some mistake. Some other dark-skinned singer posed above the caption, "Black Donatella Dies." Madame Celia had seen her own mistaken obituary and Eden's heart sank at the thought.

At the top of the clipping she read now, there was the image of an aged, and maybe infirm Celia. She was not the young, spirited, and beautiful woman who Eden had come to know in these pages through the newspaper clippings of reviews and feature articles. Disappointments, heartbreaks, and age had paled her skin, and it sagged beneath translucent, topaz eyes. She was shrunken and thin. Her white hair was pulled back, and a delicate lace shawl draped over her shoulders. Her faint smile was resigned.

Catherine must have tucked them inside the scrapbook Celia had given to her. The article, along with several other clippings, had been placed inside a yellowed envelope; the return address, the Friedlander Convalescent Home in Boston, Massachusetts. There were other papers. A notice of bankruptcy. A death certificate. A typewritten page titled "Last Will and Testament." A funeral program with a short obituary.

The will, obviously a carbon copy, spelled out her wishes:

All my music, clothing, jewelry, and personal papers are to be given to Catherine Fountaineau, New Orleans, LA.

And beneath that:

"With the exception of my scrapbook detailing my career, which Miss Fountaineau shall deliver to Mr. Arthur Flanagan of the New York Times *newspaper in New York, New York."*

And on a scrap of paper tucked beneath the will, there was a name she had never seen before, written in someone else's handwriting. Catherine's, Eden guessed.

Carl Murkison, 229 W. 43rd St., NY, NY.

That was a puzzle. Who was he? A fan maybe? A close friend she'd met in her travels? There was much more about the diva's life that she didn't know, and never would.

From the side window next to her bed came a cloud-dimmed wash of gray morning light along with the sounds of taxi horns, delivery trucks, and the backing-up beeps of waste disposal vehicles. Riffs of salsa and a radio traffic report played from an open apartment door two floors below. It was 8 a.m. She'd awakened early, unable to sleep more than six hours, her mind racing. In less than five hours, her life would be completely different. She knew it. She could feel it in her blood.

But guilt clawed and scratched at the hope in her. Her chest expanded with a deep, slow sigh, sadness eddying up in waves as she closed the book. One of the greatest singers in the world, in the end, forgotten. She died broke. A career thwarted by prejudice, diminished by time, while Eden's was just beginning.

And that was just how she felt this morning, on the brink of something so big, so wild, she could hardly stand it. She was about to become a singer. The flesh on her arms prickled; she would be famous. People all over the world would wait in long lines to hear her. She remembered last night, and Evan. How he had leaned into her, waited, then kissed her. The kiss had stirred long-buried feelings in her, feelings trapped beneath guilt, duty, obligation. But here, finally, was someone who believed in her.

She put the book of Celia DeMille's life back beneath her bed. *Someday*, she thought. *Someday when people will listen to me, I'll tell the world about you.*

Her bedroom door still closed, she listened for sounds of Reginald Jr. moving about the living room. He'd been coming in later and later, and it'd been more than twenty-four hours since she'd seen him. They kept missing each other. Since their conversation the other night after the gumbo, she had thought it best to give him room.

When she finished her shower, she fried two eggs in a cast iron skillet, made toast and coffee, and prepared to sing, the way she had for the last several days: vocalizing on vowels, slow warm-ups with scales. On the Sony Walkman Blessing had loaned her, she played recordings of the great singers he'd introduced her to: Anderson, Callas, Price, Tebaldi, singing in Italian, French, and German, languages she hoped someday to fully learn, more than the phonetic German she would sing today. The more great voices she heard, Blessings had said, the better. Great singers would inspire her, show her what was possible.

She was on the second exercise, *Ma...may...mi...mo...moo*, finding tone and pitch, increasing volume, ascending slowly and smoothly, gathering breath from her core, the way she'd been taught. The whole diaphragmatic breathing thing. She'd come to love this part of the warm-up, the way an athlete finds meditative peace in a muscle stretch.

The ring of the mobile phone startled her. It was her brother's number.

"What's up, Boo-Boo Head," she said. "Where you at?"

A beat passed. The voice on the other end, dark, gravelly, sent a chill up her spine.

"Tell your little brother he got hisself in a fix."

Eden's heart thumped. "What…who is this?"

"Tell 'im he need to make good on his debt. And he need to do it soon."

"Who is this?" Eden said. "Why do you have my brother's phone? Where is he?"

The line went silent.

Like a nerve, something twitched in her mind. Reginald Jr. was not just in trouble. He was in danger.

She dialed Evan's number. No answer. She tried four times again over the next ten minutes. When she finally reached him, she was nearly hysterical.

"Slow down," he said. "When was the last time you saw him? Did he say anything to you that would make you think something was going on?"

She said no. She hadn't seen him in at least a whole day, twenty-four hours, she told him. Or more. She thought they'd kept missing each other because of his job, her schedule, his shooting hoops, and hanging with his friends.

"You said he talked about New Orleans. Do you think he might have gone there?"

"I don't know. I don't think…I don't know. Oh, God."

She walked, dazed, into the living room. His futon was folded into the sofa position, the way he did it every morning before leaving the apartment. She opened the closet door where he hung his clothes. His jacket. His Timberland boots and sneakers. Most of his shirts and jeans. His blue duffle bag and backpack. All gone. She was sitting now at the table near the kitchen, one hand holding the phone to her ear, the other massaging the ache in her forehead.

She stood up, made circles in the living room, pulling at the ends of her hair. "His stuff is gone—he's gone. I don't know what to do. What should I do?"

"You said he had a part-time job," Evan said. "Do you know where he works? Maybe somebody there knows something."

"Right," she said. "It's called…let me see. Something 'Messenger Service.' Mid-Manhattan, that's it. Mid-Manhattan Messenger Service. Let me call you right back."

She hung up, got the number from information, and dialed.

"Reginald Malveaux?" said a young woman in a sleepy voice. "Sorry. Nobody working here with that name."

She called Evan back, now even more distraught. Her brother, she told him, had somehow found money to keep them from being evicted. When he said he was working, she believed him.

"He lied to me," she said.

"OK. OK." Evan said. "Look. What time is your audition?"

Audition? Seriously? No way could she go and sing now.

"Eden." Evan's voice was calm. "Please, you have to show up. Didn't you say this is the only day when they'll hear people? No exceptions? Please. Just go sing, or at least tell them there's been an emergency, and I promise you we will figure all this out."

Just then, her phone lit up with another call.

"Hold on," she told Evan. "I gotta take this."

It was from the 504 area code. New Orleans.

"Eden? Eden? You hear me? Shoot, I don't know how this thing works. Say what? You there?"

She heard Aunt Baby's slow drawl, with a trace of irritation. Then, Mildred's voice, "Hold it up to your ear, Baby! You don't have to keep putting it up to your mouth!"

"Sorry, baby," Aunt Baby said. "Mildred got me one of them cell phones, and I ain't had the chance to get used to it."

"Aunt Baby? Are you all right?"

"I'm fine, baby, but that brother of yours came over here last night. Some buddies dropped him off. Said he wanted to borrow some money."

"He's in New Orleans? How did he…Is he all right?"

"Yeah, child, just showed up at my door. Didn't look too good. Seemed kinda jumpy about something—eyes all shifty, sweating like a runaway slave. Anyway, I fixed him some dinner and he ate like a mule. What's going on, child? How come you didn't come with him? I guess you working. Anyway, he said he had to pay somebody some money he owed them. I didn't ask no questions, just gave him fifty dollars. And I figured by the look on his face he owed a whole lot more than that. I know he didn't come all the way down here for no fifty dollars, 'cause that's a long walk for a short drink. What's he got hisself into? I asked him if you knew he was here. He said, not exactly. Said it was kinda spur of the moment, that he was gonna tell you, but then he lost his phone—"

"Tell him to please, please call me. Somebody got his phone and used it to call me. Said he owed them money."

"Well, I figured it was something like that. I asked him where he was staying down here, how long he was gonna be here. He didn't answer me."

"Aunt Baby, he's been doing some stuff I didn't know about. He's in trouble. Just please, if you hear from him or see him again, tell him to call me as soon as he can."

After she hung up, Eden leaned forward in her chair, both hands on her head.

Dear God.

Evan called back. When she told him what she'd learned, he said, "Look, I don't blame you for being worried, but the main thing is that he's OK. Your Aunt said he's fine. Whatever he's gotten himself into… well, he's practically a grown man. He'll just have to figure it out."

"He's a kid! He's my responsibility! I've got to go down there. I've got to go find him."

"Eden. Eden. Hold on. We can figure all this out. I know you want to help him, but today, right now, there's really nothing you can do. I'll help you. I promise you. But you have an audition today. This is your chance. You're ready. This could change your life. You've got to go."

Eden sat quietly, rubbing the palm of her left hand against her knee. Her mind raced backward. Her brother's first real haircut. His missing tooth smile at seven. His growth spurt at twelve that turned his skinny legs and arms into poles. His face when she told him about his mother.

She thought of Evan. Their kiss seemed a lifetime ago. He didn't understand. He didn't get it. He didn't get her.

Sing? Now?

"You got to be out of your mind," she said, and hung up.

She sat for a moment, arms folded across her chest, rocking, thinking.

Something flashed in her mind—an instinct. She went to the bathroom. Lately, she'd worn the necklace so often, she'd not been careful to return it to the box beneath her bed. She'd taken it off and left it on the cabinet near the sink.

And now it was gone.

CHAPTER 37

"You can sit just over there," said the woman at the registration table for the Fedak audition. She pointed to a row of stuffed armchairs against the wall. "We'll come to get you when we're about ten minutes away from your time."

Eden sat in one of the armchairs and took several deep breaths. Instinctively, she felt her neck where the necklace should be. It had been her nerve calmer, her worry beads. She rubbed two fingers against the bones of her clavicle and sighed.

She had said she could not sing without it, and now singing without it was exactly what she had to do. And on top of everything else, she had not been able to warm up properly. She placed both hands against her stomach when she felt something turn inside. Sitting here now, she could barely breathe, let alone sing.

She sat alone just outside the double doors of the ballroom on the twelfth floor of the Ansonia Hotel, an elegant homage to turn-of-the-century New York on Manhattan's Upper West Side. From some distant room came the sound of a piano, then, the high-pitched trill of a coloratura. "The opportunity of a lifetime," Evan had said. She'd be crazy to not show up for it.

Eden took a swallow of the hibiscus tea with lemon she'd brought in a thermos and tried to calm the fluttering in her chest. She went over the first line of "Night and Dream," trying to remember everything she had been taught. Her blood pulsed wildly and nerves jumped and raced beneath her skin. Never had she ever felt less prepared, and more scared.

"Just go, do your best," Evan had told her, "I'll meet you right afterward. We can sit down and figure out what to do about this thing with your brother. We'll figure it out."

"Ah, there you are! Ms. Malveaux? Student of Ernest Blessing? Right."

A silver-haired woman led her down a white-carpeted hallway. The woman gave her a form to fill out and left Eden in a small meeting room to warm up. The room was freezing, and Eden buttoned the top button of her black jacket. A pitcher of water, several glasses, and a tea pot sat on a table draped with white cloth.

Eden looked at herself in the standing mirror in the corner and opened her mouth to sing a scale. Not good. Neither the way she looked (disheveled hair, shiny skin, and worry frowns prominent between her brows) nor the way she sounded (rough, uneven, and breathless). Notes came out in unsteady streams, ascending upward with breaks. And what in hell was going on with her top octave? She started again. Better, this time. She took a long deep breath to calm her shudders, then several smaller ones, inhaled from deep inside her chest and exhaled through her pursed lips. She started the exercises again.

When she was called to sing, she followed the young man who'd come for her, a boy who couldn't have been more than nineteen and was dressed in black. "Right through there," he told her, pointing to a door leading to the ballroom.

A long table sat at one end of the rectangular room with two women and four men sitting at the table. All were white except two; one of the men looked Asian, one of the women was black.

One of the men cleared his throat, then looked down at a sheet of paper in front of him. "All right! Good afternoon, Ms. Malveaux? And you'll be singing Schubert? Correct? And then the Mozart 'Deh vieni non tardar' from *The Marriage of Figaro*, and let's see, a spiritual, too? 'City Called Heaven?'"

"Yes, sir. Yes, that's right." Eden said.

"Very good. Whenever you are ready."

Eden pulled a pitch pipe from her pocket and blew the first note of the Mozart, finding the place in her throat. The warm-up in the smaller room had not gone particularly well. So, the first notes of the Mozart aria, rolling out smoothly, surprised her. *All right. Good.* In the warm-up room, she thought of everything that Blessing told her about support, breath, control, and pace. Then, she put all of that aside and focused on the music.

Or, she tried to. Everything went fairly well until the end of the second phrase. A small break in her sound—air where tone should have been—frightened her.

She stopped, looked at the judges who returned blank, waiting stares.

"I'm sorry. Can I...may I start again?"

Two of the male judges smiled. "Of course. Take your time. Would you rather start with something a little less technical? How about the spiritual?"

"Yes, I'll do that." She relaxed, closed her eyes, and began "City Called Heaven." *A spiritual, in English, thank God.* A song she knew exactly what to do with.

"I am a poor pilgrim of sorrow. I'm tossed in this wide world alone..."

Breathe. She told herself. *Just breathe.*

What had he told her? "Forget Mozart now," Blessing had said. "Sorrow. Sing your sorrow. What are you carrying inside of you? Sing it now."

Sorrow? Well, that was easy.

At last, she felt herself settling. She thought only of the sound she wanted to make. When she finished, she nearly smiled; she had done what she wanted to do. At the end of the song, she soared to a high C and held it, owned it. She played with it, a soft pianissimo, then a full, long push, a crescendo to a forte. Her eyes widened and her face relaxed into a smile. *Good,* she thought. She felt the judges' eyes on her. She had them.

"All right. And now…Schubert, is it?" one of the judges asked.

She felt a little better now. She began the next song. But again, her nerves rose and rattled. The moment the first note was out of her mouth she realized she had made the same mistake, mispronouncing the first word the way she had many times before. The mistake played in her mind, and at the end of the second phrase, like a lost child at the end of an unfamiliar street, she didn't know which way to go. *Should I ask to start again? No. You already did that. Which are the right words, the right notes?*

She started again anyway, pronouncing the word correctly, but now forgetting the next phrase. She glanced at the judges. A few looked up at her with questioning glances.

"Take your time. Would you like to go back to the Mozart?"

Eden looked down at the floor, at her shoes. Her breath was short. Suddenly, she noticed the scuff marks on the left toe of her black pumps. And then her ankles. Ashy. How could she have forgotten to lotion them? *You too brown-skinned to go out without lotioning those legs!*

Where had that come from? Her mother's voice.

Folks like to size you up from head to toe, so make sure they don't go cross-eyed at what comes out of your mouth or what you got on your feet.

Her father might as well have been in the room, talking to her. She looked at her shoes, her feet, and her ankles. What would he say?

In that moment, she wondered who she thought she was. And why she was there.

"Um…excuse me," she said. "I, uh…" Bile rose in her throat. "I'm sorry," she said. "I'm sorry."

She ran out of the room.

When she reached the street beyond the hotel's lobby door, she remembered Evan had promised to meet her there. But now he was the last person she wanted to see. She looked around to make sure there was no sign of him. Not here. Good. She headed for the bus stop.

At the corner, her phone rang.

"I'm here in the lobby. When I went upstairs, they said you'd already left. Did you sing? What happened? How did it go?" Evan sounded agitated.

"It didn't go well. It was the worst. I was too…upset, nervous. I should have never tried to do this."

Silence. Then, "Eden, I'm so sorry. Where are you now? Let's talk."

Her eyes welled up. "No, I think I'm just going to go home. I shouldn'ta come and try to sing. I wish you'da never…"

She paused. She wished he'd never…what? Come into her life? Taught her to believe in the impossible?

"I'm sorry." She didn't want to be rude. When she started to speak, she felt a fullness in her throat, a burning in her eyes. "I'm done with this," she said through her tears.

"Eden…"

"Hey, look," she said. "I know you were trying to help, but don't… just let me be."

She hung up. On the street, she walked north toward the corner and found a diner. She pulled open the glass door, headed past the counter through the thick grease-smoke, the beer and bacon smell, to the restroom, then ducked into a stall.

She tried to muffle the sound of her tears with a wad of toilet paper pressed to her mouth. *Pull yourself together, damnit.* A full ten minutes after locking herself in the stall, she placed one hand against the wall, leaned over the toilet, and retched.

CHAPTER 38

The day after the audition, after a sleepless night, she'd dragged herself to work at Maestro's, then left after thirty minutes. She couldn't sing. Her throat ached and she felt dizzy. The next few weeks were a blur. The dark waters of depression took a toll on her body—insomnia, poor diet, and stress—so the sickening head cold was no real surprise. "A summer cold is just the worst!" Janelle, the manager, had told Eden when she'd reported that she wouldn't be in for a few days. And when the cold dragged on and Eden could not get out of bed, much less sing, Janelle had even been patient. "Take your time! Get some rest!" she said and seemed sincere.

Eden attacked the virus with a vengeance. Days in bed. Long hot drinks with lemon and honey. Lozenges with echinacea, zinc, and goldenseal. But the sore throat and headaches persisted while a river of mucus, streaming from her sinuses to her throat and to her gut, wreaked havoc with her digestion and gave her a persistent, hacking cough. Laryngitis sandpapered her voice down to a husky baritone, when she had a voice at all.

After three weeks, when she felt well enough to wait tables but not well enough to sing, she called Janelle.

"The thing is," Janelle sighed, "We need you to be able to sing. Customers love you and want to hear you. The whole dinner cabaret thing is really popular, and just as many people come to hear our singers as to eat. Take a little more time. Let us know when you're ready to sing."

"Oh, OK," Eden croaked.

But days passed, and while her speaking voice came back, her singing voice had not. She thought of calling up Professor Blessing, but felt so embarrassed at her performance at the audition, she didn't have the nerve. She sent him a card, a note of appreciation for all his help and a word about how the audition hadn't gone as well as she'd hoped. She'd thanked him for everything.

Her brother was still missing. Bed-bound and steeped in self-pity and medicinal broths, she had time to fret. When Mildred called, she held her breath.

"Haven't heard from him," Mildred said. "But there was something on the news that got us both worried sick."

There had been a shooting at a convenience store in New Orleans' Central City neighborhood. Two of the suspects had been taken into custody. A third, it was reported, had gotten away.

"Might not've been your brother," Mildred said. "But could have been."

"What makes you think it was Reginald?"

Mildred paused. "The two men? That night a while back? The men on the news were the same two men who dropped your brother off at Baby's."

Eden swallowed hard. It didn't mean that it was Reginald. It could have been anybody.

He was safe. He was healthy and whole, and would get in touch with her any day now.

She would believe that as long as she could.

The change hadn't been as much of an adjustment as she'd expected.

She missed putting on full makeup and a skirt to sing at Maestro's, but with the orange Home Depot apron she and the other employees wore, she could disappear. And no one cared whether she was dressed to sing a solo or stock the high shelves with toilet seats.

She hadn't thought about singing since the cold—virus, whatever it was—left her with a throat that didn't seem to remember how. And Reginald Jr.—where he was, what he was doing—gave her enough to think about. Every horrible possibility knocked about in her rattled brain: in jail, dead, or living on the street. Late at night, wine-induced sleep dragged in after the third or fourth glass, but strong morning coffee and a day-long parade of customers—*Something you looking for? Can I help you with that? Aisle four on the left*—kept the worrisome thoughts at bay.

And when she wasn't working or thinking about her brother, she read.

Celia's scrapbook had gotten Eden into a reading routine. She remembered the books she'd seen on Evan's shelves, so she bought a dog-eared six-dollar copy of Toni Morrison's *Beloved* in a used bookstore in Harlem and started reading it on the subway rides home. Another useful distraction: *So, did that girl really come back as a ghost? What did she want from Sethe and why?* Late summer was slipping into cool nights with clean, starry skies, so the fire escape steps, a glass of wine, and a deep dive into a complicated head-spinning novel became her new refuge.

Long walks in the city calmed her. When the weather cooperated, hiking up and down Manhattan's avenues staved off a funk that would set like cement if given half a chance. Twice a week, before taking the subway home at 3:30, she went to her new favorite spot, sat on a bench, and read. The construction noises around her, the jackhammers and excavators in a part of town that seemed an eternal "work-in-progress" were oddly comforting. But especially, she loved returning to the space that Evan had shown her months ago, now turned into something nearly sacred. What had he called it? "Hallowed ground." Thousands of African souls who built Lower Manhattan were now buried beneath it, remembered in The African Burial Ground Monument.

Today was a day like that one; a jewel-blue sky and clouds white as sea-foam, the air rain-rinsed and fresh. So, she took the subway down to Chambers Street, then walked to the spot, put her coffee cup and white bag of Delton's cream-filled doughnuts on the bench next to her, and opened her book. She could think here, a point at the cacophonous tip of Manhattan, a tiny island of peace in the midst of a bigger, bustling one. A thin waterfall streamed from a metal sculpture and made a soothing, gurgling sound. Near her bench, a fountain rushed into a narrow pool. The water sounds held the traffic noise at bay.

A stillness settled over the raised mounds of earth that replicated freshly filled-in graves. *How many?* she wondered. No names, Evan had said. How many people had been buried here with no names?

A granite slab erected near the mounds read:

For all those who were lost
For all those who were stolen
For all those who were left behind
For all those who were not forgotten

She closed her eyes. Isaac. Lottie. And Celia, buried somewhere in Boston in a potter's field.

When she thought of Celia, she felt a chill. She would never see it again. She'd tried not to think about the necklace, and when she did, she tried to convince herself that her brother, wherever he was, needed it more than she did. If it meant getting him out of whatever hell he'd gotten himself into, or if it meant saving his life, he wouldn't have had to steal it; she would have gladly given it to him.

But Celia. The diva just would not let her rest. It didn't matter that Eden had literally closed the book on Madame's life. Every night in the middle of some unrelated, pedestrian dream—stocking Home Depot shelves with light bulbs or staring at grocery aisles of detergent—there she was. Celia, singing at the river. Celia, watching the opera house go up in flames. Celia, drowning in fire, calling to her:

Save me. Save me, girl.

Save her? From what?

The gold necklace—the guilt choked her. But the woman was dead. What could Celia want from her now, from the grave?

She took a sip of her coffee and looked up at the trees above until the answer came:

But at least we'll know they lived. They won't be forgotten. Better late than never. The words Evan spoke that day and the thought behind them seemed to come from nowhere. Or maybe it had been in her mind all along.

"Thank you for seeing me."

The sidewalk café near the *New York Times* building did a brisk business on most Sunday mornings, and this one was no different. They found a table shaded by a red Cinzano umbrella near the quietest corner of the street. He held a chair for her as she sat, and a waitress came to take their order.

"Two coffees, and…?"

"Just coffee for me," Eden said. "Black. Thank you."

Thick-chested and ruddy-cheeked, Walter Meyerholtz looked heavier than he had when they met in New Orleans in the lobby of The Inn, the hotel that stood on the spot where the old French Opera House had been before it burned.

Walter looked over the menu, then closed it. "I was surprised to hear from you. You didn't tell me that you lived in New York now! Before we start talking, I think it's only fair that I tell you: the anniversary pieces we planned about the hurricane, the flood…that's all done. I'd hoped that you would call and I'm glad you did, but actually, I don't think we need anything more at this point. But I'll keep you in mind."

"I called you about something else. Not the hurricane stories." Eden placed her backpack on the small table between them. From it, she pulled out the scrapbook, the medallions, the photos, and the letter written in Celia's own handwriting.

"This is what I called you about," she said. She explained to him as much as she could. The metal box left behind in the street from the flood with a scrapbook of extraordinary reviews. The famous black singer who had sung all over the world in the 1890s and early 1900s, including at the White House, for four presidents, and the king of England. The reviews that called her one of the greatest living singers, and the nickname "The Black Donatella" that replaced her own. The minstrel troupe she formed to showcase her genius, that went bankrupt. Her death after a long illness, and being penniless, forgotten, and buried in a pauper's grave. And the interest of the reporter who might have saved her career.

"She never got what she deserved. They never gave her enough credit, not like they should have. But she was really, really good."

The cold still with her, she'd stopped in the middle twice to cough, and he'd handed her a tissue from his jacket pocket.

She blew her nose. "Sorry," she said. "I got this cold."

"That's OK," he said. "Warm weather colds are the worst, aren't they?"

He seemed nice enough. But after a moment, she realized how ridiculous this was. Was she insane? Coming here, taking up this man's time? And for what? What did she think he could do?

"This is all very interesting. But I'm afraid there's nothing I can do with this. First of all, I cover travel, not the arts. Who did you say promised to write an article about her? Someone said that recently?"

"No...well. This man from the *Times*," she said. "While she was still alive, he promised he would write a big long article about her. She left all this stuff because she wanted to be remembered. And I thought, even though she's been dead for years, it might be good to have a kind of tribute to her, for history and all."

"When was this?" he said.

"Uh, I think it was 1921."

Silence. A raised eyebrow, an incredulous look, something between condescension and sympathy.

"I know," Eden said. "I know it's been, like, a really long time. But she was so famous, a genius, some people said. It's all there in those articles." She turned a few pages in the scrapbook. "See? All these, from different papers—Cincinnati, San Francisco, Chicago. Here's one in French from Paris, I think. And England. And like I said, she sang for everybody, kings, queens, President Roosevelt..."

"Well, if that's the case, I'm sure she must have been written about in our obituaries. What year did she die?"

"Uh, I think it was 1929. And no, sir. There wasn't any obituary in the *New York Times*. Only the small one you see here. And this man, Arthur Flanagan," she added. "He promised her."

He chuckled. "Arthur Flanagan? Wow, the stories about him! Way before my time, but legendary. A little eccentric. Loved peppermint schnapps, and kept a box of Cracker Jacks in a drawer by his desk. Liked to party and could drink you under the table, from what I hear. Loved singers, though. Wrote a couple of books about opera. Died in the sixties."

He looked at his watch, then buttoned the top button of his jacket. "Look. I'm really sorry. Your singer looks like she had an interesting life. Maybe if you take it to one of the black newspapers? They might be interested in doing a historical piece, a tribute. Maybe during black history month, or something."

Eden felt her throat tighten; it was sore again. She got up. "You know, I'm sorry I took up your time. It was just...this woman, this singer kind of inspired me, you could say. I just felt she oughta get her due, even if it took all these years," She paused. "I thought I should at least try."

"Well, she has been dead for, what, seventy-five years!"

"Better late than never," she said. "I felt like, whether she's alive now or not, people need to know who she was. "

"What did you say her name was again?" He looked down at one of the headlines. "'The Black Donatella?'"

Eden suppressed an irritated sigh. "Her name was Celia DeMille."

"Oh right, well, sorry I couldn't help you. I'm sure your singer was great."

She gathered the materials to put them back in her backpack. As they both stood to leave, he offered his hand. "Good luck," he said, his large palm surrounding hers as they shook. "By the way, I met some pretty interesting folks in New Orleans. And I wrote a few pieces about the city. Great place, great people. Looks like the Gulf Coast is on its way back. Most of it anyway. We'll be running pieces about it for the next few weeks. How about you? You and your family making out OK? Everybody safe?"

She blinked. These days, just the mention of family triggered a shiver of fear. She took a deep breath. *Safe?* She wished she knew.

She managed a half-smile, half-shrug. "Nice to see you again," she said. "Appreciate your time."

CHAPTER 39

She had just got off the train when Marianne called.

"You're in town?!" Eden practically screamed into the phone. "Why didn't you tell me you were coming? Oh, girl, it's so good to…tonight? Yeah, perfect! Anytime you say!"

When they met at Jimmy Solo's Pizza near Penn Station an hour later, they hugged each other like long-parted sisters. They sat in the back near the kitchen doors and talked loudly above a speaker blasting Motown hits.

"Oh, my God, it's good to be back in this big, crazy city! Yeah, I know. I didn't use to drink beer. It's all these youngsters I've been hanging out with. Students. Babies, most of them. I feel like their mama. One of the students, Hispanic boy, couldn't'a been more than twenty-eight, invited me to his place and promised to 'rock my world.' Can you imagine? I flashed my AARP card. I thought that would scare him away, except he didn't know what the AARP was."

Eden smiled. "So, what brings you back?"

In town to renew her driver's license and visit with her old roommates, Marianne told her. She and Eden had talked on the phone only once since the audition, a long conversation about her brother's disappearance.

"So have you heard from him?"

"Who?"

"Anybody. Evan? Your brother? Anything change since we talked?"

Eden gave her a glassy-eyed stare, then put both hands over her eyes as she started to cry.

Marianne reached a hand to her shoulder. "Hey, honey. Let's get out of here. Let's walk a little bit." She summoned the waiter and paid the bill. As they walked, Eden's tears subsided.

"Sorry, sorry, girl," she said. "I'm OK." Eden let out an embarrassed laugh and wiped her eye with the back of her hand.

"Believe me." Marianne put both hands around Eden's forearm as they walked toward the neon glimmer of Times Square at dusk. "I have been where you are now. There was a time when I felt my life was over."

It wasn't that she was afraid her life was over, she told Marianne. It was the opposite, that it would go on. Without her brother. Without music. Without singing.

"I told Evan I couldn't sing without Celia's necklace. When I wore it, it felt like I was connected to something big, bigger than me. Turned out it was true. I lost the necklace, and then lost everything else."

They turned a corner onto a quieter street off Broadway. Marianne said, "I can't believe you'd give up singing. As if your talent depended on somebody or something besides you and your voice."

"My voice is, like, gone. There's something wrong with it. I haven't been able to sing since before I got this cold. The thing keeps dragging on."

She told Marianne about having to quit Maestro's since she could not sing, and that she now worked at Home Depot.

"Oh, girl," Marianne said. "Did you go to see a doctor?"

"No."

Marianne shook her head. "There it is again. Nurses see this all the time—folks who just ignore whatever is wrong with them. Promise me you'll go."

See a doctor? Eden said sure, she'd go, in a tone lacking conviction, since she couldn't afford it. But what did it matter? She wasn't going to be a singer anyway.

They walked on in quiet, lost in their own thoughts, winding their way from one block to another without a destination in mind, before reaching the subway station at Columbus Circle, where they would go their separate ways.

Marianne asked her when she'd last heard from Evan. Not since the day of the audition, Eden told her. Weeks ago. She described the last evening she'd seen him, singing with him at the café, the things he'd said, the closeness between them. She was beginning to think they could have something together. And she had ruined it.

"I feel like he's done with me, and I don't blame him, after the way I treated him," Eden said. "I thought he really liked me. Maybe he did. But I think I was a project for him. He told me once he liked to find things that were broken and fix them. Well, that's me. One of those broken things he just wanted to fix."

Marianne looked her straight in the eye. "Don't give up on yourself. On any of it. You're crazy if you do, and believe me, if you do, there will come a time when you'll regret it. Take that from a middle-aged divorced woman who just entered nursing school," she added. "My regret? That I waited so damn long."

The station grew noisy as commuters gathered near the track. The approaching D train vibrated the platform. "This is mine," Marianne said. "Maybe he wasn't just trying to fix something that was broken. Maybe he just liked finding things with a beauty nobody else can see."

Marianne disappeared inside the crowded car and Eden pondered this as the train pulled away. It didn't matter now. She believed she would never in her life see Evan Smallwood again.

As she got off the train near her apartment, her phone rang.

"Hello?" she said. Fear rose in her chest like a flash of heat. Maybe, like before, it was somebody calling about her brother.

"Is this Eden Malveaux?"

"Yes, it is."

"My name is Mia Hightower. I'm a friend of Professor Ernest Blessing. I'm one of his former students."

What would a friend of Ernest Blessing's want with her? "Oh. Is he all right? I've been meaning to get in touch with him. Is everything OK?"

"Yes. He's fine," the woman said. "Listen, I would like to talk to you about something."

The woman gave no clue of what she wanted with Eden, except to say, "I was one of the judges at the Fedak audition. There's something I want to discuss with you."

Oh, Lord. The devastation of that day came back in a rush. "Ah... OK. Yes, ma'am."

"Good," the woman said, and gave her an address. "Tomorrow at 2? That work for you?"

"Oh, yes, ma'am. I'll be there."

Nerves flipped in Eden's stomach. It was one of the two women judges; the black one, she bet.

What could she want with me, bad as I was? Eden fished for a positive thought. The audition was a mess, but she had sung that spiritual pretty well. A church gig, maybe? Maybe Blessing had told the woman how desperate she was. But realistically, she came to another conclusion. As one of the judges who witnessed the most humiliating performance of her life, the woman must surely have a bone to pick with Eden. Showing up at an important audition and performing horribly was one thing. Being black and screwing up in front of the only black judge surely didn't help.

Whatever. She had to go; the woman was Blessing's friend. She would just woman-up and go meet the lady, receive whatever how-dare-you-embarrass-me-and-black-people-everywhere scolding she had coming. Eden spent five minutes in front of her nearly empty closet deciding what to wear to meet a woman whose upper-crust speech and frou-frou diction suggested attire she didn't own. She finally decided on her go-to outfit—a long-sleeved, black cotton top, black skirt, and black belt. Rich or poor, smart or stupid, black was the equalizer.

If ever there was a time when she needed her special, confidence-building necklace, this was it. But there was no point in traveling to that dark place, an express train to depression and endless thoughts of her brother. She would set aside some time later for that mud-wallowing pity party. Now, for a face-to-face with her own shame, she chose a thin, silver-plated choker that caught her eye in a resale shop window between Home Depot and the subway station. It wasn't Madame Celia's locket, but it would have to do.

It was a part of town she'd never been to before: Washington Square. When she found the building on West 10th, the woman greeted her at the elevator door. "Are you Eden? Hello," she said, and extended her hand.

"Hello, Miss, uh..." She'd forgotten the woman's name. Nerves. *Calm the hell down.*

"Mia Hightower. Come on back this way."

Nearly six feet tall, large-boned and broad-shouldered, Mia Hightower had deep copper skin set off by long lashes, dramatic bronze foundation, and theatrical-looking mascara. Her cheek bones sat high and sculpted beneath a broad forehead and expertly cut crown of short, natural hair flecked with gray. Her silk handkerchief-hemmed kaftan showed hand-painted brush strokes of red, purple, and yellow playing against a field of white. Even in four-inch heels, her stately posture transformed her stride into a floating glide, reminding Eden of a proud matriarch carrying a huge gourd of water on her head across an African landscape.

She led Eden down a long, beige-carpeted hallway with cream-colored walls and crown-molded ceilings. At the end of the hall, she opened a door. The apartment was small, tiny even, but the high ceiling created the illusion of voluminous space. A long, white, button-tufted sofa stretched against one wall, and above it hung a half dozen or so abstract modern paintings.

On another wall, Eden's eyes fell on a poster that made her jaw drop. She felt a chill.

At the audition, she hadn't realized that she had not only seen this woman before but had also heard her sing.

Mia Hightower closed the door of the apartment and gestured toward the white sofa. She still hadn't smiled at Eden. "Have a seat. Tea?"

"No, thank you."

Eden couldn't take her eyes off the poster. The woman in it, unmistakably Mia Hightower, had longish straight hair. Nothing like the close-cropped Afro she sported now.

Mia sat opposite her in an upholstered gray chair and noticed Eden looking at the poster. "Oh, yes," she smiled for the first time. "I wear a wig sometimes. It's just so much easier, especially when I travel." At the bottom of the poster was her name, an upcoming concert date, and a venue.

"I've seen you before."

Mia's eyebrows arched up. "Oh? Where?"

"The church. St. John the Divine. A friend took me there. I was there one day when you were rehearsing."

If Eden had felt embarrassed before, now she wanted to sink through the floor. She realized she had made a fool of herself trying to sing the song Mia had sung herself.

Eden's mind raced. *I should apologize. I should tell her how sorry I am, how embarrassed I feel.*

Before she could speak, Mia said, "So tell me. Are you feeling better now? You ran out of the audition as if you were ill."

Eden swallowed around the painful bulge in her throat. "Um, yes. Yes, ma'am."

Mia leaned forward in her armchair, her hands clasped on her knees. "Let me tell you something," she continued, as if Eden had not spoken. "Number one. If you are too ill to sing, then don't. Number two, your German. How long have you been studying it? Never mind, I think I know the answer to that. Number three, and this brings me to your biggest failing that day."

Eden wanted to cry. "Yes, ma'am?"

Mia folded both arms across her chest, her round eyes flashing. "You gave up! You didn't finish. Never, ever do that." She shook her head. "There may be many things you cannot control, but whether to finish or not? That is not one of them."

"I'm sorry," Eden said, holding back tears. She put a hand to her forehead. "But my brother, he's in trouble. Big trouble. I've been having some family problems."

Mia's voice lowered. "I'm very sorry to hear that."

Mia continued past the awkward silence, changing the subject. "Mr. Blessing, he's a wonderful man, and teacher, isn't he?" She'd been a student of Blessing's twenty years ago when she was just out of the Manhattan School, and now, whenever she needed a tune-up, he was her coach. She moved to Paris nine years ago to be closer to the Paris Opera, where she sang often, but recently bought this place in New York. She now divided her time between the two cities. As a younger singer, she learned from Blessing about the world she was about to enter. "'Brutal,' is how he described it. "Competition like you've never seen. You have to be ready for whatever comes."

"And *us*," she said, in a tone of presumed mutual understanding. "We have to be more than ready." She leaned back in the armchair and crossed her legs. "Now, a question for you. Are you able to sing? Physically able?"

Eden told her that after the audition she came down with a cold and her voice had been weird since then. She described her symptoms: scratchy throat, sneezing, mucus-y sinuses.

"Have you been to see an allergist?"

"No," Eden told her. "I haven't."

"Mr. Blessing told me about you, and having heard you sing, I agree with him. I have never heard anyone sing that spiritual the way you sang it. You have a great gift. Often voices are beautiful, sometimes interesting. Rarely are they both. Yours is. You have something that a thousand other singers wish they had. So, here's the deal, if you are ready for it. Forget about the Fedak. That's done. Someone has won that, and frankly, even though she was much better prepared and performed beautifully, she is not as talented as you are."

But there was another opportunity. A fall opera apprentice program in Italy trains young singers for professional careers, she explained, and one of the sopranos chosen in another audition, a young woman from Oklahoma City, had to drop out at the last minute due to her pregnancy. The American-sponsored program, Bella Voces, needed someone to take her place.

It was a full scholarship with a stipend for living costs, all travel expenses paid.

"It starts in a few weeks. The work is intense. You will learn Italian. Study French, German. You will spend six weeks working with coaches and studying in Florence, then over the next month or so sing in different cities, you and seven other singers. At the end of that time, there will be agents, producers, opera managers, and artistic directors that you will meet. There's no guarantee you'll get work, but you'll be in a good position.

"In the meantime, call this number." She handed her a card. "Pollen count is crazy right now. A lot of singers are struggling."

When Eden looked at the card, puzzled, Mia said, "He's an allergist. Works with singers all the time."

"I'm sorry, I can't afford..."

"Don't worry about that. He'll examine you and probably prescribe something. You won't have to pay. He's my ex-husband. He owes me, big time."

When the meeting ended, Mia stood up. "Professor Blessing told me you are from Louisiana, the Gulf Coast."

"That's right."

"And you say you raised your brother on your own?"

"Yes."

She nodded. "I have a younger brother, too. I know how it is. We worry about them, these boys today. But after a certain time, they have to live their lives, and we have to live ours."

Eden had been wrong about this woman; looking into her eyes now, she saw no judgment. Remove the makeup, the dress, the posture, and the backdrop of expensive furniture and modern art, and what was left was just a woman, like her. The voice in the church, at once earthen and ethereal, came from a woman with bills to pay, family issues, faults, and troubles of her own. A woman who seemed only to want the best for her.

Eden looked at the card. "I'll call him. Right away. And thank you. Thank you so much."

CHAPTER 40

By now, she had lost count of the number of times she'd tried to call Evan. Ten? Twelve?

Her long, stumbling apologies landed, unanswered, in his phone's voice mailbox. In the last few weeks, it had become clear: he wasn't going to call her and didn't want to hear from her.

She'd seen Mia's ex-husband, the allergist. A round of tests, a prescription, and in four days, her throat was better; two more and her voice was good to go, as healthy as ever. She'd missed singing as much as she might miss a toe, a finger. She dove back into the warm-up exercises to get back into shape.

She was so desperate to share her good news, she was close to stopping strangers on the street: "You don't know me, but guess where I'm going."

Professor Blessing did not seem surprised to hear from her. "You'll need to work on your German," he said. "I am available Tuesday and Thursday after five."

When she reached Marianne, her friend's joyful squeal had Eden holding the phone away from her ear, and Pastor Fleet at the Holiness Church let out a resounding "Praise Jesus!" so loud it made her skin jump. The friends she'd made at Maestro's, even Home Depot, were ecstatic. But when she interrupted Aunt Baby's and Mildred's Tuesday morning breakfast with a phone call, they were surprisingly subdued.

"That's wonderful, child." Aunt Baby called to Mildred and put the phone on speaker mode.

"We're so happy for you!" Mildred said.

She went on in detail, explaining how she met the beautiful singer, her teacher's former student. She'd gotten a packet of material two days ago and went over, in detail, the itinerary of the trip as the women listened with the phone between them: fly out of Kennedy, land in Frankfort, fly to Rome for two days, and on to Florence.

"When you leaving?" Aunt Baby interrupted.

"Two and a half weeks."

Aunt Baby paused. "Child, we were going to call you today. We got some not-so-good news."

"What?" Eden braced herself.

"Your brother. He got arrested. He's in jail."

Eden's breath stopped. Her head felt light, her heart thumped in double time.

The two men who were accused in the convenience store robbery, as Randy Marvais accurately reported, had been picked up, released, then picked up again by the police. But Reginald Jr. fit the description of someone who had been seen with the two men in the car.

"He called me yesterday," Aunt Baby said. "Arraignment's tomorrow. They'll set bail then. Even if it's only a few thousand, we just can't afford that. Doesn't have a lawyer; can't afford that either. He'll have to wait for the court to appoint him one. There'll probably be a trial and he might have to wait in jail for it. No telling when that will be. Your brother swears he didn't know those two knuckleheads were planning anything. For right now, we believe him."

Eden put a hand on her pounding chest and sighed. "OK. I'm coming. I'll come as soon as possible."

"No!" Aunt Baby practically shouted. "Listen here. You stay right where you are and we'll take care of this. Me and Mildred gonna stand with your brother tomorrow down at the courthouse. If there's anything needs doing that can be done, we gonna do it."

Mildred said, "She's right. Child, we'll handle this. I'm sure you got lots to do to prepare."

Aunt Baby spoke quietly. "It's time now. Time to let him stand on his own."

Eden protested. "I'm responsible for him. I can't let him down, not now. I promised Daddy—"

"Promised him what, exactly?" Aunt Baby's voice rose. "That you would let your own life go for your brother's sake? That you would pass up a chance to make his dream for you come true? Now get off this phone. Do what you need to do to get ready. You say you leaving in a couple of weeks?"

"Yes, ma'am."

"You got a passport? Got your clothes all lined up and packed?"

"No, ma'am."

"What you waiting for? I'ma speak for your daddy since he ain't here. You go and live your life. Go and sing and make us proud."

That night, Eden sat on the fire escape steps in her robe, legs crossed, a half glass of red zinfandel in hand and a plate of Ritz crackers and sardines on her lap. The night sky held a sliver of moon and a single star, and the chill air was still. The day had gone by in a rush; there was so much to do. The passport thing- -she hadn't realized how long it would take, but thank God, Mia's lawyer friend rushed it through. The rent was paid for another month, but she'd needed to borrow enough from Marianne to cover it until her first stipend check. Fall months in Europe evoked movie scenes of villages wrapped in snow, so with her little bit of stashed tip money, she'd gone to the Methodist thrift store on 96th and for $28.95 bought a thick, black wool winter coat and a pair of good re-soled leather boots. But she'd spent most of the day writing a long letter to her brother.

She'd only gotten halfway through it before putting it away, then pulled it out again to finish. It was a hard letter to write, her throat swelling, her words halting, searching for words to phrase a loving goodbye. She was not just leaving the country for a few weeks, she was leaving him, for real; a parting of paths, him heading one way, her another. And even if their paths converged again, it would never be the same between them. But who was she kidding? In both their minds, the separation had already begun. The physical part of it, him in New Orleans, maybe in jail awaiting whatever fate held for him, and her taking off for Europe, was just a formality.

What do you say to a brother who might be looking at years in prison? "I'll always have your back?" She wouldn't, couldn't—not now. It was time for them to live their lives apart.

The anger she felt at his disobedience, the I-told-you-sos that wanted to creep onto the page, evaporated the moment she began to write.

I'm always going to be your sister. Remember that, Boo-Boo Head, she wrote.

She wasn't in a scolding mood, but had to tell him, *I know you took the necklace. Maybe it was a survival thing, a money thing. Maybe you felt like you didn't have a choice. But you need to know what's in that little piece of history. And if you don't have the necklace anymore, like somehow you let it get away from you, you let go of more than a little piece of gold.*

And now she told him the whole story of the diva and the necklace: how it was sold in exchange for a slave girl's services. How her father, the slave-turned-free-man, had stolen it along with his own freedom, and how it reminded him of his lost daughter, Lottie.

At the end, she wished him well. *Do something good,* she said. When she finished the letter, the crackers and sardines were gone and she turned up the glass to savor the last tart sips of wine.

Before she folded the six pages and sealed the envelope, she placed something else inside it. She always carried it in her purse. It was thin now with age, its edges worn. *I don't know when I'll see you again, so I want you to have this.*

The photograph of Reginald Sr., Afro long and grin wide, with arms draped around the shoulders of two marine buddies, was the only picture she had left of him after the storm. If Reginald Jr. was sentenced to prison, he would at least have a reminder. *This was your daddy*, she wrote. *This was the man who loved you as much as I do.*

She looked at her watch. Before she headed back inside, she opened her phone and dialed Evan's number once more. *Please, answer this time.*

She listened only to his recorded voice: *Sorry I can't answer right now. Leave your name and number. And have a good day.*

CHAPTER 41

Europe, 2006

In Europe, Eden felt herself a woman slipping out of old skin into new flesh. The things to see, to learn, to explore, crowded her brain. In Italy, Eden was a child happily trapped in a dream. Forget New York. This place took her breath away: the ancient, cobbled streets behind their hotel in Florence, the flower vendors, the quaint cafés ripe with history, the squares and piazzas gaudy with fountains and sculpture, the sumptuous food, the wine, the people, the style. Here, the natives adorned themselves like works of art; women packed their thin frames into skinny jeans with scarves of colored silk and thigh-high couture boots, putting casual New York to shame. The men, too, exuded style in their slim-cut blazers, smoking cigars or cigarettes with Italian film flare, and even the ones who weren't handsome looked self-possessed and suave. She'd been warned about those fine Italians with their about-face turns on the street to admire legs and derrieres, their dark-eyed stares proposing whatever the imagination could dream. But, temptations aside, Eden and the singers were there for the work.

Before, in another life, hard work meant aching feet and a sore back from long days of double shifts, or the stress of demanding customers impatient with a slow kitchen. Or the getting on and off trains in Manhattan to navigate hordes of pedestrians bunched together into a slow-motion stampede. But this work—language classes (Italian was OK, but that German, with its strange word order, was a trip), private lessons, classes in movement, and the daily sessions with coaches and accompanists who would not let up for a minute—well, it was a kind of work with which her body and mind were not familiar. Nothing Eden had ever done before had prepared her for the fatigue of a spent, aching brain.

There were eight of them, all American-born and all hopeful artists. Of the group of sopranos and mezzos and one lone baritone from Tennessee, Eden had bonded with two: Cynthia, the only other black girl in the group, a Chicagoan in her late twenties, and Tina, a thirty-ish Latina mezzo from Atlanta. Four weeks into the grueling schedule, it was Tina who, when they were awarded a three-day furlough, said, "Let's go to Paris," in a tone befitting a trip to the movies. Why not?

If Italy was a dream, then Paris was that dream on a seventy-millimeter screen. The broad boulevards. The Arc de Triomphe and the Louvre and the Eiffel Tower looked like giant replicas—the Champs-Élysées, a coursing river of exotic wealth. The Paris Opera theater's ornate architecture and impossibly grand staircase. And the way the city looked at night—like fireworks frozen and harnessed in a frame—was breathtaking.

On their second afternoon, as the three women walked arm in arm past dazzling boulevard shops and giggled as they tried out their French nouns, Eden caught her reflection in a window.

No, that can't be me. Her posture was straight, her clear skin glowed under her makeup, and her natural curls were voluminous. The thick, well-tailored black thrift-store coat clung to her size-six frame like custom-cut skin. Framing her reflection was the city of Paris. Too good to be real, but it was. A chill went up her back, raised the hairs on her arms. *Things will be different now. This is just the beginning.*

After the brief French respite, they returned to Italy inspired and with renewed vigor, as classes gave way to recitals performed for the locals in small village churches in and around Florence. As promised, at the end of the apprenticeship in Italy, their last three days on the Continent, a bevy of opera house managers, producers, directors and agents listened to the young singers in an evening recital featuring all eight at Florence's Chiesa di Santa Monaca. The time in Europe had gone by quickly. After the concert, at the nearby Giovanni Trattoria, the group of more than thirty dined on prosciutto with melon, bruschetta with truffle crostini, beef with pasta and parmesan, and an endless supply of chianti. And afterward, at a small café near the Ponte Vecchio, Eden and her two new friends sipped wine and espresso and pondered their futures.

They were sitting outdoors on metal chairs just outside the café, well after midnight. It was a perfect evening; the moon cast a quality of light that seemed almost foreign, unlike any moonlight anywhere at home. The cobbled stone streets near the restaurant were quiet except for soft strains of an accordion on a high, unseen balcony, bellowing something that sounded like old Frank Sinatra. They complimented each other's performances ("Girl, you crushed that high E-flat!"), drank beyond their limits and deep-dived into the nature of Italian men's eyes (soulful? lecherous?) and the dubious appeal of sautéed calamari versus squid in ink. And what was that weird vegetable at the end? Artichoke, Cynthia said. The others had never seen one before.

"So, I'm staying here," said Cynthia, smiling while she turned up a glass of port. She'd landed a job in the chorus of the Paris Opera for an upcoming *Rigoletto*. And Tina, who'd met a local tenor and fallen in love, had also decided to stay, with no particular prospects in mind. "I've got a few auditions lined up," she offered. She looked at Eden, said, "What about you?"

"Uh, still thinking about it." Eden turned up her chianti and drained the glass. *Love it here, want to go home,* she thought. She'd learned just days ago that her brother's case might come to trial soon, and after more than a month in jail, he'd either be set free or sentenced to more time.

"I got family to see about," she told them. "Brother in a little bit of trouble."

No one asked for details. Cynthia said, "A brother in a little bit of trouble? Who doesn't know about that!"

After a quiet moment, Tina raised a goblet. "Here's to us," she said to the sound of clinking glass. "I don't know about y'all, but after this, I just want to sing. That's all. Here's to good gigs, and singing our asses off from now on!"

On her third jet-lagged day back in New York, Eden got a call from Janelle at Maestro's Bistro and Bar. One of the singers was returning to school. They were down a waitress, and the restaurant needed someone to fill in, at least temporarily. Eden's eyes lit up. Jet lag or not, she was ready. But the day before her return to Maestro's, she had to decline, for the best reason she could imagine.

One of the Italian opera directors Eden met abroad had a colleague in New York with a problem. A singer scheduled to sing a three-week run of *Carmen* with Opera New York had dropped out with the flu. It wasn't the starring role, but Micaela, the young friend of Carmen's lover, Don José, was a perfect role for a young singer breaking in. Eden's French was improving, and she'd studied the role in Italy. A tall order, the director said, but could she be ready in a week?

Eden didn't hesitate: she'd be ready the day after tomorrow.

"I'll be there, not opening night but as soon as I can get away," Marianne told her over the phone. "With bells on!"

It was bittersweet, Eden said. She had planned to return from Europe, then head to New Orleans to see about Reginald Jr. That wasn't possible now, not for another few weeks.

"You heard anything yet?"

"No. He's still waiting for the trial. We don't know what's going to happen. Hoping for the best. Aunt Baby and Mildred go see him as much as they can. They say he's OK. Scared, nervous. But healthy."

"And what about our friend?"

Eden had thought about Evan countless times in Europe. She'd sent a couple of postcards and a letter to his address. "Nothing."

"Well, maybe when he hears that you're singing…"

Eden blinked, let a silent beat pass. "I can't believe I said I'd do this. It's not that big of a role, but this is some scary stuff. Me, singing opera in New York."

Marianne laughed. "Yeah, better you than that other girl. She probably couldn't have done it."

"What other girl?"

"The one just up from Louisiana with nothing but a little brother in tow and a truckload of baggage. No, she never could have done it. But you? You're not that girl. I can hear it over the phone. You even talk differently! I would say it was Europe, but I was seeing it even before you left."

Eden weighed this. "Well, I hope I haven't changed too much. I'm still a Louisiana girl. I don't ever want to get too far from home, at least, inside."

But she knew Marianne was right. Something in her had shifted, and some things would never be the same. Making beds, waiting tables, stocking shelves, slouching her shoulders and shuddering at heights—all gone. Even her grammar had changed; there was nothing like conjugating Italian verbs to clean up your trashy English. She had no idea what she would do after this three-week run. But whatever she'd do, it would be with eyes ahead, not back.

Despite a slightly nervous stomach, Eden's opening night began fairly well. By the third act, when the moment arrived for her big aria, she felt calm. Taking in a breath, she opened her mouth and surrendered herself to the swells of the orchestra, folded herself and her voice deep into a space inside the opera's make-believe universe. She was no longer

Eden Malveaux, but Micaela, a young country maiden pleading with Don José to come home, to spare him the fate that awaited with the irrepressible Carmen. After her aria, "Je dis que ne rien m'épouvante," shouts of "Brava!" erupted from the faceless dark.

When the cast lined up for final bows, it was impossible to see the audience for the glare of the lights, but from somewhere, single stemmed roses landed at Eden's feet. She stepped forward, picked them up, and held them aloft as more cheers rose from the crowd.

That night, she could barely sleep, which was just as well. At 7:00, she was jolted by a phone call. It was Aaron Frankel, the manager who had hired her. "Sorry to wake you," he said. "Go get a copy of the *New York Times*."

At the kiosk on 106th, she bought a cup of French Roast and the *Times*, and turned to the arts section. On page eight, above the fold, were two photographs below the headline, A NEW CARMEN DELIGHTS AND SURPRISES. Both photos were taken during the production: one of Irina Levin, who played the role of Carmen, and the other of a young tenor named Ronald Foxx, who played Don José, along with the newly discovered soprano in the role of Micaela, Eden Malveaux.

Eden let out such a loud gasp that the man who sold her the paper nearly dropped his coffee. "Everything all right?"

Everything was fine, she assured him while scanning the article to find a mention of her name. In the third paragraph she read: "And replacing an indisposed Margaret Fairlane to make her opera debut, soprano Eden Malveaux sang with a purity of tone and richness of texture and color too seldom heard in the role of Micaela. This late stand-in was a stand-out. Ms. Malveaux is a singer to watch."

CHAPTER 42

Aunt Baby answered on the second ring. Eden was full of news to share, but her brother's situation was always uppermost in her mind. The last she'd heard from Aunt Baby and Mildred, the case, scheduled for trial, had been delayed three times. But the two women had spent the entire day at the courthouse the day before. Mildred had left her a message that things were going forward.

"What happened?" Eden held her breath.

Aunt Baby sighed. "Well, child, we got good news and then we got some other news."

Mildred rushed in with the good news. "Your brother got released! One of the two boys with him, the ones that got picked up that night, signed a affidavit that Reginald Jr. wasn't involved, that he didn't have any idea what the other two had planned to do. Reginald didn't have any priors, so that helped. The judge left it up to the prosecutor, and the prosecutor said it would be OK if Reginald went free."

Eden heaved a relieved sigh and placed a hand to her chest. *Thank God*. "Where is he? Can I talk to him?"

"Well, that's the other news," Mildred's tone darkened. "This all happened yesterday. We brought Reginald home with us. Your auntie and me fixed a big dinner and we sat and ate red beans and rice like it was going out of style—that's what your brother wanted, of course!"

"We got up this morning, bright and early," Aunt Baby said. "But your brother, he was gone. No sign of him. Just took all his stuff and left."

"He just…left? Just like that?"

"Left us a little note on the refrigerator, saying something like, 'Thanks for all you did for me. Sorry, I can't stay. There's something I gotta go do.'"

"Well, what does that mean?"

"Child, we don't know," Aunt Baby said. "We just afraid he's gonna go off with the wrong folks, you know. Get hisself in trouble again."

"Did he say anything about coming back to New York? He's got another year of school left up here. Maybe he's—"

Mildred interrupted. "Somehow, I don't think that was what he planned. He didn't have too much good to say about New York. No, my guess is he's hooking up with somebody or somebodies down here. And he didn't mention anything about enrolling in school, even if there was one for him to enroll in. Schools coming back after the storm, but it's real slow."

Aunt Baby said, "Sorry, child. I just don't know what to say, except I smell more trouble. He didn't have a phone, so we don't have no way of getting in touch with him. But he's got my number. We'll let you know if we hear from him."

Eden's good news felt anticlimactic now, but she told them about the opera, opening night, the article in the paper.

"That's wonderful, child!" they both exclaimed. "Please send it to us!"

Eden promised she would; she'd already bought a dozen copies of it.

"And please, as soon as you hear anything, anything at all, please call me," Eden said.

The conversation left Eden wanting a drink. But the zinfandel bottle on the refrigerator door was empty. Distracted by the article, she'd forgotten to go to the store. She headed out of the apartment.

Mixed emotions muddled her thoughts as she fished through boxes of frozen waffles in the freezer section of the bodega three blocks away, then bought a dozen eggs from the market next door. And to celebrate, a twenty-dollar Merlot, the most expensive wine she'd ever bought. The opera opening, the review—it was surreal. But part of her felt angry—her mind wasn't free to enjoy it. What if he stayed in New Orleans? He wouldn't be enrolled in school and those streets would eat him alive. He'd be at the mercy of the same forces that guided his life before. And if he returned to New York? People were looking for him there, too. What would happen to him? Was there anything she could have done? Anything she could do now to keep him alive and out of prison?

She tried to console herself with something Evan had told her: "You can do everything for someone, except live their life for them."

And with that, she decided to let it go. She had done all she could.

Three nights later, after the second performance of *Carmen*, Eden was removing her makeup when someone knocked at her dressing room door.

"Be right there," she said, "I'll just be a couple of minutes."

When she opened it, a very tall, slender white man, seventy-ish with a mane of thick white hair and an oddly much darker beard, extended his hand to her. "Well! Congratulations. Another fine performance," he said. "Oh, sorry. Let me introduce myself. I'm Carl. Carl Murkison. I wrote the review of the opera for the *Times*."

"Oh!" Eden extended her hand. "Thank you for mentioning me!"

He learned about her from his good friend, Walter Meyerholtz, who told him Eden's story—that she was displaced by the hurricane, and ended up in New York, where she lived now.

He handed her his card. "Walter was shocked to learn not only that you were a singer, but that you were singing in this production! I think you've got an amazing story," he said. "I can only imagine what you've been through, and to be here now—well, if you don't mind, please call when you're free. I think your story is worth telling."

Later that night, she found Murkison's card and called him.

"I'd like to talk to you about the article you wanted to write," Eden said.

"Wonderful! When would you like to do the interview?"

"Did you know Arthur Flanagan?"

"Yes, of course. He was my mentor, a dear friend."

"And did he ever tell you about a singer, born in the late 1860s, named Celia DeMille?"

Murkison paused before answering. "It's been a very long time since I have heard that name."

When Murkison was a young reporter, decades ago, the much older Flanagan told him about an extraordinary singer he had wanted to write about in a feature for the *Times*. He proposed the idea to his editor. Forget it, the editor said. He'd never heard of her, she'd never made a record or performed with an opera company, and didn't he say she was black? The issue was closed.

"But Arthur said she was one of the greatest he ever heard. Maybe the greatest singer in the world. Never really got her due. Such were those times," he said. Murkison cleared his throat. "I was young, just a kid really, when I started reporting. Before he died, Arthur passed boxes of his materials on to me. His notes for stories he never got a chance to write. There were pages and pages about your singer, Madame DeMille."

Eden was silent as her mind worked. "I'll do the interview for your article, Mr. Murkison, on one condition."

CHAPTER 43

Sis,

 Sorry it took me all this time to write. But I wanted to let you know I'm OK. I wrote to Aunt Julia and Miss Mildred too. I hated leaving them like I did, but I figured it was the best thing, them not knowing what I was getting ready to do.

 Thanks for sending me that letter. I read it over and over again a whole bunch of times. Sitting in jail for those weeks, I had a lot of time to read. All the stuff you said about that young girl, her daddy, and that necklace. But then the part about her daddy, how he decided to just take off like he did. That dude was fierce. I can't even imagine it. Strong in his body for sure, but like, really strong in his mind. Anyway, it got me thinking about how a man who didn't have nothing can just say, screw this, just change his whole damn life.

 I liked all you said about Daddy, too, about how smart he was and how hard he worked to take care of us. Thanks for that picture of him. I don't remember Daddy. I wish I did. But looking at that picture, him and his buddies, he looked strong, too. I don't know how you can miss a daddy you never knew, but I do. Sometimes when I be just sitting in my cell after they feed us, waiting for the time to pass, I just take out that picture of him. Daddy looked powerful in that picture, all built up in his chest and arms and everything, but I bet Daddy was strong in his mind too. Just looking at his eyes, he looked like somebody who knew what he wanted, and went after it.

That night you fixed that gumbo for me, you reminded me how Daddy read all the time. So, I asked Aunt Julia to bring me some books. She brought me a couple of Star Wars *books like I asked her. But then she found a paperback by that black writer, James Baldwin.* The Fire Next Time. *It was a book Daddy had. I haven't read all of it yet, but there was this letter he wrote to his nephew where he said something about knowing where you come from, like if you know where you come from, then you can go anywhere you want to go. Something like that.*

All I know about where I come from is what you told me, about Daddy, and my mama, wherever she is. I think maybe someday I'll go to one of those places that find your people, see if I can find out what happened to her, see if she might want to see me.

I don't know where I want to go. But I know I don't want to go back to nobody's jail! I said once I got out of there they wouldn't see my skinny ass there again. So even though I don't know exactly what I want to do, I decided to make some kind of plan, see what happens. So that's why I went down to the recruitment place and signed up with the U. S. Army.

I want to do what Daddy did. Now I know Daddy was a marine and everything. But I'm not much of a fighter, and I figured the army was more my style. I don't think he would of minded. I just figured I needed something they might be able to give me, you know? They told me I could get my high school diploma, and even study mechanical engineering like I been wanting to do, and they would pay for it. Seem like a pretty good deal.

One more thing. Sis, I'm real sorry I took that necklace. I thought I could hock it or sell it to pay somebody some money I owed them. I wasn't telling you the truth about what I was doing in New York after school. I guess you figured that out by now. Anyway, I owed money and when I looked at that necklace, all I could see was cash. But now I see what it meant to you. One day you're going to be like that singer, special, with your pretty voice. For you, seeing that lady and her necklace must have been like me looking at a picture of Daddy. Sometimes you just need something special to pull out, something that's got its own story behind it, to help you figure out what yours is gonna be.

So anyway, I'm staying with a buddy until we both go to basic in Fort Benning, Georgia in a few days. They're taking us by bus. They say it's tough, but I'll bet it's not as tough as this last year since the storm! Glad we got through that. I've never said this, but thanks for taking care of me. You did a pretty good job. By the way, I can't believe you got to go to Europe! Maybe I'll get there one day myself.

When I finish basic, I'll let you know as soon as I can where I'll be. The next time I see you, we'll both be different, right? You'll be a famous singer. And I'll be a soldier.

Peace out,

Your brother

The letter and a box were waiting for Eden when she returned from the Thursday night performance. After reading she folded the handwritten pages, then blotted the tears on her cheeks. *He was safe.* He'd found a path, had a plan. All the years of struggle and pain and worry bearing fruit on the pages before her: *I want to do what Daddy did.* She could not have asked for more.

The package itself, a securely wrapped shirt box in brown grocery sack paper, was wound in cellophane packing tape. Sitting at her small kitchen table she turned it in her hands, surprised by a nimble skill and elegant care for detail she didn't know her brother had. He'd written the address in large block letters in the thick ink of a marking pen. When she opened the box, pulled the necklace from a nest of Styrofoam chips, and held it to the light, the tears sprang again. She actually believed she had let it all go. Made peace with the thing being gone forever, if it somehow helped keep her brother safe, alive. Holding the cool, heavy metal, patina-ed with age but shiny and intact, she clutched it to her chest. At some point, he had weighed what the necklace could do for him against what it meant to her and she had won. How many times had she said to him over the years, "You just don't think!" Yet her hands held solid evidence. He was becoming his daddy's thoughtful son, the man their father would have wanted him to be. Now, she could let him go.

At the last performance of *Carmen*, she stood in the shadowy stage right wing waiting for her cue. The wardrobe mistress, a stout red-haired Czech woman, looked at the necklace around Eden's neck. "What is this you are wearing?" the woman frowned.

"It's the last night, and it's from family," Eden answered.

The mistress shrugged, then winked. "Go, then."

With Eden's voice in good form, the aria went better than ever before. After the applause and final curtain, Eden's dressing room was rowdy with noisy, post-performance bustle and boisterous jubilation as a dozen people crowded into a room fit for four. White and yellow mums with a card from New Orleans sat on the long counter in front of the row of mirrors, compliments of Aunt Baby and Mildred. *Come see us when you can!* the note said. Marianne brought two dozen roses, Andre from Estelle's brought See's Chocolates, and three singers from Maestro's presented two bottles of Chandon and white and purple orchids. In a corner, a champagne cork popped, sailed across the room, and landed with a *whack!* against the mirror, and plastic flutes appeared from nowhere and filled up with foamy, ginger-colored bubbly.

Airy, random laughter sparkled along with the champagne and someone offered a toast. Pastor Fleet, tall and rotund in a gray vested suit, grabbed her into a huge bear hug. "Sister, I didn't know you had all that inside you," he said, his voice pitched with emotion. Marianne held her so tightly she could hardly breathe.

When Carl Murkison appeared, Eden gave him a polite smile.

"Looks good on you," he said. At her questioning look, he nodded toward the necklace on her chest. "What are you going to do with it?"

"Oh," she said, laughing. "Sometimes I forget I have it on." She would keep it a while, she said. It would be hard to part with, but someday, a university archive, a museum. She'd see.

"Did you read it? The article?" he asked. "Sorry about the cheesy headline, but I don't control that end of it."

"Yes, I did," she said, the light paling in her eyes. "I was going to send you a note. It was...so beautiful. Thank you so much."

"I know it wasn't what you were expecting."

The article about her by Murkison had been sizable, yet disappointing. "I really appreciate what you said about me. But we talked about—"

"I know," he said. "As it turned out, we had a limited amount of space. We just couldn't write much about Madame DeMille. But I did mention her, as I promised. And I mentioned how much you were inspired by her."

It was true, he wrote a long and interesting profile of the city's newest, most improbable diva. "From the Storm to the Stage" was a compelling story that practically wrote itself: a young woman's struggle to raise her brother, fleeing a devastating hurricane and finding her way to New York, her future as well as her brother's in doubt. Her journey from waitress/singer to opera singer. But she'd thought they had an agreement. Only one sentence on Madame DeMille? "She is the reason why I sing," Eden had told Murkison. Was this man like all the others in Celia's career? Another reporter not giving her what she was due?

"I just thought it would be more about her. But I don't want to sound ungrateful. 'Cause I am grateful. Really. It meant so much to me. Thank you, very, very much."

Changing the subject, he told Eden he and his wife, who never missed a performance and was now a fan, wanted to give her a small party, a celebration in her honor. Monday evening, if she was free. He gave her a card with his home address.

"That's really nice of you," she said. "I'll be there."

The group thinned and the laughter and noisy celebration quieted. Marianne and Andre gathered all the flowers and gifts. "Car's just outside the stage door. We'll load it up and meet you there," Marianne said.

A lone figure in the corner near the restroom stepped out of the shadow. Evan looked older, thinner. His beard, thicker than she remembered, was brushed with silver, along with the hair around his temples.

"Eden," Evan said.

"You," she said.

No other words rushed to join that first one. *Stupid. Say something,* she told herself. *Isn't this what you wanted?*

Finally, Evan smiled, and reached out, pulling her into a long hug.

"I...I tried to call you," she stuttered, nearly breathless. "I tried, like, a bunch of times."

She pulled away and wiped at her eyes. "I'm sorry...I guess I can't believe you're here."

When she said she called, he looked surprised. "I haven't checked messages in weeks. Not on my cell phone, anyway. I guess I've been distracted. I had to leave town. I went to Morristown to stay at my mom's after her stroke."

"Why didn't you tell me?" Immediately, she wanted to take the words back. Why would he call her after the way she treated him the last time they'd spoken? She'd all but told him to disappear.

"Is she OK?" Eden said. "I mean, I hope she's OK. Are you OK?"

He smiled. "Touch and go for a while. She's a lot better. Minimal damage, but her left side is weak. She's getting rehab. Speech is a little trickier, but it's coming along. I took leave from work, packed up, and moved in with her for a bit. My sister Arnelle was there too."

Stroke. She'd hoped his silence was grounded in reason, but not this. But even through her guilt, she couldn't resist the relief. So, it wasn't because he hated her.

"So, I got back yesterday and I read that feature article about you in the *Times*. Europe, huh? Wow. I want to hear all about that! Figures, though. When I saw you on that stage, you looked like you'd been somewhere you'd never been before. Sounded like it, too."

She said, "Look, I'm really sorry. I kept calling because I wanted to apologize. The things I said to you the last time we talked…the way I acted."

Eyes down, he held up a hand. "You don't owe me any apologies. Hearing you sing tonight, it was…just…something. I mean I knew you could do it. I knew it."

Eden said, "I'm not sure I believed you, but it kept me going anyway. What I mean is…I, uh.." She stopped, looked down at her hands, one inside the other, and up again. "I couldn't have done any of this without you."

He smiled, put a hand over his chest. "Look, Eden, I missed you," he said. "I mean, really. You have no idea how much."

Eden said, "I missed you, too."

"How about we go out on a date, a real one? How about Monday night?"

Something fluttered in her chest. "Yes," she said. Then she remembered the Monday evening party Murkison had planned for her. "Would you go with me?"

He laughed. "A party to celebrate you? Try and keep me away."

Carl Murkison lived in the eighties on the Upper West Side off Riverside Drive, a brownstone nestled in a row of stately pre-War apartment buildings, each gated with thick wrought iron, each stoop embellished with flower boxes spilling azaleas. The late fall temperatures spawned a palette of deep rusts and golds in the tree-lined neighborhood, the blazing crimson of Japanese maples against the deep brown brick gave the facade of buildings an imperious look.

Murkison's third-floor apartment was decorated in turn-of-the-twentieth-century antiques, beige loveseats, and overstuffed chairs. A grand piano occupied a corner near a bank of windows facing the river. Murkison's wife, Arlise, a petite, well-preserved woman of seventy or so, passed trays of shrimp rollups, mini quiches, and champagne among the guests. Along with Evan, Eden had invited Marianne, Professor Blessing, and Mia Hightower. Murkison had invited a few friends, some from the newspaper, some from the world of opera managers and administrators.

Mia Hightower, in red five-inch heels and a black sheath dress trimmed in red piping, towered over her escort for the evening, Ernest Blessing.

Blessing nodded, reached for Eden's hand. "You've done good work," he said. "You were a fine Micaela."

"Yes!" Mia said. "Good job. Europe was tough, wasn't it?" she said with a knowing smile. "But it made you a completely different singer. Brava."

A completely different person, Eden thought. She looked from Mia to Blessing. "You…both of you," Eden started, "Nothing would have happened without you."

"Well, you are very fortunate to have so many people committed to your success," Blessing said. "Including your own personal angel."

"What do you mean?"

Blessing shrugged. "Well, the person who paid for your private studies."

She narrowed her eyes. "But I thought…" she began. "I don't know who you're talking about."

Blessing gave her an incredulous look. "You don't know? I just assumed it was a family member, a friend. Someone who'd decided to sponsor you."

Eden frowned. "Somebody paid for my voice lessons with you?" She had thought they were free.

Blessing nodded. "Your lessons were paid up front. Six months of study." Distracted, he looked at his watch and said, "I'm sorry, time for me to go. I promised I would play about now."

He headed for the piano. Eden was dumbstruck. *Evan. Couldn't be anyone else.*

She was still pondering this when Mia asked, "Your brother. He's OK now?"

Eden blinked and looked at her. "What? Sorry, yes, I think he's gonna be fine. Thanks for asking."

"Good. Let's get another drink and talk a minute before the toasting starts."

From the corner near the two sofas emerged the tones of a massive black Steinway, thick, sonorous chords and florid arpeggios in full volume rang throughout the room. Buoyed by the music, the din of chatter rose in the space. Mia guided Eden toward the bar near the window, where a woman refilled their glasses. "You should be really happy about that review!" Mia said, handing a glass to Eden. "So, what's your plan now?"

Plan? Up to now, there had never been a plan. Things happened out of her control, first one thing, then another. If she'd had a plan at all, it was to get through the production without embarrassing herself. "Well. I don't know. Keep studying. I guess maybe I could do some auditions, and the restaurant says I can do a few nights a week there."

"Seriously? Look, you got a good review from the *Times*. What are you going to do with that? Sing 'Some Enchanted Evening' to Midwestern tourists between prime rib entrées and drinks? I don't think so. I'll put you in touch with Tyce Davis at Alexander Artists. That's the agency I work through, and Tyce is one of the new, young agents. Sharp, smart. Hungry to make his mark—perfect for you. I'm not going to lie—there's a lot of tough work ahead. You'll need to do some serious study, and my God, you've got to get your German together.

But there's no reason why, in a few months, you shouldn't start getting some good work. Opera New York is casting for the next couple of seasons. In fact, I know there's talk about a new production of *Carmen*. You shouldn't have to wait for someone to get sick."

"Wow," Eden said. "I'd really like to play Micaela again."

Mia took a sip of her wine and frowned. "Micaela? No, no, dear! The lead is usually a mezzo, but you're a soprano who can do it. Carmen is your role now."

While the drinking and eating continued, strains of Duke Ellington filled the space, then a medley of Gershwin songs. Ernest Blessing, head bowed and back arched over the piano keyboard with the faintest possible smile lighting his face, nodded in time as he delivered a syncopated, bouncy "Our Love is Here to Stay."

Later, as he ended an Art Tatum arrangement of "The Man I Love" in a virtuosic flurry of notes, Blessing acknowledged the guests' applause with a subtle nod, then got up to have a word with Murkison. Evan, Marianne, and Eden stood in the curve of the nine-foot grand, drinks in hand.

"Great news about your brother," Marianne said.

"I'm just so relieved he's OK, you know?" Eden said. "Things are gonna be different now. But I want us to be close, me and him. My daddy, he would have wanted that."

Marianne excused herself to find the powder room. An awkward silence cut the space between Eden and Evan. They both took long sips from their glasses.

Evan cleared his throat. "I, uh, read the article, but I didn't see the review until today. Your first review, a rave. Wow, lady. You are going to be so famous."

She nodded, unsmiling, thoughtful, her eyes unable to meet his. How much had he paid for her lessons? Hundreds? More? Why didn't he tell her? And why did he do it? She didn't know what to think or how to feel, let alone what to say.

The words sounded ridiculous to her and none of them seemed right. But she knew why he had done it. For reasons so complicated and yet so simple. Someday she would ask him about it, maybe when the two of them were much older, looking back, remembering this night. But not now.

A half-hour into the evening, Murkison tapped his champagne glass with a silver spoon. "I'd like you all to raise your glasses in a toast to one of the most talented singers I've heard in a long time! Someone who, I'm sure, has a great future awaiting her."

Applause again. Eden smiled, slightly embarrassed, but lifted her glass.

He asked everyone to sit. "And now I have a special surprise. You are all about to witness a historic event. Something I promise you will make music history. Trust me, you'll be glad you were here for this."

He explained that he had promised Eden he would write about the early twentieth-century singer, Celia DeMille, who had inspired her. He gestured toward Eden, explaining that through unusual circumstances she has come into the possession of certain artifacts which once belonged to DeMille. "As you can see, she is wearing a stunning necklace, one that once belonged to the diva! In all of the photographs of Madame DeMille left to me by my mentor, Arthur Flanagan, she was never without it!"

Heads turned toward Eden. A murmur of surprise and approval circled through the room. He went on. According to the interviews she gave, Madame DeMille always lamented the fact that she never had a professional commercial recording, something that might have changed her career, indeed, her whole life. "While she lived," he said, "she was unanimously beloved as an artist. The reviews confirm that. Yet she had to deal with one fact: that the black voice was not valued the way the white one was. And therefore, even with her talent, Madame DeMille, often called 'The Black Donatella' instead of her own name, found out that the recording companies were not interested to record the voice of a black classical artist."

Murkison removed his glasses, wiped them with a handkerchief, and placed them back on. "Yet, from the reports of her performances at Madison Square Garden, Carnegie Hall, the Chicago World's Fair, several times at the White House, Buckingham Palace, and throughout Europe, she clearly was one of the world's greatest singers," he said. "But she was never invited to sing with the major opera companies, something that many in opera today, since the great Marian Anderson, may take for granted."

"And the major American newspapers, even ours, never treated De-Mille with the respect accorded others. Sadly, she died with no money and was buried without fanfare in an unmarked grave. But the errors of history can be corrected and a lost legacy can be revived. And with that in mind, I will be writing a full-page feature, with photographs, on Madame Celia DeMille, which will appear in next Sunday's paper."

By the next day, he said, Madame DeMille will be among the most talked-about singers in America, and the world will know her name.

Throughout the room, there were exclamations and applause. Murkison held up both hands. "But that's not the only news I want to share with you," he said.

He placed one hand on the piano as he spoke. Before the end of the nineteenth century, he said, Thomas Edison's company produced something called a wax cylinder on which recordings could be made. "They were eventually replaced by the more advanced disc recordings of the Victor company."

But, he continued, while the cylinders were an older technology, they had one huge advantage over the disc—someone with no recording experience could record themselves. "A person could theoretically make a recording at home, even back during the turn of the century. If an artist wanted to preserve her voice on record, she would not have to wait for a commercial recording company."

He then reached into a large cardboard box his wife handed him.

He held up what looked to be a tube or cylinder. A few smalls gasps went up from those who guessed what the object was.

Evan leaned forward, eyes narrowing. "Is that what I think it is?"

Ernest Blessing sharply inhaled, his mouth open. "I don't believe it," he said. "Impossible. This is…authentic?"

Reaching behind the piano, Murkison picked up what looked like an old box of walnut-stained wood, along with a handle and what appeared to be a cone-shaped horn. He placed it all on top of the piano. The room fell silent.

Murkison looked at Blessing. "Authentic? Absolutely."

Earlier, Mia had asked about Eden's necklace, and when she told her who had owned it, the singer's eyes had brightened. Now, she said, "No, you've got to be kidding."

Murkison smiled. "Before he died, Arthur Flanagan gave me a box of Madame's artifacts, things she wanted him to have to preserve her legacy for the future. I thought I had found everything in the box. But when I went back to it to gather material for the article, this is what I found. I would guess, given my research, this was recorded around 1915. Madame would have been at the peak of her powers."

And what you are about to hear, he told the guests, was recorded by the diva herself.

Eden and Evan looked at each other. Her hand reached for his and squeezed it—her heart thumped wildly. With her other hand, she touched the necklace. She was about to hear a revelation.

Miss Celia, finally, we meet.

The cylinder machine and horn, also dating to the 1920s, had been borrowed from an antiques collector, Murkison explained. "And now," he said, his voice low and measured, "I'm going to ask for complete quiet. Eventually, this recording will be digitalized, cleaned up to smooth out the roughness, re-recorded, and transferred to a modern disc. But tonight, you'll have to listen, not just with your ears, but with your imagination. You'll have to step back in time, listen only to the voice. The sound will be small, but Madame's voice is strong and pure. There are scratches you'll have to endure, but if you listen through them, around them, you will be rewarded with one of the great voices of history."

Chairs squeaked against the hardwood as they were pulled closer to the piano. Murkison attached the horn, slipped the cylinder into its place, and cranked the machine. Everyone in the room leaned forward, held their breath.

The cylinder spun with crackles and pops and hisses, and from beneath it all, a piano emerged. B major chords pulsed slowly, and Eden smiled through her tears. The music was instantly recognizable. How many times had she heard this song? Or sung it? Only now did she grasp its meaning.

It was the music of longing. The music of a dream.

The piano intro repeated, this time louder. Outside the window and beyond the street, while night closed in on the city, white lights flickered on the bridge spanning the river below. Eden closed her eyes. On the grand stage in her mind, a black woman in white lace lifted her chin and took a breath. She had been biding her time, her voice having waited a century before winding its way out of the dark.

"My name is Celia DeMille," the voice said. "And I will sing for you now."

AUTHOR'S NOTE

A Few Words on Sissieretta Jones

A great part of this book is inspired by the life of one of the great American singers of history, Sissieretta Joyner Jones.

When I was researching and writing my first book, *And So I Sing, African American Divas of Opera and Concert*, the great historian John Hope Franklin suggested I include Sissieretta Jones in my history of the great Black American divas of the past century. At the time, like most people, I had never heard of her. I learned she was arguably one of the most accomplished and successful singers of the nineteenth and early twentieth centuries. I opened *And So I Sing* with a chapter on Sissieretta Jones.

The daughter of a formerly enslaved Virginian, she was born around 1869 and was later educated and trained as a singer in Boston. Jones sang at the White House for four U.S. presidents, the 1893 Columbian Exposition (the first World's Fair in Chicago), Madison Square Garden, Carnegie Hall, and throughout Europe and the Americas. Praised by critics everywhere, she was a sensation, the press core likening her genius to the great white artists at the time. At one point, she was reportedly the highest paid Black performer in America. Yet, being Black, she was never allowed to sing with American or European opera companies, and even though her white counterparts were recorded on discs by such companies as Edison and Victor, she reportedly was never recorded commercially.

The press, and even her own management, called her "The Black Patti," a reference to the reigning white diva at the time, Adelina Patti.

Jones wanted so much to sing opera, she and her managers formed their own troupe of performers, exploiting the comparisons with Patti. The Black Patti Troubadours, a minstrel show featuring Black comedians, singers, and other performers, toured America with Jones as the star, performing excerpts from opera in full costume with chorus. The troupe was enormously successful, with Jones and company's tours advertised across the country with P.T. Barnum–style dazzle and panache. But when minstrel-style variety entertainment fell from popularity around the time of World War I, Jones' company went bankrupt, and the artist's career was essentially over. She returned to Providence, Rhode Island, where she once resided, and lived a quiet life, singing only occasionally in church. She went on "relief," as did many indigent Americans during the Great Depression, then died in poverty and obscurity, and was buried in Providence in an unmarked grave.

Because she was nicknamed "The Black Patti," often to the exclusion of her own name, she was confused with other singers. When another Black classical singer, Flora Batson Bergen, passed away, a newspaper obituary wrongly claimed "Black Patti" had died.

Sing Her Name is a work of fiction, loosely inspired by fact. I took many liberties with the story of this great diva: changing her name to Celia DeMille, picking and choosing truthful elements, then diverting for the purposes of plot development, narrative interest, and dramatic arc. Jones was born in Portsmouth, Virginia, and never lived in New Orleans. As far as I know, she was not the mistress of an opera company director who reneged on an offer to star in the opera *Carmen*, and though the New Orleans French Opera House did burn down mysteriously in 1919 (and to this day, has never been rebuilt), she was likely, at the time, nowhere near it. The corner of Bourbon and Toulouse, where the opera house one stood, is now occupied by the Sheraton Four Points Hotel. As far as vestiges from the famous opera house are concerned, there is only a wall of photographs of the building itself (before and after the fire), posters of performances, and photographs of Adelina Patti, who owned a house on New Orleans' Royal Street. At the time of this writing, The Puccini Bar, adjacent to the lobby, often welcomes impromptu, casual performances by opera and classical singers.

The novel's fictional constructions were the inventions of my imagination and the result of literary license. The reigning queen of opera, Adelina Patti, however, did star in *Carmen* at the ill-fated French Opera House.

To get the real story of Jones, I refer readers to an excellent biography written by Maureen D. Lee, titled *Sissieretta Jones: The Greatest Singer of Her Race*.

The character Eden, the young contemporary singer, was based on many young artists I interviewed for *And So I Sing*. Many of these gifted young women, like Eden, became successful, but some struggled to find their place in opera's overwhelmingly white world and in a field foreign to their background and experience.

In 2018, the *New York Times* launched a new series of articles titled "Overlooked No More," reaching back over a 250-year history to correct the omission of obituaries of "remarkable people" in history—artists, inventors, activists—primarily women and people of color. Sissieretta Jones was one of its first subjects. "Who gets remembered—and how involves judgment," the *Times* writes. "To look back at the obituary archives can, therefore, be a stark lesson in how society valued various achievements and achievers."

Jones may well have been called the greatest singer of her race, but she may have been, at the time, the greatest singer of any race; we'll never know. As with the violinist Niccolò Paganini, or the jazz trumpeter from New Orleans, Buddy Bolden, the mythic genius of such unrecorded artists springs from written and oral history, and the measure of their artistry lies in the province of the imagination. With no recordings, the scale of their talent is left to passionate debate that has endured for decades and centuries, and will surely continue for years to come. Yet, as we hold Jones and other artists up to the light, we measure them the only way we can, by the handed-down stories and testimonies of admirers whose hearts were moved by their art.

ACKNOWLEDGMENTS

No author has a book published alone. There is always a small, supportive army, unseen and mostly unsung, without whose help each book would not be possible.

Doug Seibold, founder and president of Agate Publishing, has believed in and supported my work unflaggingly throughout the years. Thank you, Doug. And thanks to the team at Agate, Jane Seibold, Jacqueline Jarik, Naomi Huffman, Amanda Gibson, Deidre Hammons, and the entire staff, for seeing this book through.

Many thanks to the Writers' Colony at Dairy Hollow in Eureka Springs, Arkansas, for providing "a room of one's own" and the perfect place to write.

To David Haynes and the Kimbilio African American writers' retreat at Taos, New Mexico, and especially to workshop leader Asali Solomon, I'm very grateful for your support and for valuable feedback during the earlier stages of the writing process.

To Barbara Hill Moore and Donnie Ray Albert, thank you so much for your friendship, your helpful details on singing technique, and for all the inspiration, support, and knowledge you have given to aspiring young singers over the years. Any factual errors or misrepresentations in this book about the art of singing, vocal pedagogy, or the industry itself, are my own.

To my good friend Mary Alice Rich, thank you for your encouragement after reading an earlier draft. To Janine Geisel and her fellow book club members in Arlington, Texas—Susan Blaser, Pat Morales, W. Elaine Langston, Kris Sandefur, Debbie Sandoval, and Meena Shah—thanks for your patient reading and helpful comments on *Sing Her Name*.

To Jamal Story in New York, and Vicky Sadin in New Orleans, I am grateful to you for your hospitality and for providing a wonderful place to stay while researching in those cities.

And finally, thanks to the Historic New Orleans Collection and the Museum of Free People of Color in New Orleans.

ABOUT THE AUTHOR

Rosalyn Story is a violinist with the Fort Worth Symphony and the author of the novels *More Than You Know* (Agate Bolden, 2004) and *Wading Home* (Agate Bolden, 2010), as well as *And So I Sing*, a non-fiction work about African American opera singers. She was an inaugural recipient of the Sphinx Organization's MPower Artist Grant, which helped produce the opera *Wading Home*, based on her novel and performed in Dallas, New Orleans, and South Africa. She currently teaches African American music history at Southern Methodist University in Dallas, Texas.